Dear Reader,

Welcome to the third of three books starring a brand-new group of modern-day McKettrick men. Readers who have embraced the irrepressible, larger-than-life McKettrick clan as their own won't want to miss the stories of Tate, Garrett and Austin—three Texas-bred brothers who meet their matches in the Remington sisters. Sidelined by an injury, bad-boy rodeo star Austin McKettrick fears he's got nothing left to live for—until spirited nurse Paige Remington makes him dream of the happily-ever-after he hadn't thought he wanted.

I'm also writing today to tell you about a special group of people with whom I've become involved in the past couple of years. It is the Humane Society of the United States (HSUS), specifically their Pets for Life program.

The Pets for Life program is one of the best ways to help your local shelter— by helping to keep animals out of shelters in the first place. Something as basic as keeping a collar and tag on your pet all the time, so if he gets out and gets lost, he can be returned home. Being a responsible pet owner. Spaying or neutering your pet. And not giving up when things don't go perfectly. If your dog digs in the yard, or your cat scratches the furniture, know that these are problems that can be addressed. You can find all the information about these and many other common problems at www.pets forlife.org. This campaign is focused on keeping pets and their people together for a lifetime.

As many of you know, my own household includes two dogs, two cats and six horses, so this is a cause that is near and dear to my heart. I hope you'll get involved along with me.

With love,

Paula Earl Miller

LINDA LAEL MILLER

McKETTRICKS OF TEXAS: AUSTIN

DOUBLEDAY LARGE PRINT HOME LIBRARY EDITION

HQN™

This is a work of fiction. Names, characters, places and incidents are either the product of the author's imagination or are used fictitiously, and any resemblance to actual persons, living or dead, business establishments, events or locales is entirely coincidental.

® and TM are trademarks of the publisher. Trademarks indicated with ® are registered in the United States Patent and Trademark Office, the Canadian Trade Marks Office and in other countries.

ISBN 978-1-61664-145-0

Printed in U.S.A.

This Large Print Book carries the Seal of Approval of N.A.V.H.

For Wendy Diane Miller, my daughter.
I love you.

Acknowledgments

Every book presents its special challenges, as does every series. But some touch writers more deeply than others, and require more of them in terms of creativity, energy, depth of emotion. This trilogy, The McKettricks of Texas, was such an experience. There were times of soaring joy, of course; there was also a lot of difficulty. Without the help, patience and faith of my beloved editor, Joan Marlow Golan, and the constant encouragement of my agent, Irene Goodman, the books would have been far more challenging, if not impossible, to write. My love and heartfelt thanks to both of these amazing women.

PROLOGUE

San Antonio, Texas
October

Eight seconds.

Outside the world of rodeo, it was hardly any time at all.

Add two thousand pounds of ticked-off bull—aptly named Buzzsaw—to the equation, though, and eight seconds could seem a whole lot like forever.

Standing at the bar in a little back-street, hole-in-the-wall dive a more prudent man would likely have steered clear of, Austin McKettrick reflected on the ride he'd made a few hours before and wondered why he didn't feel more like celebrating.

For months now, ever since the first go-round with that particular bull, when he'd nearly been killed, Austin had thought about little else *except* riding Buzzsaw.

Now that he'd done it, and laid a demon or two to rest in the process, he was fresh out of worthy objectives.

A flicker in the mirror behind the bar drew Austin's attention; he adjusted his hat and scanned the shadowy width of the glass with an imperceptible movement of his eyes.

Shit, he thought as he watched his brothers, Tate and Garrett, approach.

They were both cowboys, lean and tall, with broad shoulders and Clint Eastwood attitudes. Folks just naturally stepped out of their way.

Without turning around, Austin lifted his mug and took a long, slow sip of beer.

Tate, the eldest of the three, bellied up to the bar on Austin's right, while Garrett took the left side, both of them crowding into his space. As if he might not have noticed them otherwise. He grinned to himself and adjusted his hat again.

Pinky, the bartender, a woman in her

mid-seventies with her hair plaited into a long gray braid and skin that glowed with good health behind a veil of wrinkles, appeared right away.

"What'll it be?" she asked, her gaze moving from Tate's face to Garrett's, but slipping right on past Austin's as if he weren't there.

Once married to one of the wranglers on the Silver Spur, Pinky was still a friend of the family. The wrangler, on the other hand, was long gone.

Tate, always a hand with the ladies, tugged at the brim of his hat, gentlemanlike, and favored the woman with that famous white-toothed smile of his. "Nothing for me, thanks," he said, exaggerating the drawl. "How've you been, Pinky?"

"I'm holding up okay," Pinky allowed. She smiled, nodded to Garrett. "I hear there's going to be a double wedding out there on the Silver Spur come this New Year's Eve. That true?"

"Sure is," Garrett answered easily. "Your invitation will be along in the mail, Pinky."

"So you're both getting hitched?"

Pinky said after clucking her tongue at the marvel of it all.

"Yes, ma'am," Tate replied. "I'm marrying Libby Remington, and Garrett's tying the knot with her sister, Julie."

Pinky gave a long, low whistle of exclamation through her teeth. "Brothers marrying sisters. Don't that beat all? Your kids will be double-cousins, won't they?"

"Yep," Garrett said.

At long last, Pinky fixed Austin with a look. "Tate's taking a wife," she said, cutting straight to the chase. "So is Garrett. What's keeping *you* single, handsome?"

Tate and Garrett both leaned in a little, putting the squeeze on him.

Austin felt heat climb his neck, and he was glad for the dim, smoky light, because there were a few things he wanted to keep to himself.

Nobody needed to know he was embarrassed.

"I'm too young to get married," he told Pinky, employing his most endearing grin.

"Nonsense," Pinky blustered. "Marriage might settle you down a little. And you could do with some settling down, if you ask me."

Austin refrained from pointing out that he *hadn't* asked her.

It was right about then that he felt a strange squeezing sensation in his lower back, and his left leg went numb to the knee. He shifted his weight to the right, hoping to relieve some of the pressure, but it didn't help much.

"Tate and I couldn't agree more," Garrett chatted on. "Austin definitely ought to settle down. Quit bumming around the rodeo circuit, start a family, do something constructive with his life."

Privately, Austin scoffed at his brother's remark. Garrett had a hell of a nerve making a speech like that. Up until a few months ago, when Julie Remington had roped him in and then hog-tied him for good, Brother Number Two had worked for a United States senator and had his pick of smart, beautiful, willing women.

Tate hadn't exactly lived like a monk either, back in the wild days after he

and Cheryl divorced and *before* he'd
fallen back in love with Libby, his high
school sweetheart and Julie's older sister.

The way they talked now, a person
could almost imagine that they'd been
living saintly and celibate lives right
along.

Austin took a long swig of his beer
and waited for the feeling in his leg to
come back.

"Do you know what he did tonight?"
Tate asked, on a roll now, resting an el-
bow on the bar and leaning earnestly in
Pinky's direction.

"No tellin'," Pinky said with a shake
of her head. "Could have been just
about anything."

"He rode Buzzsaw," Garrett informed
the bartender, as though Austin weren't
standing right there between his brothers, both of them shoulder-mashing
him. "Managed to draw the same bull
that tore him apart last year. Took a
whole team of surgeons to sew our
baby brother back together, and what
does he do?"

Pinky's blue eyes grew round. She

stared at Austin as though he were seven kinds of a fool and then some. "Well, I'll be damned," she said. "Always said you had more looks than good sense, and now here's the proof."

Austin didn't have an answer handy, and he wouldn't have gotten the chance to use one, anyhow. Suddenly, the floor pitched sideways, and he leaned against the bar, waiting for the room to right itself.

When it did, the motion was sudden, and Austin's knees buckled.

He might have gone down if Tate and Garrett hadn't gotten him by the elbows and held him upright.

"I swear that's only his second beer," Pinky said, sounding worried.

Garrett waved off her concern. "He's all right, Pinky."

"Can you walk?" Tate asked Austin, his voice quiet now and serious.

If fierce determination had been enough, Austin would have made it across that barroom floor and outside to his own truck, told his brothers to go to hell and driven himself back to the seedy motel room he'd rented a few days before. A hot shower and about twelve hours of sleep and he'd be fine.

Unfortunately, determination *wasn't* enough, not that night anyway. Austin managed to stay on his feet, but only because Tate and Garrett were holding him up.

"Hell, yes, I can walk," he lied.

"You damn idiot," Tate muttered, as they crossed the parking lot, headed for his big extended-cab truck. With some help from Garrett, Tate muscled him into the backseat.

He'd have fought back for sure if his legs hadn't turned to noodles. He felt light-headed, too, and slightly sick to his stomach.

"My truck," he said. "I can't just leave it here. This isn't exactly the best neighborhood in San Antonio—"

Garrett cut him off. "We'll get your truck later."

"It's a classic," Austin said.

"Yeah, yeah," Garrett replied, sounding grim. "Whatever."

The world was on the tilt again, and a strange sense of urgency sent a rush of adrenaline through Austin's system.

"There's a dog," he added anxiously. "Back at the motel, I mean. I've been feeding him and—"

Tate got behind the wheel.

Garrett buckled himself in on the passenger side.

The numbness in Austin's leg washed back up his spine and turned to pain. He swore. "I can't just—leave—the dog—" he insisted.

"We'll see to the dog, and the truck, too," Garrett assured him quietly. "Let it go, Austin."

Austin passed out, woke up again. He wondered if somebody had slipped him something back at the bar.

Over the course of the next few minutes, time seemed to lose all meaning. He was in the back of Tate's truck, and then he wasn't. He was sitting up, and then he was lying down flat. Lights spun around him, a strange mix of neon and moon glow and fluorescent bulbs glaring brightly enough to dazzle his eyes.

A pretty nurse in scrubs smiled down at him. Red curls poked out around her face.

Something leaped inside Austin. Paige Remington?

No, this couldn't be Paige. His luck was neither that good nor that bad. Anyway, Paige had dark hair.

"What . . ." he began.

He realized he was on a gurney, his brothers at his side, being wheeled through a hospital corridor. It was a familiar scenario. Déjà vu all over again, he thought. Then he frowned. Wait a second. Sure, Buzzsaw had gotten the best of him that other time. He'd been airlifted to Houston, undergone a couple of different operations, fought his way back from the banks of the River Styx. But he *had* recovered.

That was then and this was now— tonight, he'd ridden that bull to the buzzer. He'd scored high enough to take first-place money, though it hadn't really been about winning, not this time.

He'd walked out of the arena, gotten into his truck and driven to Pinky's, thinking he ought to whoop it up a little.

After that, the details were a mite sketchy.

So what the hell was he doing in a hospital?

He would have asked why he was there, but for the pain. It swelled to a crescendo and then gulped him down whole, and there was nothing but darkness.

Austin came to lying in a bed with rails on either side, still dressed except for his boots. The curtains were drawn all around, shutting him in, and he couldn't begin to guess what time of day—or night—it might be.

"If the pain is under control," Austin heard a woman's voice say, "I'll release him. If not, he'll have to stick around for more tests and some observation."

"But you don't think there's any permanent damage?" Garrett asked quietly, sounding hopeful, bone-tired and completely exasperated all at once.

They were shadows against the curtain, the three of them. The lady—no doubt a doctor—and Tate and Garrett.

"That depends," the woman answered, "on your definition of 'permanent damage.' Your brother has a herniated disc. With rest and reasonable caution, he could make a full recovery."

"Austin wouldn't know 'reasonable caution' if it bit him in the ass," Tate said.

"What's *your* definition of reasonable caution, Doc?" Garrett asked.

She sighed. She could have been fresh out of med school or as old as Pinky; Austin couldn't tell by her voice or her shape. "Well," she replied, "it certainly wouldn't include riding bulls in rodeos."

Austin closed his eyes.

He was a bull rider and not much else. Who the hell would he be if he quit the rodeo circuit?

"What about horses?" Tate asked. "He can still ride them, right?"

"If you're talking about regular saddle horses," the doc answered, "that would probably be fine, once he's had some time to recover, and if he uses common sense."

The sound Garrett made was somewhere between a snort and a laugh. "*That'll* be the day."

Tate again. "What's the worst-case scenario?"

Tate, being the eldest brother, the one who oversaw the day-to-day operation of the family ranch, took himself pretty seriously sometimes. More so since their folks were gone.

The doctor didn't reply right away. That, Austin concluded, probably wasn't a good sign.

"Doc?" Garrett prompted.

Another sigh. More hesitation.

Austin tried to sit up, but his back spasmed and he barely bit back a groan.

He must have made some kind of sound, though, because he'd drawn their attention. The curtain zipped open and the doctor appeared at his bedside, peering at him.

She was young and pretty. Some consolation, under the circumstances.

"Mr. McKettrick?" she said.

Austin nodded. "That would be me," he told her.

"How are you feeling?"

If the pain is under control, I'll release

him. If not, he'll have to stick around for more tests and some observation.

"Never better," Austin said, scrounging up a grin.

She looked him over skeptically. "You're sure?"

"Yeah," he said. "I'm sure."

"You will need to see your own doctor within the next few days."

"Yes, ma'am," Austin agreed cheerfully. "I will surely do that."

Tate and Garrett exchanged suspicious glances. They'd probably figured out that he'd say just about anything he had to say to get out of that place.

"I'm prescribing muscle relaxants," the doctor rambled on. "But only for the short term. It is imperative, Mr. McKettrick, that you rest. I'm sure your personal physician will agree that, except for moderate exercise, definitely low-impact, you shouldn't move around a lot for the next several weeks."

"Whatever you say," Austin told her, sweet as pecan pie.

Garrett rolled his eyes.

Tate folded his arms and frowned

thoughtfully. "Maybe our brother ought to stay here after all," he said. "For some of that . . . observation."

Austin spoke up. "I need to get my gear from the motel room," he said, suddenly scared that Tate might convince the doc to admit him after all. He'd spent enough time in hospitals to last him the rest of his life. "And the dog. He'll be wondering where I went—"

"Will you forget that damn dog?" Garrett snapped.

"No," Austin said, leveling a look at his brother. "I *won't* forget the damn dog."

Garrett subsided, coloring up a little.

The doctor gave a few more instructions, promised that a prescription would be waiting downstairs at the pharmacy by the time Austin had been wheeled down there in a chair and signed all the insurance forms. With that, she left.

A good half an hour had gone by before they finally turned him loose. He'd scrawled his name on various dotted lines and retrieved his cell phone and wallet, along with the key to Room 3, over at the Cozy Doze Motel.

After climbing into Tate's truck—this time with no help from his brothers—he shook two pills out of the bottle into his palm and swallowed them dry.

Then he directed Tate to the motel where he'd left a change of clothes and the dog he'd found cowering in the alley the first night, slat-ribbed and down on his luck.

"Room 3," he said as they pulled up to the crumbling adobe structure. "It's around back."

Garrett turned in the front passenger seat to look at him, both eyebrows raised. "You were staying *here?*" he asked.

Austin chuckled. "The Ritz was full," he replied. Then he rolled down the back window and whistled, shrill, through his front teeth. He'd chosen the Cozy Doze because he'd wanted to keep a low profile until after he'd evened the score with Buzzsaw the night before at the rodeo. Folks in San Antonio knew him, especially around the fancier hotels, and he hadn't wanted word of his presence to get back to his brothers before he'd had a chance to make his ride. But clearly Tate and Garrett had eventually tracked him down.

Much to his relief, the dog he'd named Shep wriggled out from behind a pile of old tires all but overgrown by weeds, wagging his tail and lolling his tongue.

Part German shepherd, part Lab and part a lot of other things, by the looks of him, Shep wasn't a big dog, but he wasn't a little one, either. He was about the same size as Harry the beagle, and his coat was probably brown, although it would be hard to tell until he'd had a bath.

Austin tossed his room key to Tate, while Garrett got out of the truck to call the dog.

Shep growled halfheartedly and laid his ears back. One of them was missing a chunk of hide.

"It's all right, boy," Austin told the frightened animal through the open window of Tate's rig. "This is my brother Garrett. He used to be a politician, but you can trust him just the same."

The dog gave a low whimper, but he wagged his tail and let his ears stand up.

Austin pushed the truck door open. If Garrett tried to touch the poor critter, he'd be bitten for sure.

"Come, Shep," Austin said very quietly.

Shep sort of slouched around Garrett, then crept over to stand on his hind legs, both front paws resting on the running board of the truck.

"Let's go on home," Austin told him.

After considering the proposition, the dog high-jumped into the rig, scrambled across Austin's boots and clawed his way up onto the seat next to him.

Tate appeared with Austin's shaving kit and duffel, a five-pound sack of kibble under one arm.

"You square on your bill and everything?" he asked, flinging the works into the truck bed. He turned to take in the sorry place once more, no doubt registering the overflowing garbage bin and the broken asphalt in the parking lot, where weeds poked up through the cracks.

Tate shook his head.

"Yeah," Austin told him. "I paid in advance."

Tate nodded, crossed to the office to drop off the key.

"This is a real shit hole," Garrett observed, settling into the front passenger seat again and wearing his hotshot aviator glasses.

Austin didn't see any point in refuting the obvious. "Why did you and Tate track me down to Pinky's last night?" he asked. Shep was lying down on the seat now, and Austin ran a light hand over the animal's matted back, letting him know he'd be okay from then on.

"You're our kid brother," Garrett said, sounding tired. "When nobody sees you in a while, we come looking for you. It's what we do."

Tate was striding toward the truck now, resettling his hat as he moved. He opened the driver's-side door, got in, started the engine. Although he wouldn't have admitted as much,

Austin was glad to be headed home, and glad to have his brothers' company, even if they *were* a couple of royal pains in the ass.

CHAPTER ONE

Blue River, Texas
November

The evil brides were gaining on her, closing the gap.

Paige Remington ran blindly down a dark country road, legs pumping, lungs burning, her heart flailing in her throat. Slender tree branches plucked at her from either side with nimble, spidery fingers, slowing her down, and the ground turned soft under her feet.

She pitched forward onto her hands and knees. Felt pebbles dig into her palms.

Behind her, the brides screeched and cackled in delighted triumph.

"This is only a dream," Paige told herself. *"Wake up."*

Still, sleep did not release her.

Flurries of silk and lace, glittering with tiny rhinestones and lustrous with the glow of seed pearls, swirled around her. She felt surrounded, almost smothered.

Suddenly furious, the dream-Paige surged to her feet.

If the monsters wanted a fight, then by God, she'd give it to them.

Confronting her pursuers now, staring directly at them, Paige recognized the brides. They were—and at the same time, in that curious way of dreams, *were not*—her sisters, Libby and Julie.

Wedding veils hid their faces, but she knew them anyway. Libby wore a luscious vintage gown of shimmering ivory, while Julie's dress was ultramodern, a little something she'd picked up on a recent romantic getaway to Paris.

"We just want you to try on your bridesmaid's dress," the pair said in creepy unison. "That's all."

"No," Paige said. "I'm not trying on the damn dress. Leave me alone."

They advanced on her. Garment bags had materialized in their arms.

"But you're our only bridesmaid," the two chorused.

"No!" Paige repeated, trying to retreat but stuck fast.

It was then that a voice penetrated the thick surface of the dream. "Hey," the voice said, low and male and disturbingly familiar. "You okay?"

She felt a hand on her shoulder and woke up with a jolt.

And a faceful of Austin McKettrick.

"It just keeps getting worse," she marveled, gripping the arms of the poolside chair where she'd fallen asleep after a solitary lunch in the ranch-house kitchen.

Austin laughed, drew up a chair himself and eased into it with the care of a man much older than his twenty-eight years. His beard was coming in, buttery-brown, and his hair looked a little shaggy.

It ought to require a license, being that good-looking.

"Gee," he drawled. "Thanks."

It galled Paige that after all this time,

he could still make her heart flutter. "What are you doing here?" she demanded.

Austin settled back, popping the top on a beer can, letting her know he meant to take his sweet time answering. A scruffy-looking dog meandered in and settled at his booted feet with a little huff of contented resignation.

"I reckon if anybody's going to demand explanations around here," Austin said at long last, "it ought to be me. I *live* here, Paige."

She'd set herself up for that one. Even seen it coming. And she'd been unable to get out of the way.

Paige drew a deep breath, released it slowly. "I've been staying in the guest suite for a couple of days," she said after a few moments. "The lease was up on my apartment and the renovations on our old house aren't quite finished, so—"

Austin's eyes were a lethal shade of blue—"heirloom" blue, as Paige thought of it, a mixture of new denim and summer sky and every hue in between. According to local legend, the

McKettricks had been passing that eye color down for generations.

He studied her for a long time before speaking again. Set the beer aside without taking a sip. "My brothers," he said, "are marrying your sisters."

Paige sighed. "So I've heard," she said.

Austin ignored the slightly snippy response, went on as if she hadn't said anything. "That means," he told her, "that you and I are going to have to learn to be civil to each other. In spite of our history."

Paige recalled some of that history—youthful, frenzied lovemaking upstairs in Austin's boyhood bedroom, the two of them dancing under the stars to music spilling from the radio in his relic of a truck.

And the fights. She closed her eyes, remembering the fights, and her cheeks burned pink.

"Paige?"

She glared at him.

"Is it a deal?" he asked quietly.

"Is *what* a deal?" she snapped.

Austin sighed, shoved a hand

through his hair. He looked thinner than the last time she'd seen him, and shadows moved behind the light in his eyes. If she hadn't known better, she would have thought he was in pain—maybe physical, maybe emotional. Maybe both.

He leaned toward her, spoke very slowly and very clearly, as though addressing a foreigner with language challenges. "Whether we like it or not, we're going to be kin, you and me, once New Year's rolls around. My guess is, my brothers and your sisters will still be married at the crack of doom. There'll be a whole lot of Christmases and Thanksgivings and birthday parties to get through, over the years. All of which means—"

"I *know* what it means," Paige broke in. "And what's with the condescending tone of voice?"

Austin raised both eyebrows. A grin quirked at one corner of his mouth but never quite kicked in. "What's with the bitchy attitude?" he countered. Then he snapped the fingers of his right hand.

"Oh, *that's* right. It's just your normal personality."

Paige rode out another surge of irritation. Much as she hated to admit it, Austin had a point.

Libby was marrying Tate. Julie was marrying Garrett. Tate's twins, Audrey and Ava, were already part of the family, of course, and so was Julie's little boy, Calvin. And both couples wanted more kids, right away. Oh, yes, there would be a lot of birthday parties to attend.

"Could we try this again?" Paige asked, trying to sound unruffled.

Austin tented his fingers under his chin and watched her with an expression of solemn merriment that was all his own. "Sure," he replied, all fake generosity and ironic goodwill. "Go ahead and say something friendly—you can do it. Just pretend I'm a human being."

Paige looked away, and a deep and inexplicable sadness swept over her. "We're never going to get anywhere at this rate," she said.

Time seemed to freeze for an instant,

then grind into motion again, gears catching on rusty gears.

And then Austin leaned forward, took a light grip on her hand, ran the pad of his thumb over her knuckles.

A hot shiver went through her; he might have been touching her in all those secret, intimate places no one else had found.

"You're right," Austin said, his tone husky. "We're not. Let's give it a shot, Paige—getting along, I mean."

He looked sincere. He *sounded* sincere.

Watch out, Paige reminded herself silently. "Okay," she said with dignity.

Another silence followed. Paige, for her part, was trying to imagine what a truce between herself and Austin would actually *look* like. After all, they'd been at odds since that summer night, soon after they'd both graduated from high school, when Paige had caught the lying, sneaking, no-good bastard—

She drew another deep breath, mentally untangled herself from the past. As best she could.

They'd gotten together by accident,

in the beginning—Tate and Libby were going to a movie one Friday night, and, grudgingly, Tate had brought his younger brother along. Paige had gotten the impression that their parents had insisted, and if Tate had refused, it would have been a deal breaker.

Paige had been curled up in an armchair reading a book when Austin turned that fabled charm on her, grinned and asked if she'd like to go to a movie.

After that, she and Austin had been as inseparable as Libby and Tate.

Paige had thought he was playing some game at first, but after a few months, they were a couple. After a year, Paige was on the pill, and they were making love.

Yes, she'd been in love with Austin. She'd lost—okay, *given*—her virginity to him, along with her trust and, of course, her heart.

Ultimately, he'd betrayed her.

But all that had happened just over ten years ago, before his folks, Jim and Sally McKettrick, were killed in that awful car accident, before her own dad had died of cancer. So very much had happened in the interim and, well, Paige was tired of holding a grudge.

"You were having a bad dream before?" Austin asked presently.

"Huh?" Paige said.

"When I woke you up a little while ago?"

"Yes," she answered, smiling a little. "Thanks for that."

He grinned, making the pit of her stomach quiver for a moment, then reached for his can of beer. Raised it slightly in an offhand toast. "Anytime," he said.

The dog whimpered, chasing something in his sleep. Or running away from something.

"Shep," Austin said, nudging the animal gently with the toe of one boot. "Easy, now. You're all right."

Paige looked down at Shep. "A stray?"

Austin grinned again. This time, there was no smart-ass edge to his tone. "What gave him away? The matted coat? The dirt, maybe?"

"The poor thing *could* use a bath,"

Paige admitted. She'd always had a soft spot for animals—especially the abused, neglected and unwanted ones.

"Garrett promised to hose him down before supper," Austin said. The way he spoke, it was no big deal.

Paige met his gaze, puzzled and not a little annoyed. "Supper's a ways off," she pointed out.

"He'll keep," Austin told her. "Won't you, Shep?"

Paige glanced at her watch. She still had more than an hour before she was due to pick Calvin up in town, at day care. Although she was a nurse by profession, she was between jobs at the moment, as well as between homes. Since Julie was practically meeting herself coming and going these days, between getting ready for the big wedding, holding down her teaching job at the high school and directing the student musical production, Paige had been looking after her nephew a lot lately.

Since she adored Calvin, it was no hardship.

She stood. "I'll do it," she said.

"Do what?" Austin asked.

"Bathe the dog," Paige answered, proud of herself for not adding, *since you can't be bothered to do the job yourself.*

"I told you," Austin said, frowning. "Garrett will take care of Shep when he gets home."

"No sense in putting it off," Paige said, feeling sorry for the critter.

Shep hauled himself to his feet, watching her with a combination of wariness and hope. His tail swished tentatively to one side, then the other.

And Paige's heart warmed and softened, like so much beeswax.

She crouched, looked straight into the dog's limpid brown eyes.

"I wouldn't hurt you," she said very gently. "Not for the world."

Shep wagged again, this time with more trust, more spirit.

"Paige," Austin interjected cautiously, "he's sort of wild and he probably hasn't had his shots—"

Paige put out a hand, let Shep sniff her fingers and palm and wrist.

She felt something akin to exultation

when he didn't retreat. "Nonsense," she said. "He's a sweetheart. Aren't you, Shep?"

She straightened, saw that Austin was standing, too. If it hadn't been for the dog, the man would practically have been on top of her. So to speak.

Heat pulsed in her cheeks.

Something mischievous and far too knowing danced in Austin's eyes. He folded his arms and tilted his head to one side, watching her. She had no clue what he was thinking, and that was even more unsettling.

In order to break the spell, Paige turned and headed for the main part of the house, moving resolutely.

She felt a little zing of triumph when she glanced back and saw the dog hesitate, then fall into step behind her.

Austin couldn't really blame the dog for trailing after Paige—watching that perfect blue-jeaned backside of hers as she walked away left him with little choice but to do likewise. Still, it stung his pride that Shep hadn't waited for him.

Whose dog *was* he, anyhow?

Paige's apparently. She led the way, like some piper in a fairy tale, with Shep padding right along in her wake, and that was how the three of them ended up in the laundry room, off the kitchen.

Paige knew her way around—she rustled up some old towels and the special mutt shampoo Julie kept around for Harry—and started the water running in one of the big sinks. She spooled out the hand-sprayer and pressed the squirter with a practiced thumb, testing the temperature against the underside of her left wrist.

The sight, ordinary as it was, did something peculiar to Austin.

"Well," Paige said, dropping her gaze to the dog and then letting it fly back to Austin's face, "don't just stand there. Hoist Shep up into the sink so I can wash him." She smiled at Shep. "You're going to feel so much better, once you've had your bath," she assured the critter.

Austin had his pride. He wasn't *about* to tell this woman that he'd blown out his back and couldn't risk lifting one skinny dog off the floor because he might wind up in traction or something.

He leaned down and carefully looped his arms under Shep's belly. Set him gently in the laundry sink.

Paige introduced Shep to the sprayer with a few little blasts of warm water, and gave him time to sort out how he felt about the experience.

Austin, meanwhile, was just about to congratulate himself on getting away with lifting the dog when he felt a stabbing ache in the same part of his back as when he'd had to be half carried out of Pinky's bar last month. He drew in a sharp breath and grasped the edge of the long counter, where the housekeeper, Esperanza, usually folded sheets and towels.

Steady, he thought. *Wait it out.*

Paige, preoccupied with sluicing down the dog and apparently oblivious to the way the water was soaking the front of her skimpy T-shirt, paid Austin no attention at all. And that was fine by him, mostly.

The spasm in Austin's back intensified, a giant charley horse that he couldn't walk off like one in his calf or the arch of his foot. He bit down hard on his lower lip and shut his eyes.

"Austin?" Paige's voice had changed. It was soft, worried-sounding. "Is something wrong? You're sort of pale and—"

Austin shook his head. The spasm was beginning to subside, though it still hurt like holy-be-Jesus, but talking was beyond him.

He wouldn't risk meeting her gaze. Back when they were just kids and hot and heavy into dating, Paige had shown a disturbing ability to read his mind—not to mention his soul— through his eyes.

Not that she'd been infallible in that regard.

Or maybe, when it really counted, she'd been too mad to look long enough, hard enough.

"I'm—fine," he finally said. The pain was letting up.

Paige reached for the dog shampoo, squeezed a glistening trail of it down

Shep's sodden back and began to suds him up.

"Excuse me," she said matter-of-factly, "but you don't *look* fine."

Poor Shep looked up at him, all bedraggled and wet, but there was a patient expression in his eyes, a willingness to endure, that tightened Austin's throat to the point where he couldn't make a sound.

Paige, a head shorter than he was, bent her knees and turned to peer up into his face. "Are you sick?"

He shook his head again, helpless to do more than that.

"Austin," she said firmly, "*I am a nurse.* I know a person in pain when I see one."

When he opened his mouth to answer, his back spasmed again. He tightened his hold on the counter's edge, riding it out.

Paige simply waited, not fussing, not pressing for an answer. In fact, she rinsed the dog, soaped him up again, sprayed him down a second time.

Shep, who withstood all this without

complaint, turned out to be buff col-
ored, with a saddlelike splotch of reddish brown running down the center of
his back.

Paige congratulated the critter on his
good looks and toweled him vigorously
before lifting him out of the laundry sink
and setting him on the floor.

Austin, by that time, could breathe
again, but that was about all.

Paige turned to him, hands on her
hips, T-shirt clinging in intriguing places
from the inevitable splashing.

Austin dragged his gaze, by force,
from her perfect breasts to her face,
though not quickly enough. Paige's
brown eyes were snapping with temper.

Or was it concern?

"Some things never change," she
said.

Austin sighed. He let go of the
counter, relieved that the kink in his
lower back had smoothed out. "What
the hell do you mean by that?" he
asked. Then, without waiting for an answer, he rushed on, fool that he was.

"Okay, so I checked out your chest. I'm sorry you saw that."

Her mouth twitched. "You're sorry I caught you at it, you mean?"

"Yeah," he admitted, unwilling to elaborate until he knew which way the mood wind was blowing.

She laughed.

He'd forgotten what the sound of Paige Remington's laughter did to him, how it made him feel dizzy inside, as though he'd been blindfolded, turned around half a dozen times and then had the floor yanked out from under him.

Paige's expression sobered, though the ghost of a grin flicked at one corner of her mouth and danced like a faint flame in her eyes. "What I *meant,*" she informed him, "when I said some things never change, was that you're still too cussed and proud to let on when you need help."

"I *don't* need help," Austin reasoned, wondering why it was so important to him to make that absolutely clear.

Shep broke loose with a good shaking then, flinging moisture over both of them.

"I'm not going to argue with you, Austin McKettrick," Paige said.

He snorted at the irony of *that* statement.

"Something is wrong," she said, ignoring his reaction. She headed back into the kitchen, and Shep followed at a sprightly pace, toenails clicking on the plank floor. "If you won't tell me what it is, I can find out from Garrett or Tate."

Austin waited until he was sure he could walk without any obvious hitches before stepping away from the counter. Paige was standing at the kitchen sink, washing her hands.

She wouldn't look at him.

"Paige."

Still, she kept her eyes averted, and he knew from the stubborn angle of her chin that she wasn't going to let this go. She meant to ask one or both of his brothers what was going on with him, and they'd tell her, putting their own spin on the story.

Dammit, it was *his* story to tell and, besides, he didn't want any second-hand versions making the rounds. "My back goes out sometimes," he said very quietly. "That's all."

Paige turned to face him. "'That's all'? Why didn't you say that a few minutes ago, when I asked you to lift Shep into the sink?"

Austin tugged at an imaginary hat brim and answered, "Because I'm Texas born and bred, ma'am, and therefore averse to letting a lady do my lifting."

She just stood there for several long moments, looking at him as if she were doing arithmetic in her head and none of the sums were coming out right.

Finally, she spoke.

"You idiot," she said with some affection.

Austin opened his mouth, closed it again, entirely at a loss.

She'd just insulted him, hadn't she? And yet her tone . . . well, it made him feel all wrapped up in something warm.

Paige, oblivious to the strange effect she was having on him, checked her watch. "I've got to pick Calvin up," she said, addressing no one in particular. "Want to come along for the ride?"

Did he ever.

She's offering to let you ride in her car, fool. That's all.

He shoved a hand through his hair. Did she really want his company, he wondered, or was she just afraid to leave the invalid cowboy alone in the house?

Hard to tell, and when it came right down to it, he didn't care.

"Sure," he said. "I guess."

Paige rolled her marvelous eyes. "Well, *that* was ambivalent," she replied. "Just let me change out of this wet T-shirt, and we'll go."

"Do you have to?"

Her gaze narrowed and her hands went back to her hips, but she was trying too hard not to grin to be angry. "Have to what?"

Austin waggled his eyebrows. "Change out of the wet T-shirt?"

She widened her eyes at him, then turned and hurried off in the direction of the guest apartment.

It was all he could do not to tag along with her.

His mouth quirked. It wasn't as if she'd let him watch her change her shirt.

Damn the luck.

Every nerve in her body was on red alert, and her heart seemed to skip every other beat.

It was her own fault.

What had she been *thinking,* asking Austin, of all people, if he'd like to ride to town with her?

Now here he was, big as life and busting with testosterone, sitting in her perfectly ordinary subcompact car, sliding the passenger seat back as far as it would go. Shep, still damp from his bath and smelling pleasantly of freshly shampooed dog, sat directly behind him.

Austin was taking up more than his fair share of room, she knew that much. If she weren't careful, their shoulders would touch.

All business, Paige took her sunglasses from the holder above her rearview mirror and put them on. Then she fastened her seat belt, shifted into Reverse and almost backed into the garage door.

Austin chuckled, reached up to push the button on the remote clasped to one of the visors.

The garage door rolled up behind them.

"I would have remembered," Paige said.

"Of course you would have," Austin agreed lightly.

Paige knew if she looked at him, she'd catch him grinning. Her cheeks ached with heat, and she was grateful for her sunglasses.

"I suppose you think you should drive," she huffed, taking great care as she backed out into the driveway.

Austin spread his hands. "Did I say that?" he asked.

Paige sighed. "No."

She managed to drive out of the garage without crashing into anything and pointed the car toward the massive iron gates standing open at the bottom of the driveway.

"Why are you so rattled?" Austin wanted to know.

Paige braked for the turn onto the main road. The coast was clear in both directions, but she came to a crawling stop anyhow.

"I am *not* rattled."

"Yes, you are."

"I am not." She paused, sucked in a righteous breath. "Don't flatter yourself, Austin. Not *every* woman is susceptible to your many charms, you know."

He laughed. "I didn't say *that,* either."

Paige sniffed, indignant. "Some things," she replied, "go *without* saying."

Austin cocked an eyebrow at her as she pointed the car toward town. "No matter what I say," he ventured, "you're going to disagree. Right?"

"Right," Paige said.

That time they both laughed.

Austin folded his arms, closed his eyes, tilted his head back, the very picture of a contented cowboy. Although Paige hated to give this particular man credit for anything, she had to admit, at least to herself, that he still had the power to short-circuit her wiring.

He was so damnably at home in his own skin.

It would have bothered some men, riding shotgun instead of taking the wheel, but not Austin. Whatever he might have questioned in his lifetime, it hadn't been his masculinity, Paige was sure of that.

Tate and Garrett were the same way. Maybe, she concluded, it was a McKettrick thing.

And why shouldn't they be confident, all three of them? They had it all—good looks, money, a ranch that was large even by Texas standards, a name that commanded respect.

Heat climbed Paige's neck, her throat tightened and her heart started racing again.

Of course that was when he hit her with the question, when she was least prepared to respond to it with any kind of dignity.

"How've you been, Paige?"

The backs of her eyes scalded with

tears she'd have died before shedding. She swallowed hard.

How've you been, Paige? Since I broke your heart, I mean. Since you chased me down Main Street on a stolen golf cart. How've you been, Paige old buddy, old pal?

"Fine," she said, surprised and relieved by how calm she sounded. "I've been—just fine. Busy. How about you?"

There. The ball was in his court.

Out of the corner of her eye, she saw that Austin had turned his head in her direction, and he was watching her.

"Has it really been ten years?"

"It has," Paige said very quietly. A month after their breakup, Austin's parents had been killed in that terrible accident. She'd wanted so much to go to him, offer her condolences, ask if there was anything she could do to help.

Alas, he wasn't the only one with too much pride.

"I went to the funeral," she said. A joint service had been held for Jim and Sally McKettrick, and there had been so many mourners, they couldn't all fit into the church. People had stood in the yard and on the sidewalk and even in the street, just to be there.

He didn't ask which funeral, though they often turned up at the same ones, both of them raised in or near Blue River as they had been.

"I know," Austin said very quietly. "I saw you."

Austin had attended Paige's father's services, too, along with both his brothers. He hadn't spoken to her then, but it had helped a little, just knowing he was nearby, that he'd cared enough to put in an appearance. She'd been too distracted by grief, that one day, to smart over the loss of her first love.

There had been plenty of *other* days to cry over Austin McKettrick, and many a dark night as well.

They passed the oil wells, long since capped, though there was still plenty of black gold under the Silver Spur, according to the experts. They drove by cattle grazing on good McKettrick grass, and there was so much Paige wanted to say.

In the end, though, she either had too much good sense—or *too little* courage—to put any of her emotions into words.

CHAPTER TWO

Calvin Remington, five years old as of a very recent birthday, was one of Austin's all-time favorite people.

Going by the broad smile on the little boy's face as he ran toward Paige's car, the feeling was mutual. His aunt walked a few feet behind him, looking bemused, while Austin waited in the passenger seat, having buzzed down the window.

"Hey, buddy!" he called.

Calvin's horn-rimmed glasses were a little askew, and his light blond hair stuck out in all directions. His jacket was unzipped and he was waving a paper over his head.

"My *whole kindergarten class* gets to go to Six Flags!" he shouted to Austin.

"Because we've been really, *really* good!"

Austin chuckled. His gaze accidentally connected with Paige's, and electricity arched between them, ending up as a hard ache that settled into his groin like a weight.

"Whose dog is that?" Calvin demanded, breathless with excitement and crossing the yard between the community center and the parking lot at a dead run. "Is that your dog, Austin? Is it?"

"That is my dog," Austin confirmed. "His name is Shep."

Calvin opened the car door and scrambled into the booster seat in the back. "Hello, Shep," he said.

Paige leaned over to make sure her nephew was properly buckled in.

She looked after the boy with the same easy competence she'd shown bathing Shep, back in the ranch-house laundry room.

For some reason, realizing that cinched Austin's throat into a painful knot.

"Give Shep some space, now," Paige

told the child. "He's still getting used to belonging to somebody, and you don't want to scare him."

Calvin agreed with a nod and changed the subject. "Will you be a chaperone when we go to Six Flags, Aunt Paige?" he asked. "I bet Mom would do it, but she's got to teach school all day and help the drama club put on the musical and get ready to get married and stuff."

Paige glanced at Austin, over the seat.

Austin indulged in a wink.

Paige blushed a little, shut Calvin's door, got into the front seat, snapped on her seat belt and started the engine. All the while, she was careful not to look at Austin again.

"Will you, Aunt Paige?" Calvin persisted.

"Depends," Paige said mildly, though there was a faint tremor in her tone. "When's the big day?"

"It's the Wednesday before Thanksgiving," the boy answered eagerly. "My teacher said she'd like to know what lame-brain scheduled a field trip for the day before a big holiday like that. She likes to bake pumpkin pies that day, but now she'll probably get a pounding headache and have to spend the whole evening with her feet up and a cold cloth on her head."

Austin grinned. "Your teacher said all that?"

Calvin nodded vigorously. "She wasn't talking to the class, though," he clarified. "It was during recess, and I went inside to the bathroom, and when I came back, I heard her talking to Mrs. Jenson, the playground monitor."

"Ah, I see," Austin said very seriously as Paige started the car and backed carefully out of her parking space. There were other kids leaving the premises with their mothers or fathers, and casual waves were exchanged.

"I think this dog is pretty friendly," Calvin remarked. "Can I pet him? Please?"

"Yes," Paige answered, hitting every possible pothole as she guided the compact out onto the highway. "But no sudden moves."

They rolled along in companionable

silence for a while, but when it came
time to turn right and head back out to
the Silver Spur, Paige turned left instead.

Austin didn't comment, but Paige explained anyhow.

Women. They were always ready to
give a man more information than he
needed.

"Calvin likes to stop by Blue River
High and see his mom for a few minutes before going home," she said.

Home. Austin liked the sound of the
word, coming from Paige. He liked that
she meant the ranch when she said it—
his ranch.

He immediately reined himself in.
*Whoa, cowboy. Don't go getting all
sentimental. You're all wrong for Paige
Remington and she's all wrong for you
and you learned that the hard way, so
don't forget it.*

"Garrett says Mom works too hard,"
Calvin announced. "And you know
what?"

"What?" Austin asked, shaking off
his own thoughts to pick up the cue.

"I get a baby brother or sister *right away*."

A grin broke across Austin's face.

Paige looked his way and smiled a little before replying, "Well, maybe not *right* away, Calvin. Babies take nine months, you know."

"Garrett says all the *other* babies will take that long, but the first one can come anytime."

Austin laughed at that.

"Garrett says, Garrett says," Paige teased, craning her neck a little to catch sight of Calvin in the rearview mirror. Hers was a slender, pretty neck, and Austin ached to trace its length with his lips. "It's the gospel according to Garrett McKettrick."

"That," Austin put in drily, "would be *some* gospel."

"Hush," Paige told him, but the word was warmly spoken, nice to hear, like the way she'd said *home* a few minutes before.

They reached Blue River High School, and Paige pulled into the teachers' parking lot. Except for Julie's car, an old pink Cadillac, and the fancy white pickup truck Garrett had bought soon after he and Julie got engaged, the lot was empty.

Plenty of the kids in the drama club had cars, of course, but the students had their own parking area, on the other side of the school building.

"Calvin and I won't be long," Paige told Austin, after popping the gearshift into Park and shutting off the motor. Then her cheeks went cotton-candy pink. "Unless, of course, you'd rather come inside with us."

"I believe Shep and I will just stretch our legs a little, out here in the parking lot," he said, enjoying her discomfort.

God, it was good to know he could still shake her up a little.

Or a lot.

Don't go there, he reminded himself, but his brain was already partway down the trail to trouble.

Mercifully, Paige and Calvin were out of the car and hotfooting it toward the entrance to the auditorium in no time.

Austin adjusted his anatomy with a subtle motion of his hips, took off his seat belt and pushed open the passenger door. Shep didn't have a collar or a leash yet, but he wasn't likely to run off; he seemed too glad to have a home to try making a go of it on his own again.

As predicted, Shep conducted himself like a gentleman, and he had just hopped back into Paige's car when Garrett ambled out of the auditorium—he often visited Julie at play practice—wearing a stupid, drifty grin. He moved easily, as if all his hinges had just been greased.

Seeing Austin, Brother Number Two grinned and readjusted his hat.

"Well, now," he said, evidently surprised to see Austin not only up and around but out and about. "If it isn't the bull-riding wonder boy of Blue River, Texas."

"In the flesh," Austin retorted, keeping his tone noncommittal, shutting the car door and approaching Garrett.

Garrett took in Paige's car, threw a quick glance back at the auditorium before facing Austin again. "You must be in better shape than Tate and I thought you were," he drawled, folding his arms.

Austin didn't answer. He just waited for whatever was coming. And he had a pretty good idea what that "whatever" was.

"As of New Year's," Garrett said, at some length, "Paige will be family. Keep that in mind, Austin."

Austin leaned into Garrett's space. He hadn't done anything wrong and, back trouble or no back trouble, he wasn't about to retreat. "What the hell is *that* supposed to mean?" he demanded under his breath.

"Add it up, little brother," Garrett replied tersely. "Paige is Julie's sister. Julie loves her. I love Julie. Consequently, if you hurt Paige, that's bound to hurt Julie, too, and I'm going to be one pissed-off Texas cowboy if that happens."

Austin knew the difference between a threat and a promise. This was a promise. And while he wasn't afraid of Garrett, or of Tate, or of the two of them together, he got the message.

"You think I'm out to take advantage of Paige?" He put the question evenly, in a steely tone void of inflection.

"Going by past history?" Garrett retorted. "Yeah. That's what I think, all right. She's not one of your usual women, Austin."

Austin wanted to land a sucker punch in the middle of his brother's handsome face, but Jim and Sally McKettrick hadn't raised any fools. He was at a distinct disadvantage with that herniated disc, and Garrett wouldn't fight because of it. So Austin waited out the rush of adrenaline that made his fists clench and his hackles rise.

"What's my 'usual woman,' Garrett?" he rasped.

Before Garrett could reply to the loaded question, the auditorium doors sprang open and Paige reappeared, Calvin trailing behind her.

"Can I ride home with you, Garrett?" the boy asked, full of delight.

Garrett didn't hesitate. "Sure," he said gruffly, ruffling Calvin's hair. "You can help me feed the horses."

"Is that okay, Aunt Paige?" Calvin asked, looking up at his aunt with such hope in his eyes that Austin didn't see how she could have refused, without her heart turning to stone first. "I have a safety seat in Garrett's truck and everything."

"Of course," Paige said softly. "See you back at the ranch."

Calvin nodded and headed for the truck.

Garrett smiled, spread his hands as if to say *What can you do?* and followed.

"He's so happy," Paige murmured, watching them go. Her gaze followed the man and the boy, tender, alight with affection.

Austin wanted to take her into his arms, then and there. Hold her tight, the way he used to do, way back when.

When.

When she loved him.

When she would have trusted him not only with her heart, but with her life.

When she still believed he felt the same way about her.

"Who?" Austin asked, keeping his distance. "Garrett or Calvin?"

She smiled, and the earth shifted under Austin's feet.

"Both of them, I guess," Paige answered with a wistful look and a little shrug of her shoulders. "Calvin adores Garrett."

Austin wanted to spread his fingers, slip them into her hair. Rub the pads of his thumbs over her delicate cheekbones and then kiss her, but he didn't do that.

There were things he could have said, *should* have said, maybe. And still couldn't.

I was only eighteen, Paige. Things were happening too fast between us and the feelings were way too overwhelming and I didn't know how else to put on the brakes, so I cheated and made sure you knew it.

Even as a teenager, Paige had known exactly what she wanted. A career, first of all. Then marriage and a home and babies.

Austin, confused and scared shitless by the emotions Paige could stir in him, seemingly without half trying, hadn't wanted to go on to college, as his older brothers had, or stay home and learn to run the ranch, either.

And love Paige though he did, he sure as *hell* hadn't been ready to move into some off-campus apartment and play househusband while his bride attended nursing school. Rodeo had been his consuming passion for as long as he could remember, and its siren song was impossible to resist.

Austin came back to the here and now with a jolt, and while he was able to shake off the memories, mostly anyway, the mood remained.

Paige got behind the wheel of her car.

Without Calvin there to serve as a buffer, the connection between Austin and Paige seemed even more intimate than before. It made Austin uncomfortable, in a not entirely unpleasant way.

"Since Esperanza is away taking care of her niece for the next couple of weeks," Paige said, as though she and Austin were mere acquaintances and not two people who had been able to turn each other inside out once upon a time, "Garrett's making supper for Julie and Calvin tonight. Tate and Libby and the girls will be there, and we're invited, too."

She wasn't looking at him. No, she

was too busy backing out, turning around, pushing her sunglasses back up her nose.

"Just one big, happy family," Austin said sourly. He was still smarting a little from the exchange with Garrett in front of the auditorium. He couldn't very well blame Garrett for his low opinion— Austin had spent years living down to it.

Paige glanced his way before pulling out of the familiar parking lot onto the road. "What's your problem now?" she asked with a note of snarky impatience.

"Who said I had a problem?" Austin retorted.

In the backseat, Shep gave a little whine, as if to intercede.

"It's hopeless," Paige said.

"What?"

"Trying to get along with you, *that's* what."

"Excuse me, but it seems to me that you're not trying all that hard," Austin pointed out. Reasonably, he thought.

"What you mean is," Paige replied heatedly, "that I'm not bending over backward to make you happy!"

Austin began to laugh. He snorted first, then howled.

Paige kept driving, but she was moving at the breakneck speed of a golf cart in first gear.

"What," she demanded, "is so freaking funny?"

In the next instant, with a visible impact, Paige realized for herself what was so freaking funny. Her bending over—in any direction—was *guaranteed* to make him happy, and he could recall a few times when she'd had a pretty good time in that position, too.

The best part was, he didn't have to say any of that.

She wrenched the car over to the side of the highway, shifted into Park, and flipped on the hazard lights.

Paige sort of pivoted in the seat then, and he watched as a tremor of anger—and possibly passion—moved through that compact, curvy little body of hers and then made the leap across the console and turned him instantly, obviously hard.

"Maybe," he said, "we ought to just have sex and get it over with."

She simply stared at him.

Mentally, Austin pulled his foot out of his mouth. Shoved a hand through his hair and wished his hard-on weren't pressing itself into the ridges of his zipper—he'd have a scar, if this kept up.

"Let me rephrase that," he said.

Paige blinked.

Time stretched.

Cars passed, the drivers tooting the horns to say howdy.

Polar ice caps melted.

New species developed, reached the pinnacle of evolution and became extinct.

"I'm waiting," Paige said finally. A little lilt of fury threaded its way through her tone.

"For what?"

"For you to 'rephrase' that ridiculous statement you just made. 'Maybe we ought to just have sex and get it over with,' I think it was." She adjusted her sunglasses, smoothed the thighs of her jeans, as she might have done with a skirt. "It's hard to imagine how, Austin, but I'm sure you can make things even *worse* if you try."

It wasn't as if he had to try, he thought bleakly. When it came to Paige Remington, he could make things worse without even opening his mouth.

"It was just a thought," he said, disgruntled. "There's no need to overreact."

"Overreact." Paige huffed out the word, made a big show of facing forward again. With prim indignation, she resettled herself, switched off the blinkers and leaned to consult the rearview mirror before pulling back out onto the highway. "You are *such* a jerk," she told him.

Austin couldn't think of a damn thing to say in reply to that—nothing that wouldn't get him in deeper, anyhow.

"I can't *believe* you said that," Paige marveled.

Austin's response was part growl, part groan. He'd forgotten just how impossible this woman could be when she got her tail into a twist about something—or how little it took to piss her off.

Shep whined again.

"You're scaring the dog," Paige said.

"*I'm* scaring the dog?" Austin shot back, keeping his voice low. "*You* started this, Paige, by calling me a jerk!"

"You *are* a jerk," Paige replied, raising her chin, her spine stiff as a ramrod, her face turned straight ahead. "And *you* started this by saying—by saying what you said."

He couldn't resist, even though he knew he should. "That we ought to have sex and get it over with, you mean?"

She glared at him. Even through the lenses of her sunglasses, he felt her eyes burning into his hide.

He grinned at her. "Well," he drawled, "now that you bring it up, maybe a roll in the hay wouldn't be such a bad idea. We could get it out of our systems, put the whole thing behind us, get on with our lives."

Her neck went crimson, and she just sat there, her back rigid, her knuckles white from her grip on the wheel. "Oh, that's a *fine* idea, Austin. Just what I would have expected from you!"

"You have a better one?"

She said nothing.

"I didn't think so," Austin said smugly.

Austin had been baiting her, Paige knew that. But knowing hadn't kept her from taking the hook.

Get it out of our systems.

Put the whole thing behind us, get on with our lives.

Indeed.

Standing at the counter in Julie and Garrett's kitchen, upstairs at the Silver Spur ranch house, Paige whacked hard at the green onions she was chopping for the salad. Julie reached out, stopped her by grasping her wrist.

"Whoa," she said. "If you're not careful, you'll chop off a finger."

Libby, standing nearby and busy pouring white wine into three elegant glasses, grinned knowingly at her two younger sisters.

All three of the McKettrick men were outside, in the small, private courtyard at the bottom of a flight of stucco steps, barbecuing steaks and hamburgers. Calvin, Tate's twin daughters and the pack of dogs were with them.

"You know, Paige," Libby observed, handing her a glass, "if I didn't know better, I'd think you and Austin were— back on, or something."

Julie's eyes twinkled as she accepted a wineglass for herself and took a sip. "Or something," she murmured after swallowing.

"Stop it, both of you," Paige protested. "Austin and I are *not* 'back on.' The man infuriates me."

Libby smiled, resting a hip against the side of the counter, but said nothing. The firstborn daughter in the Remington family, Libby had light brown hair and expressive blue eyes. She and Tate were crazy about each other, and they would have beautiful children together.

"Why?" Julie asked. The second sister, a year younger than Libby and a year older than Paige, Julie had chameleon eyes. They seemed a fierce shade of bluish green at the moment, though the color changed with what she was wearing and often looked

hazel, and her coppery hair fell naturally into wonderful, spiraling curls past
her shoulders.

"Why?" Paige echoed, stalling.

"Why does Austin infuriate you?"
Julie wanted to know.

"Because he's so—sure of himself,"
Paige said. There were probably a million reasons, but that was the first to
come to mind.

Libby raised both eyebrows. "This is
a *bad* thing?" she asked.

Paige wanted her sisters to understand. Take her side. If anybody knew
how badly her heart had been broken,
they did. "He's arrogant."

Julie laughed. "No," she said with a
shake of her head, "he's a *McKettrick.*"

Paige took a sip from her wineglass—and nearly choked. She set the
drink aside and promptly forgot all
about it. "The difference being . . . ?"

Julie and Libby exchanged knowing
glances over the rims of their wineglasses.

"If you still care about Austin," Julie
said presently, after a visible gathering
of internal forces, "there's nothing

wrong with that. You're not in high school anymore, after all, and there's no denying that the man is all McKettrick."

Paige folded her arms. "Look," she said, "I know you're both madly in love with McKettrick men, and I'm happy for you—I really, *truly* am—but if you think I'm going to decide all is forgiven and fall into Austin's bed as if nothing ever happened, you're sadly mistaken."

"She's not going to fall into Austin's bed," Libby said to Julie very seriously.

"She's not going to fall *back* into Austin's bed," Julie said.

Paige stepped between them and waved both arms. "Hello? I'm in the room," she told her sisters. "I can hear everything you're saying."

Libby and Julie laughed. And they raised their wineglasses to each other.

"I give them seventy-two hours," Libby said.

"Nonsense," Julie replied matter-of-factly. "Paige will be twisting the sheets with Austin by tomorrow night at the latest."

"You're both crazy," Paige said, flustered. "Just because neither of *you* can resist a McKettrick man, doesn't mean *I* can't!"

"She's got it bad," Libby told Julie.

"Worst case I've ever seen," Julie decreed.

Paige simmered.

"About the bridesmaid's dress," Libby said, evidently determined to make bad matters worse. "I was thinking daffodil yellow, with ruffles, pearl buttons and lots of lace trim—"

"Lavender," Julie countered cheerfully. "With a *bustle.*"

That did it. "Why not throw in a lamb and one of those hoops you roll with a stick?" Paige erupted. "And maybe I could *skip* down the aisle?"

The picture must have delighted Libby and Julie, because they both laughed uproariously.

Libby refilled her own wineglass, and Julie's. Paige's was still full.

Julie elbowed Paige aside to finish making the salad. She was, after all, the cook in the family.

"You're really afraid of The Dress, aren't you, Paige?" Libby asked, her eyes sparkling with happiness and well-being.

"I'm the Lone Bridesmaid," Paige pointed out, calmer now but still discouraged. "I have nightmares about that dress."

"To hear her tell it," Julie told Libby, "neither of us has any taste at all."

"Will you two stop talking as though I'm not even here?" Paige asked. "If you'd just agree to let *me* pick out my gown, since I'm the one who has to wear it—"

"What fun would *that* be?" Libby said to Julie. "We're the brides, after all."

Paige, as the youngest, flashed back to the old days, when the three of them were kids and her older sisters had tossed a ball back and forth between them, over her head, making sure it was always out of her reach. They called the game "Keep Away."

The term seemed especially apt that night, though she couldn't have explained the idea. If ever two people had had her back, no matter what the situation might be, her sisters were those two people.

As a kid, she'd tagged after them, wanting so badly to go wherever they went, do whatever they did, to be part of their circle.

Growing up, she'd loved wearing their clothes and mimicking their voices and copying their mannerisms. Now, they were marrying brothers. Was some unconscious part of her still trying to follow in Libby and Julie's footsteps? The possibility was chilling to consider.

"That's it," Paige said decisively, though without rancor. "I'm dropping out of the wedding party. You both have plenty of friends, and I'm sure some of them are willing to make absolute fools of themselves at the ceremony by wearing some god-awful dress—lavender with a bustle, or yellow, with ruffles—"

"Maybe we shouldn't have teased her," Julie told Libby.

"Of *course* we should have teased her," Libby said. "She's our little sister."

Julie looked speculative. "If you married Austin," she ruminated, turning to Paige, "we could have a *triple* wedding, and you wouldn't have to worry about hoops and lambs and bustles, because you'd be wearing a *bridal gown.*"

Paige flung both hands out from her sides. "Why didn't *I* think of that?" she scoffed. "I'll just *marry Austin.* To hell with my goals, my plans, my personal standards. To hell with everything!"

Julie reached out to touch Paige's arm. "Honey," she said softly, "we didn't mean to upset you—"

Paige drew in a deep, sharp breath, let it out slowly. Shook her head. "It's all right, I just—I just need some time alone, that's all."

Having said that, she left Garrett's glam second-story apartment—one of three such spaces comprising that floor of the house and part of a third—and to their credit, neither Julie nor Libby called her back or tried to follow.

Downstairs, Paige crossed the main kitchen, retrieved her jacket and purse from the guest apartment and slipped out through the back door. It was dark, and stars glittered from horizon to horizon in great silvery splotches of far-away light.

On the other side of the courtyard wall, the kids were laughing, the dogs were barking, while the men talked in quiet voices.

Paige couldn't make out their words, wouldn't have tried. She needed quiet to collect her scattered thoughts, get some perspective. So she walked to her car—which she'd parked near the barn instead of in the garage as she usually did, flustered, at the time, because of Austin's close proximity—got in and started the engine.

She drove down the long driveway, through the open iron gates, and out onto the highway, headed for town. She switched on the radio, choosing a classical spot on the dial instead of her favorite country station. Paige felt too raw to listen to country music at the moment, and she was woman enough to admit it, by God.

This last thought made her smile.

Drive, she told herself. *Don't think about him.*

Between the soft piano concerto flowing out of the dashboard speakers and the semihypnotic effect of driving alone over a rural road, cosseted in purple twilight and under a canopy of stars, Paige was finally able to relax a little—and then a little more.

It was as though Austin McKettrick possessed his own magnetic field; the farther she got from him, the easier it was to breathe, to reason. To simply *be.*

Reaching the outskirts of town, Paige slowed down, drove automatically toward the house where she and Libby and Julie had grown up, with their dad. Libby had lived there, before and after Will Remington's death from pancreatic cancer, with her dog, Hildie, and had run the Perk Up Coffee Shop to support herself.

Now, thanks largely to their mother, Marva, and her questionable driving skills, the shop was gone, along with the mom-and-pop grocery store that had once stood beside it, the lot totally empty.

Rumor had it that a bank would be built on the site, but as Paige bumped along the alley toward the detached garage behind the old house, she saw no signs of construction.

After parking her car in the narrow space the garage afforded, Paige got out, walked to the back gate and let herself into the yard.

Here, there were *definitely* signs of construction. The old cupboards, newly pulled away from the kitchen walls, stood near the porch, seeming to crouch under blue plastic tarps. The bathtub, so outdated that it was probably about to come back into style again, rested in one of the flowerbeds, with the matching green toilet perched inside it.

Paige sighed as she let herself in through the back door and drew in the scents of sawdust and new drywall. She flipped on the overhead light and was gratified, and a little surprised, that it worked.

The kitchen, twice its former size, boasted a new slate-tile floor and an alcove set into a semicircle of floor-to-ceiling windows, but it was a long way from usable.

Paige shoved her hands into the

pockets of her jacket and moved farther into the house.

The living room was all new; the
floors were hardwood and the molding
around the edges of the raised ceiling
had been salvaged from an old man-
sion in Dallas. There was an elegant
marble fireplace, with an antique mantel, and the windows, like the ones in
the kitchen, stood taller than Paige did.

Black against the night, the glass
threw her reflection back at her—a trim
woman in jeans, a T-shirt and a jacket,
with dark, chin-length hair and the sad-
dest eyes.

A lot of changes had been made, but
this was still the place—the very
room—where her dad had died.

It was the same house her mother
had left, for good, when she and Libby
and Julie needed her most.

The same house where she'd waited
in vain for Marva to come back. Where
she'd cried over Austin McKettrick and
grieved after her father's death.

Julie and Libby had both signed their
shares over to her. And she would live
here, a spinster, growing stranger and

stranger with each passing year. Adopting dozens and dozens of cats, and playing bingo three nights a week, cutting beer cans into panels, punching holes in the sides and crocheting them together into hats.

Paige sank down onto the raised hearth of the fireplace and tried to make up her mind whether to laugh or cry. It was a tough choice.

CHAPTER THREE

Austin was only half listening to his brothers' conversation that evening, there in Garrett's small, well-lit courtyard; a big part of his mind was on Paige. He'd heard her car door slam, listened as she started the engine, and it had been all he could do not to let himself out through the gate and run down the driveway after her, like some damn fool in a bad movie.

Lounging at the picnic table, watching the kids and the dogs dash around in the grass, Austin sipped his beer and savored the smoky scent of beef cooking on an outdoor grill.

Julie and Libby came down the back steps from Garrett's terrace, Libby carrying a salad, Julie holding a tray of empty glasses and a pitcher of iced tea. While Austin couldn't rightly think of a place he'd rather be just then, he wished Paige hadn't left.

Remembering his manners—better late than never, he supposed wryly—he rose, crossed the yard and took the tray out of Julie's hands.

Julie thanked him. She and Libby exchanged glances, and both of them looked flustered.

Austin carried the tray back to the picnic table, set it down and turned to see both his brothers watching him.

When he realized that they thought he might have done himself permanent injury by carrying the tray, he gave a brief, ragged chuckle and shook his head.

Tate and Garrett had the good grace to look chagrined, and went back to turning steaks and talking ranch business.

The meal was served, and they all sat down at the long picnic table, kids and adults, with the dogs sitting quietly—and hopefully—nearby.

"Where's Aunt Paige?" Calvin piped

up, barely visible over the hamburger towering on his plate.

An awkward little silence fell, broken only by the distant lowing of cattle and the sound of a car somewhere down the road.

"Eat your supper, sweetheart," Julie told her son gently.

"What about *Aunt Paige's* supper?" Calvin persisted. "Is she going to have any?"

"I'm sure your aunt will be fine," Julie assured him.

Silverware clinked against dishes, and the wind whispered in the limbs of the oak trees nearest the house. It was November, and turning colder, but thanks to a pair of outdoor heaters, the patio was warm enough.

"Maybe she ran away," Ava, one of Tate's twins, speculated, after chewing and swallowing a big bite of burger and bun.

Calvin took immediate offense, stiffening and glaring across the table at Ava. *"Did not!"*

"Hush," Julie said, ruffling the boy's hair.

Ava blinked behind her glasses and then jutted out her fine McKettrick chin, stubborn to the bone. "Did, too!" she insisted. *"Maybe."*

"Grown-ups don't run away!" Calvin said.

"Sometimes they do!" Ava argued.

"Ava," Tate said quietly. "That will be enough."

Ava subsided, but not graciously.

And her sister, Audrey, by far the more outgoing of the pair, spoke right up. "Our mom ran away," she said. "She went all the way to New York City, and she's never coming back."

Another silence.

Then Libby, sitting next to Audrey, slipped an arm around the child. Over the girls' heads, her gaze connected with Tate's. "Your mother came to visit just last month," Libby reminded her softly. "She took you and Ava to the ballet in Austin, and you stayed in a ho-tel."

Tate sighed, pushed his plate away.

Austin felt a pang of sympathy, watching his brother. Tate's first mar-riage, to the twins' mother, had been a mistake from the beginning. He and Cheryl had been divorced since the twins were babies, but they still butted heads now and then over the kids. Cheryl, probably jealous of Libby, was always playing some kind of head game.

Just one more reason, as far as Austin was concerned, to stay single. And if the idea gave him a lonesome feeling, well, he concluded, nobody had everything.

Garrett, meanwhile, managed to shift Calvin onto his lap without making a big fat production of it. "Your Aunt Paige wouldn't run away," he told the boy, looking straight at Austin. "She probably just didn't feel like having steak for supper."

Austin felt color rise to his face. What was Garrett implying? That it was *his* fault Paige didn't want to join the rest of the family for a meal?

Maybe it *was* his fault.

Austin decided he wasn't all that hungry. He excused himself, as he'd been taught to do, having been raised by a good Texas mama, and left the table. Carried his plate inside and left it in the sink in Garrett's kitchen.

Shep joined him on the short walk to the door of his own apartment, just down the hall from Garrett's.

In the terrible days immediately after their folks were killed, nothing had made sense to any of the three brothers, and little wonder. They'd been eighteen, nineteen and twenty years old at the time. For the last ten years, they'd shared the main floor of the ranch house, where the big kitchen and the pool and the media room were, among other things, but back then, for reasons Austin couldn't recall, they'd divided the rest of the house into three separate living areas.

As little kids, still on their first set of teeth, Tate, Garrett and Austin had shared one wide, long room, with lots of windows. When Tate entered tenth grade, the original space was sectioned off into three connecting squares, all the same size but distinctly separate.

Now, those rooms were gone, too,

making up the wide corridor. Only the long row of tall windows remained.

Austin shoved a hand through his hair as he entered his own part of the house. The kitchen, living room and master suite were on that floor, while an office and two guest rooms shared the third with a huge attic.

Like Tate and Garrett, Austin had his own stairway.

God forbid they should have to share one.

Bleakly, he wandered to the windows, gazed out over the range, toward the main road. No question about it—he wanted to see headlights, and not just *any* headlights, either. He was looking for Paige's car.

No sign of it, though.

He finally turned away, took in the stark simplicity of his living room and longed for the old days, when things had been different. When the folks were alive and they'd lived like a family, not a bunch of strangers.

The Silver Spur ranch house had been just that, a *house,* before the folks died; a big one, granted, but still a family home, with one kitchen, one living room, one dining room.

One turkey at Thanksgiving.

One tree at Christmas.

Now, it was more like a grand hotel, or an apartment building.

It sure as hell wasn't a home anymore. Nobody really *lived* there; they were all just passing through, doing their own thing, on their way to somewhere else.

Paige woke up late the next morning, having tossed and turned until all hours. Glancing at the bedside clock, she gasped, threw back the covers, and leaped out of bed. She showered quickly, put on black slacks and a simple white blouse, gave each of her cheeks a pass with the blush brush, and sped out into the kitchen.

Garrett and Austin were there, Garrett drinking coffee and reading a newspaper at the table, Austin leaning indolently against one of the counters, wearing nothing but a pair of rag-bag sweatpants, a case of bedhead and an obnoxious grin.

Shep, wolfing down kibble from a bowl nearby, spared her a glance but went right on eating.

"Did Julie leave already?" Paige asked. "I was supposed to drive Calvin to school this morning—"

Garrett smiled easily and rose from his chair, remained standing until Paige waved him back into his seat. "Julie didn't want to wake you," he said. "She took Calvin over to Libby and Tate's to ride the school bus to town later on with the twins."

Paige was aware of Austin at the periphery of her vision, lounging like he had nothing better to do than stand around in the kitchen on a weekday morning.

And maybe he didn't.

"Have some coffee," Austin said in an easy drawl that brought back all sorts of sensory memories, all of which were purely physical. "There's no hurry now, is there?"

Garrett glanced back at his brother, and something passed between them, though Paige had no idea what.

"All right," Paige said.

Austin moved to the coffeemaker, filled a mug, brought it to Paige. His hair was a mess. His chest was bare. His sweatpants were in disreputable shape.

And just looking at him made Paige wish she were lying flat on her back in his bed, instead of standing in a kitchen awash in morning light.

"Thanks," she said out loud, taking the mug he offered.

"Guess I'd better throw on some clothes," he said without the least trace of self-consciousness in either his tone or his manner. "As Dad always said, we're burnin' daylight."

Paige didn't respond. She *couldn't* have responded, because her throat had closed.

With a nod, Austin left, heading up his set of stairs, the dog trotting behind him.

Garrett stood up again, gestured for Paige to take a seat.

She slumped onto the bench, curled both hands around the mug.

Garrett sank back into his chair. "Are you all right?" he asked.

Paige, realizing that she'd clenched her eyes shut, opened them and drummed up a smile. "Yes," she said. "But Julie was counting on me to look after Calvin and I overslept and—"

"Calvin is fine," Garrett said, covering her hand with his very briefly.

Paige sighed, and with the outward thrust of her breath, her shoulders relaxed. She felt the familiar rush of love for her only nephew; she could not have loved Calvin more if he'd been her own child.

Garrett cleared his throat subtly, and glanced toward the stairs Austin and Shep had mounted only moments before.

"Tate and I were wondering . . ." he began. But then his voice fell away, and he looked strangely shy for a man whose self-confidence seemed to rise from the cellular level.

"What?" she asked. God knew it had complicated her life when Libby and Tate had fallen in love and, soon after that, Garrett and Julie. Austin was their brother; it would, of course, be almost

impossible to avoid coming into contact with him on a fairly regular basis.

Still, Paige liked her future brothers-
in-law, and she was certainly glad they
were making her sisters so happy.

Garrett scooted his chair in a little
closer to the table. Lowered his voice,
even though Austin was nowhere in
sight and couldn't possibly have overheard.

"Julie says you're between jobs right
now," he ventured carefully.

Paige felt a brief sting of embarrass-
ment; she'd worked since high school
and being unemployed was new to her.
Fortunately, the feeling passed quickly.

"I guess you could say that," she
said with a little smile. If Julie had confided that her sister was "between
jobs," she'd explained the circumstances, too, but Paige saw no reason
to point that out. "I was supposed to
replace one of the nurses at Blue River
Clinic—Alice was planning on enlisting
in the Navy. There was some kind of
hitch, though, and it will be another few
months before she starts her training."

The expression in Garrett's McKettrick-blue eyes was kind.

He and Tate, Paige realized with a start, would be the brothers she'd never had. They had already accepted her as part of the family, and they would look out for her, if only because they loved her sisters.

Her throat ached with an emotion she was glad she didn't have to define, because there were no words for it.

Garrett gave her a few moments to recover before he tried to continue. He said his younger brother's name, hoarsely, and then faltered.

"Go on," Paige said very quietly.

"Austin—needs help. He's never going to admit that, though."

Paige nodded, waited. She knew Austin better than most people did, and nothing Garrett had said so far surprised her.

Garrett sighed again, thrust a hand through his dark-blond hair. "We—Tate and I, that is—think there ought to be somebody around to sort of keep an eye on Austin when none of us are around, just in case—"

She didn't speak, hoping the conclusion she'd just jumped to was wrong.

"Austin needs a nurse," Garrett finally said, and his tone was decisive.

"A nurse," Paige repeated dully. "Garrett, tell me you're not suggesting that I—"

Garrett merely smiled and raised one eyebrow ever so slightly.

Paige swallowed. "Don't you think that would be a little—well—*awkward?*"

"Awkward?" Garrett, the skilled political spin doctor, was probably playing her, but he sure *sounded* confused. "It's not as if you would have to bathe him or anything intimate like that."

She met his gaze and held it. "What *is* Austin's diagnosis, exactly?"

"He has a herniated disc," Garrett answered, his tone genuinely grave now.

"Will he need surgery?" The question was rhetorical; Paige was thinking out loud. Processing the implications of an injury all too common to athletes, no matter what their sport.

Garrett rubbed his attractively stubbled chin with one hand as he considered his answer. "That depends," he finally replied. "If he stays away from the rodeo, gives himself a chance to heal, there's a good chance he can avoid having an operation."

Paige felt faintly sick to her stomach. "You don't think Austin will actually go along with the idea, do you? I mean, he and I *are* making an effort to get along—for obvious reasons—but things are still pretty rocky—"

"Tate and I aren't planning on giving Austin a choice in the matter," Garrett said firmly.

"And you want me to . . . babysit."

A slow grin settled over Garrett's sensual mouth. "That's about the size of it," he said with a little nod.

"There are a lot of private nurses in the world," Paige said. "Why me?"

Austin could be heard at the top of the stairs, talking to the dog.

Paige lowered her voice and added, "You know I infuriate him."

Garrett folded his arms, and if they'd been playing poker, Paige would have thrown in any hand short of a royal

flush when she saw the flicker of triumph in his eyes. He leaned in and said
in a stage whisper, "That's the idea.
We'd make it worth your while."

Paige widened her eyes, but before
she could say anything in response to
Garrett's remark, Austin was back.

He'd pulled on jeans and a raggedy
T-shirt and his damp hair showed comb
ridges, though he hadn't shaved. That
practiced smile flashed across both
Paige and Garrett like the sweep of
a searchlight, dazzlingly bright, but
somehow distant, and distinctly cool.

Garrett looked at his watch, pushed
back his chair and stood. "Time to play
cowboy," he said. "I was supposed to
meet Tate on the east range fifteen
minutes ago—better get out there before his lid starts rattling."

Austin rolled his eyes. "Can't have
that," he said.

"Later," Garrett responded. Grabbing
the keys to his truck from the hook beside the door, he disappeared into the
garage.

Austin rounded slowly, studying
Paige. "What were you two talking

about, before I came downstairs?" he asked mildly.

Paige bit her lower lip. "Garrett offered me a job," she said.

He frowned. "Doing what?"

She hadn't actually accepted the position, but it wouldn't hurt to bait Austin a little. Paige took pleasure in her reply. "Babysitting."

Austin looked relieved. "You're already doing that, aren't you?" Not expecting an answer, he took up the mug he'd left on the counter earlier and refilled it at the coffeemaker. Turned to look at Paige again as he took a sip of the brew. "Calvin's a great kid," he observed.

"I wasn't hired to look after Calvin," Paige said.

Austin lowered the cup from his mouth, set it aside with a faint thump. His marvelous eyes narrowed a little. "What?"

"Garrett asked me to be your nurse, Austin." No need to add that she hadn't said yes.

She was enjoying this *way* too much,

but it was harmless fun, all things considered.

"In that case," Austin said evenly, "you're fired."

"You can't fire me," Paige told him, delighted by the swift blue flash of his temper and the sudden buzz in the air. "I don't work for you."

Austin shoved a hand through his hair, sucked in a breath and released it, summoned up a casual smile. Paige recognized the tactic from days of old; he was still annoyed, but she wasn't supposed to notice.

"Do I look as though I need medical supervision?" he asked reasonably, spreading his hands.

He looked like sugar-coated sin, not that Paige would have said so. "All I know," she said, trying to look and sound innocent, "is that I've been hired to take care of you."

She should have put on the brakes right then and there, admitted she was only teasing, that she thought the idea of signing on as his nurse was as ludicrous as he did.

For whatever reason, she didn't straighten him out.

Austin crossed to one of the row of fancy refrigerators, wrenched open a door and promptly slammed it shut again, without taking anything out.

Turning back to face Paige, he snapped, "Fine."

"Fine," she repeated with a nod, tucking her hands behind her back and hooking her index fingers together. Rocking back on her heels.

"Don't do that," Austin growled, storming over to another cupboard, taking out a loaf of bread, extracting two slices and dropping them into the toaster.

"Don't do what?" Paige asked.

"Don't repeat what I say."

"I was only *agreeing* with you."

"You're enjoying this," he accused.

"Enjoying what?"

"You know damn well what."

Paige smiled blandly. Watched as he ranged all over the kitchen, getting a plate down from a shelf, then a knife from a drawer, then butter and jam from another one of the refrigerators.

Such an enormous amount of fuss just to make toast.

The bread popped up.

Austin grabbed both slices at once, plunked them down on the plate, spread butter and jam.

Finally walked over to the table and stood stiffly at one end of the bench. "Sit down," he said. When Paige didn't move, he added, "I can't until you do."

Ah, yes. His manners.

The irony made her want to chuckle, but she didn't give in to the impulse.

He sat. Ate some of his toast, tore off a piece of buttery crust and gave it to Shep, who wolfed it down.

"You shouldn't give a dog people food," Paige said.

"Gosh," Austin answered, "thanks for straightening me out on that point, *Nurse* Remington."

"You don't have to be such an asshole," she told him.

He smiled as though weighing the accuracy of the accusation, then dismissed it with a shake of his head. "I don't know what it is," he said in his own good time, after chewing and swallowing, "but something about you just totally pisses me off."

She smiled back. "I feel exactly the same way about you," she said with a note of saucy surprise.

That was when he laughed. It was a ragged sound, and there was some bitterness in it, though she suspected that had less to do with her than Garrett. Austin had always been prickly about being the youngest of the three McKettrick brothers.

Paige, being the youngest of three *sisters,* thought she understood. She loved Libby and Julie with all her heart, but she did tend to compare herself to them, and in her own mind, she didn't always measure up.

"Austin," she said very gently.

He had finished his toast, pushed away his plate. When he raised his eyes to hers, she was, once again, struck by their very *blue*ness, and by the way that color pierced her in so many tender and nameless places.

"Your brothers are worried about you," she said, thick-throated. "They just want you to be okay."

Austin was quiet, absorbing that. He'd lowered his head a little, and his eyes didn't meet Paige's, not right away, at least. "My brothers," he said slowly, "ought to stop treating me like I'm Calvin's age and let me work things out on my own."

"What things?" Paige ventured. She was on thin emotional ice here, couldn't have said why she'd voiced such an intimate question in the first place.

He thrust a hand through his hair. For the briefest of moments, she thought he might answer honestly, but in the end, he simply sighed again and shook his head. The effect was so chilly and distant that he might as well have pushed her away physically.

"I don't want a nurse," he said after a long time.

Paige didn't answer.

Austin left her then, heading upstairs, Shep scrambling at his heels.

Paige just sat there, at the long trestle table where several generations of McKettricks had not only taken their meals, but argued and made peace, borne their singular sorrows alone or shared them with each other. She sat there and thought about families—how precious they were, and how complicated, and how damnably inconvenient sometimes.

It was because of her sisters and their McKettrick men that she was *in* this fix, after all. If Libby hadn't decided to marry Tate, and Julie Garrett, then *she,* Paige, would have no earthly reason to pass the time of day with Austin, let alone serve as his glorified babysitter.

Paige stiffened her spine, jutted out her chin.

After the big wedding on New Year's Eve, she could leave Blue River, start her life over somewhere else. She'd often thought about going back to school, maybe becoming a physician's assistant or even a doctor. And there were other options, too, like joining one of the international relief organizations, where her skills and experience, instead of just looking good on a résumé and qualifying her for a top-level salary, would make a real difference.

The hardest part of leaving wouldn't be parting from her sisters, though the three of them had always been close. No, the prospect that closed Paige's throat and made her sinuses burn was not being able to see her five-year-old nephew as often as they both liked.

Although Calvin's birth father was back in his life—sort of—Julie was a single mother. Libby and Paige, both devoted aunts, had done a lot of pinch-hitting, right from the beginning. Paige loved her sister's child as fiercely as if he were her own, and so did Libby.

On top of that, Blue River was and always would be *home,* at least to Paige. Like her sisters, she'd been born there, in the old brick hospital that had burned down while she was still in elementary school.

Paige stood up, determined not to follow the memory trail, but it was already too late. Even as she gathered her purse and her coat and her car keys, all with no particular destination in mind, the past unfolded in her mind.

She'd grown up in the modest house her parents had bought when they were newlyweds, probably convinced, being young and naive, that they would be together always.

Inwardly, Paige sighed.

She raised the garage door from the control on the wall and climbed into her car.

Her mom and dad had had three babies in three years. Will Remington, a born husband and father and a gifted teacher, had thrived on family life. Marva? Not so much.

Paige started the car engine, backed carefully out onto the concrete that comprised the upper driveway.

Even though years had passed since Marva had found herself a tattooed boyfriend, announced that she "just wasn't happy" being a wife and mother and hit the road with barely a backward glance, the hurt still surfaced sometimes.

Marva had eventually come back to Blue River, having made up her mind to reconnect with the daughters she'd abandoned as small children, and she'd succeeded, to a certain degree. Still a gypsy at heart, it would seem, dear old Mom had stayed long enough to demolish Libby's coffee shop by driving through the front wall and present each of her children with a sizable windfall, the proceeds of an old life insurance policy, prudently invested. With a classic my-work-here-is-done flair, Marva had then given up her apartment and returned to her retired-proctologist husband and their home in Costa Rica.

Paige had not been sorry to see her go. Not like the first time, anyhow.

Reaching the main gates, Paige met Tate, driving his flashy pickup truck and pulling a horse trailer behind. Garrett, riding shotgun, smiled and greeted her with a tug at the brim of his hat.

Paige, no longer distracted by thoughts of her mother, waggled her fingers and then backed up, so Tate could make the wide turn onto the ranch road.

The driver's-side window zipped down, and Tate took off his hat, set it aside. "Did Austin manage to run you off already?" he asked with a worried grin.

Paige laughed, though her face warmed. She refrained from pointing out that she hadn't formally accepted the job Garrett had offered her earlier. Instead she replied, "I wouldn't say that. He *is* in a mood, though."

"He's always in a mood," Tate said wearily, shoving splayed fingers through his dark hair and then replacing his hat.

Paige indicated the trailer with a nod of her head. "New horse?"

Tate nodded, and now there was a grim set to his mouth. "A little mare," he answered. "She's half starved—according to Libby's friend at the animal shelter, Molly's owners moved away, nobody's sure exactly when, and left her behind to fend for herself."

Paige's heart slipped a notch. Her sister was always finding homes for unwanted pets of all kinds—dogs, cats, horses, birds, even a few snakes over the years. Before she could make a reply, Garrett leaned from the passenger side of the truck to favor her with a grin.

"So," he said, "are you taking the job or not?"

A smile tugged at Paige's mouth. "You're only slightly less impossible than your younger brother, Garrett McKettrick," she told him. "The truth is, I haven't decided."

Tate flashed the grin that had always made Libby's heart pound. "It's a pretty tough assignment, riding herd on Austin. Not everybody's cut out to do it."

She was about to call her future brother-in-law on his attempt to manipulate her with flattery, but Libby pulled up just then, tooting the horn of a classic red Corvette Paige didn't recognize.

After parking behind the truck and horse trailer, Libby got out of the sports car and approached, beaming.

"What do you think?" she asked Paige, gesturing toward the shining vehicle.

Paige blinked. "I think it's really— red," she answered, and then laughed, not out of amusement, but out of joy. Her big sister was so happy.

Libby, meanwhile, climbed onto the

running board of Tate's truck, and the two of them exchanged a quick kiss through the open window. That done, she turned toward Paige again.

"Were you going somewhere?" she asked.

Paige sighed, shook her head. "Not really," she answered.

Tate said he and Garrett would be up at the barn, and the two of them drove off.

Libby watched them go, a special light glowing in her eyes, then smiled at Paige and gestured toward the Corvette.

"It won't do, of course," Libby said, "but it's sure fun test-driving the thing."

"Why won't it do?" Paige asked, thinking of her sister's ancient Impala, with its rust marks and temperamental engine.

"There's no room for the twins," Libby told her, with a tolerant grin. "Or for babies or for the dogs, or for groceries or feed sacks—"

Paige laughed. "I get the point," she said. Then, resigned to the fact that she wasn't going anywhere, for the moment at least, she watched as Libby walked back to the Corvette, got in and started the engine with a deliberate roar.

As soon as Libby sped by, a flash of red, Paige turned her boring subcompact around and followed her sister up the driveway.

Why fool herself?

She probably could have resisted Austin.

Resisting Molly, the rescued mare, was a whole other matter, though.

CHAPTER FOUR

It was the sight of a horse trailer that brought Austin out of the house, Shep and Harry, the three-legged beagle, Calvin's dog, scuttling to keep pace.

Garrett and Tate gave him passing nods but didn't speak. They were intent on unloading the new arrival.

Austin, curious, unable to resist making the acquaintance of yet another four-legged hay burner, hung around, watching. Garrett opened the trailer and pulled down the ramp.

The small horse lay in the narrow bed of the trailer, delicate legs turned under, barely strong enough, it seemed to Austin, to hold up its head. A black-and-white paint, under all the scruff and dried mud and thistle burrs, the poor critter had been hard done by, that was clear. Its ribs jutted out from its side, each one as clearly differentiated from the next as the rungs on a ladder.

Austin spat out a swear word and started forward just as Libby and Paige drove up in two different vehicles— Libby was driving a jazzy red 'Vette, while Paige was in her dull subcompact.

As if by tacit agreement, Tate and Garrett stepped back out of the way so Austin could climb into the trailer. Squatting beside the animal, he ran a slow hand along the length of her neck. The hide felt gritty against Austin's palm, and damp with sweat.

"Meet Molly," Tate said, his voice gruff. Briefly, he sketched in the outlines of the call Libby had gotten from her friends at the animal shelter in town, told how he and Garrett had gone straight to the sparse pasture where the mare had apparently been abandoned—they weren't sure how long ago.

Never taking his eyes off Molly, Austin listened to the account, swore again, once he'd heard it all and processed it. The mare's halter was so old and so tight that it was partially embedded in the hide on one side of her head—evidently, somebody had put it on her and then just left it. Her slatted sides heaved with the effort to breathe, and the look of sorrowing hope in her eyes as she gazed at Austin sent his heart into a slow, backward roll.

"You're going to be all right now, Molly," he promised the mare.

She nickered, the sound barely audible, then nuzzled him in the shoulder.

The backs of Austin's eyes stung. He stood and got out of the way, feeling worse than useless, so Garrett and Tate could get the mare to her feet, a process that involved considerable kindly cajoling and some lifting, too. Molly stumbled a few times crossing the barnyard, and they had to stop twice so she could rest, but finally she made it into her new stall.

Some of the other horses whinnied in greeting, watching with interest as the mare took her place among them.

Molly had spent her strength, and

she immediately folded into the thick bed of wood shavings covering the stall floor.

"Farley's on his way," Garrett said, standing behind Austin in the breeze-way, laying a hand on his shoulder.

Farley Pomeroy was the local large-animal vet; he'd been taking care of McKettrick livestock for some forty-odd years. When their dad, Jim, was ten or twelve, he'd fallen off the hay truck one summer day and splintered the bone in his right forearm so badly that he required surgery. It had been Doc Pomeroy, who happened to be on the ranch at the time, ministering to a sick calf, who treated Jim for shock and rigged up a splint and a sling for the fifty-mile trip to the hospital.

Austin nodded to let Garrett know he'd heard. If ever a horse had needed Farley's expert attention, it was this one.

Tate came out of Molly's stall, took off his hat.

Austin realized then that Libby and Paige were standing nearby.

"You'll wait for Farley?" Tate asked, meeting Austin's gaze.

Once again, Austin nodded. "I'll wait."

He was aware of it when Tate and Garrett and Libby left the barn, aware too, even without looking, that Paige had stayed behind.

Austin opened the stall door and stepped through it, dropping to one knee beside the little mare.

He didn't ask her to do it, but Paige found a bucket, filled it from a nearby faucet, and brought it into the stall. Set it down within Molly's reach. Austin murmured a *thanks* without looking back at Paige and steadied the bucket with both hands, so the animal could drink.

"Slow, now," he told Molly. "Real slow."

When she'd emptied the bucket, Paige took it and went back for more water.

Molly drank thirstily, then rolled onto her side, thrusting her legs out from under her and making both Austin and

Paige move quickly to get out of the way.

Shep peered into the stall from the breezeway, Harry at his side.

The dogs made such a picture standing there that Austin gave a ragged chuckle and shook his head. Molly didn't seem frightened of them, but he stroked her neck just to reassure her, told her she was among friends now, and there was no need to worry.

"Shall I take them into the house?" Paige asked.

"Might be better if they weren't underfoot when Doc gets here," Austin answered, not looking at her. "Thanks."

She left the stall and then the barn, and while Harry was cooperative, it took some doing to get Shep to go along with the plan. He wanted to stick around and help out with the horse-tending, it seemed.

Insisting to himself that it didn't matter one way or the other, Austin wondered if Paige would come back out to wait with him or stay inside the house.

She returned within five minutes, handed him an icy bottle of water.

He thanked her again, unscrewed the top and drank deeply. His back didn't hurt, but he knew he'd be asking for it if he continued to crouch, so he stood, stretched his legs, finished off the water.

Paige looked almost like a ranch wife, standing there in that horse stall, her arms folded and her face worried. Maybe it was the jeans.

"How can things like this happen?" she muttered, staring at poor Molly.

Austin knew Paige didn't expect an answer; she was thinking out loud, that was all. He wanted to put an arm around her shoulders right about then and just hold her against his side for a little while, but he wrote it off as a bad idea and kept his distance—insofar as that was possible in an eight-by-eight-foot stall.

A silence fell between the two of them, but it was a comfortable one. Austin moved out into the breezeway, and he and Paige stood side by side in front of the half door of the stall, both of them focused on the mare.

Soon, Doc Pomeroy's old rig rattled

up outside, backfired, then did some clanking and clattering as the engine shut down.

Austin and Paige exchanged glances, not quite smiles but almost, and turned to watch as the old man trundled into the barn, carrying his battered bag in one gnarled hand. Probably pushing eighty, Doc still had powerful shoulders, a fine head of white hair and the stamina of a much younger man.

"Come on in here, Clifton," he said, half turning to address the figure hesitating in the wide, sunlit doorway. "I might need a hand."

Clifton Pomeroy, Doc's only son, hadn't shown his face in or around Blue River in a long time. Not since Jim and Sally McKettrick's funeral, in fact.

As kids, Cliff and Jim McKettrick had been the best of friends. Later on, they'd been business partners. When Jim had shut down the oil wells on the Silver Spur, though, Cliff had objected strenuously, since he'd been making a lot of money brokering McKettrick crude to various small independents.

The association—and the friendship—had ended soon after that.

Austin's dad had never said what happened—giving reasons for things he regarded as his own business had not been Jim McKettrick's way. On the rare occasions when Cliff Pomeroy's name had come up, Jim had always clamped his jaw and either left the room or changed the subject.

Now, finding himself back on a ranch he'd left on bad terms, Cliff hung back for a few moments, sizing things up. Then, in that vaguely slick way he had, he strolled easily into the barn, approaching Austin with one hand extended in greeting. His smile was broad and a little too bright, reminiscent of Garrett's late boss, Senator Morgan Cox.

Because there was no way to avoid doing so without hurting Doc's feelings, Austin shook hands with Cliff and said hello.

By then, Doc was in the stall with Molly and Garrett. Tate and Libby were entering the barn.

Everybody clustered in front of the stall door.

Doc, crouching next to the mare, looked up and frowned. "What is this?" he demanded. "Some kind of convention?"

Doc had always been a cranky old coot, but he knew his business.

Cliff chuckled nervously, took off his baseball cap and ran a hand through his thinning brown hair. "You want a hand or not, Dad?" he asked, his tone falsely cheerful.

Austin recalled his mom saying that Clifton Pomeroy must have taken after his mother's people, since he looked nothing like his father.

Doc opened his bag and rooted around inside with one of his pawlike hands. Brought out a round tin and a packet of gauze. Catching Austin's eye, he said, "You'll do. The rest of you had better occupy yourselves elsewhere and give this poor horse room to breathe."

They all stepped away from the door, so Austin could go through.

Garrett struck up a conversation with

Cliff, and the whole bunch receded, including Libby and Paige.

By then, Doc had filled one large syringe, set it carefully aside and filled another, and his expression was so grim that Austin was momentarily alarmed.

"What is that stuff?" he rasped, kneeling next to the veterinarian, near Molly's head.

Doc's mouth twitched, but he probably hadn't smiled, or even grinned, in decades, and he didn't break his record now. "Antibiotics, a mild sedative and a painkiller."

Austin nodded, scratching lightly behind Molly's ears and speaking to her in a soothing tone while Doc administered the shots, one right after the other.

The mare flinched, but that must have been all the resistance she had in her, because she lapsed into a noisy sleep right away.

Doc used some hand sanitizer from a bottle in his bag and began pulling away the half-rotted remains of Molly's halter. Now and then, some hair and hide came away with it, and there were places where scabs had grown right over the strips of nylon.

Austin felt sick to his stomach.

"There are sterile wipes in my bag," Doc told him quietly in a tone that indicated both understanding and stern competence. "Disinfect your hands, boy, then start cleaning the wounds as I uncover them. We'll apply some ointment after that, and hope to God an infection doesn't set in."

Austin did as he was told, working quickly.

Maybe forty-five minutes had gone by when they'd finished. Molly came to right away, shook off the sedative and even scrambled to her feet.

Doc finished cleaning her up and dabbed on more ointment.

"She's a good strong girl, then," the old man proclaimed, patting Molly's flank. "What she needs now is some supper and some rest and a whole lot of TLC."

Austin fetched an armload of grass hay and dropped it into Molly's feeder, then made sure the automatic waterer in her stall was working. Doc tarried long enough to watch her eat for a few moments, then picked up his bag and left the stall.

Austin shut and latched Molly's door.

The other horses snorted and nickered, calling for room service.

"Thanks," Austin told Doc.

Doc merely nodded. He wasn't much for idle conversation.

While Austin fed the rest of the critters, Doc washed up at the sink in the tack room. Austin finished the chow chores pretty fast and washed up, too.

For some reason, Doc lingered in the tack room, rolling down the sleeves of his shirt, carefully buttoning the cuffs.

He and Austin left the barn at the same time, while Tate and Garrett came out of the main house by way of the kitchen door. Clifton was with them.

Austin looked for Paige, but there was no sign of her.

Probably for the best, he thought.

But he wasn't quite convinced.

Libby hooked her arm through his and smiled up at him. "Paige went to town to fetch Calvin," she said.

Austin chuckled, shook his head. He

liked Libby, liked Julie, too—they were the sisters he'd never had. Paige was harder to categorize.

"Did I ask where Paige got to?" he challenged, grinning a little.

Libby just made a face at him, then walked over to speak to Tate.

Doc and Clifton said their goodbyes, got into Doc's old truck and drove off at a good clip, stirring up a dry swirl of dust behind them. Libby stood on tiptoe to kiss Tate's cheek, then she got into the red Corvette and made for the main road.

That left Tate, Garrett and Austin standing in a loose circle in front of the barn, strangely quiet now that the crowd had thinned out a little.

Tate rubbed the back of his neck, looked as though he might be nursing a tension headache.

"How long's it been since Clifton Pomeroy paid his ole daddy a visit?" Garrett mused, his gaze following the departing rigs.

"Long time," Tate remarked. He seemed distracted.

Austin wondered if his oldest brother

had more on his mind than the sick horse he and Garrett had rescued at Libby's request.

Just two months before, they'd had some trouble with rustlers, and one of the thieves turned out to be Charlie Bates, a longtime employee on the Silver Spur. Charlie and a few other crooks were in jail now, unable to make bail, but nobody figured the bad guys were all in custody. Charlie didn't have the mental capacity to run an operation that big and complicated, but he wasn't naming any names and neither were any of his partners in crime.

"How are things in the cattle business?" Austin asked, keeping his tone light.

Tate frowned, and his jawline hardened. Evidently, he'd used up his daily allotment of good cheer saving the horse. "As if you gave a damn," he retorted, peevish as hell, just before he turned to walk away, vanishing into the barn.

Austin watched him go, didn't look at Garrett when he spoke. "What's chewing on *him?*"

"We're still losing livestock," Garrett replied after a long time and with significant reluctance.

Austin faced Garrett straight on. "Stolen?" Before Charlie and his gang had been rounded up, they'd raided the McKettrick herd a number of times, carted off a lot of living beef in semi-trucks. Another half-dozen cattle had been gunned down and left to rot.

"About a hundred head, as far as we can tell," Garrett replied. "A few more were shot, too."

Austin swore. "You and Tate were planning on mentioning this to me— when . . . ?"

Garrett sighed, folded his arms. Scuffed at the ground with the toe of one boot. "We figured you had enough to worry about, what with your back being messed up and everything."

"I get a little sore once in a while," Austin bit out, stung to a cold, hard fury, "but I'm not a cripple, Garrett. And what happens on this ranch is as much my concern as it is yours and Tate's— whatever you think to the contrary."

Tate came out of the barn again. Because of the angle of his hat brim, his face was in shadow, and there was no reading his mood, but Austin figured it was still bad.

As if you gave a damn, Tate had said. Where the hell had *that* come from?

Garrett thrust out a sigh. "Tate's pretty worried," he said, keeping his voice down. "And I can't say I blame him. Rustling is one thing, and killing cattle for the hell of it is another. It's hard not to conclude that somebody out there has worked up a pretty good grudge against us, for whatever reason, and we figure it's bound to escalate."

Tate waved but headed for his truck instead of joining the conversation between Austin and Garrett.

At the moment, that was fine with Austin, because he was pissed off at being left out of the loop. Okay, so he had a herniated disc. He couldn't ride bulls anymore, and for the time being, he wouldn't be doing any heavy-duty ranch work, either. But one-third of the Silver Spur was his, and he had a right to know what went on within its boundaries, whether it was good or bad.

He watched as Tate got into the truck and drove off.

Garrett started toward the house and, after a moment's hesitation, Austin fell into step beside him, but there was no more talk.

Once they were inside, Garrett headed for his part of the house, and Austin went to his, glad to find Shep there waiting for him. It made him feel a little less lonely.

A little, not a lot.

He fed the dog, then made for the bathroom, kicking off his boots and stripping down for a hot shower.

The spray eased some of the residual knots in his back, and he felt damn near human by the time he toweled off and pulled on fresh clothes. He ran a comb through his hair, put his boots back on and then went downstairs.

Shep, having finished his nightly kibble ration, went along, too, curious and companionable.

Austin searched the large storage room adjoining the garage until he found the camping gear. He took a rolled-up sleeping bag out of a cabinet—it smelled a little musty—and returned to the kitchen.

There he ate two frankfurters straight from the package, drank what was left of the milk and called it supper. If he got hungry later, he could always raid the kitchen again. Before going off to El Paso to take care of her niece and the new baby, Esperanza had cooked up and frozen enough grub to last for weeks.

He was in no danger of starvation.

The teenage actors were on a break, and Paige sat with Julie and Calvin in the front row of the small auditorium, the three of them sharing a submarine sandwich from the supermarket deli.

Paige wanted to tell her sister all about the little mare, Molly, and how gentle Austin had been with the animal, but with Calvin right there and some of the drama club kids within earshot, that didn't seem like a good idea.

"Did you decide whether or not you'll take the job?" Julie asked, finishing her part of the sandwich, crumpling the wrapper and stuffing it into the bag.

"What job?" Paige asked, momentarily confused.

Of course, the moment the words left her mouth, she remembered Garrett's offer, made that morning in the ranch-house kitchen. Basically, he and Tate wanted her to play nursemaid to Austin.

"You knew Garrett and Tate were planning to ask me to serve as Austin's nurse?" Paige wondered aloud.

Of course she had, and Libby, too. Most likely, her sisters had set her up, hoping she would fall for Austin the way they had for his brothers and make the wedding a triple.

Even after a long day of teaching, Julie's smile was brilliant. She seemed to have boundless energy, and it took a lot to catch her off guard.

"Sure I did," she replied, unfazed. "Garrett and I talked about it last night."

Paige sighed. "I see."

Julie elbowed her lightly. "Answer my question," she said.

"Right now, I'm inclined to refuse," Paige replied, taking the sandwich bag

from Julie and dropping in what remained of her supper and a couple of
wadded paper napkins. "Austin didn't
exactly take kindly to the idea."

"That's just his pride," Julie said with
a dismissive wave of one hand. "This is
serious, Paige. If Austin isn't careful,
he'll have to have surgery, and that's always a risk."

Paige widened her eyes at Julie.
"Yes," she said pointedly, "as an RN,
I'm familiar with the risks."

Julie smiled angelically. Since she'd
fallen in love with Garrett McKettrick
and the two of them had decided to get
married, she seemed to float through
life, unconcerned with the moods of ordinary mortals like her younger sister.
"It's not as if you're terribly *busy* or anything," she reasoned cheerfully. "You
probably won't have to do anything
more strenuous than make sure Austin
doesn't sneak off to enter some rodeo.
How bad could it be?"

In her mind's eye, Paige saw Austin
tending the ailing mare, recalled the
way he'd touched the animal, the gentle, rumbling tone of his voice. And she

felt new emotions, things that had little or nothing to do with the girl she'd been so long ago, and the boy that girl had loved.

She was a woman now.

Austin was most definitely a man.

And watching him that afternoon, sitting on his haunches in that stall, next to Molly, Paige had come to the startling realization that this was a whole new ball game.

"Paige?" Julie prompted in a happy whisper. "Since you seem to have something—or some*one*—else on your mind, I'll repeat my question. How bad could it be, taking care of a hunk like Austin McKettrick?"

It could be really, *really* bad, Paige figured, but again, this wasn't the time or place to talk about such things.

Paige shook her head, but she was smiling. "I think Calvin and I ought to get back to the ranch. Harry will be wanting his kibble, for one thing."

"Garrett will feed Harry," Julie said. But she stood up, and Calvin stood, too, and Julie slipped an arm around her little boy. Bending, she kissed the top of his head and then ruffled his hair. "I won't be late," she told the child, her voice tender. "Mind your Aunt Paige and wash all over when you take your bath and don't ask for more than one bedtime story, okay?"

Calvin looked up at his mother, blinking behind the lenses of his glasses. "Okay," he said in a tone of mock resignation. Turning to Paige, he added solemnly, "I won't need any help with my bath, because I'm five now, and I can pretty much read any book on my own, too, but I still like the sound of your voice when I'm falling asleep. It's almost as good as when *Mom* reads to me."

Paige laughed. "Well," she said, "I guess *that's* settled."

Julie gave Calvin another hug and then started the rehearsal again.

"I'll be glad when Mom is married to Garrett and making a baby," Calvin confided as he and Paige left the auditorium, hand in hand, walking toward her car. "The play will be over then, and she'll be at home every night, like most moms."

Paige bit her lower lip and helped her nephew into his car seat, checking to make sure that he was properly buckled up. She was behind the wheel with the headlights on and the motor going before she responded to his remark, and then she took pains to speak casually. "The musical is this month," she said. "And there are only a few performances, aren't there?"

Turning her head, she saw Calvin nod in confirmation. "Two Friday night shows and two Saturday night shows and then she's all done." He paused. "And there's the class trip to Six Flags, too. You're going, aren't you?"

Paige suppressed a sigh. She'd forgotten about the kindergarten field trip to the famed amusement park, scheduled for the Wednesday before Thanksgiving. Hadn't even discussed it with Julie yet, and of course that had to happen before she could make any promises.

"Your mom and I will talk about it," she said.

"When?" Calvin asked, sounding a little plaintive. The poor kid was tired, she reasoned, and with Julie so busy helping the drama club rehearse their play, he missed his mother.

"Tomorrow," Paige answered, pulling carefully out onto the main road, pointing the car in the direction of the Silver Spur.

"Promise?" Calvin persisted.

"Promise," Paige said with a little smile.

After that, Calvin lightened up, having conveyed his dissatisfaction with the long hours Julie had been putting in lately, and told her all about his day. One of the other kids in his class had eaten a bug and thrown up, and his teacher had a headache after that and had to rest in the teacher's lounge while the librarian's assistant took over the art program. He asked, as he often did, how long it would be, in "actual days," until he could start first grade and "learn stuff."

"You *are* learning things, Calvin," Paige pointed out, keeping her eyes on the road.

"How to weave pot holders with those stupid little loops," Calvin said.

Paige laughed. "I think those pot holders are lovely," she told him. "I use mine all the time. Your mom and your Aunt Libby love them, too."

Calvin would not be mollified. "We make hand-prints with finger paints," he went on scornfully. "I don't see how any of this stuff is going to prepare me for life."

"Calvin," Paige reminded her nephew, "you're only five. Believe me, you have plenty of time to 'prepare for life.'" She paused. "What exactly is it that you want to learn right now, *immediately,* anyhow?"

"How to ride a horse," Calvin said.

Paige smiled again. "You ride with Garrett all the time," she said. "What else?"

"Higher mathematics," Calvin replied. "World history."

"I think it's mostly simple arithmetic and the alphabet in first grade," she ventured, flipping the signal lever and starting the turn onto the Silver Spur Ranch.

"Well, that's just ridiculous," he said.

"I can already read and write and everything."

"Maybe you should just go straight from kindergarten to college, then," Paige teased, noticing that the lights were on in the barn and wondering how Molly was doing.

"I could skip a couple of grades," Calvin replied seriously, "but Mom and Garrett and my dad all said no. They say I have to put in my time as a kid, like everybody else."

"There you have it," Paige said. Calvin's birth father, Gordon Pruett, had contacted Julie a couple of months before and informed her that he wanted to get to know his son. Things were moving slowly on that front. "So many people can't be wrong."

She felt the change in Calvin before he spoke. "What's going on in the barn?" he asked. "All the chores should be finished by now."

"Let's find out," Paige said, stopping the car in the square spill of light at the entrance to the long, rambling structure housing the McKettrick horses, including the golden ponies Austin had given

Audrey and Ava for their sixth birthday, back in June.

Calvin had unbuckled himself and pushed open the door before Paige could pull her keys from the ignition and reach for her purse.

She had planned to give him a modified rundown on Molly's situation, but she didn't get the chance. Calvin sprinted into the barn.

Paige sighed and followed.

Austin was standing in front of Molly's stall door, looking deliciously rumpled. A cot stood in the center of the breezeway, with a sleeping bag spread over it and Shep curled up underneath.

"You're going to sleep out here?" Calvin demanded of Austin, sounding delighted. "You're going to *camp out in the barn?*"

Austin slanted a glance at Paige, greeted her with a nod so slight it might not have happened at all.

"That's the plan," he told the boy, reaching out to ruffle his hair.

Still impressed, Calvin climbed up the rails in the stall door to peer over the top. Austin looked ready to grab him if he slipped.

"This is Molly," he explained. "Molly, this is my good friend, Calvin."

Paige wondered why his voice made her heart flutter, weak as the first motion of a hatchling's wing.

"Hey, Molly," Calvin cried exuberantly.

By that time, Paige was standing close enough to hook an arm around Calvin's middle and hold him up so he could see the black-and-white mare without clinging precariously to the stall door.

Her arm touched Austin's, and she took a half step to the side.

Molly had been groomed since Paige had seen her last, and she was on her feet, too. There were raw strips on the animal's head, where the nylon halter straps had been, glistening with ointment.

"Can Molly be my horse?" Calvin asked, squirming so that Paige had to set him down. "I could feed her and ride her and put medicine on her cuts—"

"Calvin," Paige interceded softly, laying a hand on the boy's shoulder.

He was so excited, he was practically vibrating.

"Could I pet her?" he implored, tilting his head back to gaze up at Paige's face, then Austin's. "Please?"

Paige felt a jolt worthy of a stun gun when her gaze connected with Austin's. Again she had that odd sense that he was a stranger, that he'd never been the Austin she'd loved so much when they were both teenagers.

"If it's okay with your aunt," Austin drawled, looking at her instead of Calvin, "then sure."

Paige hesitated, then nodded her permission.

Austin unlatched the stall door and stepped slowly inside, holding Calvin by the hand.

"I can't reach," Calvin said.

Paige took a step toward the boy, intending to lift him up again, but Austin beat her to it. He paled slightly, beneath the bristle of his beard, holding Calvin in the curve of one arm.

"Austin," Paige said, reaching out to take the child from him.

He hesitated before he let Calvin go.

Calvin, for his part, was too busy petting Molly's nose to care who was holding him. He hooked an arm around Paige's neck, though, and she felt a rush of such love for her sister's child that it made her light-headed.

After a few more moments, she carried Calvin out of Molly's stall and set him back on his feet. She was aware of Austin moving behind her, shutting and latching the door.

"Can I sleep out here in the barn, with Austin and Shep?" Calvin asked, his upturned face earnest with hope.

"Not tonight," Paige told him gently.

Conveniently, Shep wriggled out from under the cot, wagging his tail, and Calvin, distracted from the camping prospect, squatted to ruffle the dog's ears.

Looking up at Austin through her eyelashes, Paige was both gratified and shaken to find him watching her.

His color was coming back, but she couldn't help wondering if he'd hurt himself, lifting Calvin up to pet Molly the way he had.

The grin came suddenly, nearly setting Paige back on her heels, dazzled.

"You know," he drawled, leaning in close and keeping his voice low, "I'm starting to think I might need a nurse after all."

CHAPTER FIVE

Once he was fairly sure Molly's visiting hours were over for the night, Austin took a couple of muscle relaxants, throwing them back with tepid tap water from the tack room sink, shut off the barn lights and eased himself down to sit on the shaky cot he'd set up earlier. He began the tricky task of taking off his boots.

With some sighing and some shifting around, Shep settled himself underneath the makeshift bed.

"Don't snore," Austin said. So far, that was the only drawback to having Shep for a dog.

Austin smiled and rubbed his chin with one hand, hoping it wouldn't start itching before morning, when he could reasonably shave.

Just sitting there, thinking his own thoughts and mostly at peace, the way he generally was around dogs and horses, he almost missed the movement in the doorway of the barn, would have disregarded it as an illusion if Shep hadn't growled once and low-crawled out from under the cot to stand guard.

"Best show yourself," Austin advised the unknown visitor mildly, rising to his feet with a lot less ease than he would have liked. "It'll save us all some grief— you, me *and* the dog."

No answer.

He rubbed the back of his neck and waited. How long would it be until the pills kicked in, anyhow? Austin wasn't exactly hurting, but he was stiff as hell, and in all the wrong places, too.

The shadow in the darkened doorway resolved itself into a small and enticing shape.

"It's me," Paige said. From the tone of her voice, she was a little surprised to find herself in that barn, after nightfall, with all the lights shut off. Maybe even more surprised than Austin was to see her there.

He felt the right corner of his mouth kick up in a grin, as his heart staggered like a drunk and slammed against his rib cage before righting itself.

A shaft of moonlight found its way in through a high window way up there in the hayloft and Paige passed through it, a goddess in blue jeans and a pullover sweater, moving slowly toward him.

Shep had long since given up growling by then, and taken to wagging his tail instead.

Paige bent to muss the dog's ears, then straightened and looked up into Austin's face. "Did you hurt yourself?"

He couldn't stop grinning. Good thing it was dark in that barn—mostly. There *was* that liquid-silver moonlight spilling in, but things were cast in angled shadows.

"Hurt myself? How would I have done that?"

She might have been flustered; there was no telling, since he couldn't really see her face and her tone of voice wasn't giving away much of anything. "Earlier, when you lifted Calvin so he could pet the horse?"

"Oh, that," Austin said. He splayed the fingers of his right hand and pushed them through his hair, just to be doing something other than grabbing Paige Remington by the shoulders and kissing her until her knees buckled. Right then, that was about *all* he wanted to do.

She saved him from temptation by stepping away to stand in front of Molly's stall door. There was enough light to see that the mare was on her feet, crunching away on the scoop of sweet feed Austin had given her just before cutting the lights.

Molly wanted for some fattening up, and a few alfalfa pellets now and again would probably do the trick.

Austin didn't move from where he stood. This was one of those pivotal moments, he figured, where one wrong move could change the whole course of his life—and Paige's, too.

"What are you doing out here?" he asked. His voice was as rough as if he'd taken sandpaper to his vocal cords. "Right now, I mean. In the barn. This late and everything."

Her laugh was quiet, brittle. "I'm not sure," she admitted.

Some of the muscles in Austin's lower back tightened ominously. Taking care not to make any wimpy sounds, he lowered himself to sit on the cot again and then questioned the wisdom of the move. What if he needed to get back up all of a sudden, and couldn't?

Damn, that would be a new low.

Once again, Paige surprised him. She sat right down beside him, on top of his flannel-lined sleeping bag, close enough that their thighs touched.

He'd felt a similar sensation once before, helping a ranch crew install electric fence lines, when he'd forgotten and closed his fingers around a live wire.

She was the one who broke the silence; Austin wasn't about to. "Molly's doing okay, then?" she asked.

"So far, so good," Austin managed, and then wished he'd cleared his throat first, because his answer came out sounding rusty.

It soon became apparent that Paige had exhausted whatever reserves of diplomacy she might have had on hand. "But you figure you ought to sleep out here? In a barn? With a herniated disc?" She was really building up a head of steam now, and it was fascinating to watch. "It's *November,* Austin."

Fools rush in, he thought ruefully, where angels fear to tread. If discretion was the better part of valor, he was just plain screwed in the valor department.

He put his hands on either side of Paige's face and he kissed her, tentatively at first. She stiffened, and Austin was prepared to back off, but then, in the next instant, the next heartbeat, she softened against him, and he deepened the kiss.

He used his tongue and *goddamn* it was good. But then it happened.

She shoved him away, hard.

And then pushed both hands into her hair and paced back and forth in front of him, muttering to herself.

Austin stood because she had, and the move was too sudden. His back seized up so ferociously that he groaned and doubled over.

And then he couldn't straighten back up.

Paige caught her breath, stopped the pacing, hurried along the breezeway and flipped the first light switch she came to, causing the overheads to flare to life. Austin stayed where he was, flat-out *incapable* of doing anything else.

Shep sat at his feet, the picture of canine goodwill, whisking his tail back and forth in the sawdust.

Austin was still bent in the middle, like an old-fashioned hairpin.

Paige returned, all professional now. Reaching Austin, she took his arm in a gentle hold. "Can you walk?" she asked.

"Hell, *no*," Austin responded, in pain and mortified that he was helpless in front of the last person in the world he wanted to think of him as weak. "Do I look to you like a man who can walk?"

She started to giggle, nervously at

first, still holding on to his arm. "Well, can you at least stand up straight?"

"*No, I freakin' cannot* stand up straight!"

"Take it easy," Paige urged, rubbing his back with one small hand. "It's probably just a spasm, like a charley horse. You'll be all right in a minute."

"Do you have any idea how much this *hurts?* And you stand there *laughing—*"

Paige's giggle turned to a chuckle, followed by a half-swallowed guffaw. Out of the corner of his eye, Austin saw her slap her free hand over her mouth. "I'm—really—sorry—" Another peal of mirth escaped her. "It's just that this whole situation—it's so—"

Bracing his hands on his thighs, he glared at her, side-long. *"Funny?"* he supplied.

She laughed again. "I must be hysterical," she said, dashing away tears with the back of her hand. "Austin, I'm *sorry.* Really. I don't mean—"

The ache seemed to be slacking off a little, but he was a long way from okay.

Plus, he felt like a damn fool, standing there, bent like a twist in the road.

"Will you just—go back in the house or something?" he said.

She blinked, shook her head. "And leave you like this?"

"I hate to say it," Austin ground out, "but you're not really helping all that much by sticking around."

"Don't be such a big baby," Paige said. Her mouth was twitching, and she still had that twinkle in her eyes. "You're not the first person whose back ever went out, you know."

He managed to hitch up a little more, but he felt as though his spine were about to split like a piece of cord-wood under the blade of an ax. "I *know* that," he said, catching his breath after another twinge of pure agony rocked his world.

"Maybe I *should* get Garrett, though," Paige speculated, looking genuinely concerned now. It was about time she showed some sympathy, by Austin's reckoning, but he didn't care for the direction her thoughts were headed.

Austin spoke through his teeth. *"Don't you* dare *bring Garrett out here."*

"Take it easy," Paige told him. Her voice was gentler now, and she was rubbing his back again. "I just thought you might need his help, that's all."

It was almost worth all that suffering, having her rub his back like that.

Almost, but not quite.

Slowly, by increments, Austin cranked himself upright.

"Just so you know," Paige informed him, linking her arm through his, "you're not sleeping in this barn. Let's get you into the house."

"I'm not going anywhere," Austin told her. He flung a hand in Molly's direction. "This horse—"

She raised her eyebrows, spoke in a deliberate and moderate tone. "Yes, you *are* going somewhere, McKettrick. Molly will be fine without you playing mother hen. Besides, you can't stay out here alone, not in the shape you're in, and I'm not sharing that sleeping bag with you. It's too damn cold for that."

"You'd do it otherwise?" he asked

hoarsely, amazed. "Share the sleeping bag with me? If it wasn't cold, I mean?"

Paige blushed.

All around them, sleepy horses looked over stall gates, probably wondering what all the fuss was about.

"I was speaking—advisedly," Paige said.

"Advisedly?" Austin repeated, amused. Carefully, he folded his arms. "Here's the thing, Paige," he went on. "If we were both stuffed into the same sleeping bag, we'd be sharing each other's body heat, so it's unlikely we'd be cold."

Her face burned even brighter.

He'd forgotten how sexy she was when she was mad as hell.

"We're going *inside,* bucko," she told him, jabbing at his chest with the tip of one index finger. "You can either come along under your own power, behaving yourself in the process, or I can fetch Garrett. Maybe call Tate, too, just in case persuading you turns out to be a two-man job. The choice is yours."

"*'Bucko'?*" he teased.

"Just a figure of speech," Paige said,

folding her arms, jutting out her chin and looking up at him with challenge sparking in her eyes. "And don't think I haven't figured out that you're stalling, Austin McKettrick. Either you come inside right now, or I'll get Garrett."

"I can handle Garrett," Austin said, starting to feel testy again. "Tate, too, come to that."

"Fine." Paige huffed, and turned on one heel, about to march off. "We'll just see, then, won't we?"

Austin blew out a sigh, caught her by the back of the waistband on her jeans.

She spun around to face him, small fists clenched.

Shep gave a halfhearted growl.

Austin flashed back to the summer night Paige had caught him messing around with her archenemy, Kimberly Johnson, in a parked car.

He hadn't meant for Paige to actually catch them in the act, but he had wanted her to find out through the Blue River grapevine that he was fooling around with someone else. It was the only way he knew to derail Paige's fantasies about marriage. She seemed to think she could study nursing and he could ride bulls and all the while they'd make babies and live happily ever after, and she just didn't hear him when he tried to tell her he couldn't commit to anything right then but following his rodeo dream.

Tipped off by one of Kimberly's malicious girlfriends, Paige had driven out to Lovers' Lane to prove it was all a lie and seen the truth with her own eyes. Austin hadn't meant to hurt her that bad—it wasn't 'til he looked into her face, contorted by pain, that he realized just how lame his plan had been.

The next day, he'd worked up the courage to knock on her door, meaning to explain, but Paige had come shooting out of her father's house like a human cannonball. She'd grabbed up the garden hose, he recalled, and turned on the spigot, clearly intending to douse him good.

Unfortunately, the scene had struck Austin as hilarious. He'd laughed and vaulted over the Remingtons' picket fence to stand on the sidewalk.

"Paige, listen to me," he'd begun,

hardly knowing what he was saying. "Kimberly and I are really—well—we're just friends—"

Paige had dropped the hose, but only because she couldn't stretch it any farther and it was useless as a weapon. She jerked open the creaky-hinged gate and bolted through it.

The next-door neighbor's shiny new golf cart sat at the base of his driveway, and Austin, backing away from Paige, bumped into the back fender and then skirted the vehicle. Even then, he'd known he ought to quit laughing, because it sure as hell wasn't helping matters, but they were both caught in a vicious cycle: the more he laughed, the madder Paige got. And the madder she got, the more he laughed.

Paige, her eyes shooting fire, had jumped behind the wheel of the golf cart, turned the key left dangling from the ignition and shifted gears.

She chased him down to the corner, then right out onto Main Street.

Clem Chambers, the neighbor, ran behind Paige, yelling for her to stop, but she paid him no mind.

Austin, now running backward, now running forward, right down the center line, was enjoying the spectacle way too much to put a stop to it.

Given that the "incident of record," as Bill Motts, then chief of police, termed it later, took place in Blue River, Texas, under a heavy canopy of blue-skied July heat, there was no traffic to speak of. Hell, even the dogs that usually roamed the community all day were curled up under porches, avoiding the glare of the sun.

Folks came out of stores and shops on both sides of the road, though, to watch the show.

So Austin ran.

Paige chased him in the golf cart.

Chief Mott jumped into his patrol car, heretofore parked in front of Willard's Bakery, where he bought three bear claws and a cup of strong coffee every morning of his working life, and switched on the lights and the siren. Used his bullhorn to order Paige to "Pull over, dammit."

If she heard the chief at all, she gave no sign of it.

Austin, a ranch kid in good shape, could have run all day. Might have kept the game going a lot longer if he hadn't known Chief Mott so well. Alternately bored with his job and miffed because in his view nobody accorded him the proper respect, the man had no sense of humor. He'd probably throw the book at Paige just for something to do and, besides, what if *she* got hurt?

Austin had led Paige on a merry chase through the middle of town, then sprinted up onto the courthouse steps and bent double, laughing.

Paige tried to drive right up there after him, but the front wheels of the golf cart bumped against the bottom step and then the motor died.

The cart's puffing, red-faced owner got to her at the same time as Chief Mott leaped out of his squad car and waddled over to yank the keys from the ignition.

"I want to press charges!" Clem had yelled, waving his arms around.

"Now, Clem," Chief Mott had said, "calm down before you have a heart attack."

Paige just sat there, on the seat of that golf cart, glaring up at him. Tears left zigzagging tracks in the dust covering her face.

The memory found a soft spot in Austin's middle and ached like a fresh bruise. Brought him back to the present with a jolt.

Dark barn. Faithful dog. Pissed-off woman.

By the time Austin had squared himself with these realities, Paige had pulled free of his grip on the back of her jeans, and she was studying him like she hoped to read his mind.

"Is your disposition still as bad as it used to be?" he asked, looking around for his boots. He didn't want to risk another spasm by pulling them on, so he decided to leave them behind and cross to the house in his stocking feet, but Paige followed his gaze and grabbed them up. Shoved the pair into his chest and looked up at him with narrowed eyes.

"What is *that* supposed to mean?" She started toward the barn door, and Austin followed.

"Just what you *think* it means," he answered. "As I recollect, *Nurse* Remington, you once tried to do me serious bodily harm with a golf cart. If that isn't an indication of antisocial tendencies, I don't know what is—"

Paige strode out into the yard, hugging herself against the chill. "You know damn well I wouldn't have run you over," she said, still on the move. Was that regret he heard in her voice? A little humility, maybe?

Nah.

Austin took off his battered denim jacket and draped it over her shoulders.

Shep trotted along at his side, tail whipping back and forth.

"I know," Austin admitted.

Paige stopped, pulling the jacket tighter around her shoulders. Moonlight caught in her eyes as she looked up at him. "You do?" she asked.

"Yeah," he confirmed. "I do." Mindful that he was bootless, and he'd given Paige his coat, Austin took her hand and kept walking. The ground was hard and the cold bit right through the soles of his socks. "Still, it *was* a pretty dramatic way of making your point."

Paige didn't answer. She walked fast, and wouldn't look at Austin again.

Once they were inside the kitchen, Shep included, he shut and locked the door.

He wanted to kiss Paige again, but since she'd pushed him away the last time, he didn't give in to the urge. No, siree, for once in his life, good judgment prevailed.

"Good night, Paige," he said. He started for his private set of stairs, and couldn't even make the first step because his lower back locked up again.

Gritting his teeth, Austin wrapped one arm around the newel post and steeled himself to wait it out.

Austin had one foot on the first stair and one on the floor, and Paige actually saw the bunching of the muscles in his back, even through the fabric of his shirt.

She hesitated, then climbed to the third step, so she could look directly into his anguished face. Although she

felt a deep pang, seeing him like this—
Austin was an intensely *physical* man, a
cowboy, an athlete, practically a legend
on the rodeo circuit, suddenly unable to
lift a dog or a child or climb a set of
stairs—Paige didn't let her sympathy
show.

"How about a swim?" she said.

Their noses were almost touching.

And his eyes were *so* blue.

He'd kissed her, out there in the
barn, and dammit, she could still feel
the buzz, all the way down to her toes.
Thank God she'd come to her senses
and put a stop to it before things went
any further.

She had a personal point of no return
when it came to Austin, and when he'd
kissed her—the *way* he'd kissed her—
she'd come perilously close to—well—
whatever.

He blinked, clearly confused. Whatever Austin had expected her to say or
do, it hadn't been this. "Huh?"

"A swim," Paige repeated, grasping
the rail for support because she suddenly felt as though she might tumble
headfirst into those sky-blue eyes and

never be seen or heard from again. "Some exercise might loosen you up a little. Make it easier to sleep."

A smile settled into his eyes and slowly made its way down to the corners of his mouth. He let go of the newel post and rested his hands on either side of Paige's waist, and for one beautiful, horrible, heartbreaking moment, she thought he was about to kiss her again.

This time, she wasn't sure she had the strength to resist.

He *didn't* kiss her, though.

He didn't move, either, except to slide his palms up her sides; she felt the sides of his fingers under her breasts.

"It would be great," he drawled, in a husky rumble, "to loosen up."

Paige's cheeks ached with sudden color.

His gaze focused on her mouth—just her mouth—searing her flesh with ice-blue heat.

Somehow, she scrounged up the presence of mind to sidestep Austin and retreat to the bottom of the stairs.

Austin stayed where he was for a long moment, then sighed and turned around to face her. Stepped down.

"What about you, Paige?" he asked. "Do *you* need to loosen up?"

She swallowed. Brazened it out by plastering on a smile. "I wouldn't mind swimming a few laps," she said. "If that's what you're asking."

He looked her over. Took in her jeans, the clingy sweater, the borrowed jacket she was still wearing. "I'll take what I can get," he said. "You have a suit?"

"I borrowed one of Julie's a few days ago," Paige replied, "and I haven't returned it yet."

Again, that insufferable grin, the one that made her reel on the inside. "Damn," Austin said in a purring growl. "I was hoping you'd have to go naked."

The words sent hot shivers rushing through her, but she could think of no good reason for letting him know that, if it could be avoided.

"Well, you're out of luck this time, cowboy," Paige answered blithely.

She walked away then, headed for

the guest quarters. The one-piece Julie had loaned her was still dangling from the showerhead where she'd hung it up to dry a few days before.

Once she was out of the kitchen, and thus out of Austin's sight, Paige picked up speed, in such a hurry to change that she practically skipped along the corridor.

Reaching the bathroom, she took the swimsuit off the showerhead, tossed it onto the counter. Then, telling herself to slow down—did she want Austin to think she was *eager?*—Paige turned on the spigots, stripped out of her clothes, took a hasty shower, dried off and wriggled into the suit. She combed her wet hair straight back from her face and studied her image in the full-length mirror bolted to the inside of the door.

The one-piece was more revealing than she remembered.

Plus it was a wild floral print, made up of screaming pinks, oranges and yellows.

Paige tugged at the shoulder straps, sucked in her stomach, turned sideways. Her butt cheeks were sticking out, so she tugged some more.

She squinted at her reflection.

Too bad her own modest, sensible black suit was in storage, along with most of her other clothes.

Resigned, Paige grabbed a towel, wrapped it around her waist like a skirt, jammed her bare feet into flip-flops from the drugstore and made her way back through the house.

There were a few lights on in the kitchen, so she was in no danger of stubbing a toe or barking a shin, and Shep was there to meet her, tail in perpetual motion, as usual.

She had to smile, and smiling relaxed her a little.

She proceeded bravely into the room where the enormous swimming pool gleamed like a giant turquoise jewel. The area around it was dimly lit, though, creating a cozy ambience.

Austin was treading water in the deep end. She had an overwhelming awareness of . . . *skin.* A lot of it. His upper body was tanned, muscular, glistening with moisture, full of controlled power. The rest of him was wrapped in shifting blue shadows.

Paige froze there on the tiled edge of that magnificent pool, keeping her towel in place with a death grip. She'd been so worried about the fit of the swimsuit that she hadn't considered what Austin might—or might *not*—wear.

Dear God. Was he naked?

Austin watched her in silence for a long moment. Then he threw back his head and gave a low bark of laughter.

Paige forced herself to walk—casually, she hoped—to the steps dipping into the shallow end of the pool, but she held fast to the towel. Her face felt hot, and she was very careful not to look in his direction again.

It was a challenge for the man to put on his own boots.

A few minutes ago, he hadn't been able to climb the stairs to his bed.

Obviously, though, he'd managed to divest himself of at least *some* of his clothes while she was showering and wiggling into Julie's tropical nightmare of a suit. She sat on the top step, swished her feet around in the water.

Austin drew a little closer; Paige felt the shift in the atmosphere even before she caught the subtle motion at the far periphery of her vision.

"What's the matter, Paige?" he drawled, and there was a teasing note in his voice. "You didn't used to be so shy."

"I'm not shy."

"Then get into the water," Austin suggested reasonably. He cleared his throat. "Might loosen you up," he added.

"I'm not the one in need of loosening up," Paige pointed out, somewhat stiffly.

Again, that gruff chuckle. "I reckon that's a matter of opinion," he said, exaggerating the words and the accent to the verbal equivalent of sweet molasses.

Paige locked eyes with Austin then, just so he wouldn't think she was rattled.

Even if she was. A little.

Austin was much nearer now. The

water lapped almost imperceptibly at his navel.

Instinctively, Paige's gaze traveled over his muscular chest, caught briefly on the surgical scars on his right shoulder, doubled back to his washboard belly, and sent the message zipping back to her brain: he was wearing boxers.

Of course he saw her looking, and it made him laugh again.

"You were right," he said very quietly, holding out a hand. "The water feels good."

Paige let him take her hand, loosening the towel and let it drop from her as he pulled her gently down the pool steps until she was facing him. "You should be moving around," she said nervously. "That's the whole point. Working the muscles in your lower back."

He rested his hands on her shoulders, dripping turquoise light onto her skin. "I can think of a few variations on that theme," he murmured.

Their proximity—not to mention the images popping like fireworks in her brain—made Paige crave full-frontal contact in every treacherous cell of her body. She didn't move forward, but she didn't step back, either.

She just stood there.

Austin curled a finger under her chin, then lifted it. His breath tingled on her mouth.

He kissed her.

His lips were soft on hers—at first.

Paige felt the pool tilt crazily to one side, then the other. She pressed her palms against his chest for a moment, then slid them up, interlaced her fingers behind his neck.

The kiss intensified.

Paige felt breathless, then dizzy, then wildly exhilarated.

By the time Austin tore his mouth from hers, she was as dazed as if she'd been catapulted right past the retractable glass roof above their heads and out into the stars.

Breathing deeply and slowly, Paige let her forehead rest against his chest. She could feel the strong, rapid beat of his heart through her skin. "Well," she said, sighing the word.

"Well," he agreed gruffly, propping his chin on the crown of her head. His arms rested loosely around her waist.

They just stood there for a while, neither one speaking. Paige's emotions were complicated, hard to separate from the sensations pulsing in her flesh; being kissed by Austin McKettrick, being held in his arms, especially in those surreal surroundings, felt like a homecoming to her body.

But her reason had a different take on things, and so did her pride.

She found the strength to pull back—it was only a few inches, but far enough that she could breathe. Far enough that she could *think.*

This was Austin. Her first love. Her *only* love, though there had been men in her life since their breakup, some of them almost special.

Trusting Austin had nearly destroyed her once before.

She'd been little more than a child then, that was true. But she'd given him her whole self—mind, body and soul—unable to hold anything back from him. She'd loved him with everything she was, everything she ever hoped to be.

They'd talked about getting married someday, when she finished nursing school and he got the rodeo out of his system.

They'd counted stars, lying on their backs in high, sweet grass, and spent hours choosing names for the children they would have.

Six of them.

And even now, after a whole decade, Paige could have recited those names, in order.

"Tell me what you're thinking," Austin urged now, cupping her face in his hands, tilting her head back, very gently, so he could look directly into her eyes.

"That we're on dangerous ground," she answered, after biting down hard on her lower lip. "The truth is, I'd really like to have sex with you right now, tonight. But I can't afford to play fast and loose here, Austin. I'm not eighteen anymore. I love my sisters. *They* love your brothers. That means we'll be running into each other a lot, you and me, probably for the rest of our lives. If we have a fling and then things fall apart, where will that leave us?"

Austin sighed. "Not in a good place," he admitted.

Paige allowed herself the fleeting solace of drinking him in with her eyes. Her voice came out sounding thick. "Not in a good place," she agreed very softly.

She moved away, climbed out of the pool, wrapped her dripping body in the towel she'd discarded earlier. Put on the flip-flops.

Without another word, or a look back, she hurried away from Austin, well aware that it was already far too late to escape.

CHAPTER SIX

Austin made it to the second floor under his own power, once Paige had carried out her strategic retreat from the swimming pool.

Maybe, he reasoned, too distracted to really give a hoot one way or the other, spending some time in the water *had* helped, as Paige had claimed it would. Eased the bunched muscles on either side of his spine, if not actually smoothing them out.

Unfortunately, there were some new knots now, of a very different variety. And they weren't in his back—no, they were in his conscience, his heart and the core of his solar plexus.

A rush of restless discontent nearly overwhelmed him, as he stood on the threshold of his quarters—a house within a house.

But not a home.

The place hadn't really qualified as one of those since his parents had died in the car crash—on their way back from watching him win yet another fancy silver buckle, riding yet another impossible bull at yet another rodeo.

He'd been just eighteen when Jim and Sally McKettrick were killed, a foolish, hotheaded kid, hurting in secret over the breakup with Paige, doing his arrogant best to convince everyone around him that he was glad he'd cut himself loose.

Bring on the women. Bring on the booze and the bad-ass bulls and the back-alley brawls. At the time, no choice had been so bad that he couldn't make a worse one.

First, he'd hurt Paige. Purposely betrayed her and made sure she knew it.

One bad choice down, one to go.

Next, he'd talked his mom and dad into putting off their vacation in Hawaii, just for a couple of days, so they could be in Lubbock to watch him ride in that damn rodeo.

Remembering, Austin squeezed his eyes shut, opened them again, forced himself through the doorway and into his Spartan living room. There was no escaping the truth, though.

If he hadn't entered *that one rodeo,* his mom and dad would be alive right now, Jim still running the ranch, Sally bustling around helping plan the double wedding, both of them enjoying Audrey and Ava, the grandchildren they'd never even gotten to see. They'd have taken Calvin straight to their hearts, too, as one of their own, regarded Libby and Julie as *daughters,* not just their sons' wives.

So many things would be different.

And the ranch house on the Silver Spur would still be a home.

Austin shook off those thoughts like a dog shaking off water. Or, at least, he tried. Got himself moving.

Reaching his bathroom, Austin took off his swim-sodden boxers and flung them in the general direction of the laundry chute, narrowly missing Shep, who seemed determined to stay close by.

He showered, letting the multiple streams of hot water pummel him, shaved hastily and then got out and toweled himself dry.

All that time, Shep waited patiently, resting on a hooked rug in front of the sink.

"Might be the best thing for everybody," Austin told the dog, squinting at his reflection in the long mirror and running the fingers of both hands through his damp hair, that being all the combing he meant to do, "if you and I hit the road for a while. Let the dust settle around here."

But Austin remembered Molly then, knew he couldn't just up and leave her, not after promising to see her through the rough part of her recovery.

And she was by no means out of the woods, that little mare.

Shep made a low, mournful sound.

"You're right," Austin told the dog, figuring he'd probably wind up as one of those crazy old bachelors who never matched up their socks before putting them on and made long, involved speeches to all manner of critters. "This is where we belong, at least for now. Right here on the Silver Spur."

Shep looked on with polite interest as Austin grabbed a pair of sweat-pants—faded and holey but most likely clean—from a pile on the floor of his closet.

Careful not to make any sudden moves, lest he screw up his back again, Austin supported himself by leaning against the bedroom wall while stepping into the sweats and went right on yammering. "No," he told the attentive Shep, as he wandered over to the long row of windows to stand looking out over the darkened range, "we've got to stick around here and tend to business, whether we want to or not. After all, we're McKettricks, you and me."

It was then that he saw—or *thought* he saw—the brief flicker of light.

Austin squinted, concentrating.

And he saw it again, clearly this time, far off at the edge of the oil field.

Something quickened inside Austin—something besides guilt over his folks' death and the unsettling realization that he still wanted Paige Remington.

"What the hell?" he said to Shep.

Shep offered no useful input.

Quickly but carefully, Austin ditched the sweatpants and got dressed, pulling on jeans, socks, a flannel shirt for warmth and his everyday boots.

Reaching the corridor, he thought about knocking on Garrett's door, letting his brother in on the plan—if you could call anything this nebulous a plan—and immediately discarded the idea.

What was he going to say? *"I saw a light over there by the oil field and like some dumb-ass in a bad horror movie, I'm on my way to check it out"?*

Austin grinned to himself. In this situation, he figured, one dumb-ass was enough—no need to go recruiting another one.

He checked the bathroom counter for his cell phone and didn't find it; figured he must have left it downstairs, in his jeans pocket, when he'd stripped to his underwear to go swimming.

He could retrieve it on the way out.

Mindful of his earlier commitment to cleaner living, Austin kicked the wet towels and the boxers into a single pile on the bathmat. Bending over to gather the stuff up so he could drop it down the laundry chute seemed too chancy, considering his new propensity for back spasms.

Ironic, Austin thought wryly, given that he was headed out into an abandoned oil field in the dark, with one skittish dog for backup.

Downstairs, he found the main kitchen empty, though one or two lights burned. He located his other pair of jeans, tossed over a chaise longue out by the pool, as expected, and rummaged for his cell phone and keys.

He mostly avoided looking in any direction except the one he meant to head in—straight on—but he couldn't help picturing Paige as she'd looked earlier, when they were both in the water, gazing up at him with her eyes all luminous and her hair and her shoul-

ders sprinkled with diamondlike droplets.

Pocketing the phone and making
sure not to jiggle the keys, lest that attract somebody's attention—admittedly
an unlikely scenario, in a house that
size—Austin proceeded to the garage.

He hadn't considered the problem of
lifting the dog into his old truck, but in
the end, it turned out to be a nonissue.
As soon as Austin opened the door,
Shep leaped nimbly onto the running
board, stepped onto the floor of the
truck and then wriggled his way up
onto the passenger seat and sat there
grinning and panting like he had good
sense.

Austin chuckled. "Born ranch dog,"
he said with approval.

A few moments later, he and Shep
were rolling down the long driveway,
toward the gates.

They were closed for the night, those
towering panels of wrought iron and
fancy brass. Austin touched a button
on the remote affixed to his visor and
they whispered open with well-oiled
grace.

Austin hung a left turn and, with another push of a button, conscientiously closed the gates behind him. He thought of his ancestor, Clay McKettrick, the original owner of the spread, and smiled.

Clay would think it was half a mile the other side of crazy, this modern setup. In his day, opening and shutting gates involved getting in and out of a wagon, or at least bending from the saddle to work a latch.

Thinking about Clay and all he'd gone through to buy and then build this ranch made Austin feel a little better about things in general and himself in particular. Whatever demons might have haunted that old-time cowboy, he'd planted his feet in the good old Texas dirt and stayed put.

Fought every battle.

Loved his wife, raised their kids, lived to see most of his grandchildren with babies of their own.

He'd stuck around and done what needed doing, Clay had, and left a legacy for the future.

Austin didn't figure he could do any

less than that and still call himself a McKettrick. It wasn't just the injured horse—Tate and Garrett had their hands full running the ranch, especially with all the rustling and such, and it was time he knuckled down and did his share, injured back or not.

As for Paige Remington—well, he'd have to figure things out as he went along. Steering clear of her would be next to impossible with both her sisters about to marry into the family and all, but maybe that wasn't entirely a bad thing. Sure, he wanted her—but every other word that came out of her luscious little mouth tended to piss him right off.

Close and constant proximity—Paige serving as his nurse, for instance— would probably intensify the physical attraction at first, on his side, anyway. But they'd inevitably get on each other's nerves, sooner rather than later, and the effect would be the same as an inoculation against some disease.

He'd be immune to Paige, and she'd be immune to him, and that would be that.

Problem solved. They'd be able to coexist, like two civilized adults, without either killing each other *or* falling into bed and screwing their brains out.

Just making a decision, albeit a convoluted one, brought Austin a measure of peace, though there was no telling how long it would last.

Probably just until he ran into Paige again, but for the moment, all he had to worry about was the possibility of armed trespassers up to no good out there in the oil field.

He and Shep drove on.

The Silver Spur spanned both sides of the road and continued for miles in three directions, but the graveyard full of rusty derricks wasn't far away.

Austin proceeded maybe half a mile, then shut off the headlights and steered the truck onto an old cattle trail. There was a full moon, allowing him to see without other light. He soon came to another gate, but this one was the old-fashioned kind—lengths of barbed wire nailed to weathered wooden posts.

He stopped, got out of the truck,

opened up the gate, hoisted himself back into the driver's seat without raising much of a sweat and bumped on through the opening. Time enough to shut the gate on his way out, he decided, leaning a little to reach under the driver's seat.

The .357 was there, in its usual spot.

He left it where it lay, nice and handy, though unloaded.

Austin sighed as he and Shep proceeded through the thin moonlight. Once, he'd been way more "cowboy" as far as guns were concerned, liked to have bullets already in the chamber, just in case, but with kids on the ranch, certain precautions had to be taken. With rare exceptions—like the .357— firearms were stored in sealed vaults on the Silver Spur, and the combinations were changed on a regular basis.

Scanning the dark landscape up ahead—the derricks reminded him of dinosaurs in the gloom—Austin didn't see the flicker of light again. He and Shep were probably on the classic wild-goose chase, but at least this way he wouldn't lie awake half the night, wondering.

He gave a low, chortling laugh. No, he'd be awake half the night thinking about *Paige,* what it would be like to make love to her again, now that he was a man instead of a boy and she was a woman instead of a girl.

Shep, meanwhile, seemed to be getting a little antsy—his hackles were up, and he kept scrabbling around in the passenger seat, making a sound that was part whimper and part growl.

In the next instant, a pair of headlights appeared at the top of the little rise just ahead, bearing down hard. Momentarily blinded by the glare, Austin cursed and, keeping his left hand on the steering wheel, put out his right to prevent the dog from slamming into the dashboard or going through the windshield.

There was a crash, but no collision.

Cracks snaked over the windshield, turning it opaque.

Austin felt an impact, and then a searing pain in his left shoulder.

At that point, he lost his grip on the

wheel and the pickup nosed into the ditch, landing hard. Shep gave a startled yelp, and then everything went silent.

The dogs were barking.

Tate McKettrick groaned and rolled onto his belly, pulling the pillow over his head.

Damn, he thought.

Libby poked him in the ribs. "Tate," she whispered, *"wake up.* Something's wrong."

He felt a rush of chilly air as she threw back the covers, knew she was fixing to go and investigate, with or without him.

Grumbling, he got out of the warm, soft bed where Libby had loved him into sweet oblivion only a few hours before, and wrenched on his jeans. Shirtless, bootless, he followed the noise.

All three of the dogs were gathered at the front door, carrying on as if Santa Ana himself were out there, with five thousand troops and a yen to level the house the same as he'd done with the Alamo.

Tate peered out through the glass oval in the front door and at first he didn't see anything but the shadows of the oaks and the sparkle of moonlight on creek water.

Hildie, Buford and Ambrose, meanwhile, turned frenzied.

"Should I get your pistol?" Libby asked, standing a few feet behind Tate.

Any moment now, the twins would be out of bed, too, and scared to death.

Tate shook his head and worked the dead bolt. He heard Libby gasp as he opened the door a crack and peered out.

Austin's dog, Shep, sat on the porch, his sides heaving and his tongue lolling out on one side.

Alarm burned through Tate like a spill of acid. Simultaneously, he silenced his own dogs with a low command and stepped out onto the porch.

"Austin?" he called.

His voice echoed back from the empty darkness.

Libby switched on the porch light, and that was when he saw the blood.

Shep looked as though somebody had sprayed him with the stuff.

Tate swore and crouched to examine the animal. As far as he could tell, the dog hadn't been injured, bloody as he was, though he gave a little yip of protest when Tate touched his right hind leg.

Libby was already on the phone to Brent Brogan, and at the same time herding their own dogs and two worried, sleep-rumpled little girls toward the kitchen.

Tate reached for Shep, wanting to bring him inside, but the animal bared his teeth and laid his ears back in warning. Clearly, he meant to stay where he was, at least for the time being.

Rushing back to the bedroom, Tate quickly finished getting dressed.

Libby appeared in the bedroom doorway just as he was pulling on his second boot. She looked pale as death.

"Brent was already on his way out here," she reported, in a stunned tone of voice, still clutching the phone receiver. "Somebody called his house

from a pay phone in town a few minutes ago, and told him he'd better get
to the oil field on the Silver Spur pronto,
that it might be a matter of life and
death."

Tate opened the gun safe bolted to
the top shelf of the master bedroom
closet and pulled out his pistol, a .38,
and a box of ammunition.

"Listen to me," he said, standing
practically nose to nose with his future
wife, the woman he loved more than
he'd ever dreamed it was even *possible*
to love a woman. "Lock the door behind me. Keep the kids close, and don't
let anybody in unless you know for sure
it's me or Garrett or Brent or—" His
throat closed then. He'd been about to
say "Austin."

"Be careful," Libby said, touching his
arm.

"Always," he replied. He kissed her,
swept his children up in his gaze. "Call
Garrett," he added, on his way out.

"Brent's doing that," Libby told him.

He went out the back door, heard the
lock turn behind him with a decisive
click.

He sprinted toward the driveway, the gun in one pocket of his denim jacket, the bullets in the other.

Austin's dog, last seen on the front porch, was waiting patiently beside Tate's truck.

Tate hesitated, then scooped the critter up and set him inside the cab, blood and all. Shep stepped over the console and the gearshift and settled himself in the passenger seat, and sat there just as calmly as if he rode shotgun every day of his life.

Paige was dressed and sitting at the table in the main kitchen, reading and sipping herbal tea, when Garrett came pounding down the middle stairway, wild-eyed, wild-haired, misbuttoning his shirt and risking his damn fool neck in his hurry to get wherever he was going.

Immediately, Paige rose to her feet. "Julie? Calvin?" she asked, terrified.

"Austin," Garrett replied, grabbing a jacket and his keys and pushing open the door leading to the garage.

Paige's heart clenched like a fist

closing around a lifeline. She didn't bother going back for her purse, but ran behind Garrett, grabbing someone's hooded sweatshirt off a hook as she passed.

They rode in Garrett's truck, descending the driveway at top speed. Midway down, Garrett pushed a button on his remote, and the iron gates slowly swung open ahead of them.

They shot through the gap with not more than an inch of leeway on either side, by Paige's hasty reckoning, and practically took the turn toward town on two wheels.

"Where is Austin?" Paige managed to gasp, holding on to the edges of the seat with both hands, even though her seat belt was securely fastened. They were moving so fast that she almost expected her face to tighten from the g-force. "Garrett, *what's happened?*"

Garrett didn't look at her. He just drove faster, and then faster still.

They heard a siren, saw ambulance and squad car lights flashing up ahead, blue and then red and then blinding white.

"Brogan got an anonymous tip a little while ago," Garrett finally replied, his voice an odd scratchy rasp. "Looks like Austin might be in some trouble, over at the oil fields." Now, briefly, he turned his head to catch Paige's eye and added, "You shouldn't be here."

A shiver moved down Paige's spine; God only knew what they might be facing, but there was no turning back now. And she wouldn't have stayed behind even if that were possible. "Well, I *am* here, Garrett, and I'm not going anywhere," she snapped in response.

The ambulance and Brent Brogan's cruiser turned onto the oil-field road, and Tate's truck wasn't far behind.

Garrett and Paige, getting there last, jostled along at the tail end.

"What the devil would he be doing out here at this hour?" Garrett muttered.

Paige didn't know the answer—she'd last seen Austin after their swim earlier that evening. Of course, Garrett wasn't expecting her to reply; he was thinking out loud, trying to make sense of the situation.

For her part, Paige leaned forward in the seat and willed the procession, slowed by the deeply rutted dirt road, to move faster.

The emergency lights cast a strange, jerky light over Austin's truck, and Paige had her door open even before Garrett stopped his rig. If he hadn't reached out and grabbed her arm, she probably would have jumped to the ground while they were still moving.

As it was, she wrenched free and bolted, her heart scalding in her throat, making it hard to breathe.

Chief Brogan got to the truck first, soon followed by two volunteer paramedics, and hinges squealed horribly as they hauled open the driver's-side door.

Seeing Paige, and well aware of her nursing skills because of earlier medical emergencies, Brogan instructed the paramedics to get out of her way.

She scrambled up onto the running board, peering in.

Both seats were splotched with blood and crunchy with broken glass, but Austin wasn't there. The passenger-side door must have been thrown open on impact; it was jammed open, partially wedged into the far wall of the ditch.

"He's gone!" Paige cried, scooting back out and jumping to the ground. A thought ricocheted through her head— she hadn't been this scared since that one Thanksgiving, when Calvin was a toddler. He'd suffered a major asthma attack, and she'd been so desperate to help him catch his breath that she'd thrust him into an icy shower.

Now, her gaze swung from one worried male face to another, all of them spookily illuminated by headlights and the swirling red-white-blue of the squad car and the ambulance.

A whimper made her drop her gaze to Shep, standing fitfully at Tate's side. His coat was matted with blood.

Pure terror rose up in Paige then. She broke away from the cluster of men and turned in a slow circle in the middle of the dark road, calling Austin's name, pausing to listen, calling again.

When Shep suddenly bolted off through the grass, Paige was right behind him. She was a fast runner, but Garrett and Tate shot past her, soon followed by Chief Brogan, fumbling with a flashlight as he sprinted along.

Shep streaked ahead of them all, barking wildly.

Finally, the dog stopped, somewhere beyond the reach of Brent's flashlight beam, and when they all caught up, Shep was turning in frantic circles, his eyes glowing yellow in the gloom, making a low, terrifying sound in his throat.

Austin was behind him, sprawled on his back, the front of his shirt crimson with blood.

Paige would have screamed in fear— she, the cool-headed nurse, trained in emergency procedures, would have lost it, right then and there—if Austin hadn't drawn up one knee and groaned, proving he was alive.

Shep wasn't going to let anybody near him—not her, not Garrett or Tate, and certainly not Chief Brogan and the two winded paramedics.

In a hoarse, somewhat strangled voice, Austin called the dog to his side, stroked Shep's back until he began to calm down.

Paige landed on her knees on one side of Austin's prone body, Tate and Garrett on the other. Shep growled again and nestled in close against his master.

"I think I'm shot," Austin said, in an almost dreamy voice.

Tate made a hoarse sound, a parody of a chuckle. "Ya think?" he asked, peeling off his coat and spreading it gently over Austin.

"Do you know who shot you?" Garrett asked, explosively calm.

Austin shook his head.

Paige, frozen for a few moments, regained her voice and her ability to move. She pushed away Tate's jacket, ripped open Austin's shirt, uncovering his chest.

Chief Brogan, the only one with a flashlight, shone the beam on the wound.

The bullet had torn into his left shoulder, only inches from his heart, but far enough away to mean he probably wouldn't die. While the paramedics ran back to the ambulance for supplies and a stretcher, Paige wadded the shirt Garrett hauled off over his head and used it to apply pressure and slow the bleeding.

"How bad is it?" Tate asked gruffly.

Paige realized she was crying. She sniffled once, shook her head. "I don't know," she replied, "but if we can control the bleeding and get him to the clinic in town—"

"Not the hospital in San Antonio?" the chief asked.

"It's too far," she said. "Austin needs treatment *now.*"

He looked up at her then and smiled ingenuously. "Are you crying over me, ma'am?" he asked. He was in shock, Paige knew, but he sounded like he was looped.

"There's no reason to cry over you, cowboy," she responded fiercely, if tremulously, "because you're going to be just fine." She leaned down, so their noses were almost touching. *"Just fine,"* she repeated.

"I hear you," Austin said sleepily.

The next couple of hours passed in a blur, at least for Paige.

She rode to the clinic in Blue River in the back of the ambulance with Austin, starting an IV. Garrett claimed the front passenger seat, while the more experienced of the two paramedics knelt opposite Paige, taking vital signs.

She was too busy to worry about much of anything except stabilizing Austin, but the dog did cross her frantic mind a couple of times.

Had someone taken care of Shep?

Austin drifted in and out of consciousness. Out was better, because whenever he started to wake up, his left shoulder felt as though it had been blown completely away from his body.

If it hadn't been for the occasional jolt of pain, he would have thought for sure he was dead. He was surrounded by blurry figures dripping light, trailing it in tumbling spangles with every move. It didn't seem possible that they were human beings, these creatures made of crackling energy.

They must have given him a pretty

powerful drug at some point, because even though the burning throb in his shoulder continued, indeed deepened and developed a rhythm suspiciously like a heartbeat, he was able to transcend it, somehow. He still had pain, but he didn't care.

"My dog," he ground out once, when he thought Paige's face passed in front of his. She looked wavery as a ghost, though. "Where's Shep?"

"I'll find out," the apparition replied.

"Good," he said, and passed out again.

When Austin finally came back to himself, he was lying in a hospital bed, as numb as if every nerve in his body were swathed in cotton balls. A light burned in the hallway, and someone—*Paige*—was slumped in a chair nearby, huddled inside a blanket.

"Paige?"

She started, gasped softly and straightened. Stood and smoothed his hair back from his forehead with a cool hand. "You're awake," she said.

He grinned. "Duh," he said, his voice husky as the call of a bullfrog.

She smiled, but her eyes shimmered with what might have been tears. "How do you feel?"

"Like somebody shot me through the windshield of my truck and everything went south from there," he answered. It was hard to talk, he discovered. His throat was so dry, it hurt.

Paige, ever the nurse, produced a glass of water with a bent straw sticking out of it and held it to his mouth.

"Slowly," she ordered.

The thirst was powerful, but guzzling through a straw was more than he could manage at the moment.

So he sipped.

"Where's my dog?" he asked, when his throat was moist enough to permit him to speak.

Paige smiled, set the glass aside. "Chief Brogan took Shep back to the ranch," she said. "Did you know he found his way to Tate and Libby's place? It's as if he actually went for help."

"Stranger things have happened," Austin ground out.

Paige laid a finger to his lips. "Shhh," she said.

It made him feel coddled, that "shhh" and the touch of her fingers against his mouth. Quickened his heartbeat, too.

"Shep is fine," she assured him, in a voice he wished she'd use all the time. "Thanks to Dr. Colwin, *you're* going to be fine, too. You were lucky, Austin— the wound was fairly minor, but you bled like a stuck pig and you went into shock. Whoever called Chief Brogan saved your life."

Austin frowned. He didn't remember anything except driving toward the oil fields, the smashed windshield, the pain in his shoulder. After that, there was a blank space, followed by a vague recollection of wondering where the dog was.

He must have gone looking, because he remembered when they found him, Paige and his brothers and Chief Brogan. He remembered poor old Shep, guarding him from all comers.

"You wouldn't lie to a cowboy about his dog, would you?" he asked. "Not even to make him feel better?"

She spilled that magical smile all over him, like fairy dust, and then she kissed his forehead. Shook her head.

"No," she said. "I would never lie to a cowboy."

He believed her, and felt a pang of deepest sorrow.

She'd never lied to a cowboy, as far as Austin knew, but a cowboy had sure as hell lied to *her,* if only by omission.

"I think I'm in the market for some competent medical care," he said.

She smiled, but a tear slipped down her perfect cheek. "At your service," she replied.

CHAPTER SEVEN

Austin had a few new stitches in his hide, along with a wad of medicated packing, a bandage over that, and a sling to support the whole mess. After two long days and three even longer nights confined to the inpatient section at the Blue River Clinic, he was finally headed home.

It was a quiet ride, just him and Paige, now officially his keeper, rolling along in her ugly little car. Shep sat silently in the backseat, with his head up, as if he were on the lookout for a fresh batch of attackers.

At least, Austin thought, cranky from the pain and the enforced immobility and all the rest of it, Paige wasn't asking questions. He had flat-out had it with questions.

How many times did he have to tell Tate, Garrett and Chief Brogan that he didn't remember anything that would help their investigation? He'd seen something out there on the oil fields and gone to check it out. Then he'd been shot.

That was the whole story.

Although the chief and the state police had gone over the oil field looking for some kind of evidence, they hadn't found anything they could use to identify the bad guys. Going by the terse reports Austin had basically pried out of Tate and Garrett, there had been an attempt to uncap one of the wells. Possibly the intruder had meant to set it afire.

As the current theory went, Austin had interrupted the process by showing up at the wrong time and, in a panic, the sneaking, chicken-shit sons of bitches had taken a shot at him when their two vehicles met on that narrow road. He'd seen nothing but that dazzle of headlights coming at him before the bullet splintered the windshield and lodged itself in his shoulder.

According to the doctors who'd treated him that night, if he hadn't leaned to the right in an attempt to protect Shep, the bullet would have gone right through the middle of his heart.

Fate was a peculiar thing, he reflected with a twinge of bitterness. Of course he was glad to be alive, but where was the lucky fluke—the wrong turn, the flat tire, the impulsive stop for Mexican food—that would have saved Jim and Sally McKettrick that night?

When that semi had jumped the median, they'd been directly in its path.

No reprieve, no mercy.

"Hello?" Paige broke into his thoughts. "Austin? Are you in there?"

He cocked a puny grin at her, slunk low in the seat and rubbed his bristly chin with one hand. His shoulder hurt, and the muscles in his lower back twitched in a vague but ominous threat of locking up. "Thanks," he said.

"Thanks?" she echoed. She was looking directly ahead, keeping her eyes on the road, and she sounded puzzled.

"For springing me from the clinic," Austin said. "And for bringing Shep along for the ride. I really missed that dog."

Paige gave an odd little chuckle, slid one brief glance in his direction before fixing her attention on the road again. "And the dog missed you," she replied in a tone meant to convey more than Austin was able to pick up on at the time.

"How about Molly?" he asked.

"Molly," Paige told him, in that same get-a-clue voice, "is healing nicely. Doc Pomeroy has stopped by twice to check on her. Calvin and I have been keeping the wounds clean and applying plenty of that special ointment Doc prescribed. Turns out my nephew has a real way with horses."

"I'm not surprised," Austin said gruffly, grinning at the thought of the boy studiously doctoring the little paint mare. "Calvin is a world-class kid."

"At last, something we can agree on," Paige said with what might—or might *not*—have been a smile. In profile, it was hard to tell. Plus, his gaze kept getting stuck on the perfect curve of her right breast.

By then, they'd reached the gates of the Silver Spur. They were open wide, and to Austin, it was like a welcoming embrace.

"When did we not agree?" Austin asked, figuring that, since they'd only been alone together for the fifteen minutes or so it took to drive from the clinic in Blue River to the ranch, they hadn't had time to get on each other's nerves.

Paige headed up the long driveway. "Just about every time we've tried to have a conversation?" she jibed, but there was a twinkle in her eyes when she looked his way.

Austin felt as though he'd been away from home a lot longer than the three days since the shooting, and maybe, at least from an emotional standpoint, he *had* been. Seeing the place again distracted him, even from the banter with Paige, and he felt things lift up inside him as he took in the barn, the outbuildings, the palatial house.

And the moving trucks.

There were two of them, parked in the massive portico.

"What's up with that?" he asked Paige, indicating the rigs with a nod of his head.

She smiled, clearly pleased to know something he didn't. "Tate and Libby and the girls are moving back into the main house," she said.

"Why?" Austin wanted to know, frowning a little but secretly happy to hear it. Tate had been so all-fired determined to create a different home for himself and Libby and the kids that he'd set up housekeeping in the old Ruiz place and started renovating like crazy.

Paige shrugged as she swung the car around the side of the house, buzzed up one of the garage doors and whisked them inside. "He's not saying," she replied, shutting off the engine, "but Libby and Julie and I figure it's the McKettrick equivalent of circling the wagons. Tate's protecting his family. What with all that's been happening on this ranch lately, he may have a point."

Whatever his oldest brother's reasons for returning to the homestead, where there was plenty of room for all of them yet with enough privacy to suit a hermit, Austin was glad. A house ought to have kids and dogs running around in it, it seemed to him, and if he and one or the other of his brothers occasionally crossed paths in the main kitchen or something, what harm could that do?

Paige parked the car, shut off the engine, closed the garage door and, finally, unsnapped her seat belt. Just as Austin was about to protest that he didn't need any help getting out of the car, he realized she didn't intend to offer any.

She stepped out onto the concrete floor of the garage, opened the rear door on her side and stepped back so Shep could leap nimbly down.

Paige didn't even glance in Austin's direction, in fact, but simply retrieved her purse, slung the strap over one shoulder and walked inside.

At least the dog waited for him.

Both amused and annoyed—a common phenomenon with him when it came to Paige Remington—Austin grinned to himself and struggled out of the car. Paused to—carefully—stretch his legs before going on.

He still had a flight of stairs to climb, and he wasn't looking forward to it.

After that, he'd have nothing to do but lie around watching TV, listening to the radio or trying to read. This last had proved frustrating since his back had gone to hell; reading was a challenge for him anyway, but the pills he had to take made concentration even more difficult, and sometimes impossible.

He wasn't looking forward to the boredom, either. Too much time to look back on things he couldn't change and regret them just the same.

All hell broke loose when he stepped into the kitchen.

Streamers flew and things popped, the dogs barked in chorus, Shep joining right in like he'd been practicing his part, and Calvin and the twins whooped, *"Surprise!"*

For one confused moment, Austin wondered if it was his birthday or something.

But Julie and Libby both approached, each of them planting a sisterly kiss on his cheek. Julie laughed, probably at the confounded expression on his face, and said, in a tone she might have used to prompt one of her drama students when they needed a cue, "Welcome home, Austin."

He looked around the big room, saw Tate opening the first of a stack of pizza boxes on the center island. Garrett, meanwhile, was calling off the kids and the dogs.

Paige was nowhere in sight.

Austin tugged at Audrey's dark ponytail, then Ava's. He ruffled Calvin's blond hair and walked into the heart of that house, and that family.

His family.

Paige stood in the larger of the two bedrooms in the guest apartment, enjoying the billow and scent of a freshly laundered, snow-white sheet as she flung it open and then watched as it settled slowly over the bed.

Until further notice, Austin would be sleeping here; Paige had carried the few belongings she'd brought from home into the smaller room that had been Calvin's, before he and Julie moved upstairs to share Garrett's place.

Until Austin's shooting, she'd been ambivalent about accepting the job as his private nurse. The moment she'd seen him lying on the ground out there in the oil field, however, losing blood at an alarming rate and more concerned about his dog's well-being than his own, there had been a seismic shift in Paige, one she couldn't fully explain, even to herself.

She was still wildly attracted to Austin McKettrick.

At the same time, she was scared to death of the things he made her feel. She wanted to run the other way, as fast and as far as she could.

She also wanted to run *toward* him.

Paige smoothed the sheet, spread a blanket on top. Fluffed up the pillows.

"Paige? Are you okay, sweetie?"

She turned, knowing Julie would be standing in the doorway. "Of course I am," she said, smiling. "Why wouldn't I be 'okay'?"

Julie rested a shoulder against the doorjamb and folded her arms. Her head was tilted to one side, and she was wearing that look of benevolent suspicion she usually reserved for Calvin. Dressed in jeans and one of Garrett's old flannel shirts with the sleeves rolled up, she'd obviously been helping Libby unpack over in Tate's part of the house.

"Well," Julie drawled in reply, "the rest of us are in the kitchen, celebrating Austin's return and about to have pizza, and you're in here, all by yourself—"

Paige turned, plunked down on the side of the bed she hadn't quite finished making. "Maybe," she admitted, somewhat testily, "I just needed a moment. Did you ever think of that?"

Julie laughed softly and crossed to sit next to Paige. Looking around the room, she sighed and, instead of answering Paige directly, mused aloud, "Who would have believed my life could change as much as it has since Calvin and I were staying in this apartment?"

Any reminder of Julie's happiness— or Libby's—made *Paige* happy, too. Smiling, she took Julie's hand and squeezed it lightly. "Garrett's a lucky man," she said.

Julie flushed. "And I'm a lucky *woman,*" she replied. Their hands still clasped, the two sisters touched the sides of their heads together briefly, then Julie got back on her feet. Smiled at Paige with genuine understanding. "I know it's awkward," she said. "Living here, I mean. Helping out with Calvin before and after school is one thing, but being in close contact with Austin, after everything—"

Paige uttered a raw chuckle and put up one hand to silence Julie. "It's good practice," she said.

Julie looked confused. "What is?"

Paige laughed. "If you could see your face," she teased. Then she stood up, and left the bed semimade behind her. In the hallway, she linked her arm through Julie's, and they both headed toward the kitchen, the pizza and those incomparable McKettrick men.

Julie smiled, but she wasn't going to let Paige off the hook. "*What* is 'good practice'?" she insisted, in a whisper.

"Being in the same room with Austin McKettrick and one, not killing him," Paige whispered back, her tone mischievous. "And, two, not jumping his bones."

Julie chuckled and shook her head.

"So far," Paige went on, still keeping her voice down because now they were almost in the kitchen, where the family had gathered to welcome one of their own back from the brink of death, "Austin and I have found two things we can agree on. The first is that Calvin is one terrific kid."

Julie beamed in obvious agreement. "What's the second?"

"That we—Austin and I—have no choice but to learn to get along, because *my* sisters are in love with *his* brothers, and vice versa, and we have to deal."

Julie gave her a one-armed hug just before they entered the kitchen. "That's right," she said. "You have to deal. *Both* of you."

With that, they stepped into the party.

By the time everyone had their fill of pizza, Austin was starting to show definite signs of exhaustion.

Paige felt a tender sting in her heart, just watching him interact with his adoring nieces, and with Calvin.

Tate and Garrett went back out onto the range, while Libby and Julie tidied up the kitchen, talking quietly about the wedding, the food and the music and—horrors!—Paige's bridesmaid's dress.

Paige found a broom and a dustpan and began sweeping up crumbs, being very careful to avoid getting sucked into the talk about the Big Event.

"We're out of school," Ava was telling her uncle Austin in a joyous tone, *"because it's Saturday!"*

"Guess I lost track of time for a while

there," Austin told his niece. His gaze flicked to Paige's face, flicked away again.

His beard was growing in, his hair was shaggy, and Paige thought she'd never seen a more attractive man in her life.

Another danger signal, of course.

She finished sweeping, emptied the dustpan, put it away, along with the broom. Grabbing a jacket from the row of hooks where a variety of such garments were kept, she shrugged into it and announced, without looking at Austin, that she was going out to the barn to see how Molly was doing.

Austin got to his feet, wan but determined. "I think I'll come along," he said, and nothing in his voice or his manner left room for disagreement.

"Can we go, too?" Calvin immediately asked.

"All of us?" Ava cried.

"And the dogs?" Audrey added.

Libby and Julie exchanged glances.

"We've got work to do upstairs," Julie told the children. "Remember?

The movers have been unloading boxes all this time, and that means we're behind with the unpacking."

None of the kids protested.

"We're helping," Ava explained to Austin. "Otherwise, we'd come out to the barn, too."

Austin smiled down at her, held the little girl's chin in his hand for a moment. "Lots of time for horse tending," he said quietly, "now that you'll be living here in the big house."

"Lots of time," Ava agreed.

With that, she and Audrey and Calvin headed for the far stairway, and all the dogs except Shep followed them.

Julie and Libby were soon gone, too, so Paige and Austin just stood there, looking at each other.

"You should lie down," Paige finally said, because they were alone and the silence made her uncomfortable. "There's a bed ready for you in the guest apartment. If anything's changed with Molly, I'll let you know."

He took a slow step toward her, one eyebrow slightly raised. "The guest apartment?" he said. "Isn't that where *you* sleep?"

Paige's cheeks instantly warmed. "You aren't supposed to climb stairs for a while," she reminded him, "so I'm giving you my room. I'll sleep where Calvin used to."

Austin had closed the space between them by then. "We'll see to the horse together," he told her, "and *then* I'll gladly climb into your bed, Nurse Remington."

The warmth in Paige's face turned to fire, probably because she didn't find the idea of Austin McKettrick climbing into her bed all that unappealing. And she *should* have, by God. After what he'd done to her—ten years, ten minutes, it didn't matter which—did it?—because once a cheater, always a cheater. She should have found the whole idea of sex with this man downright revolting.

Instead, she wanted him. Ferociously.

She knotted her hands into fists and thrust them deep into the pockets of the hooded jacket she'd helped herself to moments before, realizing only then that the garment belonged to Austin—it carried his unique scent.

"All right, then," she said, sounding a lot calmer than she was, "let's go see Molly."

Because of the sling, Austin couldn't put his left arm into the sleeve of a jacket, but he didn't seem to mind the November cold as they headed outside.

Shep stuck with them, probably reluctant to let Austin out of his sight after what must have seemed like a long absence to him.

All the time Austin was confined to the clinic, Shep had spent most of his time curled up on a pile of unwashed jeans and T-shirts on the floor of his master's closet.

Paige had tracked him there, the first morning, and worried when he wouldn't eat or drink.

It had been Calvin who finally persuaded Shep to accept kibbles from the palm of his hand and even to take some water. If Julie hadn't nixed the idea, Calvin would probably have slept in that closet with Shep, just to keep him company.

Paige couldn't help drawing a comparison between that and Austin wanting to spend the night in the barn when Molly was first brought to the ranch.

Two of the cowboys were working in the barn when Paige and Austin got there, one feeding livestock, the other shoveling out stalls. There were probably more long-term employees on the Silver Spur than on most ranches, but some of the workers were transitory, and this pair fell into that category.

Paige had never seen them before.

Apparently, Austin had.

"Hello, Tom," he said, addressing the one filling the feeders with grass hay.

Tom nodded. "Austin," he said in a friendly tone. "Hell of a thing, what happened to you. I was right sorry to hear about it."

"Thanks," Austin told him.

The other man, younger than the first, flung a pitchfork full of manure into a waiting wheelbarrow and drew idly on the cigarette between his lips.

"Told you before, Reese," Austin said easily. "No smoking in the barn."

Reese's jaw tightened, but then he grinned. He was probably in his early twenties, Paige thought, and except for his acne scars, he was handsome.

"Sorry, boss," he replied, tossing the butt down in the stall muck and grinding it out with the toe of his boot. "It won't happen again."

Austin merely nodded, as if taking the promise at face value, and went on to stand at the door of Molly's stall.

The mare was waiting to greet him; she nickered happily and nuzzled his chest.

Paige, no stranger to confrontation herself, felt vaguely unsettled by the exchange over the no-smoking rule, even though it had been a quiet one.

Still, she saw how Reese's eyes followed Austin as he moved on to greet Molly, clearly considering the matter resolved. And she didn't like the feeling that settled into the pit of her stomach.

As she walked past the man, to join Austin in front of Molly's stall, tiny prickles moved over Paige's body in a wave, and she instinctively quickened her step.

Shep, always protective of Austin, gave no sign of concern. He was with his master, and that was all that mattered to him.

Reese went back to shoveling, and Tom continued to feed.

Paige told herself she was just jumpy because she hadn't slept well since Austin's shooting. Now that he was home again, her emotions seemed to be cycling from one extreme—joy—to its utter opposite—despair.

She joined Austin inside Molly's stall and immediately felt better.

Because of his sling, Austin couldn't help out much except to stroke Molly's long nose and talk to her while Paige cleaned off the cruel marks left by the old halter with sterile wipes and then gently applied fresh ointment.

Doing all that, Paige forgot about Tom and Reese, forgot everything, actually, except for Austin and the trusting horse and the dog waiting faithfully outside the stall door.

The sense of pure belonging that came over her then was sweet and strange, something to savor and then let go of, because she knew there was no way it could last.

Austin's gaze strayed to her face and she blushed, as she often did when this man looked at her, because it seemed he could see beyond the persona she presented to the world—the competent nurse, Julie and Libby's outspoken sister, Calvin's devoted aunt.

And as much as Paige cherished her family, as hard as she'd worked to earn her professional credentials, for that one instant she could admit, if only to herself, that those things weren't enough.

She wanted a husband, a lover.

She wanted children.

She wanted a home of her own.

But if there was one thing Paige Remington had learned in her life, it was that wanting something wasn't the same as getting it.

As a small child, she'd wanted her mother to stay—wanted that with an urgent intensity she could still feel, even now, so many years later.

She'd wanted her dad to survive the cancer that had taken his life. She'd wept and prayed, but Will Remington, a brokenhearted husband, a dedicated father, had still died.

And dear God how she had wanted *Austin.*

Standing there in Molly's stall, her fingers smeared with antibiotic ointment, Paige blinked back tears. Told herself to get a grip, to be grateful for what she had—two wonderful sisters, a nephew she loved as her own child, a career that caused her soul to thrive within her. Her health was good, and she lived in a free country.

It was just plain wrong to want more. Wasn't it?

They finished with the horse, and Austin opened the stall door, waiting for Paige to precede him into the breezeway, where Shep was waiting.

They walked in silence, their shoulders almost touching but not quite, and when they stepped outside, Paige was genuinely surprised to realize that nightfall wasn't far off.

High overhead, the first audacious stars were popping out, staking silvery claims to the night sky.

Austin took Paige's hand, and she didn't pull away.

She didn't pull away. No, Paige allowed him to hold her hand.

Austin counted that as a victory, however small.

The big kitchen was empty.

He hesitated, dropped her hand. "You don't have to give up your room," he said. "I can make it upstairs with no problem."

Paige looked mildly surprised, and then obstinate. "Maybe you can, Austin," she said, "but there's no need to complicate things by ignoring your doctor's instructions, now is there?"

If loving to argue with Paige Remington was wrong, Austin didn't want to be right. "It's a big house," he said, gesturing with one hand to indicate a wide area, "and there are other bedrooms on this floor. Esperanza's place is empty at the moment, for example, and there are other options besides." He paused, knowing he was pissing her off, enjoying the fact immensely. "Why *your bed,* Paige?"

Her color flared, but then she recovered her composure. "You are being deliberately obtuse," she accused him, turning and moving on, leaving him to follow or not. And, of course, he followed.

"I'm not inviting you to sleep with me," she went on, when they stood in the modestly furnished living room of the guest quarters. Light spilled from the lamps, and dark was at the windows. "No matter how determined you may be to misinterpret everything I say."

Austin looked around, taking in the space. It was part of the original house, the one Clay and his wife had built together, early in the last century.

"This would have been the parlor," he said, thinking aloud.

Paige looked at him curiously. She wasn't quite so prickly as before, but she still generated plenty of electricity. "The parlor?"

"Yes," Austin said, moving to stand in front of the cold fireplace, tracing the design carved into the mantel's edge with his working hand. The wood was dark and heavy, scarred in places, but built to last. The clock Clay had given his bride as a wedding gift was still there, too, and still ticking away, the sound strong and true. "Once upon a time, this was pretty much the whole house—this apartment and Esperanza's, anyway. There was a loft, but no upstairs."

She watched him, arms folded, but loosely, and not like she was guarding herself from him, her head tilted to one side. He loved the way she looked when she listened. "You McKettricks have quite a family history," she said.

He nodded, offered up a lopsided grin. "Yep," he agreed. His place upstairs seemed far away, hard to get to and way too lonely. Paige's bed, even without her in it, was looking better and better.

"Come on," she said, putting out a hand. "You'd better rest."

"I'm going to need some help with my—boots," he said, looking down at his clothes and that sling and figuring he was going to need help with a lot more than his boots. Taking pity on her, he added, "I could call Garrett or Tate."

"Don't be silly," she said, surprising him again. "I'm an RN, Austin. I've undressed a lot of men in my time."

Austin's mouth twitched with the impulse to comment, but he restrained himself. From the look on her face, Paige was under a lot of strain, and he didn't plan on adding to it.

"Okay," he said.

In the bedroom, Austin lowered himself to sit on the edge of the bed. It was a four-poster, intricately carved like the mantelpiece out in the living room, and from the same era.

A lot of McKettricks had been conceived and eventually born in that old bed, and not a few had died there. It made Austin feel connected, in a strangely comforting way, to all those who had gone before.

He was not a whimsical man, nor was he particularly interested in climbing the branches of his family tree. This odd nostalgia was probably nothing more than a side effect of all the drugs he'd been given lately, and it would pass.

He'd be his old rascally self again before he knew it.

Paige bent, got him by one foot, and pulled. Vigorously.

Nothing happened.

She pulled again.

Again, nothing.

"It works better," Austin drawled, wondering how long it had been since he'd had this much fun with his clothes on, "if you turn around. That way, I can push with my other foot."

Crimson patches bloomed on her cheeks, and her eyes glittered. "Are you suggesting . . . ?" She paused, swallowed, visibly regrouped. "*Are you suggesting* that I let you put your *foot* on my—backside—and *push?*"

"Yeah," he said, and then bit the inside of his lower lip so he wouldn't laugh right out loud. "That's how it's done, Paige."

Shep, content to lie under the window and watch the proceedings, pricked up both ears and then relaxed again, resting his muzzle on his forelegs and rolling his brown eyes from Austin to Paige and then back again.

Paige didn't move.

Austin put a lot of drama into a sigh of resignation, then leaned to grab hold of his right boot, with his one working hand. He gave a mighty pull—that was real—but the gasp of pain, not so much.

Paige called him an idiot—he was beginning to read that as a term of affection—and took over the boot pulling. As instructed, she turned her back to him, held his booted foot between her knees and yanked.

Unable to resist, Austin carefully centered his left boot across her shapely, blue-jeaned buttocks and pushed.

She gave a little cry, one of indignation rather than pain, and stumbled a few steps when the boot came off.

The look she gave him over her shoulder could have been used to brand cowhide.

It wasn't as if he'd laughed or anything. He'd wanted to, though. He had *really* wanted to.

"I offered to call Tate or Garrett down here to help," Austin reminded her. "And you said you'd rather undress me yourself."

"I did *not* say I wanted to undress you," Paige pointed out, glaring. But she hauled off his second boot, the same way she'd done with the first one, and the gesture left Austin feeling a new kind of tenderness toward her.

After that, they didn't talk much.

She helped him strip to his boxers and drew back the covers so he could lie down. She didn't exactly tuck him in, but close.

"I'll get your medicine," she said stiffly.

"Thanks," he told her, wanting to laugh again.

As soon as she'd left the room, Shep crossed the floor and sprang up onto the mattress, sprawled himself across

Austin's ankles and gave a going-to-sleep sigh.

Austin grinned. "I missed you, too, buddy," he said.

CHAPTER EIGHT

Paige slept lightly, just down the hall from Austin, and when she heard a crash, followed by a guttural and rather creative curse, somewhere in the deepest, darkest folds of the night, she was awake in an instant.

She tossed back the covers on the narrow bed that used to be Calvin's and sat up, reaching out to switch on the lamp.

"Austin?" she called, but quietly, rushing into the hallway.

No answer.

Had he fallen? Reinjured himself, opened his stitches? Done some lasting and irrevocable harm to his back?

These fears and others plagued her, even as she reminded herself that she was a *nurse,* for heaven's sake, and therefore not usually prone to panic.

She tried again. "Austin?"

Paige flipped on the bathroom light, half expecting to see her charge sprawled on the floor, or unconscious in the tub or the shower stall, but the room was empty. So was the bedroom he'd occupied earlier.

Another crash sounded, then another curse. A dog, probably Shep, began to bark.

Heart pounding, Paige followed the ruckus to the kitchen.

Austin, armed with a rifle and wearing only a pair of sweatpants and his sling, was just heading out the back door.

"Wait!" Paige cried. "You can't go out there like—"

Shep darted past them both, shooting into the chilly darkness like a fur-covered bullet.

As for Austin's response, well, Paige might not have spoken at all, he paid so little attention.

"Dammit," Paige cursed, hopping and hurrying, trying to catch up with

Austin and failing utterly. The ground was cold and small rocks dug into her bare feet. "Austin McKettrick," she yelled, *"you come back here!"*

Of course, he *didn't* come back.

Garrett and Tate ran out of the house, though, half-dressed shadows passing a now-limping Paige.

The snarling started then, vicious.

Paige knew Shep was fighting for his life, maybe for Austin's.

A scream burgeoned into the back of her throat, came out as a croak of terrified despair.

Paige heard the crisp *crack* of a rifle shot, a brief yelp and pulsing silence.

Garrett appeared out of the darkness, and took Paige by the shoulders. "Don't go any farther," he said.

Fear lanced through Paige, shredding her from the inside. "Austin? Shep?"

Just then, Austin stepped, ghost-pale, into a shaft of moonlight. His sling was askew, his bandages bloody. And he was carrying Shep in both arms.

Paige looked back, saw Tate standing over the carcass of some huge animal—a wolf? A coyote? Perhaps even a panther? From that distance, she couldn't tell.

She continued toward the house, wincing as she walked but never slowing her pace.

Inside the kitchen, the overhead lights flicked on, and Paige couldn't tell who was in worse shape, the man or the dog.

Shep made a small whimpering sound as Austin laid him gently on the big table, smoothed his ruff.

Garrett was already on the phone to Doc Pomeroy.

Stricken, Paige moved to stand beside Austin.

Shep, though breathing hard, was conscious. A moment passed before Paige noticed the twisted angle of the dog's right hind leg.

"What—what happened?" she asked.

Austin swung a leg over the bench and sat down at the table, stroking Shep's side with slow, gentle motions of his right hand. He looked up at Paige briefly when he answered. "I heard a ruckus," he said slowly. "It sounded like it was coming from someplace around the barn. I went to check it out, and Shep—well, something came at us, another dog, I think, and Shep went after it—"

Tate came into the house, carrying what must have been the same rifle Austin had taken outside earlier. Paige barely registered his presence, or Garrett's. Austin and his dog stood out in bold relief for her; everything and everyone else was beside the point.

Gently, she laid a hand on Austin's bare shoulder. His flesh was ice cold—not surprising, given that he'd just been outside in the chill of a November night, wearing almost nothing. "You shot the other animal?" she asked quietly.

Austin nodded. "Shep was down," he said. "I knew he'd be a goner if I didn't do something."

"Doc Pomeroy will be here to take care of Shep in a few minutes," Garrett told his brother very quietly. "In the meantime, cowpoke, you're somewhat worse for wear yourself. Better let Paige have a look at that shoulder."

Austin looked up at Garrett, his gaze

hardening into something fierce, even primal. "The shoulder will keep," he said.

"So will the dog," Garrett answered, unfazed by the cold put-down Austin had just delivered.

Paige shook off her stupor then and got busy. "I'll need some washcloths and some towels," she told Garrett. "And a basin, since Austin isn't likely to leave Shep's side long enough to stand at the sink so I can clean him up and see how badly he's hurt."

Garrett, obviously glad to have something to do, immediately got busy.

Tate, meanwhile, sat down on the bench directly across the table—and the prone figure of the dog—his denim-blue eyes fixed on Austin's pale face.

Paige carefully removed the bandages from his shoulder and began to clean the wound with the water and washcloths Garrett had rounded up for her. The damage to Austin's thick hide was probably only superficial, Paige concluded, biting her lip as she worked. He'd popped a few stitches, which accounted for the bleeding, but she doubted he'd done himself any serious harm.

This time.

Tate's thoughts must have been running along the same lines as Paige's were, because his jaw was outlined in white, and unclamping the joints to speak cost him visible effort.

"I was right upstairs," he said evenly. "So was Garrett. And you went out there, half-naked and all on your own *because*—"

Meanwhile, Garrett had scared up a first aid kit from somewhere.

He opened the plastic case for Paige and she assessed the supplies, took out antiseptic wipes, a package of cotton balls and a small bottle of iodine.

Austin, who had been glaring at Tate, projecting the clear message that he would explain himself when and if he felt like it, sucked in a sharp breath when the iodine hit. He looked up at Paige, his expression faintly accusing, but he didn't stop stroking the dog.

Shep, for his part, seemed a lot calmer now. He lay still on the table, except for one or two attempts to reach back and lick his broken leg.

"That *hurt,*" Austin told Paige.

"It was *supposed* to hurt," she replied. "It's iodine."

He glared at her.

She glared back.

When it came to obstinacy, Paige could hold her own, thank you very much, even against a McKettrick.

She took a packet of gauze and some tape from the first aid kit and applied a fresh bandage to Austin's wound, offering no further comment. The sling was a total loss, so she chucked it into the garbage and fashioned a new one using some of Esperanza's dish towels.

Tate waited for an answer, his gaze practically pinning Austin, and one eyebrow slightly raised.

"Okay," Austin finally burst out, staring darkly back at Tate, "so maybe I should have asked you and Garrett for help. The point is, I didn't, and now it's over and if you wouldn't mind dropping the subject, *big brother,* I would be much obliged."

There was a rap at the back door, which they had unlocked for the vet, and Doc Pomeroy let himself in, lumbered into the kitchen, his gaze going straight to Shep. This time, Cliff wasn't along for the ride.

"Get back, all of you," Farley snapped, in his usual gruff voice. "Give us some room."

Everybody moved except Austin, who remained right where he was, still comforting the dog.

Paige cleaned up, washing out the plastic basin and then scrubbing her hands.

Garrett and Tate conferred with each other, in low voices, and left the house, probably to remove the body of the animal Austin had shot to save Shep. It wouldn't do for Calvin or the twins to be confronted with such a sight, come morning.

Doc murmured under his breath as he examined and treated Shep. He gave the dog an injection first, probably a painkiller, and then set Shep's leg and bound it tightly with gauze and bandages.

That done, Farley scrubbed up and then shook some small tablets out of a bottle he carried in his medical bag, dropping them into a small envelope.

"Starting tomorrow morning, give him one of these every twenty-four hours," the veterinarian directed, brusque as ever.

"Thanks," Austin said, sounding relieved.

He got up to hoist a snoring Shep off the table, but Doc elbowed him aside and did the honors himself.

"Where do you want this fella put?" the old man asked. He was big, awkward-looking, raw-boned. And yet he held that dog as tenderly as he might have held a child, and the sight touched Paige, way down deep.

Austin left the table, moving with weary grace. "This way," he said, and he led Doc Pomeroy right back to the room where he'd been before all the excitement started.

Paige took some blankets from the linen closet in the apartment hallway and made a nest for Shep on the floor, close to Austin's bed.

Doc's strength didn't falter as he dropped to a crouch and gently laid Shep down on the blankets.

"He's going to be fine," Doc said, looking Austin over. "But I'm not so sure about you."

Paige had been mainly concerned with Austin's wound, before. Now, she finally noticed that he was shivering, and there was a bluish cast to his lips.

"I'm all right," he told Doc solemnly.

Doc shook his head. "You McKettricks. I once pulled the prongs of a pitchfork out of your granddaddy's leg, back when the Silver Spur still grew all its own hay. He was bleeding like there was no tomorrow and giving me guff about how he had to get the cows and the horses fed when I asked him to let me take a look. Last thing he said before he passed out colder than a wedge was, 'I'm all right.'"

Austin cocked a grin at him. "What happened next, Doc?" he asked, in the tone of one who knew full well what happened next. "After you pulled the pitchfork out of Granddad's leg, I mean."

"Soon as old Bill came around, he doused those punctures with kerosene from a can in one of the sheds and kept right on working. Put in a full day."

"Well, then," Austin said lightly. "It must be genetic."

He sat down on the edge of the bed, then stretched himself out straight.

Paige covered him with two faded quilts and a thin blanket, thus exhausting the guest-quarters' linen supply, peered at the labels on his prescription bottles, which were lined up on the dresser on the other side of the room.

Once Doc had said his good-nights and gone, Paige went back to Austin's bedside.

He sat up—the chills were worse now—and accepted the pills and a glass of water.

"I've said it before," Paige told him, "and I'll say it again—"

"I'm an idiot?"

"That's pretty much it, yes."

Austin grinned, set the glass aside on the nightstand, and snuggled down under the blankets. "Now that we've established that," he said, his teeth chattering a little, "maybe you could do something—*nurselike*."

Paige, her emotions spent, her body aching with fatigue, blinked back tears. She spoke in the most normal tone she could manage. "Such as?"

"I was thinking you might want to get in bed with me."

"You were, were you? Why in *hell* would I want to do that?"

"Because I'm cold? I could get pneumonia, you know. What kind of nurse lets a man get pneumonia, when all she'd have to do to prevent it is share her body warmth?"

Paige sat down on the edge of the mattress, not because she was planning on "sharing her body warmth," but because she was suddenly so tired that she didn't trust her legs to hold her up.

"You know something, McKettrick?" she said, sighing the words more than saying them. "You are high maintenance. As in, a *lot* of work."

He grinned, but he still looked pale, and she knew he wasn't faking the shivers. "If you'd like," he said generously, "I could ask my brothers to give you a raise."

She couldn't help it.

She laughed, though her eyes burned.

"You're not only a lot of work," she said. "You're *impossible.*"

"There doesn't have to be any sex," he said.

"You're damn right there doesn't," Paige replied. But then she turned off the lamp and she joined him under the covers, wrapping her arms around him, settling in close.

That was when the numbness began to subside, and Paige realized that her feet were very sore—until then, she'd forgotten that she'd rushed outside without her shoes, chasing Austin.

Now, other parts of her body awakened, as things warmed and unfurled inside her.

Austin slid his good arm underneath her and used his strength to roll her on top of him.

"That's better," he ground out.

"Austin McKettrick—"

He moved his hips beneath hers, and

though she'd been aware of his powerful erection before that, now she was
*hyper*aware. "You. Feel. So. Good."

Paige tried—though, admittedly, not
very hard—to move aside.

Austin lifted his head off the pillow,
and snagged her mouth in a kiss.

She forgot to protest.

He kissed her senseless. Kissed her
until she had to come up for air or
smother, right there on top of him, with
his magnificent hard-on pressing into
her belly and his arm still locked around
her waist.

"We can't," she said.

A great sigh moved through Austin's
frame, though he had, at least, stopped
shivering. "I know," he replied.

"We'd need a condom," Paige heard
herself say, and was mortified.

"I don't suppose you happen to have
one handy," Austin reasoned, and while
there was a teasing quality in his voice,
Paige suspected that he was more serious than not.

"Of *course* I don't have a condom
handy!" she sputtered.

"Shhh," Austin said. "Everybody in the house will hear you."

Paige's cheek throbbed with heat— and so did her body. She had to get off Austin, she decided. Eventually.

"Not in *this* house, they won't," she said.

Austin was easing her nightgown upward, very slowly. "Well," he told her huskily, "if both of us can't be happy, at least *one* of us can."

Why didn't she get *off* the man? She was behaving like some kind of— *tramp.* A red-hot mama, ready to get it on.

She was naked under her nightgown—she was keenly aware of that— and if he hauled it up much farther, there would hardly be anything between her and his erection.

"Austin." The name came out as part whisper, part moan.

Skillfully, he maneuvered her upward, at the same time relieving her of the nightgown. Bared her breasts and then promptly caught one of her nipples in his mouth and began, very gently, to suck.

She groaned, and her body seemed to lengthen, while her low back arched, giving him easier access.

He tongued her, and she was lost to the pleasure, to the need he'd aroused in her. As easily as that, she was lost.

He enjoyed her breasts, one and then the other, wetly and for a long, long time. Then, just when she thought she would lose her mind, Austin slid his hand down, between them, and unerringly found the crux of her thighs. He parted her with his fingers, chuckled when she gave a little cry of joyous despair.

"Feel good?" he teased, plying her, causing her to squirm on top of him, seeking more and more contact with his fingers.

"Damn you," she gasped, "you *know* it does—"

"I'll stop any time you want me to," he declared in that butter-and-honey drawl of his, but he didn't even slow down, let alone stop.

"Don't—you—dare—" Paige groaned. He was picking up the pace, and she began instinctively to move her hips, needing more and then still more.

"What, Paige?" he asked, just before taking her nipple into his mouth again.

"Don't—*stop*—" she whimpered, shameless in her need now, grinding against him.

He sucked. He caressed. And she came, hard, and for what seemed like an eternity. Every time her body buckled in full surrender, Austin asked more of her, and then still more. Finally, she fell against him, spent, unable even to imagine reaching another orgasm.

But she had another climax, and another after that, because Austin somehow managed to get her onto her knees, and then he slid beneath her, and she rode his seeking mouth, rode the dancing tip of his tongue, into a blaze that consumed her need, her reason, her everything.

The satisfaction was complete, although Paige knew, even as she descended from the heights, that Austin could arouse her again, with a few touches, a few murmured words, a few flicks of his tongue against her earlobe, or in the hollow of her throat, or . . .

He somehow arranged her so that she was lying beside him once more, in roughly the same place where the odyssey had begun. His arm was still around her and, as she sank back into herself, with little whimpers of residual pleasure, he soothed her with low murmurs.

She cried.

"Don't," he whispered, his lips moving against her temple.

"I can't help it," she sniffled. "It was—that was—"

"Shhh," he breathed.

"So good—"

Austin chuckled. "Good is, well, a *good* thing, isn't it?"

Not when it concerns you, Austin McKettrick.

"No," Paige said. "We agreed not to let this happen, remember? Because we have at least fifty years of family gatherings ahead of us—christenings and graduations, birthdays and eventually weddings—"

"We agreed not to have sex, Paige," he said reasonably.

"Well, maybe that wasn't sex to *you,*" Paige retorted, letting herself nestle against him while she could, "but *I* had about five orgasms, so you'll excuse me if my interpretation is different from yours."

Austin chuckled. Wound a finger loosely in her hair. "Five," he said, with pretended disappointment. "I was hoping to break your record."

"Jerk," Paige said without much conviction.

She felt Austin's smile in the shift of muscles in his arms and chest and shoulder. Her body was like a tuning fork, still resonating to the chords he'd struck.

"Eight," he recalled. "That's your personal best."

Paige felt it stirring again, the quiet, insistent ember that Austin would fan and fondle until it was a roaring blaze. "I beg your pardon?" she said.

"That time we spread a blanket on the ground and made love under the stars," Austin reminisced. "You were straddling me, and you came eight times."

Should she laugh, or should she cry? It was a toss-up.

"You counted?" she challenged.

"No," Austin reminded her. "*You* did. You'd tense, and yell out a number—" He shifted, began to caress one of her breasts. *"One—two—three—"*

"Shut up."

"You were so hot."

"Stop it."

"And, apparently, you're still just as hot now."

"Austin McKettrick," Paige warned.

He laughed, but not for long.

Turnabout, after all, is considered fair play in most places.

Especially Texas.

Something cold and wet awakened Paige shortly before the sun came up.

Sprawled beside Austin in the antique bed, she opened her eyes and came face-to-face with Shep. Even with his leg bandaged so stiffly that he might as well have been wearing a cast, he'd managed to haul himself up off his blanket pile and hobble across the room.

He made a low sound and stared imploringly into Paige's very soul.

Shep might have been in pain, but she knew that wasn't his main concern at the moment.

"You need to go outside, huh?" she whispered with affection, reaching out to gently ruffle his ears.

Shep all but nodded his head.

Easing away from Austin, who was sleeping with an abandon so complete that Paige momentarily envied it, she got up, padded to the bedroom doorway.

Shep stumped along after her.

After grabbing a robe and a pair of slippers from the smaller room down the hall, where she'd expected to spend the night, Paige led the dog outside. Waited in the predawn chill while the poor critter teetered around, looking for a place to do his business.

Paige hugged herself against the cool morning air and lifted her gaze to the eastern hills, now rimmed with the first fiery pink fringe of light.

A truck rattled up to the barn, and a man got out. Slammed the door.

Shep, finished with his outdoor duties, gave a growl.

Paige bent and got him by the scruff, peering through the gloom.

More by the sense of inner alarm than by sight, she recognized the man Austin had called Reese.

Shep tried to pull away, probably set to lunge across the yard and attack, but Paige tightened her hold on his hide and whispered a firm, *"No."*

A red ember flared as Reese lit a cigarette; Paige caught the scent of it only a moment later.

She realized he'd seen her, but he didn't move, and neither did she. He stood with one foot resting on the running board of his truck and smoked.

It was cold outside, so cold that Paige could see her breath. She wasn't dressed for confrontation—she was still in her nightgown and robe—and besides that, she had to restrain Shep. Just the same, she stayed where she was until the ranch hand threw his cigarette down on the ground and made a show of grinding it out under his heel.

In the growing light, Reese spread his hands and bowed a little.

She ignored the gesture and turned, half pulling, half coaxing Shep to come along.

Austin was in the kitchen when she stepped inside, starting the coffee-maker.

As quickly as that, she forgot Reese.

"Mornin'," Austin said with a slow grin and an even slower glance that swept from her head to her toes and then back up again.

Paige blushed.

They hadn't actually *made love,* she reminded herself.

As in, they hadn't had intercourse.

She felt well loved, though.

And she'd probably howled like a she-wolf in heat.

"Good morning," she said, raising her chin and injecting a certain cool formality into her tone. But inside her head, she heard her own greedy cries of pleasure, echoing from the night before.

Desperate to be busy, Paige scouted around until she found some kibble. She scooped a heap into a bowl, and set it down for Shep. He three-legged it over and began to eat.

"Excellent," Paige said. "As soon as he has some food in his stomach, he can take his medicine."

Dividing his attention between her and the dog, Austin just stood there, taking it all in. His mouth kicked up at one corner, though, and blue mischief sparkled in his eyes.

Paige felt incredibly self-conscious, standing there in a robe and slippers, which was strange, because for most of the night she'd been wearing nothing at all, and it hadn't bothered her.

Austin chuckled and shook his head, went back to the coffeemaker and filled two mugs, even though the machine hadn't finished the brewing cycle.

"Shall we drink our coffee out here, Nurse Remington?" he asked, raising one of the mugs in an insolent little salute. "Or should we take it back to bed?"

Paige glanced nervously at all three

sets of stairs before blushing again so hard that it actually hurt a little, and whispering, "We are *not* going to bed, Austin."

He handed her one cup of coffee and took an appreciative sip from the other. Over the rim, his eyes laughed at her.

"Seems to me *that* horse is already out of the barn," he said.

"That wasn't sex," Paige told him in a furious undertone.

"And I never inhaled," Austin replied. His whole face seemed to twinkle then, not just his eyes. The effect was a sun-light-on-water kind of dazzle.

"I was only—" Paige stopped, swallowed.

"Keeping me warm?" Austin prompted. "You did that, all right."

She bit her lower lip. Remembered having to restrain the dog.

"I don't think Shep likes that one ranch hand," she said carefully.

"*Which* ranch hand, Paige?" Austin asked, turning his back to her now, looking out through the big window above the kitchen sink.

"The guy who was smoking in the

barn. He pulled in a little while ago, while I was outside with Shep, and Shep wanted to go after him."

Austin turned back. His eyes were tired, hollow with pain, but watchful, too. "Okay," he said slowly. "I don't much like the sound of that."

Paige sighed. "Me, either." It was obvious that Austin and Shep had bonded, but Shep was a stray and there was still a lot they didn't know about him. There were three children and three other dogs on the place, and if Shep turned out to be aggressive, he would probably have to be destroyed. "Austin, do you think he's dangerous?"

A grin quirked at the corner of Austin's mouth. He relaxed, took another sip of coffee, savored it and swallowed before replying. "Reese—or the dog?"

"I was referring to Shep."

"No," Austin said, frowning and setting the mug aside. He was looking at her fluffy pink slippers—not her own fashion choice, but, hey. Calvin had given them to her for Christmas, and she would wear them for as long as they lasted. "What's the matter with your feet? You keep shifting from one to the other."

"Nothing," Paige lied. "I'm all right."

Those words, she thought wryly, recalling Doc Pomeroy's story about Austin's grandfather and the pitchfork, were practically the McKettrick family anthem. And here she was, learning to sing right along with the chorus.

"You'd best stick with the truth," Austin counseled, approaching her, taking her by the shoulders, and easing her down into the antique rocking chair in the alcove, "because you're pretty sorry at stretching it."

Paige sighed. "It's nothing serious," she protested as Austin crouched in front of her, like the prince flourishing a glass slipper, and bared both her feet. "I might have gone rushing outside after you last night and forgotten to put on shoes—"

Gripping her right heel, Austin gently turned her foot and bent a little sideways to look at it.

There were a few small cuts and lots

of bruises, left by small rocks in the yard and the driveway.

Austin gave a low whistle of exclamation and checked out her other foot. "No wonder you've been dancing around like an old-time movie cowboy dodging bullets."

While Paige was still dealing with the disturbing discovery that she loved it when Austin McKettrick handled her feet, he left her long enough to retrieve the first aid kit. One-handed because of the dish-towel sling, he began to treat her injuries, minor as they were, with an uncommon tenderness.

He applied iodine, but only after holding up the bottle from the first aid kit and waiting for her to give him the go-ahead to use it.

Reluctantly, she nodded. The stuff would sting like holy-be-bingo, but it would also wipe out the germ population.

Paige braced herself, drew in a hissing breath when the medicine bit into her abrasions. Stoically endured the second round, on the bottom of her other foot.

That one hurt so badly that Paige, who was no wimp, almost cried.

Austin, noting her reaction, lifted the appendage, and blew lightly on her sole, cooling the burning sensation down a little.

It was the sort of thing her dad would have done, once upon a time. As kids, Libby, Julie and Paige were forever falling off bicycles, skinning their knees and elbows, and all the rest.

Will Remington always applied iodine, once the wound was clean, and he always blew on the sore place until the stinging stopped.

Austin, Paige thought sorrowfully, as he stood and set the first aid kit aside, would make an excellent father someday.

How would she stand it, she wondered, when the Right Woman came along, and Austin finally settled down, got married and started a family?

How in the world would she stand it?

CHAPTER NINE

As soon as he'd finished medicating Paige's feet, she slipped them into her slippers and boogied for her part of the house, blushing and avoiding his gaze.

Austin waited, sipping coffee at the kitchen table, until she'd had plenty of time to shower and get dressed and all the rest of it. Once she surfaced, he'd find a way to get into his clothes without her help—if she thought he was going to carry on like some invalid, which in Paige's mind probably meant lying around in pajamas and sipping fluids through bent straws, she was sorely mistaken—and get on with his day.

When Paige finally resurfaced, looking delicious in crisp blue jeans and a gray pullover shirt, she was doubly careful not to look at him. She got real busy fussing over Shep, who had curled up on the rug in front of the fireplace nobody ever lit up anymore, patting his head, filling his water dish and the like.

Then Julie appeared at the top of the stairway leading to her and Garrett's place, also wearing jeans and the same kind of pullover as Paige, except in a purplish color.

"Paige," Julie called to her sister, "come and join Libby and me for breakfast. We *have* to settle on your bridesmaid's dress."

Paige rolled her eyes at that, but then she nodded, because there were some battles that couldn't be won, and said, "Okay. Be there in a sec."

Julie gave Austin a cheerful wave and vanished from sight.

Paige washed her hands at the sink and then turned to face Austin, leaning back against the counter. "You should probably eat something before you take your medication," she said. Her tone and manner were so coolly professional that they might have been strangers instead of two people who'd been lovers as teenagers and gotten pretty chummy just the night before on top of that.

"Yeah," he grumbled, his mood souring a little, mainly because he wanted things to be different between him and Paige and they weren't.

She was his one-time lover, and so much more. *And* she was Libby and Julie's baby sister, the one he wouldn't be able to avoid, at least not gracefully, after the shindig on New Year's Eve.

Once his brothers and their soon-to-be-wives started having kids—it wouldn't be long, that was for sure—he'd be an uncle God only knew how many times over, and Paige would be an aunt to the whole brood.

The things that had happened between them the night before didn't have to upset the balance at family gatherings—as long as the shenanigans didn't continue. After all, he and Paige already *had* a history, didn't they? And so far they'd been able to cope with living under the same roof, hadn't they?

Paige broke into his thoughts. "Do you want me to whip up some scrambled eggs or something?"

"No," Austin said. Then, "Thanks."

"You need food if you're going to take your pills."

"I know that, Paige," he replied with exaggerated patience. "But right now I'm okay, and I'm not ready to eat."

"Suit yourself, then," Paige said, snipping off the words.

After giving a great sigh, intended to sound long-suffering, Austin rose and retreated to the bedroom where, to hear her tell it, he and Nurse Remington had most definitely and absolutely *not* had sexual relations.

Could have fooled me, Austin thought, remembering the way she'd pitched and moaned and squirmed before finally exploding in trembling satisfaction. *Oh, lady, you could have fooled me.*

Calvin and the twins were gathered in Garrett and Julie's living room, watching cartoons on TV, still in their pajamas and munching cold cereal from colorful plastic bowls, when Paige arrived.

Paige waggled her fingers and smiled in greeting, then drifted into the kitchen, where her sisters were sitting at the table, conferring over yet another goony dress, in yet another bridal magazine.

"What do you think of this?" Julie asked, jabbing at an image with one manicured index finger. The model wore something that resembled a pink cloud.

"I'd look like a giant wad of cotton candy," Paige said, meaning it.

She helped herself to a cup of coffee and stood at the counter to sip away, instead of joining her sisters at the table. She was afraid to get too close to the pink dress, even in printed form.

Libby and Julie exchanged glances and sighed in perfect unison. It reminded Paige of the dream where the two spooky brides had chased her down a dark country road, waving horrible travesties of fashion at her.

"Well, what do *you* suggest?" Libby inquired archly. "Something tasteful and form-fitting, maybe? Say, a black sheath and a rope of pearls?"

Paige imagined the outfit, drank more coffee and finally replied, "You know, that doesn't sound half-bad."

Verbally, Libby sprang. Physically, she remained in her chair. "You are *not* wearing a black dress at my wedding, Paige Remington!"

"Mine, either," Julie agreed, all huffy.

"How about red?" Paige suggested. With her dark hair, she looked especially good in most shades of red.

"If we were getting married in a *brothel,* maybe," Libby said.

The hopelessness of it all made Paige sag on the inside. She hated wearing pastels—with few exceptions, they washed her out, made her look like a plague victim.

Her sisters, on the other hand, looked wonderful in pinks and baby blues and cheery lavenders. And this was *their* big day, after all.

"Okay," she said bravely, "I'll wear the dress." She indicated the magazine, still open on the table, with a motion of one hand. "Even if it *does* make me look like something from the snack bar at the circus."

Having said that, Paige surprised not only her sisters but herself, too—she burst into tears.

Libby and Julie, both used to mothering her, immediately scooted back their chairs, got to their feet and advanced on her. Each one gripping an elbow, they ushered her to the table and sat her down, with rather more force than was strictly necessary, in a chair.

"I knew it," Libby told Julie fitfully. "We shouldn't have brought up the bridesmaid's dress so soon after the latest Austin crisis."

"You're right," Julie agreed with a big sigh, propping her elbow on the tabletop and cupping her chin.

Paige was momentarily distracted from the subject of the hour: the gown of her nightmares. "What do you mean, the *latest* Austin crisis?" she asked as Libby shoved a box of tissues at her.

Julie watched with concern as Paige wadded a tissue and scrubbed at her eyes.

"There was Buzzsaw, the bull," Libby ventured.

"And then whatever happened in that bar in San Antonio and the shooting in the oil field," Julie added.

"And now *this,*" Libby concluded.

"This *what?*" Paige wanted to know.

"All that excitement last night, with the gun and everything," Julie said, using the same tone of over-the-top patience she might have chosen to address a four-year-old learning to tie his or her shoes. "Garrett told me all about it."

"And Tate told *me,*" Libby threw in. Her blue eyes rounded. "He said there was this huge dog, and Austin had to shoot it."

All three of the Remington sisters were animal lovers, but Libby was passionately protective of critters. She'd fostered dozens of dogs and cats over the years, until good homes could be found for them, and before their mother had leveled the Perk Up Coffee Shop in Julie's tank of a Cadillac, she'd kept a donation jar for the shelter right next to the cash register.

Would she think less of Austin for using the rifle?

Paige gulped hard, but before she could figure out a way to find out, Libby went right ahead and answered her. "I know he had to do it," she said softly, squeezing Paige's hand. "Austin was defending Shep."

Another tear strayed down Paige's cheek; she wiped at her face with the back of one hand. The salt made her skin sting, and she thought she'd better get a grip and cut out all this crying before she turned into a chronic sniveler.

"How do you stand it?" she asked, looking deep into Libby's eyes and then, in turn, Julie's.

Libby frowned, clearly puzzled. "Stand it?"

"Stand what?" Julie wanted to know.

"Loving McKettrick men," Paige burst out, in what might have been called a stage whisper, spreading her hands for emphasis. "They act as though they're immortal, all three of them."

Her sisters were smiling at her.

Knowingly, too, as if she'd just inadvertently revealed some deep, dark secret.

"Stop it," she said. "It's not what you're thinking."

"What are we thinking?" Libby asked lightly.

"Who knew you were psychic?" Julie threw in, still smiling. "From now on, when I need a glimpse of the future, I'll just dial 1-800-PAIGE."

"You two are just so hilariously funny," Paige said, keeping her voice down because of the kids in the next room, "that it makes me want to *puke.*"

"Touchy," Julie said, sipping coffee.

Libby's tone was prim, though her eyes danced. "To answer your question," she said to Paige, "loving Tate McKettrick isn't hard. It comes as naturally to me as my breath and my heartbeat."

Julie sighed contentedly, her expression dreamy and faraway all of a sudden, and smiled mysteriously.

"That isn't what I mean," Paige insisted, "and both of you know it. It seems to me that Tate and Garrett and

Austin *all* take a lot of risks, compared to normal people. On top of that, they seem to have acquired some dangerous enemies. How can you sleep at night, thinking of all the things that might happen to them?"

Libby giggled. "I sleep just fine. Tate and I make love and then we both conk out until morning. It's really very healthy."

Paige blushed hard. Told herself there was no way her sisters could know what she and Austin had done the night before.

"Lucky you," she said, and there might have been *some* acid in her tone.

"Jealous?" Julie teased. These days, she always had a twinkle *and* a glow, and she made no secret of the fact that the physical part of her relationship with Garrett was working out just fine.

"Maybe," Paige admitted. She made a sweep of one hand to indicate the tabletop, which was empty except for their coffee cups and the bridal magazine opened to the hideous cotton-candy dress. "I thought you said we were going to have breakfast. Where's the food?"

Austin made the climb to his own rooms, after shutting Shep up in the pantry downstairs so he wouldn't try to follow on his splinted leg, and raided his dresser drawers for shorts and a pair of jeans. He'd planned on wearing a T-shirt, but the plan proved too painful to carry out, even after he'd temporarily removed the splint.

Carefully, and with no small amount of difficulty, he managed to get into a blue chambray work shirt, leaving the left sleeve to dangle empty.

The word *awkward* didn't do justice to the way it felt to wear half a shirt, Austin thought glumly.

He did manage to get into a pair of beat-up old boots, probably because he'd had them so long that they were starting to fall apart.

As accomplishments went, it was pretty pissant, but a man had to take what he could get.

A smile curved Austin's mouth as he thought of Paige, gasping and flexing and crooning with pleasure during the night. In that case, it hadn't been about what a man could get, but what he could *give*.

Since he didn't need a hard-on in addition to his other woes, Austin turned his thoughts in another direction: his mental to-do list.

After gathering his shaving gear, some extra clothes and the book he'd been trying to read before he'd been prescribed all those pharmaceuticals, Austin headed back down to the first floor.

He let Shep out of the pantry, put the clothes away and then stood in front of the bureau, looking at the cover of the book. Reading was a chore for him— he'd been diagnosed with ADD as a kid—but he wanted to *like* books, the way his brothers did, and he had no intention of giving up before that happened.

Even if it took until he was a hundred.

With a sigh, he set the paperback Western down and returned to the kitchen. After putting on half a jacket,

Austin stepped out into the cold, sunny morning and Shep peg-legged along behind him.

Reese and Tom were working in the barn again, along with Ron Strivens, the father of one of Julie's favorite students. Garrett had personally hired Strivens on as a ranch hand, moving the widower and his three kids into a trailer on the Silver Spur. The guy was quiet, mostly kept to himself, but he more than earned his pay.

In fact, Tate was planning to promote Strivens to an assistant foreman's job after the first of the year. In the meantime, he seemed thrilled to have grocery money coming in steady, along with a home and health insurance for his family.

Reese nodded abruptly to Austin and went on shoveling horseshit.

Tom was in the loft, throwing bales of hay down into the bed of a truck backed up to the barn. Although there was plenty of grass on the range in spring and summer, it started to go a little sparse in places in the late fall, and that meant feed had to be hauled

to different parts of the ranch on a ro-
tating basis.

Strivens, standing in Molly's stall and
applying ointment to her rapidly healing
hide, had cleaned up pretty well, as
Garrett had once remarked. The man
had cut his hair and shaved off his
beard the same day he was hired, and
he showed up every day, rain or shine,
sick or well, not just on time, but early.
His clothes were mended in places, but
always clean, and while he seemed
shy, he was friendly enough.

Austin liked him.

"Mornin'," he said, standing outside
the stall and looking in.

Strivens smiled tentatively. Nodded
his head. "Morning," he replied, wiping
his hands down the front of his flannel
shirt after he was done dosing Molly
with the ointment.

A movement at the periphery of his
vision distracted Austin; he turned his
head, out of curiosity, and saw Tom
and Cliff Pomeroy standing at the far
end of the breezeway. They seemed to
be having a serious conversation, both
of them gesturing, but their words

didn't carry far enough for Austin to pick up on the topic.

If Cliff was around, Austin reasoned idly, pondering the faintly unsettled feeling in the pit of his stomach, the one his granddad had called botheration, then Doc was probably there, too.

Austin thanked Strivens for tending to Molly and turned to head for the open doorway at the other end of the barn.

As he came nearer, Cliff flushed and worked up a smile. Tom nodded a greeting to Austin and went on about his business.

"Hello, Cliff," Austin said. The man had been away from Blue River for years, and Tom was little more than a drifter, according to Tate. Such men tended to turn up out of nowhere, wanting a job, work just hard enough to get by and quit without notice as soon as they'd racked up a paycheck or two.

Cliff's gaze moved to Austin's sling, and his expression changed subtly. "Dad wanted to stop by and check up on your animals," he said.

"We appreciate that," Austin said,

glancing down at his canine sidekick. "Don't we, Shep?" He looked his father's one-time friend over and wondered what it was about the man that troubled him.

They stepped out into the cold November sunlight.

Doc was standing at the back of his truck, with the tailgate down, and Reese was practically on top of him, yammering on about something.

Austin surely would have liked to know what that something was.

Shep, meanwhile, turned testy again. His hackles rose and he gave a snarling growl of warning.

Austin reached down and got him by the scruff of his neck just as he would have lunged, bandaged leg and all.

Reese turned his head, saw the dog and backed up a step. His neck turned a dull shade of crimson, though, while his face went pale.

It was a disturbing contrast.

Doc waved the man off and approached Austin and Shep. Cliff stood just behind Austin, and when Doc got close, it seemed that his gaze shifted briefly to his son and narrowed.

Austin made a mental note to find out what had brought Cliff Pomeroy back to Blue River after all these years. As far as he knew, the man hadn't even visited, once he'd decided to leave Blue River.

"I've come for a look at the little mare and this dog," Doc answered, and his countenance softened as he crouched to look Shep in the eye.

Uneasy, Cliff wandered back toward the barn.

Doc ruffled Shep's ears and straightened. "He gets around pretty well on that bandaged leg," the old man observed. "Poor critter will do his best to keep up with you, Austin, no matter what the effort costs him. Try to keep that in mind for the dog's sake, if not your own."

Austin registered the message, acknowledged it with a nod. Shep probably *did* need a rest, but he wouldn't light anywhere unless his master did.

"What was that all about?" he asked when it was clear that Doc wasn't going to volunteer anything about the apparent argument he'd had with Reese. "You and the ranch hand, I mean."

Doc heaved a sigh. Took off his hat, tugged it on again. Today, he was wearing a beat-up Stetson, a change from his usual billed cap with the sweat stains and the threadbare seams.

Maybe he had a hot date after rounds, Austin thought whimsically.

"Best you take that up with him, rather than me," Doc said, going around him to head for the barn, where he meant to examine Molly. "You get that dog inside the house. He needs to rest a spell, and it wouldn't hurt you to take a load off, either."

Austin agreed, but he didn't move, and neither did Shep.

"Doc?" Austin said.

Farley Pomeroy stopped. His back stiffened, and he didn't turn around or speak.

"The dog I shot last night. You got a look at him before we buried him and you came in to tend to Shep?"

Farley faced him then, but his face was screwed up against the sunlight and Austin couldn't read his expression. "Course I did. Had to make sure he was gone. Couldn't let him suffer."

"*I* made sure he was gone, Doc."

"I reckon you did," Doc allowed, not unkindly. Then he shook his head, remembering. "It was a good, clean shot, Austin. I couldn't have disposed of that animal any more humanely than you did. He was a fine specimen, though— some Mastiff in him, I think. I've seen *ponies* that weren't as big as he was."

Tate and Garrett had moved the carcass the night before, buried it on the other side of a copse of oak trees, not wanting the women or the kids to see it.

"Did you see any signs of rabies?" Austin persisted, though he knew Doc wanted to get on with it, look in on Molly, collect his son and move on to the next sick animal, on the next ranch or farm.

Doc considered the question for a long time. Could have been he was just debating with himself, deciding whether to answer or not. "He wasn't foaming at the mouth or anything like that, but he was hungry. Ribs stood out like pickets along a fence. I figure, you probably did that poor critter a favor by shooting him."

"He meant to go for my throat, Doc," Austin said. "And when my dog got in the way, he damn near killed him."

Doc sighed. "I hate to see any animal die before it ought to," he said, his voice gruff. "But there are times when something just plain has to be done, and last night was one of them. You did the right thing, Austin, if that's what you're asking me. You did the only thing you *could* do, under the circumstances."

Austin swallowed, nodded. "But the dog belonged to Reese, didn't he? That's why he was ranting at you, a few minutes ago."

"Yes," Doc finally admitted. "The dog was his. He claimed he kept the critter close to home, in a kennel he and his friend rigged up out behind the bunkhouse. Said the dog had been known to run off now and again but was tame, wouldn't hurt anybody. He's pretty riled up about it."

"But not 'riled up' enough to ask me directly?"

"I guess not," Doc said. His gaze moved to Austin's sling, lingered there for a moment. "Might be he figured that wouldn't be right, you being all bunged up and everything."

A charitable view if Austin had ever heard one. "You said you thought the dog was hungry."

Doc set his jaw hard. "He was," he said. "Critter like that never gets to be a pet. No, sir. His whole purpose in life is to make a statement for some asshole who thinks owning a mean dog makes him look tough."

Austin felt a pang of sorrow for the fallen animal, and it wasn't the first. Looked around for Reese, thinking he'd have a word with the man, but then he decided to wait.

Shep was panting, in need of water and his blanket pile, and there were too many people around anyway. He'd wait until Doc and Cliff and Ron Strivens had gone, at least.

So Austin went on into the house, and then the bedroom.

There was no sign of Paige; she was probably still upstairs, shooting the breeze with her sisters. The image of the three of them with their heads together made him smile.

He reached for the book he'd brought downstairs earlier, from his apartment, and stretched out on the bed, though he was careful to keep his boots off the edge.

Shep, once he was certain that Austin meant to stay put, curled up on his blankets nearby and shut down his engines for a while.

Austin read a few paragraphs before deciding to rest his eyes. When he opened them again, the slant of the light at the windows was different, and somebody was pulling his leg. Literally.

He opened one eye, saw Paige struggling womanfully with his left boot. The right one was already off; he could feel a breeze through the fabric of his sock.

"This is an antique quilt," she fussed.

"I can't hear you. I'm asleep."

"Right," Paige said, and if she still had a sense of humor, it was not in evidence. She finally succeeded in separating the boot from his foot, and nearly fell on her perfect backside in the process. "Honestly, Austin. What if you'd gotten mud or manure on this exquisite heirloom?"

Austin eased himself upright, far enough to sit with his back against the headboard. Grinned and set the book aside. "Then I guess that would become part of its history," he said. "'See this stain here?' some future McKettrick might say to another future McKettrick. 'Ole Great-grampa Austin himself did that, way back when. Yes, sir, went to bed with his boots on one day and damned if some woman didn't give him three kinds of hell for it.'"

Paige tried to look stern, but in the end she couldn't hold back a giggle. So she turned and crossed the room and chucked the boots willy-nilly into the closet.

Austin heard them thump against the back wall before landing.

When she turned around again, her arms were folded.

Austin peeked over at Shep, still

snoozing on his blanket pile, and raised a finger to his lips. "Tone it down a little," he told Paige. "You'll wake up the dog. According to Doc, Shep needs his rest."

She rolled her eyes.

He loved it when she rolled her eyes.

"Yes," she said. "And so do you."

"Typical medico logic," Austin remarked, wanting to keep the conversation going, even if it *was* a mite on the prickly side. "Come in here and wake me up, pulling off my boots, and then preach a sermon about how I ought to get more sleep."

A grin flicked at the corner of her mouth. "Did you take your meds?"

"No."

"Why not?"

"Because I haven't eaten anything yet and I'm not supposed to take them without food—Nurse Remington."

"Don't call me Nurse Remington," she said. She smiled, high beam, but it was all for Shep, who'd hauled himself up onto his haunches by then, yawning big.

"Why not?" Austin asked, vaguely irritated.

"Because you only say it to be a smart-ass," Paige told him.

"I say *everything* to be a smart-ass," he replied.

She sighed. "Well," she said cheerfully. "You've got me there."

He laughed. "How was breakfast?" he asked. And when she looked blank, he added, "With your sisters?"

"Turned out to be a bait and switch," Paige answered, patting Shep on the head once before starting to putter with things on top of the bureau and then the bookshelf. "They just wanted me to look at another awful bridesmaid's dress."

Austin assumed an expression of mocking horror. "Not that."

"Pink," Paige fussed, straightening out things that didn't need any straightening. "Pink, with ruffles. Tons of ruffles—"

"Hey," Austin said in a gentle rasp.

She looked at him, and he wondered if all the misery he saw in that beautiful face could really be about a bad dress.

He patted the mattress, scooted over to make room for her.

"Oh, no, you don't," she said.

"I promise not to subject you to another round of screaming climaxes," he said mildly.

Paige glanced anxiously in the direction of the door. Closed it carefully. "I did *not* scream," she pointed out in a hissing whisper.

"But you did climax," Austin teased. "Repeatedly."

"So did you."

"Once," he said. "And I definitely didn't scream."

Her face was pink—perhaps as pink as the dress she so desperately wanted *not* to wear in the wedding.

"Is this conversation going somewhere?" Paige asked.

He patted the mattress again, arched his eyebrows.

She didn't move an inch.

"I was hired as your nurse, Austin," she informed him. "Not your sexual plaything."

He gave a snorting laugh. "My 'sexual plaything'?"

She glared at him, still keeping her distance. Still with her arms folded. "If we're going to get along with each other for the next fifty years," she reasoned, "we're going to have to avoid doing what we—almost did last night."

"What we *almost* did?"

"We *didn't make love.*" She was really flustered now. "And it doesn't have to happen again."

"How can it happen *again,*" Austin wanted to know, "if it never happened in the first place?"

"You *know* what I mean."

"You mean," he replied gravely, in the tone of a man grappling with a weighty philosophical dilemma, "that what happened between us last night wasn't sex because we didn't actually—*connect.* Am I right?"

"It wasn't sex," she insisted. "Technically."

"Then why can't we do it again? Nontechnically, of course."

She looked around, probably for something to run over him with.

Fortunately, there was no golf cart handy.

"It's time for your medicine," she said, after unclamping her lips. "I'm bringing you a grilled cheese sandwich, Austin McKettrick, and you will *eat it* and take your pills and go back to sleep."

Austin saluted.

That *so* pissed her off. She stormed out.

Shep crutch-hopped it over to the side of the bed, laid his muzzle on the mattress and gave a little whimper.

Austin chuckled. Then he got off the bed and he and Shep made their way into the kitchen.

Paige was there, banging things around, making grilling a sandwich a lot more complicated, it seemed to him, than it had to be.

"Oh, Nurse Remington," he trilled.

At least he thought he was trilling it.

She turned, a spatula in one hand, and glared at him. If ever he'd seen a woman in need of at least one more orgasm, Paige was that woman. *"What?"*

"Shep wants to go outside," he told her sweetly.

"Take him out yourself, then," Paige

snapped, turning back to the sandwich-making enterprise.

"I'm only trying to be a good patient," Austin said, turning on the pathos. "Isn't that what you want?"

Angrily, she shoved the skillet back off the burner, set down the spatula and went to open the back door.

She was all sweetness and light when she spoke to Shep. "Come on, fella," she said.

The two of them went out.

Paige slammed the door.

And Austin, grinning, turned around and went back to bed.

Who knew? If he got Paige riled enough, she just might join him there.

Again.

CHAPTER TEN

Paige practically shoved the plate into Austin's hands, and it didn't improve her crazy, hormonal mood when he peeled back the bread and peered beneath it.

"Grilled cheese," she said tightly. "Just as I promised."

"I was only checking for obvious signs of tampering," Austin retorted, with a grin that made her want to slap him.

It was galling how this man could take her through an entire range of emotions with his mischievous eyes and crooked grins—even *more* galling that she couldn't seem to stop herself from going along for the ride.

And she *so* knew better.

Still, Paige's own personal, private

riot continued: she wanted to throttle him. She wanted to shut and lock the door and crawl right into bed with him. She wanted to scream and throw things.

It was dizzying. Everything in Paige's life made sense—except her penchant for this man. Maybe, she thought with alarm, she was one of those people who liked pain or, more accurately, *needed* it for some dark psychological reason.

While all these thoughts were whirling through her mind, Austin picked up half the sandwich, took a bite, chewed slowly, ponderously. Waited a long, long time to take another bite.

"I was fresh out of cyanide," Paige said with a brittle smile, spreading her hands. "So I had to resort to drain cleaner."

"It's actually pretty good," Austin told her. "Almost as good as the ones Esperanza makes. She usually chops up some jalapeño and—"

"If you don't like that sandwich, Austin McKettrick," Paige broke in, "get off your cowboy-ass and make your own."

He laughed. "You used to have a sense of humor," he said.

"That must have been before we met," she countered.

"I doubt it. We go all the way back to Mrs. Roberts's kindergarten class, remember?" Austin took another bite of the sandwich and took his time chewing, swallowing and thinking. Paige hoped he wouldn't hurt himself, trying that last thing.

Shep, the poor devil, was trying to join Austin on the bed.

Carefully, because of his injuries, Paige lifted the dog off the floor and onto the mattress.

Austin gave him the other half of the sandwich. At Paige's dark look, he said, "Point in your favor. I couldn't have fed him Esperanza's—God knows what jalapeños would do to a dog."

Paige clamped down her jaw. Austin was *deliberately* baiting her, she *knew* that. But why—oh, why—did she have to take the hook? It was like some figurative tennis game, and she kept batting the damn ball back over the net instead of just walking off the court.

What was up with *that?*

She went into his bathroom, counted out his various pills, filled a glass with water and returned to his bedside.

"Here," she said, practically shoving the meds at him. "Take these. They'll make you sleep."

"Maybe I don't *feel* like sleeping."

"Imagine how bad I might feel if I *gave* a rat's ass what you feel like doing, Austin McKettrick," Paige replied coolly.

He reared back a little, gave a low, exclamatory whistle. "Are you PMS-ing or something? Because I'll understand if you are. That's the kind of guy I am. Modern. Sensitive."

"A real *softy,*" Paige said with an emphasis on the last word. She wanted to laugh in spite of everything, but she managed to keep a straight face.

Austin assumed an injured look. "I wouldn't go *that* far," he said.

Paige smiled. Waited.

He finally took the pills from her still-extended palm, tossed them back and washed them down with a few gulps of water.

Paige's mouth twitched as she watched him set the glass aside. She *would not* laugh, by God.

She wasn't prepared for Austin's strength, or his speed. He gripped her wrist and pulled and the next thing she knew, she was flat on her back on the bed beside him, looking up into his devilish blue eyes.

With his mouth very close to hers, he breathed, "Oops. Sorry—that was clumsy of me."

Paige blinked. *Get up,* she told herself.

But her self didn't listen.

Austin slid his hand under her sweater, splayed his fingers over the bare skin of her midsection.

And she *still* didn't move.

Unless a racing heart and some very fast breathing counted as movement.

"I think it's real important," Austin drawled, his lips right against hers now, hot and firm, "that we don't have sex."

He slid his hand down a little way, popped the button on her jeans.

And, at the same time, he kissed her—deeply, gently, in a way that rocked her to the core of her being.

"No, we definitely *should not* have sex," he went on after the kiss had finally ended.

Paige was too breathless to respond, and too turned on—*already*—to do what she should have done, which was slap Austin McKettrick across his handsome, insolent face and *get off the bed.*

He bent his head and, through her sweater and bra, nipped lightly at her left nipple, and then her right.

Paige moaned, and arched the small of her back.

Both responses were utterly involuntary.

"You just tell me," Austin continued in a sleepy rumble, "when you want to stop not having sex, and that's the way it will be."

"Stop." Paige managed to croak out the word.

Austin looked into her face then, and although his mouth was serious, his eyes were laughing. "Stop what, Paige?"

"Just—stop."

He pulled his hand out of her jeans, zipped them up, fastened the button. Pretty handy for a man with one arm in a sling—but then, he'd probably had all kinds of practice getting into women's pants.

"Okay," he said.

"Okay?" she asked.

"I'm a man of my word. We'll stop not having sex."

"But that would mean—"

Austin chuckled. "Yeah," he agreed huskily. "That's what it would mean."

She managed to suck in a breath, sit up, swing her legs over the side of the bed. Looked at her watch.

Thank heavens; the pills she'd given him ought to be kicking in any minute now.

He would probably doze off.

And she could sneak out of the room, give herself a much-needed break.

Sure enough, he closed his eyes.

Paige stood up and sidled out of his reach.

He let out a long breath, turned onto his right side.

Paige waited a few seconds, then ventured close enough to cover him with the timeworn quilt one of his female ancestors had made with her own two hands.

She half expected Austin to grab her again and pull her back down beside him, but he didn't. He really was asleep, evidently.

An unspeakable tenderness filled her, just to look at him.

Why, she could not have said.

Austin McKettrick was all man, but there was a boyish abandon in the way he slept, a vulnerability he'd never willingly reveal in a waking state.

Unable to resist, Paige leaned down and lightly kissed his forehead, then turned and hurried out of the room.

Austin slept. And he slept. And then he slept some more.

He got up to use the bathroom, even gulped down a mug of soup Paige had fixed for him at one point, but he always tumbled straight back into slumber as soon as his head hit the pillow.

"How's Shep?" he would ask whenever he happened to wake up. "How's Molly?"

Each time, Paige was quick to answer that both animals were faring well—Ron Strivens took very good care of Molly and Shep was really on the mend, now that he could stay put on his blanket pile for hours at a time, recuperating, instead of wearing himself out keeping up with his master.

Biding her time, Paige sat in a rocking chair Tate brought in from the kitchen, reading, surfing the Internet on her laptop and trying, without much success, to knit a scarf. To the casual observer, she probably looked calm and proficient and relaxed—the private nurse on duty, well trained. In control.

Oh, it was true enough that she wasn't worried about Austin, though both Tate and Garrett had expressed concern about his protracted slumber. She knew he had simply used up his physical reserves—which must have

been formidable—and his body, pro-
grammed to survive, had overridden
the incessant demands of his mind, basically shutting down for repairs.

No, what troubled Paige was not
Austin's condition, but her own.

She was losing her objectivity.

What started out as a Web search for
a decent bridesmaid's dress, for instance, morphed into a fascination with
the endless array of wedding gowns
pictured online.

Paige nervously—and privately—at-
tributed this odd obsession to the fact
that both her sisters were about to get
married. Somewhere inside, she was
still that little girl who trailed after them,
wanting to do what they did.

Maybe she felt a little left out.

When Libby got her driver's license,
and Julie a year later, Paige had ached
for her turn at the wheel of the family
car.

When Libby had her waist-length hair
cut short, as a junior in high school,
Paige, lacking sufficient funds for a visit
to the Curly-Girly Salon, had taken a

pair of pinking shears to her own tresses.

She and Julie had fought constantly because she was always "borrowing" something black and dramatic from Julie's closet.

And the list went on.

Still, Paige reasoned, looking at bridal gowns was a harmless enough pursuit, wasn't it?

It wasn't until the next morning that Austin's eyes flew open, then widened, as he sat up in bed and focused on Paige.

She'd been reading his paperback Western; she set the book aside and smiled.

He threw back the covers, vanished into the bathroom and came back with his hair standing on end because he'd been shoving his fingers through it.

"How the hell long have I been asleep?" he demanded.

Paige made a point of consulting her watch—a gift from her dad and her sisters upon her graduation from nursing school—and took her time answering, because seeing him so rattled was a lot of fun and she wanted to stay in the moment as long as possible.

"Not quite thirty-six hours," she answered.

Austin's knees seemed to give out. Still wearing the original pair of sweatpants he'd fallen asleep in two days before, he sank onto the edge of the mattress and swore hoarsely before echoing, *"Thirty-six hours?* And I wasn't in a coma?"

"Of course you weren't in a coma," Paige told him. "I would have called an ambulance immediately if you had been."

"You mean I was just sleeping? For the better part of two days?"

"In a word, yes."

He was off the bed again, crossing to the dresser, where he must have stashed some clean clothes before the big sleep, because now he had jeans, shorts and a black T-shirt with no sleeves. "Why didn't you wake me up?"

"Because you needed to rest." She inclined her head toward Shep, now rising off his improvised dog bed. He was doing so well that Doc Pomeroy had replaced his first bandage with a new and much lighter one. "So did your buddy, here."

Shep stretched, yawned big and then crossed to Austin in a sort of skippy trot, wagging his tail and smiling a huge dog smile.

Austin grinned and ruffled the animal's ears, but when he looked at Paige, she saw frustration in his eyes. And a flash of that legendary McKettrick temper.

"Did you double up my pills or something?" he asked suspiciously.

The question set Paige back on her figurative heels. She rose slowly from the rocking chair, but only because she didn't want to startle Shep by shooting toward the ceiling like a geyser.

"You did *not* just ask me that question," she said evenly, glaring at Austin.

He shook out the jeans, scrounged up a pair of socks. Maybe he thought he was all better now, and he could just shower, dress, saddle up and ride the range as though his back had magically healed and so had the bullet wound in his shoulder.

He made a grumbling sound, rubbed his stubbly chin, and started for the bathroom without offering a verbal response.

Paige marched over and started stripping the sheets off his bed, and she did it with such vigor that Shep, instead of following Austin as he normally would have done, stood watching her with his ears perked and his head tipped to one side.

She heard the water go on in the shower.

After a day-and-a-half-long sleeping marathon, Paige didn't blame Austin for wanting to suds up and sluice off, but attempting the feat on his own was a stretch, after so long in bed. Having removed the sheets from his bed, she waited until she heard the shower turn off to carry them out to the laundry room and fetch replacements.

Then she left the apartment and crossed the wide kitchen to the laundry room, stuffed the sheets into the washing machine, set the controls and added soap. By the time she got back, carrying a fragrant armload of fresh linens Esperanza must have washed and dried before she went on her trip, Austin was wearing the jeans and the black T-shirt, and he'd shaved, too.

The sling had been dispensed with, and probably the bandages—which she'd changed twice while he was sleeping—as well.

Paige refrained from commenting on the absence of the sling. She'd spoken to his doctor at the clinic in town a couple of times, and he'd asked her to bring Austin in for a checkup as soon as he felt ready to make the trip.

Today, he was going to the clinic—whether he felt ready or not. If he needed more bandages and another sling—Paige doubted he would—then it would be young Dr. Colwin's responsibility to break the news.

Paige didn't plan on wasting her breath. She said nothing, but nodded and began making up the bed. Out of the corner of her eye, she saw Austin sag into the rocking chair and draw a few slow, deep breaths before putting on his socks and reaching for his boots.

"Feel up to taking a drive?" she asked, keeping her tone light in hopes that he wouldn't balk.

"I was planning on saddling a horse," he said, but he sounded uncertain.

"Plenty of time for that later on," Paige replied in that same breezy voice. "Let's take my car and go to town."

"I wouldn't mind a steak," Austin speculated.

Once again watching him at the periphery of her vision, Paige noted that he was having trouble pulling on his boot, but she pretended not to see. "It'll be good for you to get out of the house," she agreed. "Good for both of us."

"I guess it would be easier for Shep than following a horse," he allowed thoughtfully.

"I was thinking we'd leave Shep here with Libby," Paige ventured. "Otherwise, he'll have to wait in the car while you're seeing the doctor and then having that steak you mentioned."

Somewhat to her surprise, Austin did

not give her grief about stopping by the clinic. He hadn't had an incident with his back, even after carrying Shep inside the night the animal was hurt, but given that he'd been in bed most of that time, that was no sign that he'd recovered significantly. Now that he was going to be up and around again and, if he stayed true to form, behaving like a movie stunt man, she knew she'd have to stay on top of things.

So to speak.

"I guess you're right," Austin said. And when she turned around, having finished changing the bed, she saw that he was still sitting in the rocking chair, and wearing both boots.

She knew by the way he grinned that he'd been watching her as she worked, especially when she bent over to fluff the pillows and tuck in the sides of the heirloom quilt. Or, more properly, watching her butt.

She blushed, but she couldn't help smiling, because she'd missed this side of his personality, as irritating as it sometimes was.

"Of *course* I'm right, Austin McKet-trick."

He grinned, shook his head slightly, and let the comment pass.

Paige changed her clothes—jeans for jeans, sweater for sweater but, hey, *different* jeans, different sweater. She ran a brush through her hair, wished it were longer and dabbed on some lip gloss.

Shep, joined by Libby, Hildie the Lab and the two overgrown puppies, Buford and Ambrose, in the main kitchen, didn't seem to mind being left behind. For him, just leaving the bedroom prob-ably constituted a change of scene, though, of course, he'd been outside regularly, doing his business.

Libby filled his dish, and Austin in-haled a bowl of cold cereal, after swig-ging down a pint of orange juice pulled from the fridge. Then he was on the move again.

Paige found that heartening, as well as frustrating. He'd have some rocky times ahead, especially if he overdid things before he was ready, but she had to admire his capacity for rapid healing.

"I'm driving," Austin informed Paige, when she caught up with him in the garage. He dangled Garrett's Porsche keys and held the door open for her on the passenger side.

"You might have low blood sugar," Paige protested.

"I drank a slug of OJ and ate some cereal. My blood sugar is *fine. I'm* fine. And *I'm driving.*"

Clearly, she wasn't going to win this round.

"Does this qualify as grand theft auto?" Paige teased, slipping inside. Austin's truck, badly damaged by the bullet and subsequent plunge into the ditch, was still in the repair shop and he apparently didn't own another vehicle.

Austin grinned. "Only if Garrett decides to press charges," he replied.

"I'll say I was held hostage," Paige told him, grinning back.

"He'll probably believe you," Austin said just before he shut her door.

As soon as he was settled behind the wheel, he pushed the remote to open the garage door, turned the ignition, and the powerful Porsche started with a satisfying roar.

Naturally, Paige considered the possibility that Austin wasn't well enough to be driving yet, orange juice and cereal aside, but the new light she glimpsed in his eyes as he backed out of the garage stopped her from pressing the point. Her intuition told her that, while this man didn't hesitate to risk his own safety, he'd be a lot more careful with someone else's.

So they drove, with the windows up but the sunroof open, and it frightened Paige that a relatively ordinary thing like cruising over a country road in a sports car with Mr. Oh-So-Wrong could make her oh-so-happy.

"I feel like Rip Van Winkle," he said after a few minutes of silence. "Anything happen in the last day and a half that I ought to know about?"

Paige smiled. Held her windblown hair back from her face with one hand. "You mean, besides the aliens landing and taking over the government?" she said.

Austin chuckled. "Reckon that might be considered an improvement in some quarters," he said.

She laughed, wondered again at the simple fact of her happiness. "First you steal your brother's car," she said, "and now you're lampooning his line of work."

Austin shifted easily, slowing the car as they passed the oil field, where he'd been shot only a few days before. For a moment, Paige was afraid that he intended to turn off the main road and return to the scene of the crime, maybe thinking he'd find some evidence that Chief Brogan and his colleagues had missed, but it didn't happen.

"Garrett isn't a politician anymore," he reminded her. "Thank God when my brother took up with your sister, he saw the error of his ways and turned back before it was too late."

Paige was still holding her hair. "You seem pretty sure he'll never go back to it," she said. Garrett had worked for the late Senator Morgan Cox since his graduation from law school, and everybody in Blue River had expected him to be president one day.

Again, and with a purely masculine kind of grace, Austin shifted the Porsche into a higher gear. His left arm might have been injured, but his right was as strong as ever.

"Loving your sister changed Garrett," he told Paige, "in ways I wouldn't have thought possible. He's interested in changing her last name to McKettrick, helping to raise Calvin, siring a whole passel of kids and running the Silver Spur with Tate. The ranch alone wasn't enough for Garrett, any more than it was for Tate, but finding the right woman, well, that tipped the balance for both of them."

The talk was moving so easily between her and Austin that Paige almost—*almost*—let her guard down far enough to confess that she sometimes envied Libby and Julie because they'd finally figured out what they wanted, and they were getting it.

Afraid Austin might misinterpret the confidence as a come-on, an attempt to make the New Year's Eve wedding a triple instead of a double, she zipped her lip.

She nodded to show she'd been listening, and then they lapsed into a comfortable silence.

Reaching the clinic, Austin parked the Porsche, shut down the engine and offered Paige the keys.

"Maybe there's something you'd like to do while I'm seeing the doc," he said.

The backs of Paige's eyes scalded with tears she would never have shed in this man's presence. Austin could be so thoughtful, a real gentleman, as he was now, and then turn around and act like such a monumental jerk.

She had to be careful, *especially* now, when she wanted so badly to be reckless instead.

"I'd like to see how things are progressing over at the house," she said. "You know, check up on the construction workers. But that can wait—maybe we could stop in after we have supper."

"The house?" Austin asked.

Of course he wouldn't have known that she was renovating her dad's old place, planning on moving in there when Austin was well enough not to need a nurse and her new job, right here at the Blue River Clinic, finally opened up.

It was going to be beautiful, that house.

She'd been looking forward to moving back in after a decade spent in various apartments, but now the idea made her feel just plain lonesome.

She could see it all now. After a few years of living alone, she'd be an advanced eccentric. Adopt her fourteenth cat. Start knitting things like golf club cozies.

Crazy Aunt Paige, Calvin would call her, though she figured he'd use a fond tone of voice. But he'd cluck his tongue and roll his eyes when he thought she wasn't looking, and when he graduated from college, she'd probably present him with knitted golf club cozies coated in cat hair.

The whole picture was so dismal that Paige groaned out loud.

"Paige?" Austin said. "Hello?"

She blinked. Came back to the present moment with no small measure of relief. "Huh?"

"What house?" Austin repeated.

"The family place," Paige said, catching up, hoping she sounded normal. "The one Libby lived in before she and Tate got engaged."

"Oh," Austin said, pushing open the driver's-side door to get out. "Yeah, I remember."

You should *remember,* Paige thought. *You used to pick me up there practically every Friday and Saturday night for a date.*

"Let's go in and see what the doctor has to say about your shoulder," she said, pushing open her door before he could come around to open it for her. Which was what he would have done, because his good Southern mama, Sally McKettrick, had raised him to mind his manners.

Too bad he'd missed the other qualities she and his dad, Jim, had modeled: do the right thing, always. When you take up with somebody, be faithful to her. Don't betray her trust.

"I'm surprised you're interested,"

Austin remarked, without a trace of sarcasm. If anything, he seemed baffled, a little off balance.

Good, Paige thought.

They walked toward the entrance to the clinic, close enough but not quite touching. Once in a while, their knuckles bumped, but the recoil was instantaneous.

Austin held the door open for her, and she stepped through.

Dr. Colwin, the newest physician on staff, happened to be standing in the lobby when they walked in.

Seeing Austin on his feet, Colwin looked pleased.

He and Austin shook hands, while Paige just stood there, suddenly feeling awkward. She'd been so concerned about her patient's condition, but she was Austin's nurse, not his mother, which meant he probably didn't want her hanging around, especially in the exam room.

Duh. That was why he'd offered her the keys to Garrett's car.

She made a production of choosing a magazine from the fanned-out array on the coffee table and tried out two different chairs before settling on one on the opposite side of the room from the reception desk.

Austin watched all this with a wry twist to his mouth, then he and Dr. Colwin disappeared into the examination and treatment area.

Concentrating on the magazine she'd selected proved to be too much work, so she set it aside, craned her neck to see if she could spot any of the nurses and lab and X-ray techs she'd be working with eventually.

Paige wasn't much for chatting, but today, probably because she hadn't left the ranch in several days and her sisters were both so busy all the time, she felt like someone emerging from a long stint in an isolation chamber.

Now that Dr. Colwin and Austin had left the area, the place seemed to echo with emptiness. But then Mary Kate Dorten came out of the hallway that led to the rest-rooms and crossed to the reception desk. Mary Kate was a hometown girl, like Paige, but because of their age difference—Mary Kate had been in Libby's class, so she was three years older—they'd never been more than cordial acquaintances.

In fact, Paige realized, she'd been so close to her sisters, from the very beginning, that she hadn't felt a need to make a lot of friends until she'd gone away to nursing school.

She'd been so homesick, and so crushed by the breakup with Austin, that she'd gone a little wild at first, partying and generally behaving like a fool, but, fortunately for her, the demands of nursing school proved so stringent that she'd given up the weekend binges and buckled down to study.

"That's going to be some wedding," Mary Kate said happily, smiling over the desk at Paige. "I am so excited. Everybody *in town* is excited." She gave a great, swoony sigh. "It's so romantic. A double wedding—the grooms are brothers and the brides are sisters. It's—" She paused again, sniffled, and plucked a tissue from the box to dab delicately at the area under her lower lashes. "Well, it's like something out of a Harlequin romance novel."

Paige smiled. "Libby and Julie are having a great time planning the event," she said. She'd wanted someone to talk with, while she waited for Austin to come out of the exam room, but given her druthers, she would not have chosen the wedding of the century as a topic.

"I heard there would be movie stars there," Mary Kate went on, wide-eyed. "And some famous country-music people, too."

"I wouldn't be surprised," Paige said, brightly noncommittal. That particular rumor happened to be true, but Tate and Libby and Garrett and Julie wanted to keep the more sensational elements of the guest list private until the big night arrived.

That way, they wouldn't need to hire a riot squad to provide security.

Mary Kate's chair squeaked as she leaned forward, and her voice dropped to a confidential near-whisper. "Isn't it kind of weird?" she asked. "Both of your sisters being brides, and marrying *McKettricks,* for Pete's sake, and you'll just be a bridesmaid?"

Paige knew Mary Kate didn't have a mean bone in her ample body. Still, Paige's lower lip might have wobbled slightly as she framed her answer because, like it or not, this was a sore point with her.

Something she'd better get over, and pronto.

"The only *weird* thing," Paige said, putting on her game face, "is the bridesmaid's dress I'll probably get roped into wearing. It's *pink.* Organza, no less, with cascades of ruffles, puffy sleeves and a big bow in back."

Mary Kate gasped. "Oh, *no,*" she said, her dark eyes luminous with sympathy.

Paige nodded solemnly. "Oh, *yes,*" she replied.

CHAPTER ELEVEN

By the time Paige and Mary Kate had thoroughly discussed the upcoming wedding, Paige evading umpteen not-so-subtle attempts on the reception-ist's part to elicit the name of at least *one* celebrity guest, Austin had finished his examination. He and Dr. Colwin stepped into the waiting area together.

Paige almost leaped to her feet, before her pride reminded her that she was Austin McKettrick's private-duty *nurse,* not some eager-to-please flunky.

"A few more weeks, Austin," Dr. Colwin was saying, in a conciliatory tone, "and you can do everything you did before the shooting."

Austin, his left shoulder bulked up under his T-shirt because he'd gotten a new bandage, looked nonplussed. He accepted the prescription the doctor offered, however, and shoved the piece of paper carelessly into a front pocket of his jeans.

"Thanks, Doc," he said.

Mary Kate, who had been hovering, saw her chance and decided to go for broke. In a flash she was out from behind the desk and standing practically toe to toe with Austin. "Is it true that somebody famous will be at the wedding?" she asked, running the words together in a breathless rush.

Austin's eyes twinkled and the charm dial was set on High. "You mean, besides me?" he drawled, beaming down on Mary Kate like sunshine on the first real day of spring.

Mary Kate, suitably captivated, flushed and swatted at his chest with one hand. "Austin McKettrick, the things you say," she marveled, laughing.

"You'll be there, won't you, Mary Kate?" Austin asked. "At the wedding, I mean?"

"Mama and I already RSVP'ed," Mary Kate said with a quick nod. "We wouldn't miss a shindig like that for *anything.* I can't hardly *wait* for the reception, what with all the food and the fancy clothes and the music."

Austin's voice was a deep, smooth rumble. "You be sure and save a dance for me now," he said. "I'll be mighty disappointed if you don't."

Paige turned her head on the off chance that Mary Kate might see her roll her eyes. Dr. Colwin *did* see—Mary Kate remained enthralled with Austin and probably wouldn't have noticed a meteor shower—and he grinned to let Paige know it.

She chuckled. Shook her head.

Although she'd met the doctor before, when Austin was brought in after the incident at the oil fields, she had naturally been too preoccupied by the emergency at hand to notice that the newcomer was attractive, in a lean, serious-runner kind of way, with dark, close-cropped hair, nice hazel eyes and exceptionally good teeth.

"Nice to see you again," Dr. Colwin said, smiling at Paige. She didn't deliberately check out his left hand—the

way he was holding Austin's chart revealed the pertinent information.

No wedding ring. Not even the pale
line left by the recent *removal* of said
ring. But, then, not all married men
wore their wedding bands, as she'd
learned the hard way not once but
twice in her dating history.

She liked Dr. Colwin, but she didn't
feel a charge. Dammit.

"Things are a little less hectic this
time around," Paige remarked pleasantly. Sooner or later, she and Dr. Colwin would be working together, perhaps on the same shifts, and it
wouldn't hurt to get acquainted.

She was a little surprised when
Austin took her hand. It wasn't as if
they went around holding hands a lot,
after all.

"Hungry?" he asked. Now his drawl
was even more honeyed than before,
when he'd been flirting with Mary Kate.

Paige looked at him, blinked in confusion. What was he up to?

"I guess," she said slowly and with
great uncertainty.

That was evidently answer enough

for Austin; he all but pulled her out of the clinic, into the chilly sunshine.

"What was *that* all about?" Paige asked when they were both back in Garrett's car, with the doors shut and their seat belts fastened.

Austin, engaged in the process of starting the engine, backing out of their parking space with studious care, was the picture of innocence. He did, however, have the decency to redden a little along the strong line of his jaw.

"I just figured, if we're going to have steak, we'd best get on with it," he said. "We're burnin' daylight, as they say out on the ranch."

"Oh, please," Paige said, and laughed. "You just had cereal and orange juice. You can't possibly be all that hungry."

Austin sent her a sheepish glance, pausing at the exit from the clinic parking lot to look in both directions. As he put on his sunglasses and looked straight ahead, his profile was so fine that Paige felt a little twitter inside, and her breath caught.

Why did he have to be so freakin'

good-looking? she wondered. Wasn't her life complicated enough, with both her sisters getting married in a couple of months, her career in limbo and the renovations on her house taking forever and a day?

Austin shifted into second gear, careful to stay within the speed limit, then eased into third when they got to a straight stretch. Blue River had one stoplight, and it tended to get stuck on red for as long as ten minutes at a stretch, but since it happened to be right next to the police station, most people just grumbled and waited it out.

Austin, of course, wasn't most people.

Granted, there weren't any other vehicles in sight, not moving ones, at least, so he drove through.

The squad car appeared behind him instantly, as if by magic, lights flashing, siren giving one insistent whine.

"Hell," Austin growled, swinging the Porsche to the side of the road.

Paige touched her fingers to her lips, mainly to hide her amusement.

Tate, being the chief's closest friend,

had nicknamed Brent Brogan "Denzel." Though he was much younger, Brogan *did* bear a strong resemblance to the handsome actor.

The window purred down, and Austin had his good-ole-boy smile ready.

Chief Brogan bent to look through the gap.

He was not wearing a smile.

Paige bit the inside of her lower lip, so she wouldn't giggle.

"Where's the fire?" Brogan growled, pushing his mirrored sunglasses up his nose.

Austin sighed. "Come on, Brent," he said. "You know that traffic light doesn't work like it ought to."

"I know," Brogan said mildly, "that it was red when you went through it like it was green instead."

"Will it help if I admit everything and swear I'll never step off the straight and narrow again?" Austin asked.

Paige gave her head a slight shake. There were times when being a smart-ass didn't pay, and this was one of them.

"It might make me feel a little better,"

the chief quipped, "but I doubt it'll do much for you."

Austin spread his hands but said nothing.

"License and registration, please," Brogan said.

"Give me a break," Austin muttered, but he got out his wallet, extracted his license and handed it over.

Paige, meanwhile, opened the glove compartment and found the registration. She gave it to Austin, who relayed it to Brogan, who pondered it as though it were written in hieroglyphics.

Solemnly, he handed the items back to Austin.

"I'll just get my ticket book," Chief Brogan said. "Wait here."

"I'll just get my ticket book," Austin mimicked, once the chief was out of earshot. *"Wait here."*

Paige could no longer keep from smiling. "You *did* run the light," she said.

"Yes, Paige," Austin replied evenly, "I'm aware of that. And we'd probably still be sitting there, waiting for it to change if I hadn't."

"And you probably wouldn't be getting a ticket right now," Paige pointed out, keeping her tone sweet.

Chief Brogan returned. He scrawled something in his ticket book, tore the page out, and gave it to Austin.

Austin looked at it, nodded and stretched to shove it into his pocket, to reside with the prescription Dr. Colwin had given him at the clinic. "Thanks, Chief," he said.

Brogan lingered. "Aren't you going to ask me if I've made any progress finding out who shot you?" he wanted to know.

"I reckon you would have been in touch if you had, Chief."

A muscle bunched in Brogan's jawline. "I'd regard it as a personal favor," Brogan said, "if you'd be a little more careful until we get a handle on whatever's going on out there on the Silver Spur. In other words, if you see moving lights, call me before you go rushing off to investigate."

"Right," Austin agreed without much conviction.

Brogan finally acknowledged Paige.

His smile was impressive. "Hello, Paige," he said.

"Brent," Paige responded pleasantly. "How are the kids?"

"Aunt Gerbera's been keeping them in line," he answered. Brent was a widower with two children. Gerbera, his late father's sister, was a local woman, so Paige knew her quite well.

"Tell Gerbera I said hey," Paige said.

"I'll do that," Brent promised affably. Then he pointed an index finger at Austin. "Be more careful," he said.

Austin didn't answer. And maybe he shut the window a little sooner than necessary.

They zipped straight to the courthouse.

Paige waited in the Porsche while Austin went inside, presumably to pay his fine and thus clear his name after his brush with the law.

When Austin returned, the two of them conferred and decided it was still too early for the steak. So they headed for Paige's house.

Although it was a workday, the construction crew was conspicuously absent. That made Paige testy, though she managed to hide her irritation. She used her front door key and they went inside, Paige first, Austin directly behind her.

Despite all the changes—wonderful new windows, the fireplace, the overall enlargement of the space—Paige's gaze went straight to the place where her dad's hospital bed had stood during the final months of his life.

As a child, yearning for a mother who had chosen a tattoo-artist boyfriend over her husband and daughters, Paige had been hugely dependent on her father first, and her sisters second. Will Remington had done his best to fill the job descriptions of both Dad *and* Mom, but he hadn't been superhuman.

He'd been a regular man, a dedicated teacher, a loving father, doing his best from day to day.

Paige had adored him. After standing there for a moment, missing her dad with a keenness so sharp that it knifed through her heart and made her sinuses throb with heat and moisture, she dashed at her eyes with the backs of both hands, determined to move on. Go through the house, room by room, and assess the renovation progress.

But even though she was very careful to avoid Austin's gaze, he'd seen her grief and recognized it for what it was.

He took hold of her shoulders and turned her around, pulled her against his chest. She tried to stifle the sob his tenderness brought on, but the effort was a failure.

"Talk to me," he said, his voice throaty.

Her mind remembered everything about his touch, his voice, the nameless emotions he elicited. "It's nothing," she lied, but she didn't withdraw from his embrace.

Austin threaded his fingers through her hair, tilted her head back a little way. "Paige," he said, searching her eyes.

There was no hiding the tears. Well aware that Austin had lost not just one parent but *both,* in a single tragic accident, she sniffled and squared her shoulders and said, "It was worse for you and Tate and Garrett."

"Losing somebody you love isn't easy for anybody."

She watched him closely. There was no way she could disagree, and she didn't trust herself to speak.

Gently, his fingers still buried in her hair, he kissed her forehead. "I used to think one day I wouldn't miss them anymore. It's been ten years, going on eleven, and that day still hasn't come."

Paige slipped her arms around his middle, because for all that they'd been lovers, mismatched and destined for heartbreak, they had also been friends. She rested her head against his chest and breathed in the scent of his skin and his freshly laundered T-shirt. "I know what you mean," she replied softly, her voice muffled. "Every once in a while—not often—I dream that my dad is still alive. That he's still teaching his classes at school and repairing things in this old house and watching out for Libby and Julie and me."

Austin curved a finger under Paige's

chin and lifted, so that their eyes met. His mouth quirked up in that familiar grin that wasn't. "You really plan on living in a place this big all by yourself?" he asked.

Paige chuckled, though her vision was still a bit blurred. "You're a fine one to talk," she pointed out. "I've stayed in *hotels* that were smaller than your house."

"It isn't just my house," Austin replied, delaying her for just a fraction of a second when she moved to pull away. "Tate and Garrett own equal shares."

Paige was leading him toward the kitchen. "Yes. And just the part of it Julie and Garrett and Calvin live in is bigger than this entire place."

He followed, and though he was grinning, his eyes looked hollow.

The man had been seriously injured, Paige reminded herself, and he'd just slept for nearly thirty-six hours in a row. He was starting to run down.

"Maybe we should just go back to the Silver Spur," she said gently.

"Not until I get my steak," he replied. He ducked his head into the kitchen, craned his neck to look around, take it all in.

Paige had the feeling he was really *looking* at things, not just going through the motions to be polite. She made quick work of the rest of the tour, skipping the master bedroom entirely, and they went back out to the Porsche.

Two streets over and they were back at the town's one traffic light again. And it was red.

Austin made a little ceremony of stopping, gearing down, adjusting all the mirrors, resetting the radio to a station he liked. When the light still hadn't changed after all that and a few other creative gyrations, he rested his forehead against the top of the steering wheel and pretended to snore.

Paige laughed.

Someone pulled up behind them in an old car and tooted the horn impatiently.

The light remained unchanged.

Austin winked at Paige. Then he unhooked his seat belt, got out of the vehicle and strolled back to chat a while with the other driver. This being Blue River, where almost everybody knew almost everybody else, the exchange appeared to be a friendly one.

When the light finally changed, Austin sprinted back to the Porsche, climbed in, fastened his seat belt again and drove sedately through the intersection.

"Very nice," Paige teased, applauding briefly. "Chief Brogan would be so proud."

Austin merely grinned at that.

Two minutes later, they pulled into the broken-asphalt parking lot beside the Silver Dollar Saloon. A neon beer sign flickered behind a greasy window, and Patsy Cline's voice spilled through the screen door and out over the weathered wooden sidewalk that probably dated back to Blue River's wilder days.

The song was "Crazy."

Paige tried not to take it personally.

*   *   *

The hinges on the screen door screeched as Austin pulled it open. He waited while Paige crossed the threshold just ahead of him.

The Silver Dollar looked seedy inside as well as out, but the food was good. A couple of decades back, the Dollar had done a flourishing business selling beer and soda and cheeseburgers to tourists stopping off on their way to Austin or San Antonio, but trade had fallen off considerably.

A spin rack of bent-cornered postcards, bearing slogans like, "Don't Mess with Texas" and "A Big Howdy from the Lone Star State," angled for floor space with shelves displaying everything from cans of motor oil to candy bars in faded wrappers. The pool tables were in use, even though it wasn't yet noon, and the regulars already lined the bar.

Flossie Kirk, who had been waiting tables at the Dollar longer than Austin had been alive, hustled over to greet them. Giving Paige a hug that nearly squeezed all the air out of her lungs,

Flossie shouted for all to hear, "Well, it's about damn *time* you two got back together."

Paige blushed and Austin noticed that she was real careful not to look in his direction. Practically everybody in the place was looking at them.

Austin fully expected Paige to protest that they weren't "back together" at all. He decided to be chivalrous and step in.

"I've got a hankering for a good steak, Flossie," he said, automatically resting his hand against the small of Paige's back as the elderly waitress led the way to an open table. "Think you can fix me up?"

Wrinkles fanned out all around the woman's mouth when she smiled, but in her tired eyes, Austin caught a glimpse of a younger Flossie.

"From what I hear," she said, stopping in front of a table next to the window, "it took a doctor, some drugs and a needle and thread to fix *you* up."

Folks at the counter and at the other tables, all people both Austin and Paige had known forever, felt free to chime in with remarks and questions.

"What the hell happened out there in that oil field, anyhow?" boomed old Charlie Felder, who owned the feed store and sold tractors and farm implements besides. "Brent ain't talkin'."

"That's what happens when a town don't have a newspaper no more," observed one of the chronic boozers at the bar. "Folks don't get no news."

Austin pulled back a chair for Paige, and she sank onto the red vinyl seat, wearing a rueful expression. She was no doubt wishing they'd gone somewhere a little classier than the Silver Dollar, but fine-dining opportunities were few and far between in their part of Texas. About the best they could do were fast-food places and the mediocre restaurant in the Amble On Inn.

"Now, Roy Lee," one of the other midday drinkers jived, "you know you never read the newspaper even when the *Blue River Weekly* was a goin' concern."

"Who do you figure shot you, Austin?" someone else called out.

"Y'all just hush up now," Flossie interceded in the raspy voice of a lifelong smoker, "and let these young people eat in peace!"

Paige was busy studying her menu as though she hadn't memorized the thing years ago, like most of the people in town.

Flossie asked for the drink orders, and Austin, who would have enjoyed a beer, chose a soft drink instead. Paige requested unsweetened iced tea.

The more inquisitive customers, having gotten their ears pinned back by Flossie, commenced to minding their own business.

Flossie brought the drinks.

Austin, who figured he must have been craving a thick steak even in his sleep, he was so hungry, ordered a rib eye, rare.

Paige opted for the salad bar. She was up there piling a plate high with lettuce and not much else, it looked like, when the screen door hinges creaked again. Austin glanced that way out of idle curiosity and saw Cliff Pomeroy walk in.

Austin hadn't really thought about his father's one-time friend very much— he'd been a little busy—but now, waiting for his steak and for Paige to come back with a lunch better suited to a rabbit than a person, he found himself taking the man's measure.

Cliff was probably in his late forties, if not his early fifties, and though he'd always been a flashy dresser and a ladies' man, he'd lost some of his luster since the days when he and Jim McKettrick had been friends.

Watching as Doc Pomeroy's only son took a stool at the counter, Austin was hard put to say what a man like Jim McKettrick could have had in common with Cliff, besides oil. Once, Cliff had made a lot of money brokering McKettrick crude—millions, probably. Should have been enough to last him, Austin figured, even after the wells were capped for good.

While Austin was doing all this wondering, Paige finished building her salad and came back to the table, glancing over one shoulder at Cliff as she passed him.

"What do you suppose Clifton Pomeroy is doing back in Blue River?" she whispered once she'd settled into her chair again. "Even when Doc had his heart attack three years ago, there was no sign of him."

Austin spotted Flossie zeroing in with his steak, baked potato and green beans boiled up with bacon and onion, and waited until she was gone again before replying, "Folks do tend to come home to Blue River," he said lightly. "No matter how far away they roam or what plans they might have made to the contrary."

Paige picked up her fork and speared a tomato and a slice of cucumber in one jab. One of her eyebrows rose slightly.

"Did *you* have other plans, Austin?" she asked.

He added salt and pepper to the steak *and* the potato, which was swimming in sour cream and butter. He reckoned Paige would have something to say about cholesterol and saturated fat, but for the moment, she was silent on the issue.

"Did you?" he countered.

"I asked you first," Paige argued.

He chuckled. Out of the corner of his eye, he saw that Cliff was looking in their direction.

"Yeah," Austin said. "I had other plans."

"What were they?"

Cliff had slapped on a smile, and now he was headed over to shoot the breeze.

"They were none of your damn business," Austin told her pleasantly, cutting into the steak and keeping an eye on Cliff.

Paige blushed a little, but before she could say anything, Cliff was standing beside the table.

"Good to see you out and about, Austin," he said.

"Thanks, Cliff," Austin replied easily. "Join us?"

Cliff hesitated, considering the invitation, but finally shook his head. "Dad's over at the office," he said. "I promised

I'd bring back a couple of sandwiches for lunch."

Austin nodded, expecting the man to walk away.

But Paige scooted one chair over and pushed her salad plate along, too. "You may as well sit with us while you wait for your order," she said. Her tone was cheerful, but Austin knew that look. She was fixing to pry.

With an odd combination of eagerness and reluctance, Cliff gave in and sat down, scraping the chair legs against the scarred linoleum floor as he did so.

"You've been away from Blue River for a long time," Paige said when Cliff didn't launch into an immediate autobiography and outline his exact whereabouts for the last fifteen years or so. "I suppose there were more opportunities in Dallas or Houston or wherever you were."

Austin didn't say anything, but he was amused, and when he caught Paige's eye, he let her know it. Did she think she was being subtle?

Cliff seemed to sag a little, and his

smile, once easy and confident, seemed fixed, even a mite phony. "I was doing real well until my last divorce," he said. "And the oil business isn't what it used to be, either."

Again, Austin kept his thoughts to himself. He was enjoying the steak, though. It was thick and juicy and seasoned just the way he liked it.

"I know what you mean," Paige said, after taking a ladylike sip of iced tea and swallowing. "A *lot* of businesses aren't what they used to be," she added, her voice both sympathetic and cheerful. "Take my sister's coffee shop, for example. Even before our mother drove Julie's car through the front wall and literally brought down the roof, Libby was barely making it. She probably would have had to close the place anyway."

Austin frowned, chewing. Where was she going with this?

Cliff nodded sadly. "Things are tough all over," he said, slanting a look at Austin and rubbing his chin with one hand. "Of course," he added, "now that

Libby is marrying into the McKettrick clan, she won't have to worry about making a business pay."

Austin's appetite took a dip, and he put down his knife and fork. Although Cliff hadn't really said anything a man could object to, Austin realized that he *did* object.

"Your other sister is marrying Garrett, isn't she?" Cliff asked, looking at Paige.

"Yes," Paige said, with a high-beam smile. "Isn't that great?"

Cliff didn't reply. His gaze shifted back to Austin. "I guess you and your brothers are as dead-set on keeping those wells capped as your daddy was," he said.

If he'd meant to be cagey, it wasn't working for him.

"Pretty much," Austin replied.

"Still a lot of oil down there, I'd say," Cliff ventured.

Austin picked up his knife and fork again. He wasn't one to waste a good piece of beef. "Most likely," he agreed.

A little crinkle formed between Paige's eyebrows; she was taking it all in, but she didn't jump into the conversation.

"Seems like a waste," Cliff said, shifting to pry his wallet out of his back pocket when Flossie appeared with the bag containing his take-out order.

"Here you go, Cliff," Flossie said.

Cliff paid the bill and then pushed back his chair to stand. Nodded to Paige and then fixed his gaze on Austin.

"If you and Tate and Garrett ever change your mind about tapping those wells, you let me know."

Austin didn't rise from his chair and offer his hand for the farewell shake the way he normally did with almost anybody older than he was.

"That isn't very likely, Cliff," he said.

Cliff's grip tightened on the bag he was holding, so that the paper made a crackling sound. He rustled up another smile, though, and if it hadn't had an edge, it might have approached cordial.

"You never know," he replied.

With that, he turned and left the Dollar.

The screen door banged shut behind him.

Paige turned in her chair, watching Pomeroy move out of sight. Then she swung back around to Austin. There was a question in her eyes, and Austin knew what it was without her having to ask it out loud.

"It wasn't Cliff," he said. "Much as he might like to shoot me, he wouldn't have the guts to do it."

"He clearly wants the oil wells re-opened," Paige said, keeping her voice down.

"Cliff's wanted that ever since Dad decided to shut them down," Austin told her. "You know the old saying— wish in one hand—"

"Stop right there," Paige said, pushing her plate away and eyeing Austin's half-finished steak. "Are we through here?"

Austin shoved back his chair, sighed. "We're through," he confirmed.

He took care of the check while Paige stood spinning the postcard rack around, checking out the pale images.

Watching her made him smile.

The transaction at the cash register completed, Austin exchanged farewell nods with a few folks as he walked to the screen door, held it open for Paige.

Outside, she extended her hand, palm up. "Keys," she said.

Austin hesitated. He was, after all, a man.

"I'm going to insist," Paige told him, without lowering her hand.

He sighed, gave up the keys to his brother's car. "If I'd known you were going to drive home," he said, "I would have had a beer. Maybe even two."

She chuckled. Then she shrugged. "Let's go fill your prescription," she said. "Then we'll head for home."

He liked that she'd called the ranch "home," even though she probably hadn't meant anything by it.

"It's just more pain stuff," he said, referring to the prescription Dr. Colwin had given him back at the clinic.

Was Paige attracted to that guy?

"We're filling the prescription," she said in the same tone she'd used to tell him she meant to drive.

"Okay," he said, spreading his

hands. The truth was, it felt good bantering with Paige like this, just *being* with her.

Too bad it wasn't likely to last.

CHAPTER TWELVE

Even though he swore he wasn't tired, Austin hadn't been back home for more than an hour before he fell sound asleep in the downstairs guest bed, the ever-loyal Shep curled protectively at his feet.

The sight made Paige smile.

They made quite a pair, this man and his dog.

Thinking Austin didn't need so much staring at, now that he was officially on the road to recovery, Paige picked up her laptop and headed for the main kitchen. She set the computer on the table, and then headed to the counter, planning to brew a cup of tea.

It was a little after 2:00 p.m.; normally at this time of day, she would have been getting ready to pick Calvin up at the community center, making sure he had something other than fast food to eat, and then stopping by the high school auditorium so he could spend twenty minutes or so with Julie. But since she'd been working as Austin's private nurse, Libby and Garrett had been taking turns looking after Calvin when Julie was working.

Paige sighed. Her nephew lived in the same house she did, so it wasn't as if she didn't see him often, but things were still different enough to make her feel an odd and poignant nostalgia.

Their lives were all changing so fast. And they were changing forever.

"Get a grip," Paige mumbled to herself, trying to blink away the burning sensation in her eyes and concentrate on the simple task at hand.

She knew where the mugs were kept, but she opened and closed a few cupboard doors before locating the tea supply, which was sparse, probably because this had been a household of men for such a long time.

Taking comfort in measuring out the small movements involved, Paige filled the mug from the special hot-water spigot on the sink and dropped in a bag. Watched as the water darkened, breathed in the familiar and very soothing aroma.

Returning to the table, she set the cup down, took a seat on the long bench and flipped open the laptop. After logging on, Paige went straight to a popular search engine and typed in the name "Clifton Pomeroy."

Not surprisingly, a lot of people in the world went by that name, so she did some narrowing down. It took nearly fifteen minutes to find Doc's only son, but eventually, he turned up.

Paige sipped her rapidly cooling tea, studying the screen.

No deep, dark secrets here: Cliff had been married four times—apparently none of these unions had resulted in children—and he'd declared bankruptcy some fifteen years ago. Until the last divorce, final only a month before, he'd resided in one of the best sections of Dallas.

Alas, the house belonged to Wife #3, a member of a prominent Texas family, so Cliff was out on his ear. Now, possibly having nowhere else to go, he'd come home to Daddy.

Paige sighed again and squeezed the bridge of her nose between a thumb and a forefinger. She was a nurse, she reminded herself, not a detective. Okay, so Cliff had made it pretty clear when she and Austin met up with him at the Silver Dollar that he wanted the McKettrick oil wells reopened—he probably wasn't alone in that. Where there was oil, there was money—*big* money—and that was reason enough, for some people, to commit a crime.

She dropped her head forward to stretch the taut muscles in the back of her neck, and when that didn't help, put both hands to her nape and kneaded with all ten fingers.

At a sound coming from one of the staircases, Paige looked up and saw Tate standing with one arm hooked around the newel post, grinning at her.

"Job getting to you already?" he asked with good-humored sympathy. "Riding herd on Austin, I mean."

Paige chuckled, logged off and shut the laptop. "He's sleeping right now," she replied with a little shake of her head. "No trouble at all."

Tate laughed, approached the table and sat down across from her. Resting his powerful forearms on the surface, he interlaced his fingers and replied, "Austin's always been at his most tractable when he's asleep."

She smiled, got up from the bench, holding her mug up. "I'm having more tea," she said. "Would you like some?"

"I'm okay, thanks," he said with a shake of his head, starting to rise.

"Oh, for heaven's sake," Paige said, "sit down. I'm only going to the sink for more hot water."

Tate's grin was a mite sheepish, but he didn't comply until Paige was back at the table and seated.

"Old habits die hard," he said, dropping back to the bench.

Paige smiled. She remembered Sally McKettrick; the mistress of this house had been a true Southern lady, with a good sense of humor, and she'd raised her three sons to be gentlemen.

"It must be pretty ingrained," she observed. "This standing-up-in-the-presence-of-a-lady thing."

"I don't remember a time when it wasn't a reflex." Tate grinned.

Paige waited, knowing there was more he wanted to say. Her patience was rewarded. Sort of.

"Libby's worried about you," Tate said, after a few moments of silent struggle, and he had the decency to at least *seem* reluctant.

"About what?" Paige asked mildly. It was only the first of several questions she had for him.

Tate drew in a breath, sighed it out heavily. "She thinks it might be too hard for you, being in such close proximity with Austin all the time."

Paige felt a sting behind her cheek-bones and hoped it didn't show on the surface. "And my big sister didn't bring this up with me herself *because . . .*"

Tate looked distinctly uncomfortable. "She will," he said. "I just thought—since Garrett and I came up with the bright idea of hiring you as Austin's nurse in the first place, I mean—that it was sort of our responsibility to straighten things out." He cleared his throat. "And since I lost the coin toss, here we are."

Paige smiled. He was there because he'd lost a coin toss. At least Tate was being honest. "Are you unhappy with my work?" she asked.

Tate looked genuinely surprised. "No," he said quickly. "It isn't that. It's just—well—what Libby said. We might have come on a little strong, Garrett and I. Put too much pressure on you to accept the job. If you'd rather back out, we'll understand."

The poor man looked so miserable that Paige almost felt sorry for him. Almost.

"Back out? You mean, *quit,* Tate?"

His neck reddened, and he tugged at his collar, even though his white Western shirt was already open to his sternum. Had there ever been a McKettrick who wasn't violently allergic to the word *quit* or any of its synonyms?

"I wouldn't put it that way," he said.

"Of course you wouldn't. You're a

McKettrick, and McKettricks don't know what it means to quit, do they?"

"There are times," Tate allowed, "when we might be better off if we did."

"But you don't," Paige pressed.

His voice was gruff and he looked away for a moment. "No," he admitted.

Paige leaned forward and spoke firmly, but not unkindly. She wasn't angry, she just wanted to make her point. "Well," she said, "the Remingtons don't quit, either. Even when we ought to."

Tate grinned, shifted on the bench. He was quiet for a few moments, then he asked, "Austin saw his doctor today, didn't he? What's the prognosis?"

"I wasn't in the exam room," Paige said, "but he's still bandaged. His appetite is fair to good—we stopped at the Silver Dollar for lunch today, and he made a pretty good dent in a sixteen-ounce steak—"

"But?" Tate prompted when she fell silent.

"Cliff Pomeroy came in while we were there," Paige said, thoughtful. What *was* it about the man that bothered her so much? "He sat with us for a while, and the conversation came around to the oil wells. The ones here on the Silver Spur, I mean. Cliff said he'd like to see the fields operational again." She paused, swallowed. "I couldn't help wondering . . ."

Tate raised one dark eyebrow. "If Cliff might have been the one to shoot Austin the other night?"

"Someone *had* been tampering with one of the wells before he got there," Paige said, and she felt slightly defensive because she could already see Tate's answer taking shape in his face. Even before he spoke, she had a pretty good idea what he was going to say.

"Cliff wouldn't do a thing like that," Tate replied, confirming her prediction. "He and our dad were good friends, Paige, for a very long time."

"But then something happened?" Paige pressed. "Between Cliff and your father, that is. And then they weren't friends anymore?"

Tate sighed, shoved a hand through his dark hair. "What happened was, there were some environmental concerns, and Dad decided to shut down the wells. That made Cliff mad as hell, because he'd been raking in a lot of money brokering deals, and they argued. But I wouldn't say the friendship was over for good, just the partnership. They'd known each other all their lives, been buddies since they were younger than Calvin. And I never heard Dad say a word against Cliff."

Paige didn't point out that the reverse might not be true, that Cliff might have had *plenty* to say against Jim McKettrick. That maybe he wasn't just looking for business opportunities, but revenge against the family who'd cut him off.

"You know, of course," she said carefully, with a nod toward the closed laptop to indicate the source of her information, "that Cliff declared bankruptcy once?"

"About five years after the business partnership between him and Dad ended," Tate said. He paused, swallowed hard, looked away for a moment. When he looked back, his eyes were glossy. "Dad was gone by then. Mom, too, of course."

Paige reached across the table, spanned her fingers over Tate's muscular forearm for a moment, smiled sadly. She knew what it was to grieve for one parent and, in a way, for two. Although her mother was still alive, Marva had been a mere footnote in Paige's life for years.

She was still searching her mind—and her heart—for an answer, when Libby came down the third stairway, stood just where Tate had a little while before. She even looped an arm around the newel post, the same way he'd done, and Paige wondered if it was really true, the old saying that the more people were together, the more alike they became.

Tate rose to his feet after he followed Paige's gaze and realized that Libby was standing behind him, on the bottom step. "I tried to give her an out," he told his future wife, "but she wouldn't take it."

Paige smiled at her sister. "Tea?" she asked, holding her cup aloft.

Libby finally pulled herself loose from the newel post and smiled back, with a bit of a wobble to her lower lip. "Yes," she said with a little nod and a sniffle. "Thanks."

Tate, still standing, said he thought he'd go on out to the barn and see how Molly and the other horses were, maybe feed them a little early, just this once.

With that, he crossed to Libby, squeezed her shoulders and then kissed the top of her head.

Paige, meanwhile, went to the sink and filled another mug with hot water, then added a tea bag. Brought it to her sister, who had taken Tate's place at the table.

"Lib?"

Libby sniffled again, cupped her hands around the mug. "Thanks," she said.

"What's the matter?" Paige said, worried. Libby wasn't the weepy type, nor was it likely that she felt guilty for any part she might have had in throwing her kid sister and Austin together, per Paige's earlier conversation with Tate.

"Sometimes things don't happen the

way we expect," Libby said, looking up at her with a peculiar combination of misery and starry-eyed wonder that made Paige's breath catch.

"What do you mean?" Paige asked softly, still standing, holding one hand to her heart. Some of her tea sloshed over the rim of the mug and burned her fingers.

Libby gave a husky little chuckle and reached out to pull Paige's free hand away from her chest and squeeze. "I'm pregnant," she said.

Paige plunked down onto the bench beside Libby, and they didn't let go of each other's hands.

"I thought you were going to say you were sick," Paige whispered, dizzy with relief. "Or that you and Tate had decided not to get married—"

Libby bit her lower lip, stared down into her tea for a few moments before meeting Paige's gaze again. "Tate thinks we should get married right away," she confided.

"And you?" Paige asked, her voice going hoarse. *Libby was expecting a baby.*

How amazing. How miraculous. How *positively wonderful.*

Libby's lips moved, but nothing more came out.

"You're *happy* about this, right?" Paige prompted.

Tears filled Libby's eyes. "Of *course* I'm happy, goose," she said, with a moist little laugh and a bump of her shoulder against Paige's. "But the wedding—Julie and I have made so many plans, bought our dresses—and, Paige, *hundreds* of people will be converging on this ranch on New Year's Eve expecting the event of the century—"

Paige put her arm around Libby's shoulders and hugged her. "Lib," she reasoned, "you can still have the big wedding. Lots of people have a civil ceremony first and follow up with the whole white-lace and birdseed thing later. I don't really see the problem here."

Libby began to cry. Loudly. "But I'm *pregnant,*" she repeated.

"So you said," Paige replied, hugging her again.

"I didn't want it to be like this," Libby said, and now she cried in earnest.

Paige got up from the table just long enough to snatch a whole roll of paper towels from the holder near the sink and bring it back to Libby.

With a giggly sob, Libby reached out to tear off a towel and half the roll unfurled, and they both laughed. Libby pressed a huge wad of crumpled towel to her face and blew her nose.

"I didn't want it to be like this," she said again.

"Like *what,* Libby?" Paige asked. "You love Tate and he loves you. In addition to becoming a stepmom to Audrey and Ava, you're about to have a *child of your very own.* What would you change about this?"

"Nothing," Libby said with a watery smile. "I just wish this baby had been conceived later on, that's all. On our wedding night, for instance, or any time *after* that."

Paige's mouth twitched at one corner. "You *do* know what causes these things, don't you?"

Libby laughed at that, truly laughed,

and it was a wonderful sound. She flung the enormous ball of paper towels at Paige. *"Yes, Dr. Remington,"* she answered, her eyes shining with tears and joy. "I *have* figured out that much. And we were, for your information, using birth control. But—things happen."

Paige folded her arms and tried to look dour. "Well, I only have one thing to say about all this," she said very solemnly.

"W-what?" Libby asked, looking wobbly again.

Paige leaped into the air and punched at the sky with one fist. *"Yes!"* she cried.

More laughing followed, along with more crying, and certainly more paper towels.

Libby and Paige were hugging each other, and Libby was getting the right shoulder of Paige's T-shirt all wet, when the door to the garage burst open and Calvin raced in, closely followed by Julie. Garrett brought up the rear.

Both Libby and Paige were startled to see Julie home so early. The rehearsals for her play often lasted until eight or nine at night, and here she was at three-fifteen.

"Mom's taking time off to be a chaperone when my class goes to Six Flags!" Calvin announced exuberantly just as Tate came back in from the barn and Austin wandered out from the guest apartment bedroom, pausing in the big arched doorway and looking curious.

As well as hot.

Julie smiled.

Calvin turned to look up at Paige. "I love you a lot," he said. "But it will be cool to have my *mom* there."

Paige grinned, mussed up his hair. "That's great, honey," she said.

"You're not disappointed?" he asked, worried. "Six Flags is a *lot* of fun."

Disappointed? To miss out on escorting twenty-three excited five-year-olds through a huge amusement park on the day before Thanksgiving?

"I'll recover," Paige said, hiding her relief.

"You're taking time off?" Libby pressed, watching Julie closely. Her expression was mildly troubled.

"Come on," Julie protested, feathers ruffled. "You make it sound like I'm some kind of—of *workaholic,* or something. Anyway, it's only one day."

"Calvin," Garrett interrupted, after clearing his throat, reaching out to catch the little boy playfully by the hood of his nylon jacket, "why don't you head on upstairs and take Harry out the back way."

Calvin loved his dog, not to mention the man who was about to become his stepfather, so he didn't argue. He pounded up Garrett's stairs, shouting, "Harry! Harry, I'm home!"

In the distance, Harry began to bark in frenetic celebration of the news.

The adults stood around, still as a garden of statues.

Paige finally cast a sidelong glance in Austin's direction, noted that he was keeping his distance. His hair was sleep-mussed and Shep was at his side.

"I'd rather just get it out there," Julie said after she and Garrett exchanged silent communiqués. "My sisters and I don't keep secrets from each other."

"Much," Paige whispered to Libby, giving her a light elbow jab.

"I was going to tell her," Libby whispered back.

Alerted, Julie looked from Paige to Libby and back again. Shrugged out of her cloth coat, which Garrett automatically lifted from her shoulders and draped over the stair rail.

"What?" Julie demanded. *"What* were you going to tell me, Libby?"

Libby glanced at Tate.

Tate gave an almost imperceptible nod.

"Tate and I are—having a baby," Libby said.

Julie let out a squeal of joy.

Tate, Garrett and Austin all winced, but they were grinning, too. With all three of them looking that good at the same time, Paige thought, it was a wonder the ocean temperatures didn't rise.

Paige, Libby and Julie met in the middle of the floor like cheerleaders after a big win and did a lot of jumping up and down and hugging and laughing and crying. Then, when things had calmed down to a moderate uproar, Julie went to the sink, washed her hands and brewed herself a cup of tea.

Garrett went outside to keep an eye on Calvin and the dog.

Tate ambled over to consult with Austin about something.

And so the three sisters were semi-alone when Julie returned to the table with her tea and sat down.

There was more coming, Paige was sure of it.

"You both knew I was planning to take a few years off from teaching," she said, "so Garrett and I can give Calvin a brother or a sister as soon as possible."

"Yes," Paige said. "But you love teaching."

Julie sighed. "Yes," she agreed. "I do. But I love Calvin more, and I want more time with him. Things are already pretty hectic around here, and the momentum is building, and I don't want my son to get lost in the shuffle."

"Julie," Libby said, "what are you saying?"

Julie looked both happy and sad, a condition Paige well understood.

"There was a staff meeting today. There were some cuts made in next year's budget, and one teacher—if not several—will have to go. I wasn't coming back after summer vacation anyway—that's common knowledge. So I raised my hand and volunteered to be voted off the island, so to speak." Julie's shoulders slumped slightly, but her eyes were clear and her smile was genuine. "Principal Dulles jumped right on that suggestion and generously informed me that I could be of further help to the cause by going part-time as soon as the play is over and the profits have been tallied up."

"Oh," Libby said.

"Yikes," Paige added.

"All is not lost," Julie said bravely. "I'll still be teaching part-time, and now I'll have time to help the kids develop the showcase."

Over the previous summer, Julie had helped three of her best students, ranch hand Ron Strivens's daughter Rachel among them, to write and polish their own one-act plays. She'd planned to produce the three pieces and have them recorded on video, hopefully resulting in college scholarships for the young playwrights. The musical the drama club was about to stage had taken precedence, however, because it was a consistent moneymaker.

Julie looked hard at both her sisters. "Stop it," she said.

"Stop what?" Libby asked.

"Stop looking as though somebody died," Julie said. "You're going to have a baby, Libby. And if that doesn't call for a celebration, I don't know what does."

Tate and Austin rejoined the group, and Garrett returned from the yard, accompanied by Calvin and Harry.

"Sister conference!" Libby declared, raising both hands.

"*Beer* conference," Tate countered with a chuckle. He opened one of the refrigerators, extracted a six-pack and blazed a trail into the pool area.

Garrett followed with Calvin, after giving Julie a look of such exquisite love that Paige's heart danced just to see it.

Austin and the dogs brought up the rear.

When the men were gone, Paige, Libby and Julie all sat down at the table, Paige and Libby on one side, Julie on the other.

"You're *pregnant,*" Julie said to Libby.

"Yeah," Libby said.

Paige studied both of them in turn, and marveled at how much she loved these sisters of hers.

"Oh, Lib," Julie said, "that's wonderful."

Libby swallowed visibly, nodded.

Julie's expression grew more intent and she folded her arms. "Libby Remington," she said, "what's the matter?"

A little silence fell.

"How long have you known you were expecting?" Julie asked Libby.

"Since this morning," Libby answered with a watery smile, "when I locked myself in the bathroom and peed on one of those little plastic sticks from the drugstore."

"So does all this mean I don't have to wear that stupid pink dress?" Paige asked. "I mean, if Tate wants to marry Libby right away, then you and Garrett might as well—"

Julie smiled with her eyes as well as her mouth. "I'm not missing out on the glam wedding, and that's final."

"You don't think Tate and I should cancel?" Libby asked, her voice as soft as the look in her eyes. "Just have a small, private ceremony, so he can make an honest woman of me?"

Paige thought of Mary Kate, who was so looking forward to the holiday wedding, with all the bells and whistles. A lot of people would be let down if the social event of the year were canceled, or even reduced from a double to a single.

"*I want a wedding,*" Julie said, and though her tone was pleasant, her eyes flashed. "Flying doves. Fireworks. The whole county in attendance." She leaned forward a little. "And you should, too, Libby. Because, I don't know about you, but I'm only going to do this once. Garrett McKettrick is *it,* the one man I'll ever love and certainly the one man I'll be married to until the end of our lives. And there *will* be a magnificent wedding to look back on."

Libby sighed. "I wanted a fancy wedding, too," she admitted. "But Tate's pretty firm on the idea that we should make it legal right away, because of the baby." She started to cry again, just like that. Such was the power of female hormones. "You know he had to get married the first time around, because Cheryl was pregnant with the twins—"

Julie was immediately on her feet, rounding the table, sitting down beside Libby, gathering her close. "Oh, honey," she said, "this is different."

"How?" Libby asked, pulling away.

"First," Paige broke in, in a whisper, "where are Audrey and Ava?"

Libby reached for the roll of paper towels and tore off a sheet. "They're upstairs in their room, watching a movie. I kept them home from school today because they were coughing." She paused, looked back at the staircase just to make sure the twins hadn't snuck up on them somehow. "And how is this situation different? Cheryl was pregnant, so Tate put a wedding band on her finger. And as much as he loves his daughters, he resented that woman every day of their marriage. Now *I'm* pregnant. And Tate wants to do the right thing. What if he decides I trapped him, just as Cheryl did, and his feelings change?"

"Oh, for Pete's sake," Julie scoffed. "Tate was going to marry you *before* this baby was conceived, Lib. The man adores you."

Libby took that in, nodded reflectively. Sat up a little straighter. Still, she wasn't through playing devil's advocate. "People will talk," she said, and her eyes were wide.

"People are *already* talking," Julie said. "Get real, Lib. The gossips in and around Blue River marked their calendars *weeks* ago. Two sisters marrying into the fabled McKettrick clan at once? It's too juicy *not* to talk about. Heck, I'd probably be in on it myself if I weren't directly involved."

The blunt honesty of Julie's remark definitely lightened the mood.

Out by the pool, the men were laughing about something.

Libby gnawed at her lower lip. She'd always been the worrywart in the family, in Paige's opinion. Both her sisters, of course, would have awarded the title to *her* instead, but that was just because she was the most practical of the three.

No other reason.

Was there something Austin hadn't told her, after his visit with Dr. Colwin that morning?

"Won't I be *showing?*" Libby fretted, looking from Julie to Paige. "Looking like a pillow smuggler in my wedding dress wasn't part of the fantasy, ladies."

Paige laughed. "You won't show," she assured her sister. "Not unless you're way more pregnant than you seem to think."

"If necessary, you could have the dress let out a little," Julie speculated.

Paige sighed inwardly. "So the wedding is still on?"

Libby, warming up to the idea, nodded distractedly. "What if Tate insists that we go ahead and get married right away?" she asked. "He's pretty stubborn, you know."

Julie laughed. "A stubborn McKettrick? Now *there's* a concept."

Libby blushed. "You know what I mean," she said.

"If Tate insists on tying the knot, fine," Julie told her. "We all go down to the courthouse and watch the two of you get hitched and then we do it all over again, on a much grander scale, on New Year's Eve."

Libby began to smile, albeit tentatively. "I guess that would work," she said.

Paige waved a hand between her sisters' faces to get their attention. "So does this mean I still have to wear that god-awful pink dress?"

CHAPTER THIRTEEN

The house was quiet, now that Garrett and Julie and Tate and Libby had retreated to their private quarters.

Paige and Austin were sitting at one of the tables by the pool, sharing one of the many delicious entrées the housekeeper, Esperanza, had whipped up and frozen before leaving for her niece's place. Shep, as usual, was resting at Austin's feet.

"Is it just me," Austin asked casually, and with a mischievous twinkle in those insufferably blue eyes of his, "or are you starting to feel like a slacker, too?"

Paige felt as though she'd been put through an emotional wringer, and a moment or two passed before she picked up on his meaning. "No," she said, leaning in a little and widening her eyes at him for emphasis. "I am *not* feeling like a slacker. I have no wish to be part of this—*rash* of weddings."

Like hell you haven't, countered some inner voice.

"I'd say it was more of a plague than a rash," Austin remarked lightly. "Seems to be running rampant around here."

Paige pretended to be affronted, but she knew she wasn't very convincing. "A *plague?*" she repeated. "Hardly what I'd call marriages between my sisters and your brothers."

"No," Austin said, all droll now as he leaned back in his chair. "Your word was *rash.*"

"So it was," Paige admitted, trying not to notice the thin strand of sorrow woven through the genuine joy she felt for her sisters. Not only had they found the right men, now Libby was pregnant and, pretty soon Julie would be, too.

Being only human, Paige couldn't help wishing something wonderful would happen in her *own* life, as well as Libby's and Julie's. Trust Austin to notice what she didn't *want* him to notice.

If she'd been *trying* to get his attention, skywriting probably wouldn't have been enough.

"Why so sad?" he asked.

Paige averted her gaze, let one shoulder rise and then fall again, in a semblance of a shrug. "I wouldn't say I'm sad exactly," she said.

"Well," Austin pointed out, still settled back in that chair like he had all the time in the world, "you're not exactly kicking up your heels, either."

"Of course I'm happy. Libby is expecting. I'm going to be an aunt again."

An aunt. Again. But not a mother. Maybe *never* a mother.

"Actually," Austin observed, "I wouldn't put it past Tate and Libby to come across with a set of twins. Exhibit A—Audrey and Ava."

Paige laughed, even though there were tears stinging her eyes. She grabbed a paper napkin and swabbed up the spills.

"Hey," Austin said gruffly when she didn't speak.

She sniffled, straightened her shoulders and looked right at him. "I was hoping to get out of wearing that damn pink dress," she said, and then wondered at herself, because she hadn't intended to say that *at all.*

"It can't be that bad," Austin answered, smiling a little as he refilled Paige's wineglass—for maybe the third time since the meal began. "The pink dress, I mean."

"Easy for you to say," Paige retorted. "You don't have to wear it."

He laughed. "Now, that's a fact. Up until you said that, I figured the monkey suit I'll have to get into to do my best-man number was pretty much a fate worse than death. Now I know the experience would pale by comparison to flitting around in a dress—pink or otherwise."

The image his words brought to mind—Austin McKettrick *flitting* in any way—brought a giggle bubbling up from Paige's very core. She nearly choked on the sip of wine she'd just taken to steady her nerves.

In fact, Austin got worried and stood up to slap her back a couple of times.

A few hiccups came next, but Paige

finally managed to breathe normally again, and Austin sank back into his chair, looking relieved.

Paige's thoughts shifted naturally to Calvin. Although his asthma flare-ups were fairly rare, this was his reality—that panicked, desperate sensation of gasping for air. Her eyes stung again.

This time, Austin didn't speak. He simply pushed his chair back from the table a little way, took Paige by the hand and pulled her easily onto his lap.

She didn't resist—which probably meant she'd had a smidge too much wine. She laid her head on Austin's good shoulder and allowed herself to let go a little.

His neck smelled so good. Things began to stir inside her, to expand and melt.

Definitely too much wine.

"I couldn't stand it if anything happened to Calvin," she heard herself say. Where had *that* come from? Lots of people lived with asthma, and Calvin was healthy in every other way.

Austin's lips were warm at her temple. "Calvin will be fine," he said. He shifted beneath her, and she realized that he was dealing with the erection of the century.

Fire shot through her. And so did common sense. If she let things go any further, it would be a repeat of last time.

Or worse.

Paige pulled free and got to her feet. Straightened her clothes and splayed her fingers to fluff out her hair. Sucked in a deep breath and let it out with a whoosh.

Austin, breaking the McKettrick rule, did not stand up. He just sat there, watching her, looking amused. There was a sleepy ease in his blue eyes that said the game wasn't over.

"You're right," Paige said in businesslike tones, "Calvin *will* be fine."

Austin still didn't speak. He did reach out and trace the length of Paige's right forearm with the tip of one index finger.

Goose bumps rose on every part of her body, and there was more heating and spilling and spreading out inside her.

"Do you still want kids, Paige? Like

you did when we were—" He paused, swallowed. "Like you did?"

She retreated a step—a victory of sorts—but ducking into her bedroom and locking the door behind her would have been a better move, because this was dangerous emotional ground.

Austin wouldn't force her to do anything, she knew that. But then, she'd never been afraid of Austin. It was herself she feared, the desperate physical need he could so easily arouse in her.

"We don't have condoms," she blurted out, without planning to, and she was appalled at herself for saying such a thing.

"Yeah, we do," Austin replied, standing up. His hands came to rest, ever so lightly, on the sides of her waist. "I bought a box after lunch today, when we stopped to fill my prescription."

"Oh," Paige said.

He hooked a finger under her chin, lifted. "Yeah," he teased. "Oh."

"We can't, Austin."

"Why not?"

"We agreed not to, remember? Because we're going to be running into each other a lot over the next—oh, say, *fifty years?*"

"Seems to me we already crossed that particular line, Paige."

She looked up at him. "We didn't—"

But Austin laid a finger to her lips. "We *did,*" he said. "For all practical intents and purposes, *we had sex.*"

"I'm not having this argument with you again, Austin McKettrick," Paige said, substituting bravado for dignity and hoping to get away with it.

"Because we didn't 'go all the way'?" Austin asked, his voice husky, his breath tingly warm and wine-scented against her mouth. "Come on, Paige. We're not kids anymore, screwing in haylofts and fields and the backseats of cars. We're consenting adults."

"Is that what it was to you?" Paige shot back, desperate for something—*anything*—to throw between them as a barrier. "Screwing?"

The tactic didn't work. Austin kept her close, and rested his chin on the top of her head. She felt his heart beating, strong and steady, under her right palm.

"Let's take a swim," he surprised her by saying. "Like before."

"You shouldn't get your bandage wet," Paige said, and then wished the statement hadn't had the tone of a lecture.

"That's easy to remedy," he replied, tightening his embrace a little and kissing the place where his chin had been propped. "I'll take it off."

"You can't do that," Paige argued. "I'm serious, Austin. Your wound could become infected, or any number of other things could happen—"

He rocked her a little, ran his strong hands along the length of her back. Sort of settled her against him. "Shhh," he said. "I'll follow your orders, Nurse Remington. No swimming. No making love. But it's early and I've already had a few hours of shut-eye and I need something to do."

She had to laugh at his reasoning. "That's why you suggested having sex?" she asked, leaning back to look up at him. "Because you need something to do?"

Austin McKettrick didn't lack for audacity—or for much else. He ground his hips against hers, letting her know how much he wanted her.

His size, coupled with the hard heat of him, made Paige think of wild stallions out on the range, courting their mares. And her knees nearly buckled.

"I didn't suggest having *sex*," he told her, about to take her mouth now, teasing her with a couple of nibbling, ricochet kisses, making contact and then bouncing off. "I said 'making love,' Paige, and there's a big difference."

Paige felt as though she were drowning—and what a way to go.

By enormous effort, she stepped back out of Austin's arms. Emotionally, it was like bolting from a warm house to run naked through a snowstorm.

"I'm going out to the barn to look in on Molly," she announced in a shaky voice, dragging in deep breaths and letting them out as if she'd been running. "If you still 'need something to do,' you can come along."

"Gee, thanks," Austin drawled. "My horse, my barn. Nice of you to invite me."

Nice? Not hardly.

And not very smart, either.

The barn was pretty private at this time of day.

And they'd had sex—made love—*whatever*—in the hayloft of that barn, more times than Paige could count.

"You go by yourself," she said, waving him off.

"Not a chance," Austin answered. "It was your idea to pay Molly a visit, and a fine idea it is, too. We'll *both* go."

Paige sighed. Looking in on Molly *had* been her idea, and she wanted, even needed, to follow through. "Okay," she said. "But keep your hands to yourself, Austin. I mean it."

He grinned and held up both those hands, palms out, like some misguidedly jovial old-West bank teller facing an armed robber and expecting matters to turn out well for everybody. "Your low opinion of my character," he drawled, "wounds me deeply."

Paige pretended to put a finger down her throat, and that only amused him more.

They bickered all the way to the

kitchen, where they both donned jackets—his denim, hers nylon and way too
big because, of course, it wasn't hers
at all.

Shep stumped along happily behind
them, stopping once to lift his leg
against one of the posts supporting Esperanza's clothesline.

It was dark out by then, of course,
and Paige's courage faltered a little as
she remembered how Austin and the
dog had both been hurt, not fifty feet
from where they were walking right
now.

Austin must have sensed her trepida-
tion, because he slipped an arm around
her shoulder. "Don't worry," he told her
cheerfully, "Shep and I will keep you
safe. Besides, there's nobody around
anyhow."

"How can you be so sure?" Paige
asked with a little shiver.

Austin's grin flashed like bright
moonlight in the heavy twilight. "Because Shep would go ape-shit if there
was," he said.

"Oh," Paige said, looking down at

the dog with his hind leg bandaged, and feeling a little dubious.

They made it to the barn without being attacked by some snarling creature or shot at by a varmint of the two-legged variety.

Austin flipped on the lights and moved from stall gate to stall gate, greeting all the sleepy horses, one by one. Stroking their long faces, sometimes giving one of their ears a gentle tug.

Paige strode straight past him, headed for Molly.

Reaching the little mare's stall, she murmured a soft greeting and stepped inside.

Molly was already filling out. Her coat seemed shinier, her eyes brighter. Best of all, the marks left by the halter were healing beautifully.

Paige stroked the animal, found an old brush balanced on one of the boards framing the stall, and began, very gently, to groom her.

Molly snuffled happily and shook her head once, causing Paige to smile.

"How long since you've ridden a

horse?" Austin's question startled her a little; she had been too absorbed in brushing Molly down to notice his approach.

"A while, I guess," Paige said, as a lump formed in her throat.

The last time she'd been on a horse had been on this ranch, a decade before, when she and Austin were still together. Back then, she'd believed with all the naive innocence of a young girl's heart that he loved her, just as she loved him, and that one day, the Silver Spur would be her home, as well as his.

His voice, like his manner, was very quiet. "Come morning," he said, "I mean to saddle up and cover a little ground."

"Your back—" Paige began, but then she bit her lip.

"I'll be careful," he said.

"That will be the day," she scoffed, well aware that she was acting like some kind of fidgety, overprotective grandmother. The fact was, Austin, like both his brothers, had been riding since he was a toddler, first with his dad and then on his own. The fresh air, the freedom and the exercise, provided it wasn't too strenuous, would be good for him.

"I like the way you look, doing that," Austin said.

"Grooming a horse?"

He grinned. "It's ranch work, and you look right at home doing it."

"Don't get any bright ideas," Paige responded with a grin of her own. "I'm doing this because it feels good to Molly, not to impress you."

"Since when have you ever tried to impress me?" Austin asked good-naturedly.

Only every day that we were together, Paige thought. But what she actually said was, "You've got a point there. Now that you mention it, I was more interested in running you down with our neighbor's new golf cart."

Austin chuckled at the memory. Ran a hand through his hair.

He needed a shave and a change of clothes and despite all that, he was so damn sexy Paige almost couldn't stand it.

"This is nice, being out here with the horses," he said. "Just you and me."

"The horses are good company," Paige admitted, a little smile tilting up one side of her mouth as she finished grooming Molly and put the brush back where she'd found it.

That made him laugh. Again.

"Will you come with me?" he asked, blocking Paige's way as she left Molly's stall.

She looked up at him, and her heart raced. "Where?"

Austin raised both eyebrows and waggled them teasingly. "Horseback riding," he said. "In the morning."

"Oh," she said. Around this man, she was a regular conversational genius.

"One way or the other, I'm going for a ride," he told her. He'd bent his head toward hers, and she felt his breath whisper over her left ear. "Maybe you ought to come along, just to keep me out of trouble. That's what Tate and Garrett pay you for, isn't it?"

Something in his tone raised her hackles, though she wasn't sure what. "Keeping you out of trouble," she said, slipping past him and striding toward the door at a good clip, "is not part of my job description."

He caught up, walking beside her. "How about getting me *into* trouble, then?" he joked. "That sounds like a lot more fun."

"You get *yourself* into plenty of trouble, Austin McKettrick. You certainly don't need my help."

He moved in front of her, forcing her to stop or try to duck around him again.

She stopped.

"I'm leaving right after breakfast," Austin said. "Around six-thirty or so. If you want to come along, you're more than welcome. If you don't, I'll see you when I get back."

"Do you have anything else to say?" Paige asked coolly.

"Yes, ma'am," Austin replied. "I surely do. You and I are bound to bed down together for real, sooner rather than later. I figure it's inevitable. But you need to know that I won't press the matter—the *when* and the *where* of it all, that's up to you. You have my word on it."

"How about never?" Paige retorted, her tone sugary sweet.

Austin merely laughed. "You *know* it's going to happen," he said. "But you'll probably still be denying it when you're yelling my name, clawing at my back with all ten fingernails and rolling your eyes back in your head."

Seething inwardly, Paige managed to appear calm. Or, at least, she *hoped* she appeared calm. She set her hands on her hips and glared at him.

"You are one arrogant, pigheaded son-of-a—"

Austin's mouth quirked up in a grin that would have done the devil proud. "Watch it," he said. "My mama was a good woman."

Paige gave a strangled cry of pure frustration and stormed toward the open doorway of the barn. This time, he let her pass.

"That went well," Austin told Shep when the back door of the house slammed behind Paige.

Shep gave a sympathetic whimper.

Inside the vast and echoing kitchen,

Austin took a can of beer from the fridge and headed, out of habit, for the stairs leading up to his apartment.

His back was okay, but he felt a head-spinning dizziness when he started the climb, and he had to turn around. This did not bode well, he figured, for the horseback ride he planned on taking in the morning, but it would take more than a little light-headedness to keep him from going. He'd been immobilized, cooped up, for too long. He needed, even craved, the feel of a horse under him, hooves flying, gobbling up ground.

Austin put the beer back in the fridge and ran a glass of water instead. Reaching his room, he eased out of his jacket and dutifully swallowed the pills Paige had counted out neatly into a little plastic container with a box for each day of the week.

He hadn't seen one of those since before his granddad died, when Austin was seven.

Shep sank gratefully onto his blanket pile and yawned big.

Leaving the dog behind in the morning would be a wrench, but for Shep's own good, Austin meant to do exactly that.

He was thinking about all these things, and a few more, as he ambled into the bathroom, planning on taking a shower before bed.

He was too far in to go back when he realized that the water was already running in the shower stall, and the flesh-colored shadow behind the frosted glass door was Paige.

It wasn't as if he'd never seen a woman in a shower before.

Hell, if there was a woman in *his* shower, he was generally in there with her.

Until now, that is.

Until Paige.

He turned on one heel, hoping to sneak back out without her seeing him, but he hadn't even crossed the threshold before she gave a little shriek.

Poor old Shep, thinking there was an emergency only a crippled dog could handle, immediately bounded into the room.

"I'm sorry," Austin said, keeping his back to Paige.

Warm, beautiful, sweetly responsive, *naked* Paige.

Something, probably a wet wash-cloth, struck him mid-spine, with a soggy plop. His molars clamped together. In all his born days, he had never encountered such a prickly and impossible woman.

He walked away.

"I might have overreacted," Paige said, standing beside Austin's bed, twenty minutes after the shower incident. She was wearing both a nightgown *and* a bathrobe, and she still felt grossly underdressed.

Austin, sprawled on top of the covers in his jeans and his attitude and nothing else, didn't look up from the pages of his paperback Western.

"Ya think?" he asked tartly.

"You walked in on me, Austin. I was startled."

He touched the tip of his index finger to his tongue, turned the page. And he still didn't look at her. "Sorry about

that," he said, with an utter lack of conviction.

She flung her hands out from her
sides, let them fall again. "I tried," she
said. "The shower is all yours, Austin.
I'm going to bed."

"Good night," he said, and turned
another page.

Austin, Paige knew, had always
struggled with reading. Unless he was
channeling Evelyn Wood, he was faking
her out with all that page turning.

She grabbed the book out of his
hands.

"That," he said drily, "was not cool."

Paige sighed. "You're right," she
said, giving back the book. "It wasn't."

"What do you want me to say,
Paige? I walked in on you. I'm sorry. I
think I said so at the time."

"I didn't believe you," Paige said.

"That's obvious," he replied. "And it's
discouraging, too, considering that
we've known each other since kindergarten and I just made that big speech
out there in the barn. All about how it
would be *your choice* when we finally
make love."

Paige folded her arms. Old hurts sneaked up and ambushed her. "You've made other speeches in your time, Austin McKettrick," she said. And then she turned on one heel and started to walk away.

Only, Austin caught her by the back of her bathrobe and stopped her in her tracks. "Hold it," he said. "You don't get to make a remark like that and then just walk away, Nurse Remington."

She turned on him. "You said you loved me!" she cried, and then wished she had the courage to literally bite off her tongue.

Austin sat up, resting his back against the headboard of the antique bed. "I did love you, Paige," he said very quietly. "That's why I did what I did."

Paige's eyes stung fiercely, and her breath came in short, rapid gasps. "Liar!"

"We were kids, Paige," he said. "Things were moving way too fast. We were eighteen and headed hell-bent for a lot of stuff we couldn't possibly have handled. I'd do things differently now, but at the time, I swear to God I didn't know any other way to save either one of us. But I'm sorry I hurt you, really and truly I am."

The ache that rose within Paige in that moment threatened to split her heart wide open. She couldn't speak, and that was probably a good thing, because anything she said would have been even more painful to hear than it was to say.

She left the room, and Austin let her go.

In Calvin's old room, she threw back the covers, laid herself down and curled into a fetal position.

A whimper behind her made her turn, and there was Shep, with his muzzle resting on the side of the mattress and his eyes luminous with sympathy in the dim moonlight coming in through the window.

That did it. Paige began to cry. In earnest. She rolled over, patting Shep's smooth head, and sobbed.

He waited, that sweet dog, for the storm to pass. Didn't move, didn't make a sound.

After a few minutes of hard grieving for things that might have been and never would be, Paige began to recover some of her composure. She continued to stroke the dog's head, and he kept his vigil, too. He didn't move even once. Just stood there, with his furry chin resting on the bottom sheet and his eyes shining with the hang-in-there kind of love he probably knew a great deal about.

"Thanks," Paige said, when the worst of the weeping storm was over.

Shep whined once, low in his throat, and then he turned and limped out of the room, no doubt returning to his master's side.

After a very, very long time, Paige slept.

"Wake up."

The voice was Austin's.

Paige struggled toward the surface of a dream. "Wh-what?"

"It's six-fifteen," Austin said. "Breakfast is ready."

"B-breakfast?" Paige blinked her eyes rapidly. Sat up. "Austin, what—?"

Then she remembered. The horse-back ride.

She sank back into her pillows and pulled the blankets up over her head.

Austin only chuckled. "Go or stay," he told her, and she knew by the sound of his voice that he was walking away. "That's up to you. You have fifteen min-utes, at the outside, and then I'm gone."

Paige moaned.

He laughed and she listened to the sound of his boot heels grow fainter and then fainter still.

The aroma of fresh coffee reached her, even through the fabric of the bed clothes.

She tried hard—maybe *too* hard—to go back to sleep.

But waking life intruded. Paige re-membered how it felt to ride a horse through a crisp autumn morning.

She also remembered that, techni-cally, she was Austin's nurse.

There would be no persuading the damn fool to stay home, but what if he was out there all alone and he had a back spasm, or even got thrown from the saddle and reinjured his shoulder?

What if whoever had shot him before tried again?

Sputtering a swear word, Paige flung back the covers and sat up. Ran both hands through her hair and dragged in a deep breath.

After that, she took a very quick shower, dressed warmly in heavy jeans and a wool sweater. She didn't own a pair of boots, so her sneakers would have to do for footwear.

When she reached the kitchen, Austin was still there, rinsing his plate and placing it neatly into the dish-washer, along with the silverware he'd used. He'd brought Shep's blanket-pile bed out and set it down in front of the unlit fireplace, and the dog looked set-tled there, as though he'd accepted that, this time, he'd have to stay home.

With a twitch of a grin, Austin looked Paige over and then nodded his head in the direction of the middle staircase.

A pair of brown boots waited there, well-worn but still sturdy, along with two pairs of wool socks, wound up into balls.

"Those were my mom's," Austin explained. "I think they might be a little big for you, but the extra socks should help."

A complicated emotion rose inside Paige, and she didn't even *try* to give it a name. It was too damn early and she hadn't even had coffee yet.

She walked over, sat down heavily on the step, kicked off her sneakers and the footies she'd worn beneath them, and donned both pairs of wool socks, then the boots. She stood, walked around a little. The fit was perfect.

The complicated emotion swelled again, then ebbed and faded as Austin held out a cup of hot coffee.

She accepted the cup, took a cautious sip.

Her eyebrows rose. "Did you make this?"

Austin laughed. "Yeah," he replied. "I have other talents as well."

"I think it would be better," Paige allowed, after more coffee, "if we didn't discuss your talents."

"Your loss." He grinned, gesturing toward the table. "Sit down. You need to eat before we go."

Paige shook one foot and then the other, getting used to the boots. "I'm not hungry," she said.

"Too bad," Austin replied. He dished up some scrambled eggs, took two thick slices of buttered toast out of the oven and set them on top, and put the whole works on the table. "Eat."

Paige sighed, but she washed and dried her hands at the sink, she sat down and she ate.

The surprises just kept on coming: it turned out that Austin was a halfway decent cook.

CHAPTER FOURTEEN

Austin crouched in front of Shep's dog bed in the kitchen and flopped the critter's ears around a little with a light pass of his hand. "You stay here and guard the house," he told the animal solemnly. "We'll be back in a couple of hours."

Standing in the middle of the room, bundled up and wearing Sally McKettrick's boots, Paige felt an odd little pinch in her heart. It was hard to believe this tough yet tender man was the same person who'd betrayed her in such a cavalier way ten years ago.

Words he'd said the night before replayed in her head.

I didn't know any other way to save either one of us.

Paige bit her lower lip, watched carefully as he straightened, looking for the smallest sign that he wasn't up to riding horseback. She saw nothing in Austin but calm confidence, a man at home in himself, no matter what was going on in the outside world.

Shep didn't make a sound, nor did he try to rise from his resting place.

Paige and Austin exchanged glances as he passed her, but neither one spoke. She followed him outside, into the first pinkish-purple shimmer of a new day, felt revitalized by the snapping chill in the air.

Up ahead, the barn glowed with light, and Paige could hear the horses stirring inside, snuffling, whinnying and nickering as they greeted each other.

Two horses stood in the breezeway, a pinto gelding and a bay mare, both saddled. Garrett smiled at Paige, held the bay still and used his free hand to steady the stirrup. He was wearing jeans and an old faded shirt and the kind of boots country people call "shit-kickers."

"Mornin'," he said.

"Morning," Paige replied. Then she

nodded, grabbed hold of the saddle horn and stuck her foot into the stirrup, silently praying that she wouldn't make a fool of herself by not landing smoothly in the saddle.

She succeeded on the first try, though, much to her relief, and looked over to see that Austin was already astride the gelding, the reins resting easy in his left hand as he adjusted his hat with his right.

"Obliged," he told Garrett, who must have saddled the horses.

Garrett gave a semisalute and asked Austin, "You got your cell phone?"

Austin chuckled and shook his head. "Now, it just ain't cowboy," he joked, "asking a question like that."

"Somebody tried to kill you a while back," Garrett responded easily. *"Have you got your cell phone, Austin?"*

Austin reached into the breast pocket of his denim jacket, pulled out a slim phone, held it by two fingers for Garrett to see.

Garrett sighed. "Get out of here," he said.

Austin ducked as he rode through

the doorway of the barn, even though there was no danger of bumping his head.

Paige rode behind him, feeling anxious—it had been a long, *long* time since she'd been in the saddle—but exhilarated, too. She'd missed riding, missed the unique company of horses.

Out in the barnyard, she leaned forward until the saddle horn pressed into her stomach, closed her eyes and breathed in the familiar smell of the animal's hide.

When she straightened and opened her eyes again, smiling, she saw that Austin had stopped the gelding, turned sideways to watch her. His expression was cryptic, partly because the brim of his hat cast a thin shadow over his features. He reined his horse toward the lower road that ran along the inside of the fence line, letting his mount walk.

Birds were beginning to sing, and Paige could hear the creek flowing in the near distance. It struck her that it was possible to be perfectly happy, not all the time, of course, but in these golden moments that arrived only at their own bidding.

The bay mare—one of those horses that are not content to follow—picked up speed, bent on closing the gap of a dozen yards or so between her and the gelding.

Paige bounced a lot for the first few seconds, then found her stride, bracing her feet in the stirrups, not quite standing, but rising into the rhythm of the animal's movements.

Once alongside Austin and the gelding, the mare was happy.

Austin gave Paige a sidelong grin and adjusted his hat again.

"What's her name?" Paige asked, referring to the mare she was riding.

Austin flashed her a grin that made things quicken inside her. "Betty," he said. "She's pretty tame, but she does like to keep up with the herd."

Paige laughed and patted the mare's neck. "Betty," she repeated. "I'm not sure I've ever met a horse by that name before."

"Audrey and Ava named her," Austin answered. He was quiet for a while, turning his head to scan the rolling land in front of them. Then he cleared his throat and said, "I'm glad you came along, Paige."

She knew he wanted to nudge the gelding to a trot and then a gallop and then a run—she could actually feel his restraint in her own body—but he continued at an easy walk. Probably, Paige figured, the restraint was for her sake.

"Me, too," she said, and the words came out sounding odd and a little squeaky.

They rode alongside the creek for a while, and then Austin pointed toward the bank on the opposite side of the road.

"Ready to climb?" he asked.

Paige nodded, leaning forward in the saddle so she wouldn't slide right off Betty's back when she followed the gelding's lead up the side hill. At the top, the land leveled out, and the sight of all that sky and grass and wide-open space snagged Paige's breath in the back of her throat.

They didn't talk, but it struck Paige that talking wasn't necessary anyhow.

They were a man and a woman riding two good horses over home ground, and that was communication enough.

When the old mining camp, with its Quonset huts and dry riverbed, came into view, Paige felt a vague prickle of alarm. She stood in the stirrups to stretch her legs and silently scolded herself for being silly. Still, even in the first fresh light of morning, the place was spooky.

Austin seemed to sense her reluctance, and he glanced back at her with a question in his eyes. Stopped the gelding and then loosened his hold on the reins to let the animal graze for a few moments.

Paige did the same. And a shiver moved down her spine. Knowing Austin had seen, she said, "Do you believe in ghosts?"

Austin took off his hat, held it for a while, leaning forward in the saddle a little way. His grin held both mischief and lively interest. "Nope," he said. "Do you?"

She smiled. Shook her head. "No," she said, looking around, taking in the lonely desolation of that once-lively patch of ground. When the mines were running, long before her and Austin's time, there had been a town on this site. Even a schoolhouse and a church. "But I do believe in energy. I think it can linger in a place, especially after something important happens."

Austin straightened, put his hat back on. "Back when we were kids," he said, "Garrett and Tate and I, along with some of our friends, used to camp out here. Pretend we were old-time cowpokes—sometimes outlaws—either driving a herd north into Montana or fixing to steal it."

This brief insight into Austin's boyhood felt sacred to Paige, even as it made her smile. She sensed there was more and held her tongue, not wanting to stem the conversational tide.

"Once the campfire went out," Austin went on presently, "and everybody else had gone to sleep, I used to lie there in my bedroll and just listen to things. A time or two, I would have sworn I heard that river flowing, even smelled the water, but it's probably been dry for ten thousand years."

Paige smiled. Here was another perfect moment, and she meant to savor it.

Austin chuckled hoarsely. "There were some other things, but Tate and Garrett were behind the more creative stuff. Back in those days, they liked to scare me."

"Did they succeed?"

He turned his head, grinning, and his eyes were the same color as his denim jean jacket. "A couple of times," he admitted. "But mostly, I just went along with the game. Fact is, I knew something they didn't."

Paige raised one eyebrow, waited.

The grin intensified to the kind of high wattage that can short-circuit female wiring. "Dad—or Pablo Ruiz— used to camp out somewhere close by, out of sight, to make sure we were safe."

Sadness touched Paige's heart lightly, like a soft breeze. They were both gone now, Jim McKettrick and his long-time ranch foreman, Pablo Ruiz. And so was her father.

The world, for all its compensations, wasn't the same place without those three men, and it never would be.

Austin rode close, then stopped, so that their horses were side by side, with his facing in one direction and hers in the other. He reached out and cupped her chin with one hand, brushed a lock of windblown hair back from her cheek with his thumb.

"I'd really like to kiss you right about now," he said.

Even as Paige's better judgment entered a silent protest, something took wing inside her, and soared.

"I think I'd really like to *be* kissed right about now," she responded.

With a slight grin, Austin leaned in, touched his mouth to hers. He smelled of good grass and sunshine and wide-open spaces, and the kiss . . .

Well, *the kiss.*

It rocked Paige so thoroughly that she clung to the back of Austin's jacket with her free hand—the other was clasping the saddle horn for dear life—

sure she'd tumble right off the horse if she didn't hold on.

Austin chuckled, the sound low and gruff, as he drew back. "I guess we'd better get moving again," he told her. "Because if we don't, I might wind up doing my damnedest to seduce you, and that would be breaking my word."

Paige struggled just to breathe. As for the concept of Austin breaking his word, well, it was probably better that she didn't now possess the necessary lung power to say anything at all, right at that moment.

Don't talk to me about breaking your word, Austin McKettrick, cried the silent but powerful voice of her anger and her pain and her pride. *You promised to love me forever.*

With the grace and ease of the lifelong horseman he was, Austin turned the gelding and started him in the direction of the dry riverbed.

Paige would have liked a few moments to recover her composure, but she didn't get them. The mare, Betty, not to be left behind, bolted after

Austin's gelding and nearly unseated her.

She had barely regained her balance when the animal did a *Man from Snowy River* down the steep, rocky bank, pitched her headlong into a midair somersault that seemed to last forever and barely missed trampling her.

Paige lay flat on her back, the breath knocked out of her, dazed.

Austin was off the gelding and crouching beside her in what seemed like an instant. "Don't try to move, okay?" he said quietly. "Just lie still."

Don't try to move.

The injunction struck Paige as funny. She wanted to laugh, to tell Austin he could quit looking so worried, because she was okay. But what came out of her mouth was a barely audible, "Is Betty all right?"

Austin was pale behind his cowboy tan, and his blue eyes also revealed his worry, but his mouth crooked up at one corner. "The horse is fine," he told her. "Do you hurt anywhere?"

Paige took a thoughtful inventory of her body, starting at the back of her head, which was beginning to throb a little, and scanning down her neck, her spine, across her shoulders, over her stomach and her hips and her pelvis, then both thighs and both knees.

She didn't run into trouble until she got to her right ankle.

"Owwww," she moaned.

Austin practically blanched. "What?"

She answered by sitting up, bending her right knee, and grasping at her ankle. "It's—probably—just a sprain," she told him, "but it hurts like holy-be—ya-hoo."

Austin helped her up, and she leaned against him, keeping the injured foot off the ground.

"Help me get back on the horse," Paige said.

He gave a raspy guffaw at that, and there was no humor in it. "Hell, no," Austin replied, flashing his cell phone. "I'm calling an ambulance."

Tears of frustration and pain stung the lining of her sinuses and the spaces behind her eyes. "Don't be silly," she said. "I don't *need* an ambulance."

"This is all my fault," Austin muttered.

Paige tried again. "No," she said. "It's nobody's fault, Austin. Please, just help me get back on Betty so we can go back to the house—"

Austin hooked his arm around her waist, clasping her against his side, and, with his free hand, fumbled in his coat pocket for the fancy cell phone. A moment later, he barked, "Garrett? We're out at the old mining camp and we need help."

Paige closed her eyes against a wave of pain-related nausea.

"No, it's Paige," Austin went on. "I think she's busted her ankle."

"It's only a sprain," Paige insisted.

"Yeah," Austin said in reply to whatever *Garrett* had said. All Paige could make out was the thrum of a masculine voice on the other end. "Somebody will need to bring the horses back home." Another pause. "Yeah. Thanks."

"Let's see if we can make it over to that fallen log over there," Austin told Paige, after he'd dropped the cell phone back into his pocket. "You ought to sit down."

"There might be snakes—or bugs—" Paige fretted, hopping along beside Austin.

He chuckled. "Snakes might be a concern," he allowed, "but I can't see why somebody ready to ride five miles with a bum foot would worry about a few ants and spiders."

The landscape tilted a couple of times before she and Austin reached the log. After feeling around for a solid place, he sat her down, leaning over her and taking a firm grasp on her shoulders when she wavered.

That was when she realized he was wearing a shoulder holster under his jacket. No wonder he wasn't worried about snakes—he was packing heat.

"Is that a gun?" she asked. It was a stupid question, she realized as soon as the words were out of her mouth.

Austin laughed. "No, ma'am," he lied. "I'm just glad to see you."

"Ha-ha," Paige said, but she couldn't help smiling.

He sat down beside her. Dear God, it

felt good having that strong arm of his around her.

"You're sure the horse isn't hurt?" she asked, rocking slightly because the pain was beginning to say "fracture," not "sprain."

"I'm sure the horse isn't hurt," Austin assured her, his voice both gruff and, at the same time, tender. He rested the side of his head against the top of hers. "Paige," he said, "I'm so sorry."

"It was an *accident,*" she said, almost whimpering the words. If the pain didn't let up soon, she was probably going to barf all over the man. Talk about making an impression.

He didn't answer. He just sat there, holding her until Garrett showed up, having raced overland in a ranch truck, hauling two cowboys along with him.

All three men—Paige noticed uneasily that one of them was the man she knew only as Reese—came skid-heeling it down the bank in their rough boots, sending pebbles rolling and dust flying.

Reese and the other cowboy cast a

few curious glances in Paige's direction, then silently mounted the gelding and the mare and started back toward home.

Garrett crouched in front of Paige, looking up at her, scanning her face with those McKettrick-blue eyes of his. A worried grin kicked up the corner of his mouth and indented a dimple in his cheek.

"We'll get you to the clinic in town," Garrett said gently, and very slowly, because she was having trouble tracking the simplest things. "They'll patch you up, and you'll be good as new."

Paige bit her lower lip again and nodded. *Please God,* she prayed silently, *don't let me throw up.*

Garrett straightened and, after a brief glance at Austin, bent to scoop Paige up into his arms.

Inside the truck, she sat on Austin's lap. By now, the prayer had become a litany.

Don't let me throw up. Please, *don't let me throw up.*

By the time they arrived at the clinic in Blue River—Dr. Colwin and two of the nurses met them in the lobby—the ache in Paige's ankle was pounding in time with her heartbeat, like a giant toothache.

"Do something," she heard Austin bark, probably addressing the doctor. "She's in pain!"

"Easy, Austin," Garrett said.

There was some jostling—which hurt plenty—and then the prick of a needle in the fleshy part of her arm.

Surely she hadn't been given an injection through the thick fabric of the nylon jacket she was wearing. When had they removed her jacket?

Goose bumps raced up her arms. Yep, definitely bare skin.

Paige grappled with her situation for a few moments, as if trying to fight her way out of a bad dream. When clarity returned, she realized she was lying on an icy table in the X-ray room.

"Is it broken?" she asked.

"Probably," Dr. Colwin replied calmly, one medical professional addressing another. "Are the pain meds taking effect yet?"

Paige had to take another inventory,

and it was a surprisingly slow process. "I think so," she said.

She closed her eyes, just to rest the lids, and when she opened them again, she was in another, warmer place. *Mostly* warmer, anyhow.

Someone was tucking a heated blanket around her.

Bliss.

"Some people," a familiar female voice said, "will do anything to get out of wearing a perfectly suitable bridesmaid's gown."

Julie's face came into focus.

"What are you doing here?" Paige asked.

Julie chuckled, smoothed Paige's hair back from her forehead. "Well," she said, "it seems my baby sister took a header off a horse. How do you feel, honey?"

Paige sighed, grateful for the blanket. "Stupid," she said. "I feel really, really *stupid.*"

"You're not stupid," Julie informed her. Her tone was sunny, so Paige figured she probably wasn't dying, or crippled for life. Even if her sister *had* left work in the middle of the day, which was a drastic step on Julie's part.

Paige raised herself up a little, but she couldn't see her feet.

"Did they amputate?" she asked.

Of course she was joking. Almost entirely.

"No," Julie said. "As soon as the swelling goes down enough, you'll have a cast."

A belated shiver rattled its way up Paige's frame. "Cold," she complained. "Julie, I'm so *cold.*"

"That would be the ice packs around your ankle," Julie told her. Then she piled on another heated blanket, tucked it in around Paige. "You could have broken your neck, you know." Tears sprang to Julie's eyes, and she sniffled. "Thank God you're all right, sis."

The swelling took its time going down. By the time Paige's ankle had been set, she was already sick of being a patient.

Dr. Colwin—or Joe, as he'd asked her to call him while he was attending to her ankle—seemed amused by her testy mood.

Julie had left by then, but Libby had taken her place.

Paige secretly wondered if Austin was around. Probably not, she decided. It was getting dark out, and they'd set out on their fateful horseback ride early in the morning. Conclusion: she'd been at the clinic for hours.

But when Joe Colwin finally said Paige could leave, and Libby wheeled her out into the reception area in a wheelchair, her gigantic fiberglass-encased foot sticking straight out, Austin was there.

He looked tired and he needed a shave and Paige could have kissed him for waiting; though, of course, she didn't.

"There'll be some pain," Joe warned, "once the shots wear off." He held out a written prescription, and Libby took it. "You'll want to have this filled before you head home. And I'd like to see Paige again in a couple of days."

Paige nodded.

Garrett came through the front entrance; Paige could see his big extended-cab truck through the glass doors. He shook hands with Joe and landed a brotherly kiss on Paige's forehead.

A few moments later, he was lifting Paige out of the wheelchair and into the backseat of the truck, while Libby fussed and flitted around, urging him to be careful.

Austin climbed in beside Paige, fastened her seat belt for her—a tricky undertaking, as it turned out; she was sitting at an odd angle, in order to accommodate the bulky cast.

Garrett helped Libby into the passenger seat, then went around to climb behind the wheel. When they stopped to fill the prescription, Austin waited with Paige while Garrett and Libby hurried inside the drugstore.

"Looks like it's *my* turn to take care of *you*," Austin said when he and Paige were alone.

A light, drizzly rain began to fall, forming little beads of moisture on the windshield. The droplets took on the hazy red of the drugstore's neon sign.

Paige sighed. "Hardly," she said. "I can take care of myself."

Austin arched one eyebrow. Rubbed a hand over his beard-bristled chin. "Don't be so damn stubborn," he said, and while his voice sounded like so many rusted bolts rolling around in the bottom of a bucket, there was a thread of amusement running through it, too.

Inexplicably, the tears returned. Not that she let them fall. She had *that much* pride left, anyway. "I'm not being stubborn," she said.

"Just cranky as hell," Austin teased. "That's okay, though. You have cause to be a little on the cantankerous side."

"Gee," Paige said, widening her wet eyes at him. "Thanks."

He laughed, but it was a weary sound. Then he shook his head. "You're welcome," he said.

Garrett and Libby came back to the truck. They'd filled the prescription and Libby had a stack of magazines and a couple of paperback books.

"You're going to be laid up for a while," she told Paige.

Paige rolled her eyes. She had no intention of being "laid up." Joe Colwin had given her a pair of crutches before they left the clinic, and she planned to be getting around on them ASAP.

The windshield wipers made a *swipe-swipe-swipe* sound as they drove toward the Silver Spur, and all of them kept their thoughts to themselves.

Back at the ranch house, the windows glowed with golden light, and dogs and kids rushed to greet Paige when Garrett carried her inside.

"Can I sign your cast, Aunt Paige?" Calvin immediately asked.

"Can we sign it, too?" Ava wanted to know.

"Calvin goes first," Audrey declared.

Julie had a nice fire going on the big hearth, and she'd cushioned the rocking chair with several timeworn quilts, faded and soft. "Later," she told the children.

At a nod from Libby, Garrett set Paige gently in the rocking chair.

She felt a little leap of gratitude, despite the problems she knew a broken ankle would inevitably present in the days and weeks ahead, because she wasn't alone. She was in a warm, fragrant kitchen, with a family around her, and a fire crackling in the grate.

Shep made his way over and rested his muzzle on her thigh, looking up at her as if to say he knew how she felt, with one foot wrapped up tight, compromising her mobility.

Touched, Paige laid a hand on the dog's head. When the time came to leave the Silver Spur and get on with her life, she was going to miss Shep something terrible.

"Dad's making spaghetti," Ava told Paige, inching up to her side and peering into her face. "It's his specialty. Do you like spaghetti?"

"I love spaghetti," Paige answered, smiling at the little girl and still stroking Shep's head. She was aware of Austin in every cell of her body, but she made it a point not to look for him.

Ava's eyes—as blue as those of her father and uncles—were solemn behind the lenses of her glasses. "Does your foot hurt?" she asked.

"Not right now," Paige answered gently.

Calvin, after scrounging through several drawers, approached with a marker. "Can I write my name on your leg now?" he asked, beaming.

Paige laughed. "Sure," she said.

Shep gave a little dog sigh and turned to trundle away. He curled up on his blanket pile in front of the fire and settled down to warm his bones.

Calvin concentrated hard as he printed his first name on Paige's cast, taking great care with each letter.

After he was done, Ava signed, then Audrey.

The kitchen was a busy place for the next hour or so. By the time Paige had eaten as much of Tate's spaghetti as she could manage and then taken a dose of pain medication, she was ready for the day to be over.

Libby contributed a warm flannel nightgown from her stash upstairs, and she and Julie helped Paige get ready for bed.

Each of them bracing her up by putting a shoulder under one arm, they walked her to the room she'd slept in originally.

Someone had changed the sheets, made the bed up crisply and turned back the covers. A bouquet of pink roses stood on the bureau top, artfully arranged.

The sight of it all choked Paige up a little.

Like her sisters, she prided herself on her independence, but that night, it was lovely to have some TLC.

Of course, she would have to sleep with her casted foot outside the covers, and the thought of going to and from the bathroom during the night was a little daunting, but Paige refused to whine, even to herself.

The crutches leaned against the wall, between the mattress and the bedside table, within easy reach.

Libby made sure her pills were handy, too, along with a bottle of water.

Tired as she was, Paige had a hard time settling down, and when she finally did sleep, she dreamed she was pitching off over the mare's head again, landing hard on the dirt of the riverbed.

Startled, she woke with a gasp, flailing her arms in a vain attempt to break the fall.

The room was dark, except for the shaft of thin moonlight slanting in through the window. It revealed Austin, sitting in the quilt-lined rocking chair that usually lived in the kitchen.

"You hurting?" he asked in a raspy, waking-up voice.

"No," Paige said. Her throat went so tight, she figured she wouldn't be able to swallow if she tried.

"Bad dream?"

She nodded, though she wasn't sure he could see her. In fact, she hoped he couldn't, because she had tears in her eyes. Again.

What was up with all this *crying?* She—practical, sensible Paige Remington—seemed to be wearing her heart on her sleeve these days.

"You know how it is," she croaked, trying to sound normal, "when you're asleep and it feels like you're falling and you have to catch yourself . . . ?"

"Yep," he said. "You need anything, Paige?"

She had to pee like the proverbial racehorse, she suddenly realized, but she'd be damned if she'd let Austin McKettrick, of all people, steer her into the bathroom and wait while she tinkled away.

"I wouldn't mind a cup of tea," she said, not because she needed tea in the middle of the night, but because she wanted him to leave so she could grab the crutches and hop to the toilet.

Austin unfolded himself from the rocking chair in stages, it seemed to Paige, making that lusty, stretching sound as he raised his arms over his head. He switched on the bedside lamp after that, and Paige saw, without surprise, that Shep was in the room, too, curled up on the hooked rug in front of the big, antique bureau.

The bulb cast a kerosene lanternlike glow over the room, and Paige had the strange sensation that she and Austin and the dog might have been transported back in time, somehow. Back to a night when the Silver Spur ranch house was much smaller, and new.

"I'll be right back with that tea," Austin said.

Paige nodded.

As soon as he was gone, she scrambled out of bed, reached for the crutches and stood up.

Turned out, using crutches was harder than it looked. She swayed a little, barely caught herself before she would have landed on the floor in a heap. Determination carried the day—or the night—however, and she made it into the bathroom, then returned minutes later to find Austin standing in the middle of the room, waiting for her. His arms were folded and he was grinning.

With a shake of his head, he took her arm and helped her back into bed. Handed her the steaming cup of tea waiting on the nightstand.

"You can go now," Paige told him, after taking a sip from the cup. "I'll be fine."

Austin kicked off one boot, then the other.

"I'm not going anywhere," he informed her.

And then he went around to the other side of the bed and stretched right out on top of the covers as though he meant to stay put.

CHAPTER FIFTEEN

Austin supposed he should have been a mite more grateful than he actually was when Joe Colwin, M.D., stopped by the ranch bright and early the next morning and announced that he'd come to look in on Paige.

"Libby—that's Paige's sister—is in there with her right now," Austin said, stepping back so the doc could come into the house.

"How's the shoulder?" Colwin asked.

The shoulder, as it happened, was a little on the sore side, since Austin had ditched the bandage and stopped taking his pain meds because they made him feel a bit woozy. "It's okay," he said. He gestured toward the table. "If you're not in a hurry, you might just as well sit down and have a cup of coffee."

Colwin nodded. "Thanks," he said, taking a seat on one of the benches. There was an earnest look in the doctor's eyes as he watched Austin fill the coffee mug and bring it to the table.

"Need anything to put in that coffee?" Austin asked, folding his arms.

Colwin shook his head. "Black's fine," he replied.

Austin hauled back the chair at the head of the table and sat down. "You're not from Texas," he remarked thoughtfully, and then felt stupid for saying it out loud.

Colwin's grin was a little wan. "No," he said. "I'm originally from Indiana." He took a sip of his coffee and set the cup down with care. He cleared his throat then, and focused the kind of straightforward look on Austin that commanded respect. "You and Paige . . . ?"

Austin sighed. Rested his forearms on the tabletop and interlaced his fingers loosely. "You're going to have to ask Paige about that," he said very calmly, though a part of him wanted to warn the man off, grab him by the shirtfront and shake his teeth loose from his gums.

"You probably ought to have some physical therapy for the shoulder," Colwin said after a short, uncomfortable silence.

"I'll keep that in mind," Austin answered.

Libby came into the kitchen then, and she smiled when she saw the doctor.

Austin stood, and so did Colwin.

"Hi, Joe," Libby said warmly. Her gaze scooted to Austin, bounced back to Colwin. "I hope you're here to see Paige. For a nurse, she's having a hard time accepting that she can't just go on as if she didn't get thrown from that horse."

Colwin smiled. "Doctors and nurses usually don't make the best patients," he replied. "We're used to taking care of people, not the other way around."

Austin felt a flick of sorrow at the back of his heart, reminded that Paige and Joe Colwin had a profession in common. Some people would even say a calling.

Libby showed the doctor to Paige's room, and Austin, needing to be busy, picked up the fireplace poker and took a few jabs at the chunks of wood in the grate, causing sparks to fly.

Shep, never very far away, got up off his blanket pile and put some distance between himself and the blaze, contained though it was.

Libby's voice startled Austin because he hadn't heard her come back into the room.

"Cheer up," his future sister-in-law said gently. "Paige will be all right."

Austin put the poker back into the rack and shut the glass doors on the fireplace before he answered. Even then, he wasn't ready to turn around to face her.

"I couldn't carry her," he said. "After she was hurt, I mean. I needed Garrett to do that."

Libby rested a hand on his shoulder. "It's not wrong to need other people's help sometimes, Austin," she said. "Especially your *brother's* help."

He faced her then. Swallowed hard. "If I hadn't persuaded Paige to go along on that horseback ride—"

"Stop," Libby interrupted, her eyes kind as she studied his face. "Things like this happen, Austin. Nobody knows why. Maybe there *isn't* a reason, even. But I can tell you this much—Paige is already talking about getting back on a horse. She'd climb back in the saddle today, if we let her."

Austin gave a confounded chuckle. There was so much about Paige that amazed him, and this was just the latest in a long line of small mysteries he wanted to solve.

"You're not serious," he said.

Libby grinned, nodded. "Of *course* I am," she replied. "My little sister is worried that she'll be too scared to ride again if she waits too long."

Austin shook his head, looked past Libby's shoulder, toward the entrance to the guest apartments. He wished he could be in there with Paige and the doctor, without coming off as some jealous idiot.

It wasn't as if the two of them would

be getting it on or anything like that, but there were much more subtle ways for a man and woman to connect—a look, a touch of the hand, a shared laugh.

"*Relax,*" Libby said, gripping Austin by the shoulders now.

He sighed, thrust a hand through his hair. "I'm trying," he said. "Trust me, Lib, I'm doing my best here."

She smiled. "You look like a man who could use some breakfast," she said, and moved away to cross the room, open one of the refrigerators, poke around inside for a dozen eggs, green onions and a block of cheese. "Sit down, Austin."

He sat, feeling more like some old codger than a man who hadn't even seen thirty yet. Sleeping beside Paige the night before, fully dressed except for his boots, and on top of the covers, too, had left him sore all over and feeling as though he hadn't rested at all.

"So," he said, making sure Libby had her back to him before stealing another glance at the doorway to the guest apartment. He frowned, because as far as he was concerned, Joe Colwin had been in there plenty long enough. What was he doing, anyhow? Putting a whole new cast on Paige's ankle?

"So," Libby repeated, chopping green onions now.

Austin took a sip of his coffee, left behind on the table, and found it cold. Shoved it away.

"Paige," he said, "would probably be happy with a doctor."

Libby turned her head quickly, so that her glossy light-brown hair flew around her shoulders, and a bubbly laugh escaped her. "Austin McKettrick," she said, "what was *that* supposed to mean?"

Austin hadn't meant to say what he had, hadn't even run the words through his head first to get an idea of how they might sound. He felt heat climb his neck, throb under his jawbones, cinch his throat up tight.

He looked toward the fire because he was too embarrassed to meet Libby's gaze. "Damned if I know," he muttered.

Libby laughed again, went right on chopping stuff over there at the

counter. But she didn't pursue the matter, and for that, Austin was profoundly
grateful.

By his reckoning, he'd made enough
of a fool of himself for one day.

Dr. Colwin finally emerged from
Paige's bedroom while Libby was still
sautéing onions for the omelet she had
under construction. She invited the doc
to stay and join them for the meal, but
after a glance at Austin, Colwin shook
his head, thanked Libby and said he
had to be getting to work.

Maybe next time, he said.

If Austin had his way, there wouldn't
be a next time.

Okay, it was crazy, because he didn't
have any kind of claim on Paige Remington, and even if he had, he wouldn't
have been within his rights to insist that
she find herself another doctor.

An old one, maybe. Or a woman.

But for all that, he felt edgy as hell
until Colwin had left.

Paige poked at the channel changer on
the remote control for the small TV Tate
had set up for her that morning before

heading out with Garrett, to ride the range, or whatever it was they did out there.

There was *nothing* on. Five hundred channels, and nothing to watch. How screwed up was that?

"Hey," Austin said with a tired grin. He stood in the doorway, holding a plate in each hand. "Lib built an omelet. I brought you some."

Paige narrowed her eyes. Gave up on television, maybe forever, by hitting the off button and tossing the remote to the foot of the bed. "I'm not hungry," she said.

"You've got to eat," Austin told her reasonably, moseying over to hand her the plate and three pieces of silverware all wrapped up in a cloth napkin, "if you want to be strong enough to ride Betty and stay in the saddle."

She looked down at the food for a long time, not wanting Austin to see that there were tears standing in her eyes.

"You're enjoying this," she said miserably.

He settled himself in the rocking

chair, with its quilts for cushioning. "Nope," he said. "I don't like seeing you or anybody else in pain."

Something in his voice made her look up, forgetting that she'd wanted to hide her tears. This whole crying-for-no-reason thing was *really* getting out of hand. "That isn't what I meant," she said truthfully, but in a barely audible voice. "I was hired to be *your* nurse. And here you are, bringing me food, keeping me company even though I'm beyond crabby—"

Austin chuckled, but there was something broken in the sound. "It's called being a friend, Nurse Remington."

She took a bite of Libby's omelet and realized she *was* hungry, after all. "I hate this," she said.

"The omelet?" Austin asked, raising one eyebrow. He knew damn well she wasn't talking about the food—she could see the knowledge in his eyes.

"Being an invalid," she said, perhaps a little more snappishly than she might have intended to sound.

"Amen," Austin said. "Been there, done that. It sucks."

Paige looked at him more carefully then, remembering, and really registering, that he spoke from experience. It wasn't just the most recent problems, the back spasms and the bullet wound; he'd been in the hospital and then in rehab for many weeks after that bull-riding accident at the rodeo.

"It certainly doesn't seem to be doing much for my disposition," she admitted, feeling sheepish and bored and weepy and sorry for herself all at once.

"No," Austin agreed, smiling, "I wouldn't say it is." He paused, and the light of that smile lingered in his eyes, even though his mouth had turned solemn. "Libby tells me you want to get back in the saddle right away."

She nodded. "You know what they say. If you get thrown from a horse, you've got to get right back on."

His mouth crooked up at the corner. "Yeah," he agreed after chewing and swallowing a bite of his omelet, "I know the saying, Paige. It's generally meant for people who didn't break any bones when they landed."

She studied him, recalling what Libby and Julie had told her, about how Austin couldn't stand it until he proved—not to the rodeo world, but to *himself*—that he wasn't afraid to ride the very bull that had nearly killed him.

"Were you scared?" she asked.

Austin frowned slightly, set his plate aside. He looked comfortable, sitting there in that old rocking chair, as though it had been built to fit his particular frame. "When?"

"When you rode that bull again— what's his name?"

"Buzzsaw," Austin said. And then he really *did* surprise her. "Yeah," he admitted forthrightly. "I was scared sh— I was plenty scared."

"Really?"

Austin chuckled, amused and puzzled, both at once. "Really," he said.

"Then why did you do it?"

"For the same reason you want to ride Betty, I guess," he answered. "I didn't give a damn what anybody else thought about my being afraid to take on that particular bull again, but I sure as hell cared what *I* thought. And I knew if I didn't at least try to ride him, I wouldn't have much use for myself from then on."

"It's hardly the same thing," Paige pointed out, secretly fascinated by this unexpected glimpse into the workings of Austin McKettrick's mind. "Betty is an ordinary saddle horse. Buzzsaw is a rodeo bull, specially bred to throw any cowboy, anywhere, anytime."

Again, that crooked grin, the serious expression in those blue, blue eyes. "When you get right down to cases, Paige," he said, "it *is* the same thing. You'd rather deal head-on with what you're scared of than carry that fear around inside you for the rest of your life, and I respect that. I respect it a lot."

Paige put her plate and silverware on the bedside table and slumped back against the many pillows Libby had fluffed out for her, trying to process all the new emotions Austin's words had aroused in her.

"You do?"

He got up out of the rocking chair, crossed to the bed and bent down to kiss the top of her head. "Yeah," he said. "I do."

With that, he picked up both their breakfast dishes and, without another word, left the room.

Paige wriggled until she was lying prone and surveyed her enormous, casted foot, resting prominently on a stack of pillows provided by Libby. According to Dr. Colwin—*Joe*—she'd be up and around in a few days, albeit on crutches.

At that point, *a few days* seemed more like forever.

She was glad to see Shep when he came stumping into the room, grinning happily, as dogs will, and panting. He approached the bedside, laid his muzzle on her arm and rolled his eyes toward her. His meaning was so clear that he might as well have spoken aloud. *"How ya doin'?"*

Paige smiled and ruffled his ears. "Well," she replied, as though the dog *had* actually asked the question, "the truth is, I've been wallowing in self-pity and now I'm just going to snap the heck out of it and start acting like a grown-up."

Shep rolled his eyes away, rolled them back.

"After all, you've got a hitch in your get-along, and *you're* not complaining."

Shep gave an enormous sigh and moved away from the bed. He curled up on the hooked rug in front of the bureau and yawned.

It was infectious. Paige yawned, too.

Shep went to sleep.

And so did Paige.

When she woke up, Libby was standing next to her bed with a tray and a sisterly smile. "Lunchtime," she said.

"Already?" Paige pushed up onto the pillows behind her. Looked for her crutches.

"Hold on a second," Libby protested good-naturedly, when, with the aid of the crutches, Paige started to get up. "Let me help you—"

"You're not helping me go to the bathroom, Lib. You are absolutely *not* doing that." She was on her feet. The tops of the crutches dug into her armpits. "There is such a thing as personal dignity, you know. I have to draw the line somewhere."

Libby set the tray down on the bedside table. "But what if you fall?"

"If you hear a crash," Paige said, "feel free to barge right in."

Libby sighed and folded her arms, clearly not amused, but she didn't follow Paige out of the room.

In fact, when she returned, Libby was sitting patiently on the edge of the bed. Seeing Paige, she jumped up and flung back the covers.

Lunch, Paige discovered, once she'd settled back into bed and let Libby put the tray in her lap, was a tuna salad sandwich, chips and a glass of unsweetened iced tea.

Libby sat in the rocking chair, watching her.

"Is there going to be an early wedding?" she asked. First off, she really wanted to know and, second, she wanted to distract her big sister from worrying too much.

"We haven't decided," Libby said,

rocking. A sweet little smile settled on her mouth, and she laid one hand on her abdomen, as though she could already feel the baby moving around inside her. "We go back and forth. One moment, we're thinking we ought to go ahead and get ourselves married. The next, we're reminding each other that it's only six weeks until the big day and what's the use of doing it twice?"

In *four* weeks, Paige reflected, munching on her sandwich, she would be out of her cast. Just in time, it would seem, to put on the ugly pink dress and stroll down the aisle ahead of her sisters, the team brides. She chuckled and shook her head. There was, evidently, no escaping bridesmaids' hell.

"Anyway," Libby went on with a sigh, slowing the rocking chair a little. "Tate has plenty to worry about right now besides gossip."

The instant Libby had uttered those words, she looked as though she would have given a lot to take them back.

"Meaning . . . ?" Paige prompted, raising one eyebrow.

"You know," Libby said, throwing out her hands. The chair had come to a complete stop now. "The rustling, Austin getting shot—"

"The rustling is still going on, then?"

Libby swallowed, nodded. She glanced toward the doorway and, seeing no one there, lowered her voice just the same. "If anything, it's worse," she said. "More cattle have been slaughtered." Pain filled her face, and a moment or so passed before she could go on. "Tate and Garrett don't want Austin to find out," she finished.

"They're keeping secrets from him?" Paige asked. "Now *there's* a recipe for trouble if I've ever heard one."

"Austin was *shot,*" Libby reminded Paige, as though she, his erstwhile nurse, needed reminding. "He has a herniated disc. If he knew about the rustling and the—the rest of it, there would be no stopping him from putting his life in danger all over again!"

Paige sighed. "Lib," she reasoned. "I don't want to see Austin—or Tate or Garrett or anyone else, for that matter—taking any unnecessary chances with their lives. I'm just saying, Austin is going to be *seriously* pissed off when he finds out—he'll figure he has as much right to know as either of his brothers, and it would be hard to argue with that logic. He's a grown man, after all."

Libby sat up very straight, her chin high. "They're only looking out for their brother," she said, sounding a mite defensive. Which probably meant she had some of the same doubts Paige did, though it was unlikely she'd ever admit as much.

The Remingtons, in their own way, were as cussedly stubborn as the McKettricks.

"Really?" Paige echoed, and there might have been a certain tartness to her tone. "Does that mean they're looking out for *each other,* too?"

"Tate and Garrett aren't injured," Libby pointed out, miffed. "Austin *is.* As his nurse, I should think you would see this from our point of view."

Paige sighed. "I certainly don't want Austin chasing after a bunch of modern-day rustlers any more than the rest of you do," she said, wearying of the argument. While she and her sisters often disagreed, they were rarely short with each other. She held out a hand, and Libby crossed the small distance between the rocking chair and the bed to sit on the side of the mattress and intertwine her fingers with Paige's. "Have they learned anything new— Brent and the state police, I mean?"

Libby shook her head. "Tate and Garrett think it's an inside job," she said, "but they can't prove anything."

Instantly, Paige thought of Reese. She disliked the man, but there could have been a million petty and subconscious reasons for that, and it wasn't fair to finger him as a crook just because something about him rubbed her the wrong way.

On the other hand, what about instinct? What about woman's intuition?

"What's being done to protect the herds?" Paige asked. "And the oil fields?"

Libby's shoulders tensed visibly under her lightweight blue sweater, worn with slim jeans and a pair of boots that had seen better days. Most likely, big sister had been paying regular visits to Molly, out in the barn, making sure the mare was recovering.

"They've hired extra ranch hands to keep an eye on the cattle," Libby said. "As for the oil fields—"

Paige waited. Her sister was an intelligent woman. She didn't need to be told, any more than Tate, Garrett or Austin did, that a fire in one or more of those wells could be a disaster of epic proportions. Oil fires could burn underground for *years,* and the environmental ramifications of that might well be staggering in scope.

"As for the oil fields," Libby finally went on, "Tate and Garrett hired a special security firm to keep an eye on the wells, but until they arrive—"

"Until they arrive," Paige repeated woodenly, "those two yahoos are guarding the property *themselves,* aren't they?"

Libby swallowed, nodded miserably. "What else can they do?" she asked when she'd had a few moments to gather her composure. "Chief Brogan

476 McKETTRICKS OF TEXAS: AUSTIN

doesn't have the manpower, and neither do the state police. And it's not the kind of job you can just turn over to a bunch of rent-a-cops, Paige."

"So when are these hotshot security people supposed to show up?"

"Any time now," Libby said, with a mix of defiant hope and utter defeat. "They've been busy in the Middle East or somewhere."

"Oh, great," Paige retorted. "God knows, it's just a hop, skip and a *jump* to the Middle East. They ought to be here any minute!"

A tear slipped down Libby's cheek. "Do you think I like this any better than you do, Paige?" she asked, almost in a whisper. "If anything happened to Tate—or to Garrett—"

Paige raised herself far enough to hug Libby hard. "I still think it would be better if Austin knew about all this," she said. "Who knows? He might even have sense enough not to rush off half-cocked and take on the bad guys single-handedly."

Libby laughed, even as she swiped at her tears with the back of one hand.

"Or not," she replied. "We're talking about the same man who saw lights in the oil field one fine night and took off to investigate all on his lonesome. If they hadn't been so scared he'd die of his gunshot wound, I *swear* Tate and Garrett would have killed him themselves."

Paige chuckled at the irony of that statement, and so did Libby. But Paige was entirely serious when she said, "Talk to your man, Libby. And tell Julie to talk to hers. I know Tate's and Garrett's hearts are in the right place, but if something goes down that Austin could have prevented—or even *thinks* he could have prevented—there will be hell to pay."

Libby sighed, nodded. "I'll try. But reasoning with a McKettrick is like trying to reason with—"

"One of us?" Paige asked gently, smiling. Touching the side of her head to the side of Libby's before her sister rose to her feet.

"Yes," Libby agreed with a feeble grin. "It's a lot like that."

"Try," Paige urged.

* * *

Try.

Paige wanted Libby—and, by extension, Julie—to persuade Tate and Garrett to tell him, Austin, what he *by God* had a right to know in the first place.

He hadn't meant to eavesdrop; he'd come back to the guest apartment to find Shep, who'd settled himself on the hooked rug in Paige's room, because Doc Pomeroy was there and wanted to examine the dog after he'd finished with Molly out in the barn.

Now, stung to the quick by what his brothers were keeping from him, even though he understood their granny-assed reasons, Austin turned on his heel and got out of the guest quarters as fast as he could.

Reaching the kitchen, he grabbed a denim jacket from one of the hooks beside the back door and muttered a curse at the pain that shot through his left arm when he forgot the bullet wound and shoved his hand through the sleeve as though nothing were wrong.

Doc Pomeroy's old truck stood in the

barnyard, but there were no human beings in sight. Austin had barely closed
the door when he heard a scratching
sound from within and opened up
again so Shep could join him.

The vet was busy checking Molly
over, and there was no sign of Cliff.
Since Doc's son had accompanied him
on every visit to the mare or to Shep so
far, Austin noticed, preoccupied as he
was.

"Cliff go back to Dallas?" he asked in
the cowboy shorthand he'd grown up
with, coming to a stop outside Molly's
stall.

Doc started slightly, reminding Austin
of the old man's age, making him wish
he'd given some indication that he was
approaching.

"Damn," Doc complained. "What's to
be gained by sneaking up on a man like
that?"

"Sorry," Austin said, and though he
spoke lightly, he meant it.

"Cliff says he's under the weather,"
Doc said, in belated reply to Austin's
original question. "You ask me, he's
just hungover from trying to drown his

sorrows last night at the bar in the Silver Dollar."

"What kind of sorrows would those be, Doc?" Austin asked quietly, leaning on the stall door, watching as Doc ran skilled eyes—and hands—over the parcel of ill-used horseflesh that was Molly.

"Ones he made for himself, I reckon," Doc said, not looking at Austin. "About like the rest of us."

"Amen to that," Austin said, thinking of all the things he'd change about his own life, if only he got the chance.

He'd tell his folks not to bother driving out to Lubbock for that one rodeo, that was for sure. And instead of deliberately hurting Paige the way he had, he'd just tell her, straight out, that they were too young to know what love *was*, let alone how to make it stick.

He'd have asked her to wait for him. *Wait, Paige. Wait for me to grow up. Wait for* yourself *to grow up.*

Austin knew then, in that moment, that he loved Paige Remington—that once he'd begun to love her, albeit with the love of a boy, rather than a man, he'd never really stopped.

Doc didn't say anything more about Molly, *or* about his son. He just picked up his worn-out medical bag, pushed open the stall door when he got to it and came out to join Austin in the breezeway.

They walked in silence, out of the barn and toward the house.

The fire on the kitchen hearth had gone out, but Shep's blanket bed was still in front of it, and Doc gently herded the animal in that direction. Opening his bag, the seasoned veterinarian spoke to the critter in a cordial undertone. The man definitely spoke fluent Dog.

Shep allowed him to cut away the old bandage without so much as a whimper of protest.

"Well, now," Doc said, when he'd un-covered the shaved leg and taken a good look, "you're a McKettrick dog, all right. Mending about twice as fast as most." With that, he slanted a wry look in Austin's direction and spared him one of his salty grins. "Unless my eyes deceive me," he drawled, "you're doing pretty well yourself."

Austin shrugged, though a big part of his mind was on Paige, and his feelings for her, the old ones and the new. Sorting through all that was going to be one hell of a job, and besides that, he still had to confront Tate and Garrett about cutting him out of ranch business the way they had. He owned a third of the Silver Spur, and that meant he had an equal share in the problems, as well as the profits.

Doc put some ointment on Shep's injured leg, then wound it up in fresh gauze and tape again. This time, at least, the bindings left the dog's paw bare, which meant it would be easier for him to get around.

Once Doc had gone, Austin resisted the urge to look in on Paige, appropriated the keys to Garrett's Porsche, and grinned to see that Shep was standing at his side, looking up at him with luminous hope.

"Come along, then," Austin said.

Since the sports car was low-slung,

Shep got in easily, with just a little boost from Austin.

The garage door rolled up at the push of a button, as usual.

Austin started the Porsche, taking a certain satisfaction in the powerful roar of the engine as it sucked up a couple of gallons of gas before turning a wheel, and backed out into the yard.

"One of these days," he told Shep, who was sitting bolt upright in the passenger seat, like a dog accustomed to riding shotgun in a Porsche, "you and I are going to have to break down and invest in a fancy car of our own, and a new rig, too. Reckon it's probably best to award the old truck a purple heart and put it out to pasture."

Shep seemed to agree, though of course it was hard to be sure.

The gates were open, and Austin pulled through and stopped to decide which way to go.

"Now," he mused aloud, "if I were either one of those numbskull brothers of mine, where would I be right about now?"

Of course he could have called one

or the other of them on his cell phone, but there was no guarantee they'd welcome his company, given that they obviously considered him an invalid. Besides, he wanted to surprise them.

Thinking back on what he'd overheard Libby telling Paige, Austin decided the oil fields might be a good place to start. Hoping he wasn't putting old Shep, and himself, right back in harm's way, he made a left turn.

"We definitely need a truck," he told his dog.

CHAPTER SIXTEEN

"Just help yourself to my car whenever you want it," Garrett snapped, leaning to peer through the passenger-side window of the Porsche when Austin lowered it. He had to bend to see around the dog.

"Thanks," Austin replied, deliberately missing the sarcasm and checking out the immediate area. "I will."

Being back at the oil field, the memory of last time still fresh in his mind, his gut *and* his wounded shoulder sent a shiver dripping like cold water down his backbone. He hid the reaction with a grin and shoved open the door to get out.

Shep crossed the console and the gearshift to follow.

Brent Brogan was present and accounted for; he'd brought one of his deputies along, and the two of them were busy pacing something off while Tate stood with his hands shoved into the pockets of his denim jacket, watching.

Garrett rounded the car to stand in front of Austin, temporarily blocking his way. "Wait a second, will you?" he said.

Austin put a hand to his brother's chest and pushed just hard enough to let him know he was pissed. "Get out of my way, Garrett."

Garrett set his jaw and, for a moment, it looked as though he'd push back, but in the end, he didn't. *Can't hit baby brother,* Austin figured he was thinking, or something along those lines, *his being crippled and all.*

"Austin, listen to me," Garrett said.

Austin was in no mood to *listen.* No, sir, he wanted to *talk,* not listen. "Screw you, Garrett," he bit out.

Tate was approaching with long strides, Austin noticed out of the corner of his eye.

Good. He wanted *both* his brothers

to hear what he had to say, loud and clear.

Austin sucked in a breath, held it for a beat or two, and then let it out. It was an anger management trick he'd learned somewhere along the line, and sometimes it even worked.

This wasn't one of those times.

Tate had a howdy grin on his mouth and a watch-out look in his eyes. "Nice car," he said drily, indicating the Porsche with a slight nod.

Austin glared at him, folded his arms. He'd been practicing his speech ever since he'd accidentally eavesdropped on Libby and Paige, back at the house, and learned that not only were the troubles plaguing the ranch—and thus the family—getting worse, that knowledge was being kept from him.

Now, standing face-to-face with his brothers, Austin discovered that he was half again too mad to say anything at all.

Tate and Garrett exchanged glances, Garrett still hard-jawed, and then Tate spoke.

"There's nothing you can do, Austin," he said quietly. "Except get better."

A wave of frustration washed over Austin; he waited for it to pass. At his side, Shep sat down and gave an uncertain whimper. The dog's ears were perked up, and he kept looking from one of the three men towering over him to the next.

Austin managed to get a grip on his temper, though just barely. "I'm two years younger than you are," he reminded Tate, "and *one* year—twelve months—younger than you, Garrett. The way you two act, a person would think I was still wet behind the ears." He swept them both up in a single scathing glance. "This ranch is as much mine as it is either of yours, and I *do not* appreciate being treated like some junior partner."

"You know damn well why we didn't tell you," Garrett growled, reddening in the neck and under the bristle of beard covering the lower half of his face. "You haven't got the sense God gave a road apple!"

Austin stepped forward.

Tate eased between them. "Now, boys," he said in a smart-ass, singsong tone. "Let's not go losing our heads, throwing punches and saying things we'll regret later. We're all on the same side, here."

Chief Brogan meandered over. "Do I need to call out the riot squad?" he asked. His tone said he was kidding, but the look on his face was all business.

The thought of Blue River with its own riot squad was ridiculous enough to drain off some of the bad juju infecting the moment.

"Well, now, Denzel," Tate told his best friend, slapping Brogan on the back, "my kinfolk and I seem to be in the midst of a disagreement. Garrett and I are trying to keep our lit—*younger* brother alive and well, but he sure as hell doesn't make it easy."

"I could lock him up, if you want him off the streets for a while," Brogan offered.

He was probably joking, but Austin was ticked off just the same. "On what charge?" he asked.

Brogan shifted his gaze to the Porsche, grinned. "Grand theft auto?" he ventured smoothly.

Garrett nodded thoughtfully. "How long could you hold a car thief, if I were to press charges?"

Like he didn't know, Austin thought furiously. The man had a goddamn law degree.

"Long enough, most likely," Brogan drawled in response, looking speculative.

Austin swore under his breath and shifted his weight from one foot to the other.

Tate held up both hands. "Hold everything," he said. "We've got serious business to attend to, if the pissing match is over." Then, resting a palm lightly between Austin's shoulder blades, he gave him an eloquent little shove. "Come on, Austin. I'll show you what we're up against."

Garrett fell into step beside Austin. A wicked grin twitched at one corner of his mouth. "Know why the folks had you?" he asked.

"Maybe they figured the third time

would be the charm," Austin replied, "and they'd finally get it right."

"Nah," Garrett said, with a shake of his head, "they were just trying to get a girl."

Around two that afternoon, all slept out and unable to bear being cooped up in the bedroom for another moment, Paige ransacked her limited clothing supply for a black broomstick skirt, since jeans wouldn't fit over her cast, and decided on a long-sleeved white pullover for a top.

Putting these garments on proved to be a challenge—she was nearly wrestled to the floor by her own bra, and *forget* underpants—for a person on crutches.

After drawing and releasing a few deep, calming breaths, Paige regained her common sense. She sat down on the side of the bed and pulled the skirt on over her feet, grateful for the garment's stretchy waist. After that, she flailed into the pullover, a task that proved incredibly arduous, considering how simple it should have been, and wiggled the toes of her good foot into a bedroom slipper.

She stood, wobbled until she caught her balance.

As a nurse, she'd taught a lot of people how to manage a pair of crutches, and it was just plain ironic that she was having so much trouble with the process herself.

By the time she stumped out into the kitchen, there was no one around. Julie was still at work, and Libby, having brought Paige's lunch and given her a pill, was probably upstairs, in the section of the house she and Tate and the girls shared. There was no sign of Austin, or his dog.

Everybody had things to do, it seemed, except her. She crutched it over to the counter, got out a mug and ferreted around until she found the tea bags. Every time she went looking for the canister, it seemed to her, it was in a different place.

While she was waiting for the tea to brew, she happened to glance out the kitchen window and see Reese entering the barn. She might not have thought anything much about it, given that the man worked on the ranch, if he hadn't stopped and looked around in a way that was just furtive enough to bother her.

Paige swung her way over to the back door, took a jacket from one of the pegs and gyrated a little, balancing on one crutch, then on the other, as she poked her arms into the sleeves and used one hand to straighten the collar.

After that, zipping the thing up just seemed like more trouble than it was worth.

Paige opened the back door and made her way along the concrete walk, across the top of the driveway, where the going was tougher because the tips of her crutches sank deep into the gravel.

As she labored on toward the barn, she asked herself what the hell she thought she was doing. She didn't have a sensible answer, just a bad feeling in the pit of her stomach.

Molly was out there, all by herself, since the other horses had been turned out into the pasture for the day.

And Paige didn't trust Reese.

When she reached the doorway of the barn, she had to pause for a moment, wait for her eyes to adjust to the dimmer light.

Reese stood with his back to her. As she watched, he struck a wooden match against one of the timbers supporting the roof.

"There's no smoking in the barn," Paige said clearly, and firmly.

The ranch hand spun around, shaking out the match as he turned. Paige hobbled forward, finding the sawdust on the floor of the breezeway even less receptive to her crutches than the gravel in the driveway had been.

He must have pulled the cigarette from his mouth without her seeing, and as he walked toward her, he was smiling.

Paige felt for the light switch, flipped it on.

Reese was practically right in front of her when she stopped blinking away the dazzle of sudden illumination.

His hair needed washing, and he smelled of smoke and sweat, but it was the glacial look in his eyes that made Paige's heart bounce up into the back of her throat for a moment.

"You givin' orders around here now, ma'am?" Reese asked. He took off his hat, in a parody of good country manners, and looked her up and down in a way that would have earned him a slap across the face if she hadn't needed both hands to stay upright on those damn crutches.

Paige simply repeated what she'd said before. "There's no smoking in the barn."

He gave an edgy little chuckle and hooked his thumbs through the belt loops of his jeans. "It ain't like some poor horse is going to keel over from breathing in a little secondhand smoke," he said.

Paige wanted to flee, but she stood her ground. Hitched her chin up a notch and tightened her fingers around the handles on her crutches. If Reese came any closer, she would either jab at his groin or swing at his head. "Secondhand smoke isn't the problem," she said mildly—*and you damn well know it, you son of a bitch.* "Fire is."

Reese made a production of looking all around, still smirking. "I guess you've got a point there, little lady. With all this hay and sawdust around, why, the place could go up—" he thrust his hand under her nose and snapped his fingers sharply "—like *that.*"

Paige flinched, startled and, for the moment, speechless.

Reese leaned in, and she felt his breath on her face, fetid and hot. *"He killed my dog,"* he said.

By then, Paige was operating strictly on bravado. "What are you talking about?" she asked, stalling.

"Austin McKettrick shot my dog," Reese repeated.

Paige cleared her throat. "The animal attacked," she said.

"So he says," Reese argued, still way too close for Paige's comfort. If she swung a crutch at him now, he'd be able to block the move easily. "You sleepin' with him?" He raised his hand, ran his knuckles lightly down the side of her cheek. "A man's got land and money, he can have his choice of the women, and you sure are that, little lady. Choice, I mean."

Adrenaline rushed through Paige's system, and she managed to lever herself back a couple of steps. "You are *way* over the line, mister," she warned. "Don't touch me again."

Reese grinned, apparently amused, but his pleasure was short-lived.

Behind her, Paige heard the distinctive sound of a rifle being cocked.

"Touch my sister again," Libby said, "and I'll have to put you out of your misery."

The man spread his hands in a conciliatory gesture. "Nobody has a sense of humor anymore," he said to no one in particular.

Libby was at Paige's elbow by then, and she sure enough had a rifle in her hands. Furthermore, she looked like she knew what to do with the thing, which was more than Paige could have claimed.

"Get out of here," Libby told Reese. "If you've got any money coming to

you, you can pick it up in town tomorrow."

"You're firin' me?" Reese asked. The
grin was still in place, but his eyes had
hardened and taken on a flinty glint.
"You got the authority to do that,
ma'am? Just because you're sleepin'
with one of the high-and-mighty Mc-
Kettricks?"

"I've got the authority," Libby replied
evenly. She gestured toward the door
with the barrel of the gun. "Go on," she
added, "get out."

"I came here in a ranch-owned vehicle," Reese said, less cocky now but
just as furious, "and I've still got personal belongings over at the bunkhouse. I'm not leavin' here on foot."

It appeared to be a standoff. Until a
rig pulled up outside the barn a few
seconds later, that is.

Ron Strivens walked in, stopped in
his tracks when he saw Libby pointing
the rifle at Reese. "What the—"

"I forgot the rules and started to have
myself a smoke," Reese told the other
man, his tone wheedling now. "The

ladies here, took serious issue with that."

"So I see," Strivens said.

"He's fired," Libby put in. "Mr. Reese has some things to collect from the bunkhouse, then he'll be needing a ride into town."

Strivens looked at the rifle, smiled slightly and swung his gaze to Reese's furious face. "You heard the lady," he said. "You're through here. Go get your stuff—I'll give you a lift to the bus station or wherever else you need to go, soon as you're ready."

Reese hesitated, then stormed out of the barn, giving the three of them— mostly Libby—a wide berth as he passed.

When he was gone, Strivens held out a hand, not speaking.

Libby surrendered the rifle.

"It's probably none of my business what just happened here," Strivens said, "but when there's a gun involved, I'll be asking just the same."

Libby sighed, ran her hands down the thighs of her blue jeans, glanced at Paige, then turned back to Strivens. "I happened to see my sister leave the house," she said, "just after Reese drove up and went into the barn. When Paige didn't come back right away, I got worried and came out here to make sure she was all right."

"With a gun?" Strivens asked.

"Call it woman's intuition," Libby said.

Strivens chuckled, shook his head. Deftly, he unloaded the rifle, dropped several shells into his coat pocket and handed the weapon back to Libby.

"Will you be calling the boss to let him know what happened," he asked her, his eyes full of friendly admiration, "or shall I do it?"

"I'll call Tate," Libby answered. "Thanks, Ron."

He nodded and left the barn, and neither Libby nor Paige spoke or moved until he was gone.

The moment they were alone, though, Libby turned to Paige with fire sparking in her eyes. "Paige Remington, what in the *world* were you thinking?"

Paige looked pointedly at the gun. "I

was about to ask you a similar question, Annie Oakley," she replied, feeling a little shaky now that the rush of fight-or-flight chemicals was ebbing. "Since when do you pack heat?"

"Since I moved in with Tate," Libby responded, straightening her shoulders and lifting her chin up a notch. "He says anybody who lives on a ranch needs to know how to shoot."

Paige was fascinated. "Really? Why?"

With a sigh, Libby gestured toward the door. The company truck Strivens drove started up outside, drove away. The bunkhouse was a good distance from the main house. "Because of snakes," she explained, with exaggerated patience.

"Reese certainly qualifies as one of those," Paige observed, sort of flinging herself into motion. She was not going to miss those freakin' crutches when it was time to hang them up for good. "Will you teach me?"

They stepped into the cool sunlight of a November afternoon. A plume of dust rolled behind the ranch truck as Strivens and Reese drove toward the bunkhouse. "Teach you what?" Libby asked.

"To shoot," Paige answered.

Libby sighed. "Sure," she said, going snarky now that it was all over but the shouting. "It's at the top of my to-do list. 'Teach Paige to fire a gun.'"

"That man is dangerous," Paige said, distracted. "Reese, I mean."

"What gave you your first clue, Sherlock?" Libby countered. Maybe it was the cold breeze, and maybe it was the high of being a gun-totin' mama, but she looked flushed.

"You don't have to be snippy," Paige told her.

"Evidently, I do," Libby replied, pausing to wait because Paige was necessarily moving at a much slower pace.

"Does this mean you won't teach me to fire a gun?"

"I'm a novice myself," Libby admitted after a deep sigh. "I have no business passing on my incompetency to somebody else."

It was a relief to reach the kitchen. It was warm there, and safe. Plus, Paige could sit down. Her knees felt like jelly.

Wishing that the rocking chair hadn't been moved to her room, she maneuvered herself around backward and plunked down onto one of the long benches at the table.

Libby disappeared through the doorway to the dining room and came back unarmed, having stowed the rifle wherever such things were kept.

"I'm impressed," Paige said admiringly. For a moment, she was fourteen again, gawky and too smart for social approval, and Libby was seventeen, gorgeous and popular, with a place on the honor roll and Tate McKettrick's class ring hanging from a chain around her neck. "If you won't teach me to handle a gun, do you think Tate might?"

Libby sighed, stomped over to the cupboard and brewed two cups of tea. Paige's first batch had gone cold, of course, and she dumped that down the sink before approaching the table.

"Speaking of Tate," Libby said, completely ignoring a perfectly reasonable question, "I'd better call him right now, and tell him I just fired one of the ranch hands."

"You were magnificent," Paige said with a teasing grin.

"Be sure and tell Tate that, will you?" Libby answered, frowning as she walked over and picked up the receiver for the cordless phone. "Because he's going to be five kinds of pissed off when he finds out about that rifle."

Clearly, the situation was not good.

Someone had tried to uncap one of the wells, and without the equipment required for pumping oil, there could only be one reason for that. They'd planned on setting a fire.

"This happened the night I was shot?" Austin asked, looking from Garrett to Tate. Brogan and the deputy had already gone back to town, and the three of them were standing around by the well in question.

Tate nodded. "Probably."

"Damn fool tried to use a crowbar," Garrett observed.

Austin gave a dry chuckle at that. Shep leaned into him, and he bent, carefully, to pat the dog on the head. "When are the security people going to get here?" he asked.

Tate was about to answer, but his coat pocket rang.

He extracted his cell phone, saw the caller's number and rasped, "Libby?" instead of barking out his name, as was his custom.

Her voice was a high, nervous vibration on the other end of the line. There was a definite charge in the air, too— from the look on Tate's face as he listened, Libby hadn't called to ask him to make a quick run to town for milk and bread before he came home, that was for sure. Both Garrett and Austin tensed, waiting to find out what was going on.

"We'll be right there," Tate finally said when he could get a word in edgewise. She said something else and he answered, "No, just stay in the house for now. Garrett and Austin are with me— one of them can wait for the kids to get off the school bus and bring them up to the house."

He said goodbye, dropped the

phone into his pocket and started for his truck at a sprint, offering a brief explanation as he went. Libby and Paige had had a run-in with one of the ranch hands out in the barn, and Libby had intervened, with a rifle. She'd fired the man on the spot, and asked Ron Strivens to take things from there.

What the hell was Paige doing in the barn? Austin wondered. She had a broken ankle, for God's sake. The last time he'd seen her, she hadn't even been dressed.

The three of them had a short conference just before Tate jumped behind the wheel of his truck and started the engine.

It was decided that Garrett would take the Porsche and go to meet the school bus carrying Audrey, Ava and Calvin home to the ranch. Austin and Shep rode with Tate.

When they reached the house, Tate slammed out of the truck and disappeared so fast that Austin had to scramble to catch up. By the time he got there, Tate was standing nose to nose with Libby, who was half furious, half terrified.

He asked if she was all right and she nodded, wobbly-chinned, and her eyes brimmed with tears.

Austin scanned the room, was relieved to see Paige sitting at the table. She'd tucked the crutches beneath the bench and, as far as he could tell, she was none the worse for wear. In fact, her eyes shone and her cheeks glowed pink; except for the bulky cast, she was the picture of well-being.

Tate and Libby headed upstairs, arguing one moment, reassuring each other the next. Watching them go, Austin envied them a little. They might bicker with each other for a while, but then they'd make up.

That would be the fun part.

"Are you going to tell me what happened here," Austin asked, filling a bowl with kibble and setting it down for Shep to gobble before joining Paige at the table, perching beside her on the bench, "or do I have to wait for the six o'clock news?"

She smiled at him in a way that

seemed wistful to Austin, watching the stairs where Tate and Libby had been until a few moments before.

Paige told him how she'd been brewing herself a cup of tea an hour or so before, she'd glanced through the window above the sink and she'd seen Reese get out of a ranch pickup and head for the barn. She hadn't been suspicious until she'd seen him turn his head, looking to see if anybody was watching him. Worried, she'd pulled on a jacket and headed out there to investigate, all by herself, on crutches, with one foot in a cast and the other in a bedroom slipper.

From there, according to Paige's account, things went downhill, fast.

She and Reese had argued, and then Libby had showed up, armed with a rifle. They'd had hard words, Libby and Reese, and she'd told him to get his things and hit the road.

Ron Strivens had gotten there just in time to defuse the situation, but it was clear from the look in Paige's eyes, even before she went on, that she thought Reese still presented a threat.

"He said you killed his dog," she finished miserably, her voice small and fretful.

Austin moved to touch her face, half expecting her to flinch away. Instead, she closed her eyes as he stroked her cheek, then her hair.

I love you, Paige Remington, he thought with such conviction and clarity that, for one horrifying moment, he was sure he'd said the words right out loud.

Paige probably wasn't ready to hear them.

"I was afraid to tell you what happened," she said, surprising him again. That seemed to be happening on a regular basis.

"Why?" he asked, puzzled and a little alarmed.

"Your *temper,* maybe?" she reminded him, with another of those little smiles and a luminosity in her eyes that struck him as a sadder thing than tears.

"Paige." The name came out scratchy and hoarse. Austin hesitated, then took her hand, ran the pad of his thumb lightly over her knuckles. "You don't think—I wouldn't hurt you—"

"Not physically," Paige said. There was tension in her now, and her spine was very straight. "Austin, of course I know that. That isn't what I meant."

He closed his eyes, let out his breath. *Not physically,* she'd said. She knew he wouldn't lay a hand on her in anger, then, and that was a consolation. But he'd hurt her in other ways, and she was too honest to pretend that he hadn't.

He felt her fingertips come to rest on his arm.

"Austin," she said very softly. "Look at me."

He opened his eyes. Met her gaze as directly as he could. "I'm looking," he said with an attempt at a grin when she didn't say anything right away.

"I was afraid you would go after Reese and get hurt again," she finally blurted out. And when he started to protest that, damn it all to hell, he could take care of himself, she pressed an index finger to his mouth to prevent it.

"*That's* what I meant when I said I was worried about your temper."

Austin sighed. Shoved a hand through his hair. "Would you mind doing me just one little favor?" he asked.

"Depends," Paige responded, with a note of mischief in her tone. Her eyes were tired, though, and he'd have bet money her ankle was hurting.

"I want your promise, Paige," he said, serious as all get-out and determined to get that across to her. "Give me your word that, next time you think there's trouble, you'll tell me or Tate or Garrett, and not just go barreling straight into the middle of it, all by yourself."

Paige lifted an eyebrow. "Fair enough," she said. "As long as you're willing to promise me the same thing in return."

He narrowed his eyes. "There's a difference," he said.

"What difference?"

Austin leaned in until his forehead touched hers. "I'm a man," he told her. "And you're a little bit of a thing—on crutches. What if Libby hadn't seen you

follow Reese into the barn, Paige?
What if she hadn't gone out there to
make sure you were all right?"

"She *did* see me go into the barn and
she *did* come out there, Austin," Paige
pointed out.

"You could have been hurt," Austin
insisted, straightening so he could look
into her eyes.

"Anybody can be hurt," Paige retorted. "It's a chance we all take, every
day of our lives."

"Give me your word, Paige," Austin
said darkly.

"Give me yours first," she countered.

They were sitting there, staring each
other down, neither one of them willing
to give an inch, when the door leading
into the garage swung open and
Calvin, Audrey and Ava burst into the
kitchen, followed by Garrett.

Paige smiled and turned on the
bench to greet them, holding her arms
open wide.

All three kids rushed her, and she
laughed with delight and widened her
embrace to make room for everybody.

Watching her, Austin felt a lump form

in his throat, then sink down into his heart.

He'd loved her as a boy. Now that he was a man, he loved her even more. He'd loved her all the years in between.

He could tell Paige all of that, and it would be the truth, and she wouldn't believe it in a million years.

CHAPTER SEVENTEEN

Gradually, the rest of the family gathered in the big kitchen—Libby and Tate came down their stairway, both of them looking a lot more relaxed than when they'd gone *up* it an hour before. Julie, no doubt having heard Garrett's account of the Reese incident that had taken place out in the barn that afternoon, decided to stay home and let the assistant director take charge of the musical rehearsals for that evening. The first performance was coming up the following weekend, and the student performers were now engaged in tech rehearsals. She arrived with several buckets of take-out chicken and all the trimmings.

The kids giggled and chased each other. The dogs chased the kids. The noise and the happy confusion were wonderful.

Paige, having gotten exactly no-where in the standoff with Austin, crutched off to the guest apartment. There, she got out a long sleep shirt and moved on to the bathroom, where she undressed and then sat down on the lid of the toilet seat, methodically wrapped her cast with a plastic trash bag from the box she found in the cab-inet under the sink, cinched the thing shut using red twist ties and finally rose, teetering a little, to start the shower running.

The bag was hardly leakproof, but if she kept it out of the direct line of the spray, it ought to do well enough.

The flow of hot water felt better than perfect, soothing the tension out of Paige's muscles and warming her to the marrow. She lathered up her skin and shampooed and conditioned her hair and shaved her legs and under-arms, all while standing on one foot, like a crane, and holding on to the han-dle of the shower door for balance.

And when she'd finished, she felt human again.

The garbage bag had served its purpose, and she removed it and hung it on the hook on the back of the bathroom door so it would be ready for next time. Maybe she'd secure it with duct tape before she indulged in another shower, just to make sure the cast didn't get wet.

Rather pleased with herself, Paige hummed as she checked her cast and found it dry—well, dry *enough,* anyway—then pulled the clean nightshirt over her head. She got caught inside it, just as she had become entangled in the pullover shirt earlier, and when she finally poked her head through the neckhole and opened the door to let some of the steam roll out, she gave a small, startled gasp.

Austin was standing in the hallway.

She glared at him. "What do you think you're doing?"

"Libby sent me," Austin answered with a cocky little grin tugging at his mouth. "With your supper."

Through the slowly clearing fog,

Paige saw that he was holding a plate in one hand, piled high with chicken, potato salad, biscuits and an ear of corn.

"And you thought I'd want to eat in the bathroom?" she asked.

He chuckled. "I heard the shower running and waited," he said. "Just in case you yelled for help or something."

Paige would have sent him packing, but for the sudden realization that she was hungry. *Very* hungry.

The chicken smelled so fattening and so good.

The corn dripped with butter, and so did the biscuits.

"You're lying," Paige accused, reaching for her crutches and wedging them under her armpits, where they bit into her flesh like teeth. "Libby would have brought the food herself, thinking I might have been—"

"Naked?" he asked, almost purring the word.

"I'm not naked," Paige pointed out, feeling testy. It had been a long and trying day, after all, and she just wanted some supper, an hour or two of brainless TV, a pain pill and a decent night's sleep.

Austin ran his gaze slowly over the sleep shirt, as if he could see right through the fabric, and stepped back out of her way.

"Thanks for bringing the food," she said, reaching the bedroom. "You can go now."

Again, that grin. "I'm not going anywhere," he said. "I'm injured, remember? I'm not supposed to climb the stairs."

Paige huffed out a breath. He didn't look to her as if he'd have any trouble with a set of stairs, but he *had* been shot very recently. "You can sleep in Calvin's old room, then," she said.

He didn't answer until she'd gone through the awkward process of setting the crutches aside, climbing into bed, arranging the blankets and all the rest.

By the time she'd finished, she was breathless from the effort.

Austin watched, amused. When she was settled, he handed her the plate and some plastic silverware wrapped in a napkin and sat down in the rocking chair to watch her eat.

Shep wandered in, circled the hooked rug three times and collapsed in comfort.

"I'll be fine now," Paige told Austin. "Really. You can leave." A pause. "Any time now."

He chuckled, rocked idly in the sturdy antique chair, obviously intending to go nowhere. "I'm fine right here," he said.

"That," she replied, "is a matter of opinion."

"I'm spending the night," Austin informed her. "In that bed. With you."

Paige hoped he couldn't tell by looking at her that she found the idea almost as intriguing as it was annoying. "Look, I appreciate your concern, but I'll be *fine.* There's no need—"

"Oh," Austin said, in a throaty drawl, when her voice fell away, "I wouldn't say there was no need. I wouldn't say that at all."

Paige's heart skittered over a couple of beats. "We agreed—" Again, she couldn't finish the sentence.

"I know what we agreed," Austin replied, low and easy. "And all I'm planning on doing for sure is holding you in my arms. Anything happens beyond that, it will be your choice."

Her face burned, not just with indignation, but with desire, too. And no matter how much she might deny the fact, even to herself, she felt scared and shaken and very much in need of holding.

"We're not having sex," she said. "I mean it, Austin. *We are not having sex.*"

"All right," Austin replied affably, raising both hands a little way, palms out. "No sex." He paused. "Unless, of course, you decide that's what you want."

"I won't," she told him too quickly.

He grinned. "We'll see," he answered.

"You think you're irresistible, don't you?" Paige challenged, after gnawing a few bites off a drumstick, chewing and then swallowing. Swabbing the grease from her mouth with a wadded paper napkin. "Well, I've got *news* for you, Austin McKettrick. You are *highly* resistible. I can resist you with one hand tied behind my back."

"I wasn't planning on tying you up," he said, deadpan. "But if that's your thing, we could probably work something out."

Paige blushed crimson. "I *meant*," she said, after unclamping her back molars, "that not *every* woman is going to fall into bed with you just because you're—sort of attractive."

"Sort of?"

"Not so much, right now. Here's a flash for you, McKettrick. I'm immune to your famous charms."

"Here's your chance to prove it," he said easily.

Paige glared at him. Waited until she was breathing normally before she answered. "You're on, buddy," she told him. Then she finished eating in silence, set her plate aside on the bedside table with a thump, squirmed down onto her back and pulled the covers up to her chin.

Austin laughed and shook his head, but he didn't comment. He just got out of the chair, picked up the plate and left

the room with it, Shep following hopefully in his wake.

As soon as they were gone, Paige
sat up, grabbed her crutches and
sprang out of bed again.

In the bathroom, she squeezed paste
onto her brush and scrubbed her teeth,
and finally swished mouthwash back
and forth between her cheeks, holding
her own gaze in the mirror above the
sink.

She would not give in to Austin Mc-
Kettrick. She *would not* let the man
make love to her—no way.

No matter how much she might want
him to do exactly that.

She'd hoped to get back to bed before Austin returned, and she made it,
but just barely.

Determined to ignore him for as long
as she could, she groped for the remote and turned on the TV. The sound
was muted, which was fine with Paige,
because the characters in the "reality"
show playing out on the screen were
obnoxious enough without being audible. A bunch of women with silicone-
enhanced breasts, big hair and too

much makeup, were sipping wine in a private dining room at some fancy restaurant in New York or Los Angeles or Palm Beach or wherever, and Paige didn't need to read their chemically plumped lips to know they were arguing.

With any luck at all, Paige thought, oddly detached and yet keeping her eyes fixed on the unfolding drama, there would be a brawl. It would be a chance to vent her own anger, vicariously.

No harm done.

Austin, meanwhile, opened one of the bureau drawers and took out a pair of gray sweatpants. Paige saw all this out of the corner of her eye.

Not that she cared what Austin McKettrick wore to bed.

He vanished into the bathroom and the water in the shower came on.

Paige unmuted the TV.

"You're sleeping with my husband, you bitch," one of the big-haired women said to another.

The two women squared off, though they didn't get out of their chairs.

Paige rolled her eyes. "He's not worth it," she told the misguided females.

"He loves me," the other one said.

There was no question that the scene had been staged. The bad acting ruined any illusion of spontaneity, and yet Paige sat there, watching.

The onscreen bickering escalated.

A commercial came on, and another rollicking segment of Real Life followed. The drama dial was definitely being cranked into the red zone.

Presently, Austin ambled out of the bathroom, wearing the sweatpants and nothing else, unless you counted the damp sheen of moisture on his chest.

Another commercial began and ended, and then the catfight began in earnest. The two women lunged at each other and rolled the length of the table, knocking over glasses and wine bottles and breadbaskets as they went. Far from breaking up the donnybrook, the other three women dove in. The screaming, kicking, clawing, hair pulling and name-calling commenced.

Austin stood in the center of the

room, watching with casual interest. "I saw something like that happen in a bar in Phoenix once," he said. "It was awesome."

Paige glanced at him. Thumbed the mute button again.

"I'll just bet you did," she said after a beat or two.

"There must have been ten females involved in that brawl," Austin recalled, as though Paige hadn't said a word.

She wouldn't eyeball him. She just wouldn't.

No matter how good he looked with his hair curling from the shower steam and his chest bare and his face freshly shaved.

"I suppose that happens a lot around you," she said, and then could have kicked herself, theoretically, anyway. Under current circumstances, kicking of any kind was way beyond her capabilities.

"What happens a lot around me?" Austin asked, still watching the now-silent battle as it unfolded on the screen. That was probably why he sounded distracted; his attention was engaged by all those skirts riding up, all those flailing limbs.

A high-heeled shoe flew through the air, and then a wig.

"Do they really think those boobs are fooling anybody?" Paige grumbled, feeling positively flat-chested in comparison. She certainly hadn't meant to say *that* out loud, but what the hell? She was on a roll; might as well keep going.

Austin winced as one of the women made the most of her fifteen minutes of fame by emptying the contents of a vase over a waiter's head when the poor man tried to intervene. "I don't think they care one way or the other," he said, grinning. Then he shook his head and looked at Paige. "If this is your idea of entertainment," he drawled, "I'm pretty sure I have a better idea."

"Television *sucks*," Paige said, frantically thumbing the channel button now. Infomercials flashed by, along with reruns of stupid comedies, people cooking things, a smarmy-looking man selling gold-plated jewelry and police shows featuring actors who had long since died or left the cast.

Austin approached. Gently removed the remote from her hand and turned off the TV.

What a concept.

"Now what?" she asked weakly, looking up at Austin and wondering how in the world she was going to resist the man for an entire night, with him in the same *bed*, for heaven's sake.

On the other hand, he might stay on top of the covers, as he had before. Not bother her at all.

Shep, snug on the rug, yawned noisily.

Austin reached out and shut off the lamp on the bedside table, stood there, gilded in moonlight, looking magnificent, like some half-naked god fresh from Olympus. "Now," he replied, "I hold you."

Oh, hell. He was going to hold her. How was she supposed to ignore that?

Tears burned in Paige's eyes, and she was glad he'd turned out the light, because that meant there was a chance he wouldn't see that she was crying and want to know why. She couldn't have answered, because she didn't know. Even making up a lie would have been too much to ask of her, at this point.

Austin walked to the other side of the bed, and Paige felt the covers move and then the mattress shift under his weight. When he stretched out beside her, she was nearly overwhelmed by the heat and the strength of him, by the delicious scent of his hair and skin.

All that, and they weren't even touching.

Yet.

Paige sighed.

Austin chuckled. "Relax," he said, his voice a quiet rumble in the silver-tinged darkness. He slid his good arm under her, bent the elbow so that she folded into him, wound up with her cheek resting on the hollow of his throat.

She felt his pulse, strong and steady.

"That show sort of reminded me of high school," she said. Although she'd never been in a fight like that herself, she'd helped break them up in the girls' locker room a couple of times.

Austin chuckled, but she felt him tense up, too. "Seems to me," he said slowly, "that a *lot of things* remind you of high school."

Paige sat up awkwardly. "Was that a dig?" she demanded.

She saw his shoulders move slightly, as if he'd meant to shrug but didn't want to expend the effort.

"I'm just wondering when you plan on *graduating,* Paige."

Her temper sizzled. "Are you calling me immature?"

Austin raised himself onto an elbow. He looked damnably casual for a man who'd just started an argument that might end in nuclear warfare. "I'm saying all that happened a long time ago. I've been as honest as I could be, telling you why I did what I did, and I haven't just said I was sorry, I've proved that I still care about you. And that I'm not that boy who hurt you anymore, but a man who can care for more than just himself."

Paige blinked, picturing him with Calvin and Audrey and Ava. With the little mare, Molly, so terrified of human beings, and with such good reason. And with Shep—he'd taken that bedraggled stray straight to his heart, made a real commitment to the animal. And Paige knew he would keep that commitment, come hell or high water.

She began to cry. "You're right," she admitted, between sniffles.

He massaged the back of her neck. Grinned, his teeth flashing white, and cupped a hand to his ear. "Hold it," he said. "I thought you just said—"

Paige turned to him. "You were *right,*" she repeated brokenly.

"Would you mind repeating that statement in front of a witness?" he asked.

She pushed at his chest. "Stop teasing," she said. "It's over. You've changed and so have I. It's time to move on."

Austin drew her down, so her head rested on his good shoulder, and he kissed her temple. "I'm not sure I like the sound of that," he said. "The part about moving on, I mean."

"Who are you kidding?" Paige countered. "As soon as you've had time to heal up, you'll hit the road again."

"What makes you so sure of that?" He spoke easily, his voice husky in the darkness, and he wound a finger loosely in a strand of her hair as he waited for her answer.

"It's your pattern," she said.

"It might have been, once," Austin allowed. "Like you said, Paige, I've changed. Tate and Garrett wanted to keep me out of the game for a while— you don't have to defend them, I know their intentions were good—and that brought me to recognize a home truth. I love this ranch. It's as much a part of me as my blood and bones. As much a part of me as—" He paused, swallowed, changed course, leaving Paige to wonder what he'd stopped himself from saying.

As much a part of me as you are? It was too much to hope for.

A girl could dream, though.

Presently, Austin went on. "Anyhow, I want to do my share to protect the Silver Spur, Paige. See that it thrives, so it will be here for all the McKettricks who come after my brothers and me."

They were both silent for a while, and that, too, seemed right.

Paige thought about his words, thought about the boy Austin had been when he loved her, and the man he was now.

As a teenager, Austin had been fearless, popular, everybody's friend—the geeks, the jocks, the rebellious misfits, the boys and the girls. He liked them all, and they liked him right back. The parents liked him, the teachers liked him.

Paige had been as smitten with the youngest of the McKettrick brothers as any other girl in her age group, but they hadn't had much in common. She was bookish and took pride in her high IQ, while Austin had trouble concentrating on any endeavor that required him to sit still longer than five minutes.

She was shy; he'd never met a stranger.

She saw the world as a place to be taken seriously and approached with caution; he saw it as a playground.

And perhaps, for him, it had been.

After all, Austin had been born a McKettrick, part of a large and confident clan, with land and money and a proud family history.

Paige had been the third daughter of a poor schoolteacher. Her own mother hadn't cared enough about her or Libby or Julie, or all three of them put together, to stick around and be a regular mom.

They'd had some heartfelt talks, back then during high school and the summer after graduation. Austin worried that they were moving too fast, that they were in too deep. He wanted to follow the rodeo for a while, instead of going to college, and he'd had a few go-rounds with his folks over that. Jim and Sally McKettrick had thought Austin and Paige were too serious and, God knew, they'd been right.

Paige, naive and starry-eyed, had firmly believed that love conquered all. She would go to nursing school. Austin could follow the rodeo during the season. Somehow, they'd make it work.

It wasn't to be.

Paige closed her eyes, remembering how shattered she'd been. Her face was wet, and Austin smoothed away her tears with the sides of his thumbs. His blue eyes glowed in the combination of shadow and moonlight.

"If you've got to cry, Paige," he murmured gruffly, "then you go right ahead. I just don't want you crying over me— not ever again."

With her broken heart and her fractured ankle and all the rest of the physical and emotional damage, Paige felt a lot like Molly in those moments. She craved Austin's touch, strong and at the same time, heartrendingly gentle.

"You said—" She paused, bit her lower lip. "You said if we were going to make love tonight, it would have to be my choice—"

He grinned. "That's what I said, all right."

"Make love to me, Austin."

He just looked at her, without speaking, for so long that Paige began to worry that he'd changed his mind. That he didn't want her after all.

But then he lowered his head, and

their mouths joined, and then the kiss deepened until heat blazed through Paige like fire from a flame thrower.

This was the kiss of a man, not a boy.

And it left Paige so shaken that she could only lie there, gasping and yet wanting more, when it ended.

"If you're going to change your mind," Austin told her solemnly, "then you'd better be quick about it. Because I'm fixing to have you, lady, and once the ride begins, it won't be over 'til it's over."

A sweet tingle of anticipation sparked inside Paige. She answered by plunging her fingers into his shower-damp hair, craning her neck to nibble at his mouth.

Austin groaned, and then stretched, reaching across her, and she heard the drawer of the nightstand open. Dazed, she remembered the box of condoms.

"What about your foot?" he asked after some fumbling on his part and a telltale snapping sound.

Paige was breathless, but she managed a giggle. "I didn't think we'd be using my foot," she said.

He laughed, and he kissed her, gently at first, and then with power, with need, with a passion that was almost a consummation in itself.

The kissing went on for a while—just that made Paige feel as though she might climax—but then Austin got down to business, so to speak.

He slid her nightshirt up and off, over her head. Threw it aside. He kissed her neck, nibbled at her earlobes, traced the ridges of her collarbones with the tip of his tongue. When he drew one of her nipples into his mouth, she arched her back and cried out, glorying in the sensations as he suckled.

Austin took his sweet time, pleasuring Paige. He tasted and teased, he whispered and tempted. Time and again, he brought her to the verge of satisfaction, then left her trembling on the precipice. Each time she fell away moaning, having come so very close.

Finally, when she could bear the waiting no longer, when not having him inside her would have been like holding her breath for too long, she pleaded and her hips rose to meet his and in a single masterful stroke, he took her.

The pleasure, already almost beyond her tolerance, grew and grew. With every plunge of his hips, he possessed her more thoroughly, and then more thoroughly still. Their bodies rocked together, slowed, rocked again. Paige began to fidget and fret, frantic in her need, but Austin's self-control was formidable. At one point, he even withdrew entirely, though he continued to caress every part of her with his hands.

She tossed her head from side to side on the pillow, repeating his name over and over again, pleading.

After a very long time, Austin finally relented. He moved his hands beneath her buttocks and raised her high to receive the hardest, deepest thrust yet.

She came apart in his arms, crying out his name, her body flexing and buckling like a thin cable in a high wind.

Not long afterward, Austin let himself go. With a hoarse shout, he conquered her and surrendered to her, both at the same time.

She quivered, arched beneath him, still straining as the seemingly endless orgasm clenched within her, relaxed, clenched again. Finally, exhausted, sated, jubilant, she sank into the mattress, gasping for breath.

Austin eased down beside her, his own breath coming hard, sawing in and out of his lungs.

They were still for a while, except for the violent struggle for air, and then Austin got out of bed, rolling to his feet, disappearing into the darkness.

He was back within a couple of minutes. "Close your eyes," he said. "I'm about to turn on the light."

Paige pulled the covers over her head. "Why?" she complained, her voice muffled. She could see a dim, golden glow through the weave of the sheets and the blanket and the bedspread. "Why do we need a light?"

"Because I want to find my sweatpants," Austin said.

Paige stuck her head out, blinking at him owlishly. "Well, *that's* romantic," she said.

He grinned. "It was a trick," he said,

pulling back the covers. Except for her cast, which hardly counted as clothing, Paige was completely naked—and in full view.

"You're beautiful," he said.

Paige tugged at the covers. "It's cold," she protested.

"So I see," he agreed, touching one of her rock-hard nipples. But then he let her pull the blankets up.

"You *did* use a condom, right?" she asked.

"Talk about romantic," he teased. Then he produced the empty wrapper, showed it to her.

Well-being suffused Paige. She stretched. "Why do you need sweat-pants?" she asked.

"I'm headed out to the barn to check on Molly and the other horses," he said. "Baby, it's cold outside, and pants are bound to come in handy."

"I'm going with you," Paige said, sitting up.

Austin eased her back down. "No," he said. "You're not."

"But what if—"

He kissed her forehead. "Shep will

look out for me," he said, as the faithful dog rose and stretched, instantly alert.

Paige imagined all sorts of things happening while Austin was out of her sight, and none of them were good.

Finally, when she could stand the waiting no longer, she got up, found her nightshirt and pulled it back on, used the crutches to get to and from the bathroom and was just about to head for the barn when Austin came back.

They met in the kitchen.

Seeing her, Austin laughed and shook his head.

He looked fairly comical himself, Paige thought, taking in his work boots, those gray sweatpants he'd worn to bed and the misbuttoned flannel shirt beneath his denim jacket.

"Going somewhere?" he asked mildly, arms folded, one eyebrow quirked up a little.

Paige blushed. "I was getting hungry," she lied.

Austin laughed again. "Why can't you just admit that you were worried about me?"

"Okay," Paige allowed. "I was worried about you."

"And that you were lusting after my body."

"You're pushing it, McKettrick."

Austin stood his ground, looking smug. "Are you or are you not lusting after my body?"

Paige's cheeks ached as the heat intensified. "Okay," she said. "I might be lusting after your body. A little."

He came to her then, slipped his arms around her waist, neatly bypassing the crutches. "Only a little?" he muttered. "I'm going to have to see what I can do about that."

She smiled a sultry smile, because he was back in the house, because he was safe, because he was about to do his damnedest to make her want him *a lot,* not just a little.

"I'll be interested to see what your strategy is," she said.

Austin cupped her face in his hands, smiled down into her eyes. "You're going to be way too busy," he murmured, about to kiss her, "to be concerned with my . . . strategy."

"Is that so?"

He turned her around, pointed her in the direction of the guest quarters, but gently, and slowly, because she had to wield the crutches.

As turned-on as Paige was, the care Austin took moved her deeply, made her throat ache and her nose burn.

Shep, as loyal as ever, came along, settled himself on the hooked rug in front of the bureau once they'd reached the bedroom and sank back to sleep.

"Molly was all right?" Paige asked, standing next to the bed.

Austin took the crutches from her, one by one, supporting her easily the whole time with a hand under her elbow.

"Molly," he replied very slowly, "is just fine. All the horses are fine."

Paige trembled with anticipation, with need, a little daunted because she knew the lovemaking would be more strenuous this time. There would be more foreplay, for one thing, and Austin wouldn't be satisfied until he'd driven her crazy.

Still holding her up, Austin tugged the nightshirt up—and up. And off.

He eased Paige down onto the mattress, sideways this time, with her legs dangling. And then he knelt between her thighs. Lightly, he kissed her right knee, and then her left. Paige, knowing what was about to happen, groaned his name.

He leaned over and kissed the soft flesh of her belly. "Tell me what you want," he said.

Paige told him exactly what she wanted.

And she got it.

CHAPTER EIGHTEEN

It had been nearly a week since Austin and Paige had come to terms and decided maybe they'd try again. Or maybe not.

The private cemetery on the Silver Spur was a peaceful place, set high on a ridge overlooking miles of McKettrick land. There were oak trees all around, and stone benches scattered among the graves.

Austin took off his hat as he approached the fancy marble marker with an intricate frieze of running horses chiseled above the inscriptions.

James Angus McKettrick. Sally Fletcher McKettrick. There were dates underneath, bridging the too-short span of their lives.

He knew his folks weren't hanging

around that graveyard, nor were any of the other departed family members, but sometimes it comforted him, coming here. Not that he'd visited in a long time, because he hadn't.

High up in the sky, a hawk wheeled in a wide, graceful circle, and Austin paused to watch it for a few moments before clearing his throat and turning his attention back to the graves, two among some fifty or sixty final resting places.

"I guess you most likely already know this," he told his mom and dad quietly, "but I need to tell you anyhow." Again, he paused. Swallowed hard. Shep, who'd come along for the ride, bouncing along on the seat of one of the ranch work trucks, sat down in the grass beside Austin and leaned heavily against his leg. "There are a few things I'd undo in my life if I had the chance, and one of them is talking you two into driving to Lubbock to watch me ride in that rodeo instead of heading for Hawaii, like you planned on doing." He choked up then, had to stop and shut his eyes until the burning let up a little.

"Right or wrong, though, feeling bad and wishing things had been different won't change what happened. And I've been feeling real bad, for a long time."

Shep made a soft sound, part whimper and part yip.

"I figure it's time to put all that aside," Austin went on, "as much as I can anyway, and get on with things."

He looked up at the brittle-blue sky again, took it in from horizon to horizon, and it seemed to fill his chest and ache there, as though he'd breathed it in somehow.

They'd made love every chance they got, he and Paige, and they'd done a lot of talking, too, but so far the most important words had yet to be said, by either one.

Austin didn't have any doubt whatsoever that he loved Paige Remington.

As a boy, he'd loved her in the best way he knew how—by driving her off before they wound up hog-tied and hating each other.

As a man, he wasn't sure how to go about loving Paige at all, beyond pleasing her physically, of course. That was an easy matter, because Paige was all woman, ripe and responsive, fiercely generous in the giving and in the taking.

She was a lot of other things, too, though.

Paige was smart and sassy, with plans and goals and plenty of opinions, many of which directly opposed his own. She had that house in town, and the job she meant to take at the clinic in Blue River, when it finally opened up, and she flat-out didn't need him or any other man to do just fine for herself, thank you—any more than Libby needed Tate that way, or Julie, Garrett.

None of the Remington women *needed* their men.

But wanting was another thing.

Austin squared his shoulders. "I plan on asking Paige Remington to marry me," he said. "And I don't have any idea what she'll say. Maybe yes, maybe no. She's pretty bullheaded, if you recall." He stopped, grinned. "Guess she'd have to go some to beat me when it comes to bullheaded, though," he admitted. "Anyway, that's what I wanted to tell you. That after all this time, I still love that woman so much it scares me, and that I'm real sorry for the other part, too. The accident, when you were coming back from the rodeo, I mean."

Again, his throat closed up tight.

He knew Jim and Sally McKettrick would never have held that accident, or anything else, against him. They'd been steadfast, loving parents, both of them, but it was always understood that their first commitment was to each other. Instead of making Tate, Garrett and Austin feel shut out, the solidarity of the elder McKettricks had engendered a quiet and unshakable sense of security in their children.

Austin stood still for a while, remembering, appreciating and, yes, missing his mom and dad. Finally, he nodded a farewell, turned and walked away, putting his hat back on as he went. Shep, eager for whatever might be next on the agenda, pranced along beside him. Now that Doc had replaced the bandage on his hind leg with an even smaller one, that dog was as spry as a pup.

When they got to the pickup—Austin still hadn't found the time to buy himself a rig to replace his old truck, now back from the repair shop and parked in one of the sheds alongside some old-time haying equipment—he went around to the passenger side and opened the door.

Shep needed only a little boost to scramble inside as far as the floor, and he made it onto the seat all on his own.

Austin went around to the driver's side, but before he climbed behind the wheel, he turned to look back at the cemetery.

His parents and grandparents and great-grandparents were all buried there, starting with Clay McKettrick and his wife. In that place, the generations doubled back on each other and created a sort of circle, because, of course, even his great-grandparents had been somebody's children, once. Every resident had been a McKettrick, by birth or adoption or by marriage.

Austin sat for a few moments before

he started up the truck. Paige was waiting for him back at the house, and probably getting fidgety—the longer she had to wear that cast, the harder she was to get along with. He enjoyed trying, though. There were plenty of fireworks, but that only made the making-up more fun.

Tonight's event *was* a big one—the final performance of Julie's high school musical, which had been a spectacular success by Blue River standards, and the whole family was fixing to gussy up and attend.

Still, Austin took a moment to reflect a little. Someday, he'd be laid to rest in that cemetery, like the rest of his Texas kin. He just hoped he'd have plenty of time to live and love before that inevitable day came. He wanted to herd cattle and argue with his brothers and make babies with Paige.

He wanted to see those babies grow up to fall in love, marry and have babies of their own.

He wanted to dance with Audrey and Ava on their wedding days, and shake Calvin's hand when the boy genius graduated from some fancy college with top honors. He was bound to do big things, and the twins, too.

First, though, before Austin could begin living his way through the life he was planning, he'd have to ask Paige if she'd have him for a husband. As much as she enjoyed tangling the sheets with him, it might take some persuading to convince her to make it legal and binding.

It was, after all, one thing to love a person—and Austin was pretty sure Paige loved him, just as he loved her—but it was another to *trust* someone. Without trust, love wasn't going to be enough for the long haul, no matter how passionate it was, and Austin wasn't willing to settle for anything less than a lifetime with Paige.

He sighed. He'd ask her. If she said no, he'd wait a while and then ask her again. Eventually, she'd come around.

He shifted the truck into gear and gave it some gas. As he drove down the cemetery hill, Austin could see the oil field, now staffed with security guards, in the distance, along with the main house and the barn, the old Ruiz place, where Tate and Libby had lived with the twins until recently, and the staff trailers standing along one side of the winding creek.

It all looked familiar and, at the same time, different. Of course, the ranch hadn't changed all that much, but he had.

He was sure of some things he hadn't been able to pin down before, like how he felt about Paige and living out the rest of his life on the Silver Spur. He'd loved his years in rodeo, thrived on the competition and excitement, but now he was content to make the switch from participant to spectator, and let other men ride the bulls and the broncs.

As for Tate and Garrett, well, he supposed they'd always see him as their little brother, at least some of the time. That didn't bother Austin so much anymore, because now he knew he could stand toe to toe with one or both of them if the need arose, and hold his own. The other side of that coin was the bone-deep certainty that his brothers always had his back, just as he had theirs.

Whenever he'd needed them, they were there, and the reverse was true as well. Being a McKettrick was a blood-bond, something that went way beyond common loyalty and family feeling.

For the first time, Austin had a glimmer of what it would mean to carry that pride into the next generation, to be a strong link in the chain.

And the only woman in the world he wanted was Paige.

Paige took real pride in being Julie's sister that night, when the auditorium next to the high school filled with a closing-night crowd. There were so many people in attendance, even though there had been several previous performances, that the massive sliding doors separating the main theater from the annex had to be opened and folding chairs set up.

Austin sat beside her, wearing crisp jeans, good boots and a starched white shirt. He'd taken her hand, and though his grip was easy, Paige knew he wouldn't let her go, no matter what, and there was solace in that.

She felt a buzz of excitement, down deep, that had little to do with the play. The closest she could have come to defining the sensation was to say that there was a new certainty in her, a new kind of strength, lasting and good.

The McKettrick bunch took up a whole first row, and there was a lot of standing up and shaking hands as they greeted friends and neighbors. Folks inquired after Austin's shoulder and Paige's foot, and said they didn't know what the world was coming to when a man wasn't safe on his own oil field, and never mind the time of day.

Brent Brogan came, along with his aunt, Gerbera, and his two children. He looked extrahandsome, having donned a natty black suit instead of his uniform.

Like Austin, Garrett and Tate wore more casual jeans and cotton shirts, and Calvin wore a miniature version of the same outfit. He had a little hat, boots and a McKettrick belt buckle, recent gifts from Garrett.

Libby, like Paige, wore a long skirt and a lightweight sweater, and Audrey and Ava were all done up in their "Thanksgiving" outfits—pretty, velvet dresses, one red and one blue, and cut differently—with their hair in French braids.

They'd talked Libby into letting them wear the dresses early, even though Thanksgiving was still a week away.

Folks settled into their seats and quieted, faces bright with expectation. The lights went down.

The band members, fidgeting in the orchestra pit until then, launched smoothly into the prelude. Except for a few squeaky notes, to be expected of high school musicians, they did an amazing job. All that dedicated practice was paying off.

The costumes, designed and sewn at home in most cases, were splendid. The dancing, much-rehearsed if still a little on the awkward side at times, was impressive, and so was the singing.

Paige watched and listened, delighted, as her sister's project went off without any significant hitches.

When it was over, the audience leaped to its feet, whistling and stomping as well as clapping and the actors, crew and band members all took well-deserved bows.

Julie was the woman of the hour, though, and as she took the stage, she looked very glamorous in her simple black dress and the double strand of creamy ivory pearls Garrett had given her earlier in the evening. Her reddish hair glinted in the lights, and her changeable eyes looked silver-gray. Her smile sought and found Calvin and Garrett, sitting together, and rested softly on them for a moment.

Julie thanked everyone who had been involved in the production—from actors to stagehands to volunteers and school staff—and said what an honor it had been to share in the whole process. One of the drama club mothers joined her onstage, carrying a giant bouquet of yellow roses, and placed them in Julie's arms. The applause began again and climbed to a thunderous crescendo. Julie positively glowed.

She was still surrounded by a delighted and grateful community when Austin retrieved Paige's crutches from under the seats and then stood to help her to her feet. She caught Julie's eye and winked, and Julie winked back, smiled and mouthed the words, "Go. I'll see you at home."

Home.

The word made Paige feel slightly melancholy as she let Austin guide her up the aisle, opening the way for both of them as beaming audience members streamed in the opposite direction, bent on offering their congratulations to the team of people who had made the production possible.

They'd borrowed Tate's Jaguar for the evening, because it was easier for Paige to get in and out of it with her cast, and Austin stood watching her with shining eyes as he held open the passenger-side door. Getting settled inside was quite a process, but between the two of them, they managed.

"Guess what," Paige said sunnily when Austin was behind the wheel, buckled in and starting the motor.

He slanted a grin at her. "What?"

"The renovations on the house are finally done," Paige said. "I can move in any time."

Austin didn't immediately respond, and that was something of a disappointment to Paige, although she didn't acknowledge the fact.

"Of course," she went on, keeping her tone bright, "I can't start my new job at the clinic until I'm out of this cast, but there will be plenty to keep me busy anyway, between the wedding preparations and picking out new furniture and getting settled and everything."

He was quiet, navigating the darkened, almost-empty roads that were so familiar to both of them.

"Austin?" Paige prompted.

He tossed her a grin—it didn't seem to have the usual juice behind it, but that might have been because of the low light—and said, as if she'd called roll, "Right here."

"The play was marvelous, wasn't it?"

Austin chuckled. As he turned his head to check for oncoming traffic at the stop sign, Paige noticed that his neck was sun-browned above his snowy-white shirt collar. "Quite an accomplishment," he agreed. "For Julie *and* for that bunch of rascals she's been riding herd over all these weeks."

"Is something wrong?" Paige asked after a little pause. She sensed a shift in Austin since they'd left the auditorium and the crowd of people.

"Nothing is wrong," Austin replied.

"You're awfully quiet."

He chuckled. "Yeah," he agreed. "That's because I'm from Mars and you're from Venus."

Paige laughed. Straightened the loose-fitting skirt she'd bought specially for the occasion. Because of the cast, she couldn't wear most of her regular clothes, but she'd developed a new fondness for wearing skirts and dresses—she liked the femininity of the soft, floaty fabrics.

"Austin McKettrick, did you actually *read* that book?"

"Hell, no," he responded good-naturedly. "I traveled with a rodeo groupie for a while, once upon a time, and she read it aloud to me thinking it might inspire me to talk to her more."

The image amused Paige, and that was an interesting development in itself. Once, the thought of Austin with another woman, groupie or not, would have made her want to chase him down Main Street in a golf cart.

"Did it?" she asked sweetly. "Inspire you, I mean?"

"Not to talk," Austin replied.

They both laughed at that.

And then they were silent for a while, comfortably so, letting the Jaguar roll over the dark, sometimes-bumpy roads, taking them back to the place that was, for one of them at least, a true home.

When they reached the ranch house, Austin parked the Jag in its assigned spot in the garage, got out of the car and came around to open the door for Paige and offer his hand.

It was the usual thing, Paige thought, and yet she felt oddly jumpy inside, practically buzzing with anticipation. In a little while, she and Austin would be in bed, making love.

And that was fine by her.

But first, Shep needed to go outside, and Austin wanted to check on Molly and the rest of the horses before they called it a night.

Inside the house, Shep greeted them with happy yips and some tail chasing in front of the back door.

Austin, who had been looking down into Paige's face, about to say something, chuckled and shook his head. "Duty first," he said.

"I'm coming with you," Paige told him.

For a moment, Austin looked as though he might argue the point, but in the end, he didn't. The three of them, man, woman and dog, ventured out into the night.

Stars twinkled overhead, millions of them, as though pricking through a vast, arching canopy of dark velvet. Looking up, Paige felt the same awe and wonder she had as a child.

Were there other places like Earth out there? Were there other people, and animals, gazing in their direction and speculating about similar mysteries?

Paige and Austin waited while Shep did what he had to do, and then they all moved on toward the barn. There were no vehicles around, and Shep didn't seem at all agitated.

Molly stood, cozy, in her stall, enjoying an evening snack from her feeder. Paige felt a rush of joy just looking at the little mare. Molly had come so far in such a short time. Eventually, with a lot more care and training, she would be Calvin's horse. For now, the little boy reveled in helping Garrett and Austin with the animal's day-to-day care, and there was definitely a bond forming between the two of them.

Austin went into Molly's stall, shut the door between him and Paige, who wasn't wearing the right shoes—or, more accurately, *shoe,* singular—to be walking in manure.

Come to think of it, neither was Austin, who was wearing his good boots tonight, but that didn't seem to bother him. He murmured to the horse, running his hands over her, his touch as knowledgeable as the sweep of his gaze.

Watching Austin with a horse or a dog or, for that matter, a child, fascinated Paige. Moved her nearly to tears at times. It was, she supposed, that combination of strength and gentleness that made Austin McKettrick the man he was. The man she loved.

He reached over the stall door to plop his hat onto her head, then rolled up the sleeves of his white shirt, picked up a brush and began to groom Molly, speaking softly to the animal as he tended to her. His every touch was sure and firm, and yet indescribably tender, too.

Paige pushed the hat to the back of her head so she could see better, and she felt a familiar awakening inside her, because she knew Austin would be touching *her* soon, in all the most intimate places.

He might have known what she was thinking—the slightest reflection of a grin would touch down somewhere on his expressive mouth every so often—but he didn't say so.

No, Austin took his time brushing down that horse, just the way he always took his time with Paige, preparing her for their lovemaking. Why, sometimes he'd start getting her worked up hours before there was any hope of privacy, with a touch or a glance or a sound he made sure only she could hear.

There certainly was no hurrying him.

Considering these things, Paige felt her nipples harden under the fabric of her bra, and then there was that melting heat that meant her body was readying itself to take him inside.

Finally, Austin finished with the chore, put the brush back where it was kept, patted Molly's flank in farewell and stepped out of the stall. In the breezeway, he chuckled and curved an arm around Paige's waist, easing her against him. The hat fell off when he kissed her, and neither one of them were in any big hurry to retrieve it.

"I guess it's about that time," he drawled when the kiss finally ended.

Paige had to struggle to catch her breath. "Time to go to bed, you mean?"

she asked, and then blushed. After all, he could have been referring to something *besides* sex.

Austin grinned. "Time to make love," he replied. "In or out of a bed." He tasted her mouth again. "I've got something to tell you," he added, "and something to ask you, but I want to wait until you're all warm and soft and pink-skinned from the best climax I can possibly give you."

Her heartbeat speeded up, and so did her breath. "You say the most outrageous things, Austin McKettrick," she said, but her voice trembled with excitement, because the only things more outrageous than the ones Austin said were the ones he *did.*

He took the crutches from her, leaned them against one of the poles supporting the barn roof. Then, as easily as if she weighed nothing at all, he swept her up into his arms.

"Austin," she gasped. "Your back—"

He ignored her protest—it *was* pretty halfhearted—and carried her along the breezeway and into an empty stall at the end farthest from the door. Mares used that space when they foaled; it was large and closed off from the rest of the building, and the floor was laid with mounds of clean, fragrant wood shavings.

There was an overhead light, a single bulb dangling high in the rafters, and Austin left that burning, but shut and latched the door, to ensure their privacy.

Paige stood with a hand resting against the wall and watched him, searching inside herself for the courage to say it straight out, the thing that burned inside her, night and day.

I love you, Austin McKettrick. I want to be your woman, for all time, and for you to be my man. I want to have your babies. I want to take your name, let the whole world know that I belong to you and you belong to me.

"What did you want to ask me?" she murmured.

He spread his jacket over a bale of hay, without speaking, and sat her down on it.

Paige trembled, but not because she

was cold. The stall was well insulated against the chill of the night beyond.

Austin crouched in front of her, slid her skirt, now pooled around her feet, up above her shoe and the cumbersome cast, above her knees to the middle of her thighs.

Paige groaned. "Austin," she said.

He moved at his own pace, as always, uncovering the parts of her he wanted with methodical ease. He freed her breasts from her bra, and he kissed and fondled them, and weighed them in his calloused hands. He chafed the nipples with the sides of his thumbs, and when Paige began to whimper and moan, he smiled and went right on driving her out of her mind.

Finally, Austin turned Paige sideways on that bale of hay—she felt the prickles even through his jacket and didn't mind at all—and laid her down on her back. He raised her skirt and he took her panties down, and Paige was already lost, already well on her way to the first peak. Sometimes, she even had spontaneous orgasms with Austin, when he was kissing her deeply, or sucking her breasts, or simply nibbling at her earlobe between throaty descriptions of everything he meant to do to her.

He parted her, and stroked her with the lightest, most fiery passes of his fingertips, and when he finally took what he wanted, Paige cried out and erupted into an immediate climax, one that made her shout and buck against Austin's mouth.

He showed her no quarter at all, but drew every last tremulous whimper out of her while her body flexed and spasmed, helpless with ecstasy.

Gradually, while he murmured to her, and stroked her thighs, Paige descended from the heights, drifting like a skydiver. Floating, hanging up, every few seconds, on a smaller climax.

When the fall was complete, she sighed, winding a finger in Austin's hair. "Ummm," she said, when she had the breath to make any sound at all. "That was—nice."

He chuckled. Kissed her bare belly, and immediately began teasing her with his fingers.

"'Nice'?" he murmured, pretending to be offended.

"Austin," Paige moaned softly, "you said—"

She'd been about to remind him that he wanted to tell her something, ask her something, but then she was back in his mouth again and all coherency was gone. All she could do was cry out as the pleasure seized her, over and over again.

She didn't know how long it had been when he finally let her rest. He smoothed her skirt for her, sat her up, righted her bra and the front of her sweater.

She just sat there, on that spiky bale of hay, grinning like an idiot, boneless as a drunk. Austin seemed to waver in front of her, like an image reflected on water; Paige had to blink a few times before he came into clear focus.

"Ummm," she said again, setting her hands on his shoulders, leaning forward so her forehead rested on the top of his head. "You *do* know how to treat a lady, Austin McKettrick."

He chuckled, curved a finger under

her chin and lifted, so she had to look at him. "Listen to me," he said.

She blinked, very slowly, literally dazed with contentment, drunk with a satisfaction so thorough that it seemed impossible that she'd ever need him again. But she knew she would, and it would be sooner, not later.

"I'm—listening," she said.

Austin held her face in his hands. Touched the tip of his nose to hers, then drew back, though not far.

"I love you, Paige Remington," he told her. His voice, like his expression, was solemn, almost grave. His eyes threatened, by their very blueness, to break her heart. "You might have trouble believing that, but it's true."

Happy tears stung her eyes. "Oh, Austin," she whispered.

"I love you," he repeated, as though fearing he might lose his momentum if he didn't keep right on talking. "And I'm asking you to marry me, and have our babies and live on this ranch with me from now on. Will you do it?"

"Of course I will," Paige answered softly. "I love you, too, Austin. And I can't think of any better way to spend the rest of my life than with you."

Austin's eyes widened—was it possible that he'd expected her to *refuse?*

In the next moment, he confirmed that with, "You mean it?"

"I mean it," she said.

A sort of joy suffused his face, and he let out a whoop of pure exultation. "Let's go inside, then, and I'll give you the ring."

Paige laughed—and cried. She put her hands on either side of his face and felt the first stubble of a new beard coming in. "There's a ring?" she asked.

Austin pretended indignation. "Well, *of course* there's a ring, woman. What do you take me for?"

"A man who needs to be made love to?"

His eyes shone. "I reckon I fit that description," he said. "But we're going inside first. I just brought you in here because I'd been thinking about doing what I did all night long and I couldn't wait any longer."

Just outside the door, Shep made a whiny sound.

Austin grinned and helped Paige back to her feet. With his arm around her waist, she easily managed to move, hop-skippity, back to where they'd left her crutches.

Shep, glad to be in human company again, trotted happily beside them.

Down at the main gates, two sets of headlights indicated that Garrett and Julie and Tate and Libby, along with the three kids, were home.

Austin and Paige were about halfway between the barn and the house when the deafening boom came, so loud it had a physical impact, nearly throwing them to the ground.

"The oil field," Austin gasped, both arms around Paige, as though to shield her from anything that might come at them, from any direction.

Paige looked in that direction, saw what Austin had already seen.

A tower of flame rose hundreds of feet into the air, and even from that distance, they could feel the heat.

Paige pressed a hand to her mouth, trembling, clinging to Austin with both hands, her crutches forgotten on the ground.

Tate and Garrett were out of their trucks within a moment of stopping, running toward them.

"Are you all right?" Garrett yelled.

At least, Paige *thought* it had been Garrett; in the darkness and confusion, she couldn't tell.

Austin didn't answer his brother directly. He nodded to Libby, who bent to retrieve Paige's crutches and hand them back to her.

"Keep her here," Austin said.

Libby said she would.

Sirens screamed in the distance, and the night had taken on a hellish orange tint.

Tate, Garrett and Austin were gone all at once, racing away in Tate's truck, with God only knew what kind of fate awaiting them.

CHAPTER NINETEEN

The blazing oil well was like the heat
from a blast furnace, and for all their
hurry, Austin knew they couldn't get
any closer.

"Where the hell are the security people?" Garrett yelled. The fastest talker
in the bunch, he was always the first to
break a silence.

"How the hell am I supposed to
know?" Tate yelled back.

Austin, shielding his eyes the way he
would have done in bright sunlight,
tried to see. By the looks of that fire, he
figured the so-called security people
would probably be dropping from the
sky in charred chunks for the next hour
or so.

A movement off to his right caught
his attention. Somebody was alive, he

thought, and headed that way at a sprint, orbiting the edge of the blistering, throbbing heat.

Tate and Garrett followed, though whether they'd seen something, too, or just wanted to stop him from getting hurt, he didn't know.

The flames cast an eerie glow ahead of him as he ran, as if to light his way. And the trail led straight to Cliff Pomeroy.

Clothes blackened, hair singed away, but seemingly unharmed otherwise, Pomeroy was trying desperately to drag something—*someone*—to safety. He must have been farther away when the blast came.

It was, Austin soon noticed, too late for Reese. Only a portion of his face remained; the rest of him was literally cooked. Austin figured he'd never forget the smell, and he gagged as he took hold of Cliff's arm.

Austin hadn't needed the rumble under his feet to tell him that there was another explosion coming, with no telling how many more to follow. There were a total of seven wells on that stretch of land, and the pools of crude underground might well be intercon- nected.

Nobody really knew how far the de- posit extended, or in what directions. It was entirely possible that the house it- self sat on top of a hundred dead di- nosaurs, transformed into oil over mil- lions of years; it might even reach as far as downtown Blue River or beyond.

Tate and Garrett bolted out of the darkness, and both of them yanked a weeping, blathering Cliff into motion.

"Goddammit," Tate yelled at Austin. *"Run!"*

They ran, made it a hundred yards or so before the next blast roared against their eardrums like the crack of doom. The impetus of the explosion sent them all sprawling, scrambling back to their feet, covering as much ground as they could before the next horrific boom, and the one after that.

The four men took shelter in the shadow of another derrick, a thing rem- iniscent of a giant insect in the weird flashes of light and heat.

"Cliff," Tate choked out, crouching in front of the man, "talk to me!"

The sirens were closer.

Austin pictured Blue River's antiquated fire engine rolling up, with a cartoonlike aplomb, and all the volunteers bumbling into each other, tripping over hoses. The image brought a smile to his face.

A blaze like this one, if it could be put out at all, called for an elite team of specialists, firefighters trained to handle the hottest kind of fires—those fed by gas and oil.

"We've got to go back and get Bobby!" Cliff wailed. "I lost sight of him before the well blew—"

It was hard to tell if Cliff was hurt and, if so, how badly. Yes, his hair was gone and his clothes were in scorched tatters, but he didn't seem to be in pain.

Shock, maybe, Austin thought glumly.

"Bobby's gone," Tate said bluntly but not without a certain understandable regret. "There was a security team out here, Cliff," he pressed, in the next moment. "What happened to them?"

"I figure Bobby must have shot one after he ran off and left me at the truck," Cliff sobbed out, getting all tangled up in his own words. "The other guy, he took off for town for some reason, and we saw our chance—"

"Bobby?" Garrett asked, his voice real quiet.

"Bobby Reese," Cliff said, between long, horrendous shudders he couldn't seem to control. "He was my boy, my stepson—"

"Why, Cliff?" Tate persisted. "Why would you and—Reese—do a thing like this?"

Cliff, sitting on his haunches now, seemed to siphon some kind of strength right up from the ground, the way a good well drew oil. "We didn't have any choice!" he all but bellowed. "This is your fault!" he shouted, as Brogan's squad car and the ambulance pulled up, lights splitting the flaming night. "Shutting down perfectly good oil wells! You McKettricks, you've got all the money in the world—what does it matter to you if everybody else does without?"

"You set this fire to pay us back for capping the wells?" Garrett asked, appalled.

Austin waited, knowing there was more.

"Your daddy and me, we were partners. We had a deal. And he just cut me out, left me high and dry!"

"Cliff," Tate reasoned, probably wasting his breath. "You must have made millions from that partnership. How much would have been enough?"

"You don't understand," Cliff went on. "I had obligations."

"You and Bobby," Garrett said quietly. "The rustling operation and the slaughtered cattle—you were behind those things, too, weren't you?"

Cliff laughed. It was a horrible sound to hear, like a shriek of pure agony. "Charlie Bates and the others took the fall. I made sure they knew we'd get them, even in jail, if they sold us out." He paused, looked from Tate to Garrett to Austin, taking them all in. Clearly, he'd transferred his hatred and resentment for Jim McKettrick to his sons. "By *God*," he wrapped up, "I hope that oil burns until hell freezes over. I hope there's a honeycomb of the stuff, running under this whole ranch, all of it burning—"

Garrett let out a long sigh, shaking his head.

The ground shook again, and there was another blast, but this time it was more sound than fury.

Brogan stumbled over to him, guided by the glare and by a flashlight, looking incongruous in his uptown suit. He was accompanied by several deputies, some men from town and Dr. Joe Colwin.

"If I didn't know better," Brogan yelled over the whooshing growl, "I'd think the devil himself split the ground clear from hell to the surface!"

Joe glanced at Austin, nodded grimly, and supervised while the paramedics loaded Cliff onto a stretcher, as carefully as they could, and the deputies searched the fringes of the heat for more casualties.

They found the murdered security agent and what was left of Bobby Reese.

The Blue River fire engine came, too, but the spectacle was bleak. Austin couldn't imagine how he'd ever thought it could be funny.

After the ambulance had gone, taking Cliff with it, and the coroner had arrived to collect the remains of the two dead men, there wasn't much point in hanging around. Tate made a few calls and arranged for a firefighting team to come out from Dallas.

Back at the main house, the women were waiting up, though the kids and the dogs had all settled down for the night.

Libby and Julie had made a mountain of sandwiches, rightly anticipating that a crowd would gather, and Paige had fired up two industrial-sized coffee pots usually reserved for roundup, when there were always a lot of extra people on the ranch helping out.

"Look at you," Paige said, taking in Austin's soot-covered clothes. Her eyes filled with tears. "Are you all right?"

Austin smiled and touched his mouth to hers lightly, but with a charge of private electricity that arched between them. "I am now," he answered. "I am now."

Paige let her forehead rest against his chest, heedless of the sweat and the dirt and even the other people milling and talking in that large room, and silently thanked God that he and Tate and Garrett had all come back safely, this time.

They led dangerous lives, all three of these McKettrick men, just as their forebears had, and loving them meant accepting that, and making the most of every moment they got to spend together. It meant celebrating every heartbeat, every breath, sharing every joy and every sorrow—for as long as forever lasted.

"Is this what it's going to be like, Austin McKettrick, being married to you?" she asked in a whisper.

His grin was a white slash in his filthy face. "Probably," he said.

"What happened?" she asked after swallowing a couple of times. Wild surges of emotion kept welling up inside her, overflowing in tears and making it hard to talk.

Standing very close to her, Austin told Paige what he knew. At that point, it wasn't much.

Folks stayed around—many still in their good clothes because they'd been to see the play at the high school earlier in the night—eating sandwiches and drinking coffee and swapping stories about wells that had caught fire and burned for months, or even years.

Just after dawn, two bits of news arrived at nearly the same moment. Tate got a call on his cell phone, telling him that the firefighting team had arrived from Dallas and were busy setting up operations over at the oil field. And Chief Brent Brogan arrived in person, showered and wearing a freshly pressed uniform, though he didn't look to Paige as though he'd had any more sleep than the rest of them, to announce that Cliff Pomeroy had died during the night.

It hadn't been Cliff's burns that killed him, though—those had proved to be fairly minor. After arriving at the clinic in

Blue River by ambulance, he'd been cleaned up and treated, and the doctors, Joe Colwin included, had conferred and decided to keep him overnight, for observation, instead of letting him go to jail. He'd asked for rice pudding and calmly given a full confession to the chief, who was guarding the prisoner. He smiled when he talked about shooting down those cattle, just to spite the McKettricks. Reese had been the one to put a bullet in Austin that night, but Cliff took the credit for making the anonymous call to report that someone might be hurt.

Over half an hour or so, Cliff had supplied a lot of information, and he'd named names. Thanks to the state police, a number of the suspects had already been rounded up.

Around 3:30, Cliff had seized his chest with both hands, suffering what turned out to be a massive coronary, and Brogan had shouted for help. A medical team fought to save Cliff's life, but there was no bringing him back.

The task of waking old Doc Pomeroy with the news that his only son was dead had fallen to Chief Brogan, that being the nature of his job. Brogan had driven directly to the ranch after speaking with Doc, not to carry word of Cliff's passing, but because the older man had asked him to let "somebody out there know" that he wouldn't be able to stop by that morning, the way he'd planned, to look in on the dog and the little mare.

Doc had sad business to attend to.

After that, people began to leave the house, saying their quiet goodbyes, offering help if it should be needed, talking among themselves about what might be done to help ole Doc through the hard days ahead.

Tate, exhausted, insisted on driving over to the oil fields to see what was happening with the fire, promising Libby he wouldn't be gone long. Garrett and Austin went with him.

The head of the firefighting team spoke frankly. They could probably contain the blaze, but it would take time and cost plenty.

No surprises there, Austin thought wearily.

Home looked as good as it ever had, when they got back. Maybe better, because Paige was inside that sprawling house, waiting for him. Libby was waiting for Tate, and Julie for Garrett.

The three brothers parted ways in the kitchen, tired, saddened, but grateful, too, and in need of the sweet solace they knew awaited them, in the arms of their women.

Austin took a long shower, washed away as much of the dirt and sweat and sadness as he could. When he stepped out, Paige was waiting, and she handed him a bath towel.

With a sigh, Austin wrapped the towel around his waist without bothering to dry off. He was a great believer in evaporation.

"I still want to ride that horse," Paige said.

"As soon as you're out of that cast," Austin replied, too tired to grin full out, but too amused not to try. "You can ride the horse that threw you." He sighed, cupped her face in one hand. "Woman," he added, "you are a piece of work."

"But you love me," she said. She was pretty perky for somebody who had been up all night long.

He leaned in. "I definitely love you," he murmured, tasting her mouth.

"Let's get some sleep," Paige said.

Austin chuckled. "Sleep?" he echoed. "Sure. Eventually."

She tried to look stern. "You must be exhausted."

"And you aren't?"

"I'm just glad you're back, safe and sound," she replied. She stretched to kiss his mouth. "Come on, cowboy. You and I are going to hit the hay."

He chuckled. "I'm there," he told her.

Their lovemaking was slow and quiet, a soothing dance of two tired bodies, and Paige gave herself up to it completely, well aware that she might so easily have lost Austin that night, just as Libby could have lost Tate, and Julie, Garrett.

Afterward, Austin sank into a deep sleep, and Paige lay on her side, propped up on one elbow, and simply watched him for a long, long time.

She memorized the strong line of his jaw, his cheekbones and those eyelashes, wasted on a man. His mouth intrigued and invited her, even in repose.

With a sigh, she shimmied down into the softness of the sheets, a delicious juxtaposition to the hard length of his frame.

She awakened much later, but very suddenly, aware only that something was different.

She opened her eyes and sat up, in a mild panic, but Austin was there, fully dressed and sitting in the rocking chair, watching her with a smile crooking up the side of his mouth. Shep, as always, was nearby, ears perked, alert and eager.

"We were interrupted last night," Austin said. "I wasn't through proposing."

Paige laughed, so full of joy and well-being that she couldn't help herself. "Well," she purred, remembering how thoroughly he'd satisfied her, both in the barn and in the very bed where she was now, "you could have fooled me."

He took a small velvet box from the

pocket of his shirt, moved to sit on the mattress beside her.

Paige's breath caught and her eyes burned, and the only sound she could make in that moment was a little strangled, "Oh."

Austin raised the lid of the box, revealing an exquisite diamond ring in an antique setting. "Clay McKettrick put this ring on his bride's finger when she agreed to marry him, way back when they founded this ranch and this family." He paused, cleared his throat. "You could probably do a lot better than me, Paige Remington, but you'll never meet a man who loves you more than I do. If you throw in with me, I'll spend the rest of my life proving you made the right decision."

Paige put a hand to her throat, waited for her heart to resume its normal rate again. Her vision blurred, and a tear slipped down her cheek. "Oh, Austin, I love you so much—"

"Is that a yes?" he asked. "I know you said *yes* out in the barn, but you were sort of—well—under the influence at the time."

The phrase was apt. She'd definitely been "under the influence at the time," all right—still spinning in the backwash of a tidal orgasm. Paige put out her left hand, ring finger raised. "It's a yes," she confirmed.

She would have sworn that some sweet charge went through her the instant Austin put that ring on her finger, but there was no time to ponder it.

He kissed her then, and she kissed him back, and it wasn't long until they were *both* under the influence.

EPILOGUE

New Year's Eve
The Silver Spur Ranch

The grounds surrounding the ranch house looked like some vast and exotic camp, with colorful canvas pavilions everywhere and dozens of potted trees twinkling with *millions* of tiny fairy lights. It looked to Esperanza, peering out through the darkening window above the sink, like an international convention of fireflies.

As if all those heated tents weren't enough, a stage had been erected, with row upon row of folding chairs set up in front of it. After the triple wedding, timed to wind up exactly at midnight, several of the most famous country singers in the world would perform with their bands.

Guests had been arriving since the day before, filling up every spare room in virtually every house for miles around, taking over hotels as far away as Austin and San Antonio.

The children hadn't been forgotten; out there in the pasture, a real Ferris wheel glowed, neon green and pink, against a clear but wintry sky. There was a carousel, too, and several other rides.

Esperanza, who had been directing workmen of all sorts since the day after Christmas, wiped her capable hands on the little towel stitched specially into the waistband of her apron and beamed.

"These McKettricks," chimed Maria, one of the housekeeper's many nieces, hired to help out with the house and the children and the dogs when the three happy couples left for their various honeymoon destinations, "they never do anything halfway."

"No," Esperanza agreed, blinking away tears as she thought of Sally and

Jim McKettrick—how proud they'd be of their sons, and their future daughters-in-law, of the twins and Calvin, how thrilled over the baby Libby was already carrying under her heart. "To a McKettrick, if something is worth doing at all, it's worth doing with everything they've got."

Caterers and their assistants moved around the kitchen in swirls of activity, but Esperanza paid little attention to them. They'd been around all day, and she was used to hubbub anyway. Working for the McKettricks, she'd learned to thrive in chaos.

"I heard there's going to be a spread about this wedding in *People* magazine," Maria said, brown eyes twinkling. "Ron Strivens says there are reporters and photographers asking to camp out *in the barn.*"

Esperanza sighed and shook her head. She supposed an event like this one was bound to attract the media, and she didn't really care, as long as those three couples ended up properly married in the eyes of God and man.

Call her old-fashioned, but Esperanza was going to feel a lot better about all this when the gossips finally had to shut up about how this venerable old ranch house had turned into a hotbed of sin since the Remington women had moved in with the McKettrick men.

She crossed herself and turned just as Calvin came rushing down the center stairway. He was the official ring bearer, and already wearing everything but the jacket of his miniature tuxedo. His blond hair was slicked down, and the lenses of his glasses, usually smudged, gleamed with cleanliness.

"Mom sent me down here," he said, coming to a stop directly in front of Esperanza and tilting his head back to look up at her. "I keep asking her when we can ride on the Ferris wheel, Audrey and Ava and me, and she says she needs a break from all those questions."

Esperanza hid a smile. She drew back one of the high stools at one of the counters and patted the seat. "Climb up here," she told the little boy. "There are some extraspecial cookies hidden away, just for you and the twins."

"Do *you* know when we can ride the Ferris wheel?" Calvin inquired.

Esperanza laughed. "Not specifically," she said. "And why are you in your wedding clothes already? The ceremony doesn't start for several hours— suppose you get dirty?"

"Well, I'd change if it meant I could ride the Ferris wheel," Calvin said.

Esperanza put three small and very fancy cookies onto a plate and set them in front of him. "I'm sure you would," she said with a smile.

Audrey and Ava arrived next. Unlike Calvin, they were still wearing their regular clothes—flannel-lined jeans and the bright red sweaters they'd gotten at Christmas. They would be flower girls in the wedding, clad in pink dresses as soft as any rosebud, and they were practically vibrating with anticipation.

"Come and have cookies," Esperanza said gently.

The girls scraped stools back from beneath the counter and climbed up onto them, perched on either side of Calvin.

"Daddy wants to see Libby in her wedding dress," Ava confided, "and she won't let him."

"She locked him out of their bedroom," Audrey added. "She's never done that before."

Esperanza crossed herself again, asked silently for guidance. "There's nothing to worry about," she told the child, patting her hand. "Everybody's just excited about the wedding, that's all."

Calvin nodded sagely. "Have you heard anything about when we get to go on the Ferris wheel?" he asked the twins, his mouth full of cookies.

Esperanza sighed, thinking of the elegant ceremony ahead, and all the photographs that would be taken. She fetched a dish towel from a drawer and tied it around Calvin like a bib.

"How about right now?" a masculine voice asked.

Everyone, including Esperanza, turned to see Garrett standing just inside the back door. To look at him, in his torn jeans and his old shirt and those boots that had no business touching her spotless kitchen floor, no-body would ever guess that he was about to get himself married.

All the kids cheered, jumping down off the stools, and the cookies were forgotten.

Calvin bounded for the door, and Garrett caught him easily by the waist, spun him around once, and set him back on his feet. "Whoa, buddy," he said. "If I let you go outside in those duds, your mother will nail my hide to the barn door."

Calvin went big-eyed at the idea.

Esperanza gave Garrett a disapprov-ing look. "Honestly," she said, with a cluck of her tongue. "Garrett McKet-trick, children take statements like that *literally.*"

Calvin had moved on. "Well, what am I supposed to *do?*" he cried, flinging his little hands out from his sides for emphasis. "Mom sent me down here because I'm underfoot up there where she is, and I don't know how I'm going to change into different clothes if I can't even *go upstairs*—"

Esperanza ducked into the laundry room and returned momentarily with an entire set of clothes for Calvin—jeans, a heavy sweatshirt to keep him extra-warm, and even a pair of high-top sneakers.

"Thank you!" Calvin fairly shrieked at such a fever pitch of joy and excitement that he snatched the garments right out of Esperanza's hands and ran wildly for the nearest bathroom, so he could switch outfits.

By then, Audrey and Ava were already bundled up in their play jackets and the family dogs were converging on that kitchen like something out of a Disney animal movie.

Old Hildie and the two pups, Buford and Ambrose, clattered down Tate's stairway, while the beagle sidled down Garrett's on his three strong legs. As if on cue, Shep descended Austin's steps, tail switching, eyes bright.

Garrett laughed and took the whole bunch of them, kids *and* dogs, outside, into the gathering twilight.

The intercom buzzed.

Esperanza made her way over to the device and pushed a button. "Yes? This is Esperanza speaking."

Julie was on the other end. "Did I just see Garrett crossing the yard with three kids and five dogs, headed for the Ferris wheel?"

Esperanza drew a breath, took the time to let it out slowly. *Very* slowly. "Yes," she said. "You did."

"Was Calvin wearing his tuxedo? I've made him take it off at least twice already, but he keeps putting it back on." Julie didn't sound angry, just nervous.

Esperanza smiled. "Calvin is wearing play clothes," she assured the fretful bride. Since both of Julie's sisters were also getting married, and all three of them had decided against having bridesmaids, there was only their mother to fuss over them, and Marva had been dashing from one section of the house to another all day. "Is there anything you would like for me to do for you?"

"You're busy overseeing the caterers

and the extra staff," Julie said with a brave sniffle. "I'll be fine."

Esperanza rolled her eyes, but she loved Libby, Julie and Paige like daughters. They were the best thing that had ever happened to those rascal men of theirs. "I am right here if you need anything," she said gently.

Julie thanked her kindly and ended the conversation. She'd barely turned to walk away when the device buzzed again.

This time it was Paige calling from the rooms upstairs. She and Austin had been sharing them ever since her cast was removed, just ten days before. She'd rented out her house in town.

"Hello? Is anyone there?"

Esperanza smiled. "I'm here," she said. "What do you need?"

"I need for this wedding to be over," Paige replied. "I just want to be married, for heaven's sake. Why does this whole thing have to be such a circus?"

"Now, now," Esperanza said soothingly. "It will not be long now."

"You're right," the youngest bride

conceded, with an extended sigh. "Have you seen our mother?"

"I believe she may be with Libby," Esperanza replied. "Shall I send someone to find her, and ask her to join you?"

"God forbid," Paige said. "I was going to ask you to give Marva some job to do, so she'll leave us alone. She's driving me crazy!"

Esperanza chuckled. "Have patience," she counseled. "She is not merely the mother of one bride, but of *three.* The poor thing must feel as if she's being pulled in every direction, and I'm sure she's doing the best she can."

Paige made a strangled sound of pure frustration and signed off.

Esperanza smiled and went back to the preparations. There was still a great deal to do, after all.

11:45 p.m.

Tate, standing on a low platform in the largest of the pavilions, the space lit with candles and carpeted in pink, yel-

low and white rose petals, watched as
Libby appeared in the doorway at the
top of the aisle, holding Garrett's arm.

There was a hush, then the music
began, and the hundreds of guests
rose from their folding chairs and
turned to watch. To Tate, they were
barely more than a smear of color at
the periphery of his awareness.

Then his daughters came into sharp
focus. Audrey and Ava fairly skipped
along the aisle, in their carefully chosen
dresses, carrying baskets filled with still
more flower petals and flinging them
around like confetti. They did just
enough grandstanding to elicit a grin
from Tate and a ripple of fond laughter
from the gathering.

Reaching the platform, Tate's daughters hiked up their skirts—more amusement from the crowd—and hurried over
to him with their baskets.

He smiled and bent to kiss the tops
of their heads, and sent them to stand
in their appointed positions, as previ-
ously rehearsed. They made a production of finding the spots where they
were supposed to stand—the wedding

planner had marked the floor with two Xs of pink tape.

Next came Calvin, standing up as straight and tall as he could in his little tux, carrying a thick red velvet pillow with three wedding bands gleaming on top. Each band was tied with a different-colored ribbon—Libby's ribbon was blue.

Calvin, unlike the twins, used the steps to mount the platform, and took his place, looking as solemn as a little judge. Although he'd said nothing could ever be as special as the day he'd spent with his mom on the class trip to Six Flags, it was clear this wedding day was going to create a lot of precious memories for the precocious youngster.

The organist struck a more decisive chord then, and Tate knew the moment he'd been waiting for, for so long, had finally arrived.

Libby, the woman he loved more than his life, was moving toward him, resplendent in her vintage ivory wedding dress. Even through the veil covering her face, Tate could see that her blue eyes were glistening with tears.

He adjusted his tie, which was choking him, and reminded himself silently that women cried when they were happy.

It was just one of many divine mysteries.

Garrett brought Libby to Tate's side, and then turned and waited as Julie stepped into view, her gloved hand resting on Austin's arm. Looking at her, in that wild confection of a white gown, with its yards of silk and lace, its sprinkling of tiny crystals, he felt his throat close up tight and his eyes burn.

"I love you," he mouthed to Julie.

And through the sparkles of her veil, he saw her touch her fingers to her lips and blow him a kiss. Austin escorted Julie to Garrett, then added his own touch by kissing Julie's cheek, then Libby's, right through their veils, before finding his mark—a slash of masking tape—and standing on it.

*   *   *

Brent Brogan, looking mighty out of his element in his rented tuxedo but spiffy just the same, filled the opening to the pavilion, practically pulling Paige to his side.

Paige's wedding dress was floor-length but fitted, and instead of a veil, she wore a round-brimmed hat the same shade of white as her dress with all sorts of gauzy stuff and flowers on the band. Her beautiful face was clearly visible.

God almighty, Austin thought, looking at her. *I'm the luckiest man who ever lived.*

She swept up the aisle, holding Brogan's arm, and never looked to the right or the left the whole way, but only straight into Austin's eyes. Straight into his soul.

I love you, he told her, with everything but words.

Paige was in a daze throughout the ceremony—she knew Julie and Libby were, too—but she managed to respond correctly whenever it was her turn to repeat some vow. Her heart was full as she and her sisters married the men they loved. Paige knew that love, so deep and true, would sustain them through life, adding to their joys and taking the edge off their sorrows.

At approximately one minute before midnight, the pastor pronounced them "men and wives," much to the cheering delight of the community of friends and family gathered to witness the marriage of three brothers to three sisters.

Right on cue, the roof of the pavilion rolled back, revealing a black velvet sky, and the first fireworks whistled high overhead and burst like a flower blooming and then dissolved into sapphires, falling like rain.

* * * * *